I0819866

KILLER FOG

Treachery, Greed, And Jihadi Fanatics

A Clay Cantrell Mystery Thriller

BY BRUCE WETTERAU

This book is a work of fiction. Names, characters, and places are used fictitiously or are products of the author's imagination. Any resemblance to actual places, or persons, living or dead, is purely coincidental.

Book design and cover by Bruce Wetterau

Printed by IngramSpark

Printed in the United States of America 2015

ISBN: 978-0-692-56511-7

Gone but not forgotten. This book is dedicated to my father, who suffered the misfortune to die a young man, and my mother, who soldiered on to raise three children on her own and become a highly respected college textbook production editor.

ACKNOWLEDGMENTS

I owe a heartfelt thanks to a number of individuals who helped make this book possible by giving generously of their time and expertise.

Ted Mason, a principal at Eastwind Power Partners (full disclosure: and my uncle), put me onto the field of Low Energy Nuclear Reactions (LENR), a lead that wound up being central to the book. Tim Fulk, CW4, an Army medivac helicopter pilot, helped me construct the scenes with helicopters, and Barton Gibson, a former Marine infantryman, provided insights into combat. My friends Alice DeWitt and Charlie Bishop, and a new acquaintance, William Mears, provided helpful background information, as did Staunton attorney John Hooe III and civilian pilot and aviation mechanic extraordinaire, Ken Peterson. Fellow author Bryan Bunch and I consulted, and commiserated, on the vagaries of book publishing today. David Kane and Franci Ferguson, friends who are proprietors of American History Press, also kindly shared their publishing expertise. And I should not forget Patrick McMillan, who volunteered to be the ominous silhouette you see on the front cover.

Writing the words is only half the battle. Someone has to read them to complete the act, and here again I am grateful to those who gave of their time to read the manuscript and offer their comments and corrections, notably Rob Mason, Jody Grogan, Helmut and Irene Filacchione, Larry and Michelle Rasheed, and Joe Rotunda. Thanks to all!

Last but not least, I want to thank my friend Paul Fargis, these days a publishing consultant, for his encouragement, savvy advice, and unflinching candor.

--Bruce Wetterau

KILLER FOG

"The only thing necessary for the triumph of evil

is that good men do nothing."

-- Edmund Burke

"...They are here, and they will kill anyone who stands in their way. We know they believe the will of Allah has no greater enemy than hi-tech America....

Chatter picked up in recent foreign intercepts indicates an attack on our technological infrastructure is imminent, but as yet gives no specifics on the intended target.

We suspect that a cell of radical sympathizers is harboring the attackers within our borders, effectively hiding their identities and true mission until they are ready to strike. We advise you issue a nationwide Imminent Threat Alert soonest possible."

--Excerpt from a classified Threat Analysis, prepared just ten days before and transmitted to the Secretary of Homeland Security, Leeland Walters. He immediately issued the warning that a terrorist attack somewhere in the U.S. is imminent.

1

PEA SOUP

"Cla-a-a-y!" Susan cried out, "You're worse than my brothers!"

"Yes dear," he deadpanned and then laughed as she gave him a playful push on the shoulder. His grin lingered as he scanned the cone of light probing the road ahead. Thick woods--shrouded in black this moonless, early October night--closed in on both sides of the darkened interstate. The outstretched tree limbs, shadowy fingers curling overhead, seemed poised to claw at the edges of the highway. A herd of fallen leaves stampeded across the pavement, driven by a rogue gust of wind. For the moment, Clay and Susan were alone, riding in the only car to be seen on this section of I-64's two west-bound lanes. Their destination, Staunton--home--lay a half hour's drive beyond this lonely stretch of rural Virginia countryside west of Charlottesville, Virginia. Not another soul was in sight, but right now their isolation, their aloneness, were the last things on Clay's mind.

The reason, of course, would be Susan. He couldn't help teasing her sometimes. It was just too tempting when she behaved like this, a nervous teenage girl, instead of the self-assured, twenty-nine-year-old woman she was. He glanced at her, but she pretended to ignore him and idly tucked a lock of her shoulder length hair behind her ear.

Susan Stratton was a ravishing brunette, a classic beauty in her prime. Certainly that didn't hurt, but everything else had clicked too when they met that night four months ago. They both were old enough to have been around the block, and at thirty-three, Clay had seen enough to know she was the kind of woman for him. Strange, though. With her, he already felt they'd known each other all their lives, yet their relationship still seemed fresh, alive, and fascinating. Teasing her was fun, but so was seeing her happy. That made him smile. Then his smile widened as he thought about her staying with him tonight at his place.

"Susan, so far as mom and dad are concerned, you can do no wrong."

"I want to believe that, Clay. But this dinner is so important. Everything has to be perfect."

"That dress you bought today *is* perfect, honey. I promise, my parents are going to love you."

"Will you be putting in a good word for me?" she asked with a sly grin.

Clay turned to look at her and caught the impish look in her eyes. He grinned back at her. "Well, I suppose I might be persuaded."

Susan's hand slid softly to his right thigh and she began idly tracing small circles with her forefinger. "Are you sure?" she teased.

The warmth of her hand, and those soft circles on his leg, kindled a familiar fire. Clay's mouth opened as he turned to answer her with a heartfelt pledge of allegiance. But no words came out, his testament being rudely interrupted by flashing headlights. An oncoming car repeatedly flicked its brights up and down.

"What is with that guy?" Clay grumbled at last. Looking at the rearview mirror, he watched the car swoop up behind them fast, then quickly switch to the left lane to pass. The light-colored, older model Mercedes four-door sedan, slowed sharply as it pulled up alongside and then wavered, edging dangerously close.

"What the--? Is this some kind of joke?" Clay growled as he and Susan focused on the driver. The old man had turned on the interior light so that they could see him mouthing words and signaling with wild gestures.

"What's he saying?" Clay asked, turning his attention back to the road. The Mercedes was definitely too close. This was Susan's Volvo they were in and she wouldn't appreciate getting it banged up. Clay edged farther to the right.

Startled, Susan put her hand up to her throat. "I think he's saying 'Help.' Something's really wrong, Clay."

Clay checked his rearview mirror. The road behind them was dark, not another car in sight.

"Call police," Susan said after a moment, then exaggerating, nodded her head *yes* to the man. The old man immediately floored the Mercedes and disappeared with a roar into the darkness.

"Oh dear, I left my phone at home. Can I use yours?" Susan asked after nervously rummaging through her purse.

"Mine's at home too. The battery was dead, so I left it."

"Can't we get to a phone?" Obviously worried now, she added, "That poor man looked like he really was in trouble."

Something *was* going on, but Clay couldn't be sure just what. Suddenly he was all too aware that they were indeed out in the middle of nowhere, a long way from home. They wouldn't be able to get to a phone for about ten minutes, until after I-64 took them up and over the Blue Ridge Mountains at Afton. The way the old man was driving, he would get there way ahead of them. So there wasn't much Clay could do but wonder what the old man's emergency was.

Clay glanced up at the rearview mirror as a new set of headlights stabbing the darkness closed fast. "Jeez, another one! He's really hauling too," Clay exclaimed, edging Susan's Volvo rightward again. Light filled the Volvo's passenger compartment as the speeding car whooshed by at what seemed like 120 mph. The airstream rocked the Volvo, forcing Clay to correct to bring it back into the lane. Angered by that driver's recklessness, Clay's first instinct was to floor it to try catching the S.O.B. This wasn't his Corvette, though. Susan's Volvo wagon just wouldn't cut it in a car chase. Clay willed the muscles in his right foot to relax.

"From the look of the taillights," Clay said, "I'd say that was an old Dodge Charger. With a big eight from the sound of it. Guy's in one hell of a hurry."

"Maybe he's chasing after that old man. We really should call the police."

"Could be, but I don't know what the heck is going on. I didn't even get his license plate, and for all we know, the old guy could have gotten off at the Crozet exit."

"I still think we should stop and call," Susan said.

"Okay, but there isn't any place around here where we can get to a phone. We're past the Crozet exit, so we'll have to wait until we get over the mountain. I'll get off at Waynesboro and call from a gas station."

"Thanks, honey. It wouldn't be right if we didn't do something to help." Relieved, she sat quietly, watching him as he concentrated on the road.

They were heading uphill now, climbing the long grade up the east side of the Blue Ridge Mountains, and what had begun as a thin, wispy mist was quickly thickening into dense fog. Crossing over the mountain in fog was not one of Clay's favorite experiences, since it could get thick as pea soup up around the top. Clay slowed to fifty to keep his distance from the two blurry taillights of a car in front.

"Looks like it's going to be really thick tonight," Clay said as much to himself as Susan.

"Maybe you should slow down, Clay."

"I just did. Can't go any slower or somebody will get me from behind. I'm going to follow those taillights. If he hits something then I'll have time to stop."

"Oh, great! It took me a long time to pay off this car, Clay. Please don't wreck it."

"Not going to happen, Susan. Just have to be extra careful that's all. We'll be fine."

Being extra careful was getting harder to do, though. With the fog closing in, Clay could barely see the taillights up ahead and his headlights did nothing to pierce the thickening billows of silky white mist. Clay felt like a cocoon of blinding white had descended around him, allowing only fleeting glimpses of dim shadows here and there--of highway signs, an overpass, eerie unidentifiable forms.

"Shouldn't we pull over Clay?"

"We'd be sitting ducks, Susan," Clay answered matter-of-factly. "Sooner or later somebody would lose the road and run right into us."

He was having trouble now keeping to the center of the lane, even though I-64 had nothing worse than gentle curves going up the mountainside. The visibility was so bad Clay was navigating partly by what he could see, partly what he remembered from his many trips up this mountain, and partly by the sound of his tires drifting onto the road's rumble strip.

The first time he hit the strip, Susan put her hand on the arm rest as if to brace herself. Clay knew she was worried. But he wasn't about to let anything happen to her. So he doubled down on his concentration, focusing intently on the blinding white, looking for even the slightest hint of a shape in the murky white froth. The mist swirled, now a solid wall of white, now thinning enough to see a little farther ahead, as Clay pressed on at fifty, keeping pace with the taillights leading the way, his guiding star.

Though it didn't seem possible, the fog got even worse as they approached the top of Afton Mountain. Both Clay and the car ahead slowed to forty mph. The red taillights now sometimes disappeared altogether and Clay couldn't see much beyond the Volvo's hood. *That* was nerve-racking. Twice more he drifted to the right far enough to hit the rumble strip before edging back to the center of the lane. He turned the windshield wipers up to high, a futile gesture, he knew, but he needed every bit of visibility he could get. The dim shadow of an overpass appeared in the mist like a sudden realization and, Clay, relieved as he passed under it, knew they were finally getting close to the top.

"Almost there Susan. This fog should thin out as we head down the other side into the Valley."

"I hope so, Clay. I can't see a thing."

Neither could he, but he didn't want to say that. He edged closer to the car in front to keep the taillights in view, but the fog only thickened again, completely blanketing the red blurs here and there. Faced with a solid wall of white and a few fleeting shadows, Clay was simply guessing where the roadway was now, trusting to blind luck until the dim red of the taillights reappeared in the heavy mists.

Then they were gone. Clay saw the faint shadow of another overpass before the realization hit him.

"We're on our own now, Susan. Our guiding star just got off at the Afton Mountain exit."

Clay barely had time to think about the tight curves coming up as I-64 headed down the Valley side of the mountain. A strange flickering light in the thick white wall caught his eye. His foot jumped to the brake pedal, but it was too late. The outlines of two wrecked cars splayed across the two westbound lanes popped out of the mist right in front of him. Flames spewed from the left one.

"Oh Jeez! Hang on, Susan!" Clay exclaimed and desperately swerved toward the right shoulder. A strange mix of shock, fear, and anger swept through him as he spun the wheel. This was not supposed to happen. Not to him. Not to Susan.

Susan's cry of "Clay!" hit him at the same time the adrenaline surged into his veins. Everything seemed to be moving in slow motion now and he became strangely detached from it all. He had almost cleared the wreck when the Volvo lost traction on the wet pavement and slid sideways. He knew it immediately but there was nothing he could do. With a tremendous bang the Volvo hit the Camry, crumpling the Volvo's rear quarter panel. Clay spun the wheel the other direction to miss the shadow of the guardrail now coming right at him. The Volvo's back end kicked out to take the brunt of that glancing blow and now the Volvo slid, screeching metal against metal, along the guardrail. Clay saw Susan being thrown against her door. Again, nothing he could do. Another shadow popped out of the fog. Dead ahead. Wide-eyed, Clay watched Susan's Volvo slam into a wrecked Chevy pickup so hard that he felt the Volvo's rear end lift up off the ground.

The deafening bang! as they hit nearly drowned out Susan's scream. Clay's seatbelt dug into his shoulder as he lurched forward and then bounced back against the headrest. The billowing airbag slammed into his face. For an instant he sat there disbelieving, then found himself staring at the Volvo's now uplifted hood as the airbags deflated. He shook his head and came around. It had all happened so fast.

"Susan, are you all right? Susan!" She was dazed, but turned her head at the sound of his voice.

"I--I think so, Clay. Where are we?"

"In the middle of a big accident. Looks like a chain reaction pile-up, and I don't think it's over yet. We'd better get out of the car. Can you open your door?" He turned off the ignition as he watched her. She lifted the handle and banged her shoulder against the door but it was no use. Clay tried his, but he succeeded only in getting it unlatched. Something kept it from opening.

Feeling trapped, Clay's attention shifted to flames leaping out of a wrecked delivery van. No way, he thought. We're getting out of here. He pushed himself over to Susan's side of the car.

"What are you doing, Clay?" she cried out. He practically shoved her against her door and then dragged his legs out from under the steering wheel.

"Got to get that door open," he grunted and, swiveling his legs up onto the driver's seat, starting kicking the door with both feet. On the third whack, the door sprung open and he slid out.

"Give me your hand," he called out and helped Susan slide out the driver's side. "We'd better get on the other side of the guardrail. It's not safe standing out here."

"Clay, this is awful," Susan gasped, looking at the mist-shrouded shadows of three or four wrecks vaguely illuminated by the flames engulfing the van. The noxious smell of burning oil, plastic, and rubber assaulted their nostrils. Stifling a cough, Clay took Susan by the hand and together they stepped over the guardrail. He turned to look at her. "Are you sure you're okay?" he asked, pushing her hair back to check a scratch on her forehead. She was shaking, so he wrapped his arms around her and hugged her gently.

"I'm okay now," she said after a minute. "I was just really scared. You holding me is what I needed."

"Thank God you're all right. I saw you getting banged around in your seat."

She settled her head back on his chest, gazing at the flickering lights in the mist. "Those two people out there might be hurt, Clay. Shouldn't we do something?

Clay spotted the shadowy outlines of two people sitting on the ground next to their wrecked car. "If you're okay, I'll get them to come over here."

Clay yelled at them, then let go of Susan, and stepped over the guardrail. With mist swirling around him, he walked out into roadway to help. Both women were pretty badly shaken up, but otherwise seemed okay. After helping them get to their feet, Clay herded them toward the guardrail.

Heading back out onto the roadway to check another wreck, Clay heard a dull thud and turned to look uphill. A wrecked car whipped sideways and suddenly Clay found himself staring into the headlights of yet another car coming out of the fog. It slid directly at him at thirty mph, wheels locked and skidding.

Clay heard Susan scream and did the only thing he could. At the last instant he jumped up in the air to come down with a crash on the car's hood. His head banged against the windshield, putting him almost nose-to-nose with the terrified driver. Dazed but still conscious, Clay hung on for dear life, locking his fingers on the back edge of the hood below the windshield. The car slid another fifty feet, coming to a stop within spitting distance of a burning fuel oil tanker lying on its side.

"Quick, mister. Get out, and get over on the other side of the guardrail," Clay yelled at the driver after sliding off the car's hood. He yanked open the driver's door and helped the man out, almost shoving him toward the roadside. The dazed man walked uncertainly for a few steps, then turned to watch Clay head toward a burning wreck.

Clay heard Susan yelling for him and then another thud and breaking glass farther up the roadway. Then two more, and a horn started blaring. "I'm okay, Susan! I'm over here. Come down here, but stay behind that guardrail. They're still coming, but they're hitting farther up the hill."

"Clay, you should come over here too. That truck, it's burning."

Heating oil, Clay thought, not much chance it's going to explode. *He hoped.* Then another wreck lighted by that fire suddenly caught Clay's eye. An old model Mercedes sedan lay flipped over on its roof. Could that be? Clay wondered. Two men knelt beside the driver's side window, apparently having trouble pulling out a struggling man. Clay hesitated for a second or two, waiting to see if they needed help. Then he called out, "Hey, I'll give you a hand," as he started toward the Mercedes.

Now half in and half out of the driver's side window, the old man growled angrily and seemed to be trying to punch the men. One of them, with dark hair and a dark full beard, stood as Clay approached. Incredibly, the other quickly pulled out a knife and plunged it twice into the man's chest. Shocked, Clay couldn't believe his eyes. Square in the middle of this carnage, the stark realization raced through his mind, *They're murdering him!* He heard the sickening sound of the knife slicing into flesh and the man's gut wrenching cry in response to the horrible pain.

Anger, outrage welled up in Clay as he broke into a run. He had to stop those bastards, beat them senseless for their wanton act of brutality. The one standing saw him coming and yelled a guttural warning cry. Both men then fled, sprinting downhill into the fog-draped night. Clay wanted to follow, but he had no choice. He had to help the old man.

Clay clapped a hand over a stab wound pumping out blood, then pulled up the man's shirttail to use as a compress. Blood was everywhere. Clay had had enough first aid training to know that the man was bleeding internally as well. And that he couldn't do anything to stabilize the wounds. The old man had already turned pale and shocky, and from the sound of his voice, he was fading fast.

Kneeling beside the man, Clay leaned in closer. He noticed a yarmulke that had fallen off the man's head during the struggle. "Who did this to you? Who were those men?"

The old man shook his head from side to side weakly. He breathed the words, just barely audible, "Find Blake's Hill. Stop them before they...."

Clay tried to comfort him. "Hang in there. You'll be all right. Help is on the way."

The man just repeated, "Find Blake's Hill." His eyes closed for a moment.

"Hey, stay with me," Clay yelled and shook him gently. The man's eyes opened and he tried to say something, but his jaw went slack and all Clay heard was a gentle sigh. That breath was the old man's last. Clay put his other hand on the man's neck to check for a pulse, but there was none. He lifted his hand from the wound. The blood had stopped flowing.

"Clay! Are you all right?" Susan called from somewhere over by the guardrail. "I hear sirens; help is coming."

"Stay right there, Susan. I'll come over to you." Moments later, he stepped over the guardrail and the two shadows became one as she hugged him tightly.

"I saw them murder him," he said quietly. "I still can't believe it. In the middle of all this. One of them pulled out a knife and stabbed him twice. I couldn't do a damn thing to help him but be there when he died." Suddenly aware of the blood on his hands, he tried wiping it off on his pants before Susan noticed.

"Murdered who, Clay?" Susan demanded. "Are you hurt?" she asked in alarm as she pulled back from him. "Your shirt. Are you bleeding?"

"I'm all right. It's the old man, the one who wanted us to call the police. He's dead. I saw his car, the old Mercedes, flipped over. Two hadjis--" Clay caught himself slipping into the slang from his Army days. "Arab bad guys, terrorists, were trying to drag him out of the car. I went to help, but they saw me. One of them pulled a knife and stabbed the old man before I could stop them."

He tried wiping the sticky blood off his hands again as he replayed that moment in his mind. This wasn't like the killing he'd seen in Afghanistan. That was war in a far away place. *This* was cold-blooded murder--so completely unexpected, and so close to his home, that the stark brutality stung him. It wasn't supposed to happen here, so far from a war he'd put behind him over five years ago now.

"Oh my God, Clay. That's terrible. Did they come after you?"

"No, they ran off," he said vacantly.

"Thank heavens you're all right, Clay. I saw that car hit you. I couldn't believe it. How in the world did you manage to walk away from that!"

That brought Clay out of his daze. He laughed, and remembering that scary moment as the car came at him, he joked, "Banged and bruised, but still kicking. Nine lives, honey, and still three dozen to go." Making light of it made that close call less frightening, even to him.

She looked up at him. "Now you're a math whiz?"

"You were right about that old man, Susan," he said coming back to that. "He was in real trouble."

"Who were those men? Did he say? We should tell the police." Then Susan mumbled plaintively, "Why did I leave my phone at home?"

"There isn't much we could have done. My bet is that this was a hit. He had a yarmulke, which means he was Jewish. He knew he was in trouble and those two looked like assassins to me. Olive skinned, dark beards and dark hair. Maybe Palestinians, or Muslim terrorists."

"Clay, this isn't Afghanistan. What in the world would they be doing here, trying to kill an old man?"

"I don't know, Susan. Not a clue, but that's what it looks like. All the old guy said was 'Find Blake's Hill.' Which doesn't make any sense. What could a hill have to do with any of this? Maybe he was out of his head."

"Let's find a policeman. I heard the sirens back up the hill."

Bringing along the dazed man Clay had pulled out of his car, they followed the guardrail back up to the Afton Mountain entrance ramp onto I-64. There they found a line of ambulances, fire trucks, and police cruisers--a blinding crescendo of red, white, orange, and blue lights flashing in urgent disharmony. One ambulance was already turning around to take the first of the injured people to the county hospital. Here and there state troopers interviewed disoriented and frightened looking people who, despite blankets draped around their shoulders, shivered in the evening cold. Clay left Susan and the dazed man with an ET, and walked over to a nearby trooper who wasn't already busy taking statements. The officer did a double-take when Clay told him about the murder. Collecting himself, the trooper focused on Clay's bloodstained shirt, suddenly spun Clay around, and cuffed him.

"Hey, what the hell are you doing? I didn't do anything." Clay protested.

"Sure mister. We'll figure that out after I've read you your rights."

"Officer, what are you doing?" Susan yelled as she hurried over from the ambulance.

The trooper was just digging out his Miranda card, when his sergeant came over, adding to the confusion.

"Ed, what have you got here?"

"Man just walked up to me and reported a murder, sergeant. Farther down the hill. Look, he's got blood all over him."

"I told him I just *saw* a murder being committed," Clay protested. "Two guys stabbed an old man and ran off. I got this blood on me trying to help the old man. I'm just trying to report a murder and this idiot cuffs me." Clay couldn't help being angry at the stupidity of being cuffed after everything else he'd been through tonight.

"Hold on now mister," the sergeant shot back. "We don't know anything for sure yet. Just settle down while we get this sorted out."

"He was trying to help," Susan exclaimed. "He chased them off."

"Who are you?" the sergeant asked Susan.

Drawn by the commotion, the dazed man, now with a bandaged forehead, entered the fray. "Two men. I saw it too," he said as he approached the sergeant. "They were dragging somebody out of an overturned car. This man went over to help, but before he got there, one of the other men stabbed the guy. Then the two of them ran off."

"Where is the victim?" the sergeant asked.

"I can show you," Clay offered, "if you'll take these damn cuffs off me."

Soon after, the two troopers and Clay disappeared into the fog, leaving Susan on her own. By the time Clay got back, she had already found warm blankets and coffee for herself and Clay, and had borrowed a phone to call Mac Harper, Clay's friend and partner in C&H Construction Company. Handing Clay a steaming container of coffee, she reported, "Mac's already on his way. He's going to meet us farther down Route 250, as close as they'll let him."

"Thanks, Susan. Glad you thought of that," Clay said. "The sooner we get out of here, the happier I'll be." He took a slug of coffee. *"That is so good."*

"You didn't lose it, did you?" she asked quietly.

Clay tapped his front pants pocket. "No, got it right here. It's okay. I checked."

Wet, cold, and still keyed up, Clay and Susan began walking arm-in-arm down the hill toward Waynesboro. A good ten minutes passed before they cleared the roadblock police had set up on Route 250 and found Mac's pickup parked on the side of the road. Clay pulled open the passenger side door to let Susan in first. The blast of heat coming from inside felt good, like the first breath of the return to normalcy.

"Hey Mac," Clay said wearily, "Boy, have we got a story to tell you."

Susan was about to climb in when she stopped and turned to Clay. "My dress. My beautiful new dress. It's still in the car," she cried, "I forgot all about it!"

"We'll get it tomorrow. Promise," Clay said as he wearily helped her up into the cab.

* * * *

The following afternoon, over on the northern edge of Staunton's city limits, two cars raised a plume of dust on a long gravel drive as they approached a looming, four-story stone mill house. Nestled in the cleft of hills rising on either side of it, the big mill occupied a secluded dell, well off paved roads and hidden from view by great swaths of rolling pastureland belonging to the surrounding farms. Some years earlier, Clay, with Mac's help, had restored the mill and converted the third and fourth floors to living spaces, which Clay now called home. The cars slowed as the drive curved around the glass-still millpond and the low hanging weeping willows clinging to its banks. Running up the short rise, the cars stopped in front of the main entrance to the mill house, on what was actually the third floor.

Mac Harper, Clay's partner in C&H Construction, climbed out of his three-month old, sculpted Lexus LS Sport and disdainfully examined the thin coat of dust on what was an otherwise gleaming dark green paint job. Jimmy Campbell clambered out of a bright red

’67 Corvette, which except for the color, was a twin to Clay’s midnight blue ’67 Vette. One ride in Clay’s had convinced Jimmy he absolutely had to have one just like it--an impossible dream for a high school history teacher, until that is, Clay, Mac, and Jimmy got lucky and recovered a lost horde of Confederate gold. That treasure hunt had turned out to be a life changing event for them all.

“When is Clay going to pave this driveway?” Jimmy complained jokingly to Mac, or rather up at Mac. Of average build, Jimmy looked small next to Mac, a big-boned, barrel-chested bruiser. At six-five, Mac made most people look on the small side.

“He’s got the money now,” Jimmy continued. “Hell, he’s always had the money!”

Mac grinned as the two turned to the path leading down to a deck on the low side of the mill house, the pea gravel crunching under their feet. It was a beautiful Indian summer day in mid-October. The sun, lower in the sky now, shone with a gentler warmth and softly lighted the bright red leaves of a massive oak across the driveway. The small deck overlooking the millpond lay around the corner of the building from the idled mill wheel, and farther upstream a thin sheet of water cascading over a dam provided a soothing background melody of rushing water.

“Hi guys.” Clay waved from his seat at a table with Susan. Both Clay and Susan were dressed casually in shorts and tee-shirts. Clay had his black Orioles baseball cap pushed back on his head, revealing a good-sized bruise on his forehead. Mac and Jimmy wore polo shirts and long pants for this casual meeting of now very rich treasure hunters.

“You two had quite a night last night,” Jimmy offered as he sat down.

“Kind of hairy. Susan’s Volvo was totaled,” Clay said solemnly.

“No offense, Susan. But it was lucky you weren’t in the Vette. A classic car like that, totaled? That would be a real tragedy.”

"Thanks a lot, Jimmy," Susan grumbled. Jimmy winced. "Some people just need a car for work, you know. Well, anyway, Clay is buying me a new one." She smiled at Clay.

"You didn't have insurance?"

"She did," Clay interjected. "But her Volvo was five years old and her insurance covers only what that was worth. I'll make up the difference on the price of a new one. I broke it; I'll buy it."

"It wasn't your fault, Clay," Susan insisted.

"So, what took you to Charlottesville in the first place?" Jimmy asked, trying to get off the wrecked car.

"Oh--" Susan said, and then hesitated. She shot a coy look at Clay and continued, "Just some shopping. And Clay took me out to dinner."

"Clay, you made the papers again--front page," Mac interrupted, pulling a newspaper clipping from his pocket. "Listen to this:"

Fog Shrouds Murder Amid 50-Car Pileup

AFTON--State police reported early today that an elderly man, driving one of the fifty cars involved in the chain reaction pileup in fog last night on I-64, was stabbed to death by two unidentified attackers. The driver of another car in the pileup, Staunton contractor Clay Cantrell, courageously drove off two men, but not before they had fatally stabbed the victim.

Police are withholding the victim's name, pending notification of next of kin.

Miraculously, that was the only death in last night's chain reaction crash, but 17 people were hospitalized, five of them with serious injuries, police reported.

Cantrell and two partners made headlines last summer when they uncovered a cache of Confederate gold coins that had been abandoned 150 years ago in a in Highland County cavern. The estimated worth of the horde is about $12 million....

"They made you out a hero, even though the old man died."

"That's my guy," Susan announced proudly.

"I don't know about that 'courageously drove off' bit. As soon as they saw me coming, they stabbed him and took off. I suppose *if* I'd tried to chase them."

"They might have turned on you," Jimmy said, completing Clay's sentence for him.

"It was awful," Susan exclaimed. "The accident--we were lucky we weren't killed. All those cars smashing into each other. It was like something out of a bad dream. And that poor old man. Imagine, surviving that crash and then being stabbed to death."

"Was it a robbery? Jimmy asked.

"I think something else was going on," Clay said, and then told Jimmy the story about the old man signaling them.

When Clay finished, Susan got up and announced, "I've got some really delicious apple cider to go with our sandwiches. We've also got beer."

"Beer," Clay piped up.

"Beer," Mac ordered.

"Beer," Jimmy said with a grin.

Miffed, Susan said, "I should have known with this crowd." All three men grinned and then offered to help. "Sit," she said firmly, "I'll bring it out."

"Okay, Jimmy, what have you got for us?" Clay asked as Susan went inside. "And what? Is that a Rolex you're wearing, Jimmy? Timex not good enough for you anymore, teach?"

Jimmy managed only a desultory "Hah-hah," before opening his sleek, and probably very expensive, new briefcase. Out came a sheaf of papers that he shuffled before beginning.

"I met with your lawyer, Clay, that Mr. Jarndyce--he was very helpful--who recommended I contact a well-known numismatist named Kenneth Wilson. Ken was kind enough to talk with me about how to market our gold coins, and he suggested hiring Joseph Eagleberger for that. Eagleberger has handled the sale of several big finds, and if what Mr. Wilson told me is true, we can kill the value of our coins if we dump them all at once. Eagleberger's services will cost us, but in the long run he'll be worth it, I think. We're talking about an estimated value in excess of $12 mil, more if the coins grade out the way I think they will."

"Agreed," Clay said. Mac nodded his approval as well. Just then, Susan arrived with three bottles of beer and her apple cider. A platter of sandwiches came out next. "You're not having a beer?" Clay asked.

"There's a whole gallon of cider in your fridge, Clay dear. Somebody's got to drink it before it goes bad."

Clay smiled but chose to ignore the poke. "Well okay, Jimmy, do you have more on the marketing?"

Jimmy finished chewing his bite of a sandwich and washed it down with a swig of beer. "Yes, once the coins have been officially graded, Eagleberger's plan is to break up the collection and sell it in lots to specific dealers best qualified to market them."

"What was the verdict on the coins we handled?" Mac asked.

"Not great. It was a good thing that we only dumped out a few bags of coins. We don't have an official ruling on the condition yet, but it seems likely most or all of our horde was in mint condition, or pretty close to that, when we hauled it out of the cavern. Out of the 380 octagonal $50 gold pieces, we probably handled about sixty pieces; of the 750 $20 gold pieces, about a hundred. If the oil from our fingers corrodes the mint sheen, which it could, that will knock the value down."

"I don't care," Mac declared. "It was worth it just to finally get our hands on it."

Clay laughed. "Amen to that, partner. There were times when I wondered...."

"So, should I hire Eagleberger and arrange the grading?"

"As far as I'm concerned, yes, but we'd better talk about his fee before you seal the deal. How about you, Mac?"

"I'm all for moving this along. I'm paying interest on the cash I got from my bridge loan. Soon as we get some money coming in, I can pay it off. You're probably in the same boat, Jimmy."

"You bet. What did Professor Adler say about the cavern, Clay?"

"I heard from him earlier this week. He definitely wants to handle the excavating and cataloguing of whatever else is in the cavern. He and his students will do the work, once we get the main entrance open. In return, the university will receive a twenty percent share of the proceeds. I don't know yet when we'll get to the job of opening the tunnel, but if you are right about that antique furniture in there being worth a lot, we could still be in for nice chunk of change. Whatever we decide to donate to the university will be eligible for a tax write-off as a charitable donation. Our accountant says we're going to need some write-offs, maybe a lot of them."

"Nice problem to have, I'd say," Mac said with a hearty laugh.

* * * *

Lights blazed against the night at the far end of a long, one-story brick building at the rear of Halston Technological Park in Loudon County, on the outer fringe of Washington, DC. With the stroke of midnight fast approaching, two suspicious-looking men hugged the shadows, crouching as they darted from tree to tree for cover in the parklike grounds surrounding the building. They spoke in hushed tones as they worked closer and closer to the lighted windows.

Suddenly, a massive explosion inside the building blew out the laboratory windows with a thunderous roar, sending glass and debris flying. The two men hit the dirt as smoke billowed from the blown-out windows.

"Allah akbar!" the bearded man exclaimed to his clean shaven comrade as the two scrambled to their feet.

"What has happened?" the other exclaimed.

"I do not know, Abdul. It is the first time I have ever seen a building blow up before we've even touched it. It must be truly evil that Allah would strike it with his own hand. But that is not for us to question why. We must remove ourselves quickly now. Police will be coming soon." With that, the two retreated into the shadows and disappeared into the night.

At the far end of the building, Professor Willard Wentworth jumped out of his chair in his office at the sound of the explosion, then sank back with a deeply distressed look. That was not good, he thought, and then slowly got to his feet. He remembered, painfully now, the maxim he'd heard from other scientists many times before, "When you work at the cutting edge, you are likely to bleed."

Fifty-eight years old, bespectacled in his thick, black horn-rimmed glasses, and bald except for a narrow strip of close-cropped gray hair that had retreated to just above the tops of his ears, Prof. Wentworth was beyond question a gifted scientist. He held degrees in nuclear physics, chemistry, and chemical engineering, but he was coming to the end of his career without having been able to fulfill the promise of discoveries made in his early years, now decades past. To say he was unlucky would be nothing short of an understatement. Some years ago, he was on the verge of publishing what was to be his crowning achievement, only to come in a corroborating second to a bright young researcher in Switzerland.

After that, he was dogged by an unfortunate series of failures in phenomenally expensive experiments to find the elusive subatomic particle Higgs boson. That cost him his prestigious position as a research fellow at CERN, leaving him no choice but to retreat to private industry. Then a string of unhappy positions at chemical companies here in the U.S. had brought him to this last desperate hope--a poorly funded, long-shot research project in the backwaters of a huge international conglomerate--Babcock Chemical Corp. Prof. Wentworth had reluctantly signed on for what was clearly the high risk, pet project of a mid-level executive at Babcock--one Robert Newsome, Second Vice President of Research and Development for Babcock's Mid-Atlantic Division. The risk, as Wentworth later discovered, was all his. If he succeeded, Prof. Wentworth would finally have his triumph, and Newsome would surely move up to first vice president.

But Newsome clearly was no fool. He kept a tight lid on the project: Prof. Wentworth was to report only to him, all lab notes and associated documents were to remain at the laboratory, and under no circumstances was there to be any mention of the project outside the lab. Use of the internet, fax, or any other electronic communication was strictly forbidden. Complete containment, Prof. Wentworth was told, was necessary to prevent industrial spying. Others were indeed working in this area in several different countries, but Prof. Wentworth knew the real reason for the security clampdown. If his experiments failed, as this latest explosion hinted might yet happen, Newsome would simply destroy all evidence of the project, bury the embarrassment with some form of creative accounting, and move on. Prof. Wentworth, of course, would be fired on the spot.

Prof. Wentworth, for his part, still believed he would triumph in the end. He was nothing, if not determined, and they were getting close; he knew that. The explosion tonight was a setback, but he only had to keep Newsome in the game a while longer. He toyed with the idea of simply not reporting it to Newsome, but he knew that would not be wise. He would have to endure that phone call tonight, as soon as he had assessed the damages. The acrid smell of smoke wafting into his office startled him back to the present moment.

"My God! Babeesh? Valerie?" he suddenly cried out loud. A minute had passed since the explosion and he had been so wrapped in his own concerns, he hadn't gone to see if his lab assistants were hurt. Racing down the hallway now, he pushed through the lab door, which had been knocked off its hinges. "Babeesh? Valerie? Are you okay?"

"Over here," Valerie said as she stood up from behind an overturned lab bench. "Everything's ruined."

Prof. Wentworth stepped past the thick-walled safety station and into the lab proper. The three heavy lab tables with soapstone tops lay overturned on their sides, an oppressively acrid smell overhung the lab, and broken glass and twisted metal littered the floor. Both Valerie and Babeesh were hunkered down on their haunches on either side of a still smoking gallon-sized container, half of which had disintegrated.

"Are you two all right?"

"Yes, but that new calorimeter is ruined," Valerie reported. A buxom redhead, Valerie was in her late twenties, had an attractive face, and apart from those thick ankles Wentworth used to call "piano legs" in his college days, she had a great body. Even though she'd been out of college for several years, she still came to work dressed like a student in fitted jeans and soft, curve hugging tee-shirts. Not that Prof. Wentworth minded that.

"Fifty thousand dollars, gone just like that? What happened?"

"We don't know," Valerie responded with a perplexed expression. "Until two hours ago, Babeesh had nothing but normal readings. Output gradually increasing the way it has been for the past couple of days."

"Valerie had just come to relieve me," said Babeesh, a dark-skinned, expatriate from the Indian subcontinent. His slightly sing-song syntax and native version of the British accent he'd learned in his homeland usually amused Prof. Wentworth. But not tonight. Not in the midst of this disaster. "Suddenly the output spiked. Ouh, yes. Went off the meter! Happened so bery, bery fast. Super quick. I shut down everything, but it wouldn't stop. Then *Boom!*, it blew up. Bery, bery bad!"

"I think the cathode vaporized," Valerie added.

Prof. Wentworth rubbed his face with both hands. Another failure, he thought. They'd have to start all over with a different catalyzer, possibly even a different material for the cathode. And new equipment. Newsome wasn't going to like this. Not at all. "All right. Please get started cleaning this mess up. I'll be back to help after I've called off the Fire Department and reported this to Mr. Newsome."

Valerie watched him leave the lab and then muttered to Babeesh, "Yeah, I'll bet we don't see him again tonight."

"Why do you hate him so?" Babeesh asked as he struggled to right one of the heavy lab tables.

"Because he's using us. Well, more me than you. You're his pal. You men all stick together."

"What makes you say that, Valerie? He gives us work, pays our salary, doesn't he?"

"Yes, but you get the day shift and I have to work nights. And you make more than I do."

"Valerie, I have a family to support," he sputtered. "I've been working with him a long time. I'm doing my post-doc, so I should get more."

Valerie slammed a feed pump onto the now righted lab table. "Yeah, he helped you. But all I get are excuses."

"Maybe he just can't right now."

"Won't is more like it."

2

PORTENTS OF THINGS TO COME

Susan fidgeted nervously the whole way from Staunton to Clay's parents' estate, Bentley, a sprawling hundred-acre property lying west of Charlottesville in a tony area of large houses, horse farms, and vineyards. This was to be her first dinner at Clay's parents' house, but that was not all. Clay, decked out in a sport coat and tie in honor of the occasion, had done his best to reassure her, told her she looked fantastic, and that she'd be a big hit. But she was not be consoled, and his inevitable teasing didn't seem to help either. Her eyes widened as Clay turned onto the long straight driveway leading up to Bentley, an imposing three-story mansion perched on a small rise and surrounded by fenced pastures. A matched pair of chestnut mares in sole possession of a great swath of grass bounded by a white, four-board fence, perked up at the sight of Clay's Vette arriving. Swishing their tails dismissively, they returned to their grazing in the late afternoon sunshine.

Clay saw the thunderstruck look on Susan's face. "Home sweet home, Susan."

"Clay, it's so big," she protested.

"Enormous is more like it, but Susan honey, they're still just Mom and Dad."

"Well that's the part I'm worried about Clay dear."

"Susan, this isn't the first time you've met them."

"That was dinner out, Clay. But this is my--our first time at their house as a couple. They hardly know me at all. And what will I think when...?"

Pulling to a stop under the porte-cochere at the side of the mansion, Clay turned to look at her. She was a beautiful brunette, subtly sensuous, not flashy or provocatively sexy. Her deep blue dress clothed, but did not hide, her youthful figure and the modestly cut neckline provided the perfect canvas for the string of pearls she wore.

Even in distress, Clay thought, the lady can't help being beautiful. He reached over to touch her shoulder and looked into her deep brown eyes. Her soft lips curved up into a slight smile as she returned his gaze. He knew what was bothering her, couldn't blame her for that.

"Susan, I know they're going to love you. But I want you to remember something," he said gently, "that no matter what, you've given *me* lots to be thankful for."

"Oh, Clay," Susan sighed and melted. She put her hand on his chest and kissed him lightly on the cheek. A moment later she was far away again, instinctively turning the rearview mirror toward herself to check her hair and makeup.

Clay watched her primping for a moment. "Right. Ready now troops? Forward, march!"

"Oh hush, Clay. Can't a girl go before the firing squad without a lot of jokes?"

"Not in this household, honey. Come on, we'll take the front door by storm."

Clay put his arm around her as they walked back around to the front porch. Clay's mother and father, both smiling, met them at the grand double front door, which opened onto the columned porch.

"Mom, Dad, you remember Susan."

Carl, Clay's father, wore a brass-buttoned blue blazer and striped tie. He stood eye-to-eye with Clay, but he had a thinner, lanky frame, and a full head of gray hair. He reached out and shook Susan's hand.

"Of course we remember, dear" Catherine said, giving Susan a hug. Tanned, slim, with her gray hair pulled back into a bun, Catherine wore a white blouse and black skirt. "So nice to see you again." She pulled back to look at Susan. "Your dress, Susan. That shade of blue looks beautiful on you. Where ever did you find it?"

"Oh, Charlottesville. The blue matches Clay's eyes, don't you think?"

Catherine smiled warmly at that.

"Come inside. It's chilly out here," Carl said, interrupting. He held the front door open for them. "William and his family are gallivanting around France at the moment, so we'll have the place to ourselves."

"I don't think you've met Clay's older brother and his family yet, have you Susan?" Catherine asked.

Susan shook her head and smiled as Carl led them through the domed, ornately tiled vestibule. The large center hallway beyond it was dominated by a wide curving staircase leading down from the floor above. The intricately parqueted floor creaked as they crossed it to enter a sitting room off to the right. Susan did her best to avoid looking like a gawking tourist while trying to take in as much of the elaborate furnishings as she could. Carl, for his part, wasted no time in getting drinks in everybody's hand. Clay and Susan sat together on a leather settee, while Carl and Catherine settled into wing chairs on their right. A low fire crackled warmly in the massive, tiled fireplace, while the twelve-foot-high ceilings and shafts of late day sunlight streaming in through the tall windows lent the room a grand, old world atmosphere.

Carl, raising his glass, smiled warmly, "To you, Susan. I hope this will be the first of many visits here."

Clay turned to her, winked, and cheered, "Here, here!" Susan flushed a bit and smiled broadly. "This is really such a beautiful house. You must love it out here."

"If Carl has his way, it will be our last resting place," Catherine joked.

"Catherine dear, you love it here too," Carl scolded gently. He turned to Susan. "She has plenty of room to ride her horses, we're out in the country, and yet it's only a few minutes into town. Best of both worlds."

"Sounds ideal. And I've always liked Charlottesville."

"Do you ride, Susan?" Catherine asked.

"No, I never really had the chance to learn."

"If Clay isn't hogging all your time, why not come over one afternoon and we'll go for a ride. I'll show you the ropes. It's really exhilarating--such a liberating feeling."

"And a great way to break your neck," Carl added.

"Oh pish, Carl, not if you know what you are doing." She paused and looked over at Clay. "I never could get him up on a horse either. He won't ride anything that doesn't have an engine."

Clay grinned sheepishly. "Saddles, bridles--you've got to do a ton of stuff before you can go anywhere. If I can't stick a key into it to start it, I don't want to deal with it."

Catherine gave him an amused, that's my Clay smile, and let the subject drop. Carl jumped into the void, "Susan, if I remember, you're an agent at Thompson Realty. Is that right? Are things picking up over there in Staunton?"

"Yes, Thompson. It's better, but we're still struggling. We're getting more traffic these days, and I've had a closing this month, which is great. But we need to get more houses on the market. Sellers are holding back, waiting for prices to recover."

Turning to Clay, Carl said with a sly grin, "Guess you're happy with the price of gold these days. You certainly picked the right time to come up with a treasure horde. Have you started selling those coins yet?"

"Jimmy's making the arrangements on that. He's lined up experts to advise us."

"I've got to give you credit, Clay, that was quite an adventure. You handled it really well and came out on top. Susan, you should be very proud of him."

"Oh, I am. I just try not to let him know," she said with a grin.

"She gangs up on me all the time," Clay joked. "But seriously, none of this would have happened, Dad, if we hadn't bought Fairview and found that diary. Just plain luck, I guess."

"How is the work coming on Fairview?"

"Okay. The heat of that fire wrecked the foundation--turned the cement to powder. But the foundation work is done and the framing is going up now."

"That fire was awful," Catherine lamented. "How could that horrible little man burn down that beautiful house. All that history."

"Well, he's going to pay for that, and a lot more," Clay said pointedly. Then he smiled at Susan. "But that day wasn't all bad. That's the day I met Susan."

"Cla-a-a-a-y!" Susan protested. "We met at that party at Midway a long time before!"

"Yes, dear." He said it dutifully while Susan grimaced. Carl and Catherine laughed.

"Sounds like he's learning who's boss," Carl prodded.

"Yes, she's working on me," Clay replied without losing a beat. He turned to Susan and asked, "Should we tell them now?" Then to his mother, "I think she'll explode if we don't soon."

Susan gave him a playful shove, then mouthed a silent "okay." If she could have crossed her fingers without being seen, she would have. Instead she held her breath.

"Mom, Dad," Clay began in a serious tone. "We've been keeping it a secret until now, because we wanted you to be the first to know. I've asked Susan to marry me and she's said yes. We're engaged."

Susan deftly spun the engagement ring around on her finger to display a big, sparkling diamond. "He gave me this," she proudly announced.

Catherine's hand went to her chest in surprise and then she cried out, "Oh my! Susan, Clay, that's wonderful. I had no idea! Carl, this calls for champagne." She smiled approvingly at Susan. For her part, Susan smiled and, relieved at Catherine's obvious approval of the engagement, secretly took a deep breath. After all that had happened on the day they had picked up the ring in Charlottesville, Susan had been secretly worried that this might wind up the same way.

"Absolutely! Champagne it is." Carl got up to fetch the champagne, and as he went by Clay, paused to put a hand on his shoulder. "Well done, son. You never were any good at fishing, but she's quite a catch. You are lucky to have found her."

"I'll say," Susan quipped. She and Clay grinned at each other.

"Carl, how can you--" Catherine scowled. "Oh, never mind. Have you two set a date yet?"

"We're thinking about that," she said, giving Clay a sideward glance. "I like June, but he hasn't made up his mind--yet!"

"June is such a nice time for a wedding," Catherine gushed.

Carl returned with two bottles of Dom Perignon Rose 2002 and four elegant Waterford crystal champagne flutes. The toasts to health, happiness, and *more grandchildren* lasted through both bottles, while a very nice Merlot carried the celebration through dinner, featuring a succulent roasted leg of lamb.

After dinner, Catherine took Susan on a tour of the house. As they topped the curving staircase and began the tour of the second floor bedrooms, Catherine gave Susan a sideward glance.

"You know, Susan, Clay's been awfully chipper lately. I thought it was all that gold he dragged out into the daylight. But now I know it was you!"

"Well, part of it. From what Clay told me, he and Mac had a real adventure down there in those caves. *He* called it fun...," she said rolling her eyes for effect.

"He would. I never could slow that boy down. Well, that's your job now, Susan."

"That's one of the things I love about him. Reminds me of my brothers, I guess."

"I think you said you have two. Is that right?"

"Yes, Victor is older than me and Tom is younger. I was outnumbered, but I learned how to handle them. Strategy," she added with a knowing smile.

"I guess you've met Rita, Mac's wife. She's a real gem. Clay and Mac have been thick as thieves since grade school. We tried to tell Rita, when she married Mac, that she was getting Clay too. I'll bet she'll be pleased to know help is on the way."

Meanwhile, Clay lingered at the dinner table, watching his father fill and tamp his pipe, a straight-stem black briar. The thick, sweet smell of pipe tobacco reminded Clay of when, as a little boy, he became fascinated with this ritual. Clay smiled at the memory, and a few moments of silence passed as Carl puffed contentedly on his pipe.

"You know, Clay, you've always had good luck with the ladies, but I think you've topped yourself with Susan."

"Yes I did," Clay responded without hesitation. "I feel like the world's luckiest guy. She's smart, loving, and, well, it's like we were made for each other."

"You mean she puts up with you?" Carl asked with a sly grin. Clay laughed at the poke.

"Yeah, that too."

"Even so, there will be times. Marriage, when it works, is a forever proposition and you do have to work at it, son. Because needs, for both of you, will change over time. Just remember how important she is to you, and that you have to listen to her, even when she isn't talking."

Clay smiled. "Is that how you and Mom did it?"

"I like to think so, Clay."

39 • KILLER FOG

It was late that night by the time Clay and Susan left Bentley to return to Staunton. The steady rumbling of the Corvette's big V-8 conspired with an evening of dinner and drinks to lull Susan into a placid, sleepy silence as they sailed along the I-64 straightaways at seventy-five. They were virtually alone on the two westbound lanes with nothing but woods on either side of the highway. It wasn't until they passed the Ivy on-ramp that Clay noticed the headlights in his rearview mirror. A semi was coming up fast behind them in the right lane, Clay guessed. The guy had his brights up, filling the Vette's passenger compartment with glaring light.

The rude intrusion of bright light surprised and irritated Clay. But he just signaled, shifting to the left lane to let the truck pass on his right. Clay assumed the driver was highballing it to make up lost time. Or maybe he was on a return leg with an empty rig. Suddenly, for no apparent reason, the big truck shifted to the left lane and came up right behind Clay, filling his rearview mirror with the truck's square grill. It was so close the red Kenworth KW logo was clear as day, and then the truck's horn blared a bone-rattling blast of sound.

"What the hell?" Clay exclaimed as he almost jumped out of his socks. He downshifted in a flash and hit the gas, pulling away from the truck and as he did so, moved back to the right lane. That put some distance between him and the truck, so Clay slowed back down to seventy-five. But whatever the truck driver was up to, he wasn't going away. Clay watched in his rearview mirror as the semi changed to the right lane and sped up fast. Before Clay knew it, the big rig was hugging his bumper again.

"Clay, what's going on?"

"I don't know Susan. That semi behind me--I think the driver must be high on bennies or something. Here he comes again."

Seconds later the truck's grill again filled Clay's rearview mirror, this time bouncing up and down as the trucker hit the gas and backed off, nosing ever closer to Clay's rear bumper. Clay accelerated again and changed back to the left lane, leaving the trucker in the dust for the moment. This time Clay put a quarter mile between himself and the charging semi before slowing back down.

"That should take care of him," Clay said, as his heart rate settled back down. But it didn't last long.

"He's catching up again, Clay," Susan reported anxiously, having turned around in her seat.

"I see him," he said, checking his rearview mirror again. Getting angry now, Clay tightened his grip on the steering wheel and stick shift. The trucker was really barreling along this time and as he closed, he again shifted lanes to get behind Clay.

"What is with this guy?" Clay growled. He waited until the semi again loomed in his rearview mirror, and then downshifted and hit the gas. But this time only until he saw that gigantic grill hop upward, signaling that the trucker had put the pedal to the metal. Clay looked quickly to his right, and in a split second put the Vette into the right lane. Then he slammed on the brakes. The semi shot by before the trucker even realized what had happened. Clay hit the gas again and pulled up behind the semi. He stayed in the slot behind the semi as the trucker at first slowed down to a crawl, then started to speed up.

"Get ready to start writing, Susan. I want to get this guy's license plate number." He'd called out five of the many plates plastered on the back of the trailer before the trucker pulled off onto the Crozet off ramp and disappeared into the night. Clay resisted the urge to follow, deciding it would be best to stay out of trouble.

"That was weird," Clay said as they whipped past the Crozet exit.

"Do you think it has anything to do with what happened the other night?"

"If it does, those people have a pretty good organization behind them. I suppose it wouldn't have been too hard to track me down from the news reports, but to set this up? That truck would have to have been waiting for us at the Ivy on-ramp tonight."

"That's scary, Clay, to think those two murderers could be following us around."

"It's more likely they are long gone, Susan. What happened could be nothing more than a ticked off trucker looking to scare the hell out of somebody."

"He did that."

"That's definitely not the way I wanted tonight to end," he said to console her. "And I really doubt we'll hear from those two again."

"If the police don't catch them, we'll never know why that poor man was killed."

"The cops could still get a lead from the victim--who he was, who might have had it in for him, that kind of thing."

"Then maybe what he said will be important."

"'Find Blake's Hill? Maybe. But what could a hill have to do with anything? He was probably out of his head. I think that old guy himself is the key. I wonder if Lt. Youngblood could help us find out who he is."

"Us?"

"Well yeah," he said, "I'm kind of curious, you know. Something's going on, and I don't have a clue what it is."

"Clay, this could be dangerous."

Clay smiled benignly at her, which did nothing to allay her concerns.

"Did you bring your phone?" Clay asked.

"Are you kidding? After what happened last week? I'll never go anywhere without it again."

"Wise decision. Let's report that trucker to the state police."

* * * *

The next day, about a half hour's drive south of Staunton, Clay swung his Vette off the narrow country road outside of Bell's Crossroads and onto the long curving drive to what, before the arson fire, had been the historic Fairview mansion. The stunning westward view of the Allegheny Mountains off in the distance--the million dollar view--lay well beyond the reach of the fire and so remained untouched. The tall oaks nearest what had been the old mansion still showed signs of the fire's searing heat, but they would recover. And now, so would the mansion itself. Clay and Mac's construction crew had nearly completed framing for the first floor, a raw, pine-colored skeleton of 2x4's, 2x8's, and 2x10's awaiting a coat of flesh. The old mansion was rising up from the ashes to reclaim its former place in the landscape, and Clay couldn't help being excited by the sight. For a time, that hadn't seemed possible, but the proof was there now in the bones of what was the grand old mansion. He and Mac were going to do it, and George Kilgore would rot in hell, if there were any justice in the world.

The popping sound of nail guns and the shrill whine of power saws greeted Clay as he pulled up behind Mac's pickup in the cobblestone circular drive out front of the mansion. Meanwhile Mac, having seen Clay arrive, threaded his way through the maze of upright 2x4s forming the interior walls of the first floor.

"What do you think, partner?" Mac asked as he greeted Clay.

"We've got something to look at now. That's what I love about framing a house. It seems to jump up out of nowhere."

"We lay the second floor joists tomorrow."

"Did Ev nail up the extra bracing on the back wall?"

"Yup. First thing today. We're good to go on that, but you'd better take a look at what we found this morning."

Clay hoisted himself up onto the first floor--the porch and steps had yet to be installed--and followed Mac into the big open space that would become the formal living room. Ev, Everett Weaver, the recently hired project foreman for C&H Construction, wore a somber expression as he pointed at the spray painted graffiti on the plywood subfloor. It was a big, black rectangle with white painted Arabic letters.

"Never thought I'd see anything like this way out here," Ev said. "They must've done it last night sometime." Ev was the short stocky type, weathered from growing up on a farm in the Shenandoah Valley and years of working construction.

"*The Silent Man Keeps His Tongue*," Clay said, reading out loud the spray painted message in English below the flag-like rectangle. "Mac, do you remember this too?"

"Yeah, partner, that flag's a jihadi calling card. Looks just like what we saw in Afghanistan. They're all using that black flag now, though. I saw on the news where the Islamic State fighters fly the black flag too."

Clay's face reddened with anger. "I don't like anybody trying to intimidate me," he said while unconsciously clenching his fists. "Especially when the bastard doesn't have the balls to do it to my face. Second place, we don't need any more problems here."

"First that trucker, now this. Do you think it's connected with what that old guy told you?"

"I don't know, Mac. Could be. Those guys were definitely Muslim types, and this would be their style. Ev, tell the guys to keep an eye out for anything suspicious. Let me know right away, even if they're not sure," Clay said.

"Think we should call the cops?"

"Yeah. I'll call them. I'm getting to be way too popular with these damned hadjis."

A good two hours passed before a plain clothes car bearing two Augusta County detectives finally showed up at Fairview. Clay and Mac were already out front when the detectives eased out of the car, gawking at the construction site.

"Awh, Jeez, Mac. It's Armstrong. That's the last thing I need."

"Be civil, Clay. Won't do any good to pick a fight with him now."

Armstrong and his partner were both in their forties, just under six feet tall, burly and bull-like. Armstrong's graying hair was brushed up into a crew cut, a constant exclamation of surprise, while his partner was cue ball bald. Both wore shades and possibly permanent scowls, but it was Armstrong, who held a simmering grudge against Clay, who did all the talking.

"So it's you, Cantrell."

Clay glared at Armstrong but bit his tongue and replied gruffly, "It's over this way." Clay, Mac, and the two detectives clambered up onto the mansion's nascent first floor and a moment later Clay pointed at the painted black flag.

"Is this it?" Armstrong whined, "You dragged us all the way out here for this?"

"Hey, some weird stuff has been happening lately. Maybe you haven't heard."

"In your head, Cantrell." He turned to his partner and muttered, "Rich kids." Then back at Clay, "You've got a lot of nerve, I'll give you that."

"Hey, do your job, Armstrong," Clay growled, seething mad. He and Armstrong had been at it off and on for years. "Something hinky is going on around here. What's it going to take to wake you up, some juiced-up terrorist driving a damn car bomb into the county courthouse?"

"What! You expect me to believe that B.S.? Terrorists around here? Man, that's crazy. That kind of thing doesn't happen way out here. This," he growled, stabbing a finger at the black flag, "is just some kids playing a joke on you. Or maybe you pissed off one of these guys working for you. This is a bullshit waste of time."

"It's that attitude, butt head, that got the twin towers destroyed."

"Oh yeah. Maybe *you* did this," he spit the words out, poking his finger angrily in Clay's chest. "I think you're just setting things up so you can burn this place down a second time."

Clay took a step toward Armstrong, but Mac grabbed Clay's arm and pulled him back.

"Easy, Clay. *He's* an ass. No sense getting into it with him." Turning to Armstrong, he barked, "Take your damn picture of it and get the hell off our jobsite."

"Nothing but one of those damn sissy rich kids," Armstrong said loudly to his partner as they walked away.

"Just don't say anything," Mac told Clay.

Clay stood there with fists clenched until Armstrong and his partner drove off. Meanwhile, the silence on the jobsite was deafening. All work had stopped and everyone stood in place, staring at Clay in anticipation of a knock down, drag out fight.

"Thanks, Mac. Lost my head for a minute there," Clay admitted somewhat sheepishly. Then he bellowed, "All right you guys. Show's over. We've got a house to build. Let's get back to work."

"Hey, Ev," Clay shouted to his project foreman over the renewed whine of saws, "How about getting two guys to tear up the flooring that's been painted. Put down new plywood."

"We could just paint over it. Finish flooring will cover everything anyway," Ev suggested.

"No," Clay answered with irritation. "I'd know it was there. Throw that plywood on the burn pile."

"Looks like those two you ran into the other night really are hadji terrorists," Mac said.

"Yeah, that's their M-O, all right. Intimidate the population so they can get away with whatever they want. I'll tell you, Mac, I sure don't like thinking that a couple of hadjis are on the loose around here. But I guess I shouldn't be surprised the way things are going. I mean, what is it about Muslim culture that makes so many bloodthirsty fanatics? It's been breeding truckloads of them and training them to hate us--the Iranians, Iraqis, Yemenis, jeez even our good buddies the Saudis. Al Qaida would love to bloody 'the Great Satan' one more time for Allah. Do I look like a damn Great Satan? Do you?" He paused then grinned. "Armstrong, maybe."

Mac laughed. "It's a holy war, Clay. That's what they claim, anyway."

"Holy War, my ass. They're just stone cold killers."

Later that day, Clay and Mac stood out front at a makeshift table looking over blueprints specifying the framing for the mansion's second floor. They both looked up when a worker named Billy, at that moment up on a ladder facing the road leading to Fairview, called out and pointed.

"Hey boss. That black limo out there's been by two times this afternoon."

Clay turned and saw a black Mercedes stretch limo with tinted windows now stopped at the head of the driveway, as if considering whether to turn in or not. "Okay, Billy, thanks," Clay called back and waved. Then he turned to Mac, and trying for the positive, quipped, "Maybe it's a prospect." Mac nodded as they both watched the limo make up its mind. A full minute passed, then the limo gently rolled forward into the driveway and came straight for them. When the limo stopped, a youngish, starkly blond-haired man in a trim black suit stepped out. He had the same athletic build as Clay and at six-foot-one, about the same height.

"Good day," the man said in a noticeably German accent. "Are you the ones in charge here? My employer would like to speak with the owner."

Clay grinned at Mac. "That would be us."

"Excellent. My employer, Mr. Conrad Nebel, is interested in your property and would like to know more about it. I noticed the plaque at the head of the driveway. Fairview. Is this the mansion that burned down last summer? Are you rebuilding it or doing something different?"

"We're rebuilding it as it was, with some interior modifications," Clay said, "but it will be true to the original Samuels's mansion in every other respect. The house comes with fifty acres."

"I see," the man said, looking out to the mountains beyond.

"A million-dollar view, wouldn't you say?" Clay teased.

The man smiled. "Impressive, yes. But perhaps not quite that much."

Clay laughed and extended his hand, "I'm Clay Cantrell. This is my partner, Mac Harper."

"Gerhard Krieger. My employer is a businessman with interests here and abroad. Do you plan to offer the property for sale?"

Clay nodded as Krieger handed him Nebel's card. "Then Mr. Nebel asks that you call him at that number to discuss the particulars. He will be at his estate near Lime Springs for the next few weeks."

"We'd be happy to talk with him. Tomorrow morning at nine, if that suits."

"I'm sure that will be fine. I'll let him know to expect your call. Thank you gentlemen." Krieger almost clicked his heels together as he straightened and turned to get back into the limo. A moment later, the limo crept forward and gradually accelerated up the drive.

"Well," Mac said beaming, "your good luck comes through again, partner. I've always said you'd find us a buyer for this place."

"Might be," Clay said smiling broadly as he itched his right palm. "Looks like he's got plenty of money, that's for sure."

"That's a good sign." Mac said, pointing at Clay itching his palm. "That itchy palm always means money is on the way."

3

TAKING CARE OF BUSINESS

Clay snapped his flip phone shut and smiled at Mac, who slouched on the sofa in Clay's living room, one arm resting on the back of the sofa and his long legs fully extended straight out from it. Half empty coffee mugs and a couple extra donuts in an open box rested on the low table between them. The morning was off to a good start.

"That went well," Clay declared as he returned the phone to the holster on his belt. "Mr. Nebel wants us to come out to his estate, show him the plans, maybe talk terms. Krieger is supposed to call us with the time and directions to Foxhaven. Should be in the next couple of days."

"That quick? Good. Do you think he wants us to finish building the mansion, or has he got his own people?"

"I think he's leaving that hanging. He probably wants us to do it, but I'll bet he'll sweat us some to get a lower price."

Mac rubbed his chin. "I don't think we should lowball the job. This is still early in the game. Fairview's a honey of a project, even if it is only a replica, and I'd like to see it through. You don't get many chances to work on one like this."

"Agreed. If he pushes us, let's hit him with a high price. See if he goes for it. Just figure it's a market test."

Mac smiled. Clay turned to look out the window as a car pulled up. "Who's that?" Mac asked.

"Don't know. I wasn't expecting anybody. Has that look of government issue though. Not a local cop either."

Clay was at the front door by the time the man knocked. After waiting a short count, he opened up to greet a middle aged man with disappearing brown hair, average height, average build, and a dark suit with a narrow black tie. The credentials already open and extended toward Clay said FBI. Behind him stood Clay's longtime friend from the Staunton Police Department, Lt. Rick Youngblood, a short, stocky fireplug of a guy with prematurely white hair.

"Mr. Cantrell?" the FBI man inquired politely. Clay nodded. "Dave Parker, FBI. I think you know Lt. Youngblood here. If you don't mind, I'd like to ask you some questions about that murder you witnessed up on Afton Mountain."

"Sure, come on in." Gesturing toward Mac, "This is my business partner, Mac Harper. "Rick, I know you want coffee, how about you Dave, er, Agent Parker. There's some donuts here too."

"Yes, thanks. Black, two sugars." He ignored the doughnuts.

"Rick, how's about giving me a hand."

Youngblood snatched a donut from the box as he followed Clay out to the kitchen. Alone now, Clay asked, "What's this all about Rick? I gave 'em everything in the first place."

"I know. But they ID'd the victim and now it's a federal case. You're coming up in the world, Clay."

"Oh great," Clay hissed sarcastically. "Who was the old guy?"

"A scientist, research chemist of some kind."

"Is that what got him killed?"

"Hard to say. He's been retired for over twenty years, so it doesn't really fit. He did work for the government during World War II on some secret stuff, then NASA for a while on rocket fuel research. He spent the rest of his career doing research at that big chemical company, Babcock Chemical Corp. I'd guess they've done plenty of government work, but I don't know what it could be. Parker hasn't said one way or another."

Clay poured the coffee into the waiting mugs, then he and Youngblood carried them out. Parker walked Clay through events of that terrible night up on Afton Mountain, and Clay gave as good a description of the two men as he could.

Clay then told him the story of the brush with the semi on I-64, and Parker seemed to perk up. But Clay admitted he never did get a look at the driver, being too busy trying to keep clear of the semi. Parker took down the name of the policeman Susan had given the license plate numbers to.

"Turned out the truck was stolen," Clay said, "so I can't give you any more help there either."

"It may not be connected, but we'll check it out. You're sure that the man who was killed said 'Find Blake's Hill'? Nothing else?"

"Yes, that's it. I don't suppose you can tell me who the man was."

"I'm not supposed to, but I would be surprised if your friend Lt. Youngblood hasn't already. He's a retired research chemist, Benjamin Weiss." He smirked as Youngblood cringed a bit.

"He sounds foreign."

"He was an American. Naturalized. He emigrated from Germany back in 1938 to escape the Nazis. He was Jewish.

"Oh. Maybe that was...."

"We haven't made any connection based on his religion, or for that matter his work history. But something may turn up. Meantime, we appreciate your help. Lieutenant, if you're ready, we should head out. Thanks, Mr. Cantrell. If we get anything on the trucker, we'll contact you as soon as we know."

*   *   *   *

That evening, long after the vast bulk of government office workers had fled downtown Washington, DC, for the suburbs, two black suburbans pulled up next to each other on the top floor of a now deserted parking garage in the Capitol district. It was after ten o'clock and the top deck was shrouded in darkness as a man in western clothes, but with the appearance of Indian or Pakistani heritage, left the driver's side of one suburban and got into the passenger seat of the other.

"What have you got for me?" the driver of the second suburban, a slim, young looking oriental man, asked with a slight accent. He had turned sideways to look at the man next to him. In the dim light, the Chinese man's hair looked almost white.

"They are making bery great progress," Babeesh answered with a slightly sing-song cadence. "Ouh yes indeed, the laboratory was much damaged, but Prof. Wentworth will be ready tomorrow to try the new combination of cathode materials. Yes, for sure."

"Aren't you just fooling yourselves with these endless experiments? All the failures?"

Babeesh felt a twinge in his gut at the thought his secure source of ready cash might be threatened. He had, after all, six kids, a second marriage and a hateful ex, and was deep underwater on a balloon mortgage on his house in Arlington. "No, I tell you, it is real," he insisted fervently. "Don't you know that Thomas Edison tried many, many--ouh yes--many different filaments before he found the right one for his light bulb? Before that, there was no-o-o such thing as a light bulb; it was not real yet, you see. Now they are eberywhere, like puddles in a rain storm. Prof. Wentworth, he is bery bery close, you know, but it takes time to work through the possibilites."

"And money, especially if he keeps blowing up the laboratory."

"Ouh yes, bery unfortunate. The operating temperature got too high. Temperature is so bery critical. The cathode must be the correct one at the correct temperature, you see. Otherwise, boom!"

"All right," the Chinese man said as he handed a thick envelope to Babeesh. "We'll meet again in two weeks. But if anything important happens, you call the number."

Babeesh took the envelope and, relieved, slipped it into his suit jacket pocket. "Ouh yes, bery bery definitely. Thank you bery much."

* * * *

A few days later, Clay stood on the second floor of the renascent mansion at Fairview, admiring the framing of the walls and ceiling joists. Good, solid work, all plumb and square, a job well done and satisfying in a way only those in the building trades can really know. Tomorrow they would set the ridge beam and begin framing the roof. They were well within the schedule and he would have been riding high but for a nagging concern. He didn't want to overreact and look like a fool; it could easily be nothing. But given what had happened lately, he couldn't take a chance. Clay opened his flip phone and dialed Mac's number.

"Hey Mac. It's Clay. I'm out here at Fairview. Ev says Maggie at the Bell's Crossroads Store told him two young guys, Arabs with black beards, were asking questions about me today. Asking if she'd ever seen me working late out here. They told her they were looking for some after hours work. Yeah, definitely. Young guys. Ev thinks probably in their twenties. Maggie said they spoke pretty good English, but didn't look like they'd done much construction work.

"I don't know. Maybe it's the same guys who spray painted that black flag out here. I suppose they could have found out I talked to the cops again. Anyway, I don't buy that it was only a coincidence. I'm thinking we should start being careful, like hiring some armed security out here for the nights. I sure don't want to see this place go up in flames again, especially with a buyer sniffing around. I'll call a security company to get it started, but they won't get anybody out here by tonight. What do you say to standing watch with me? We might catch those guys trying something.

"Okay, it's four now. I'm going to run back to Staunton to pick up some stuff. You want me to pick you up? Okay."

About midnight, Clay checked his watch. Time was dragging. It had been a long time since he'd had to stand a watch, and the night air had a definite chill to it. Clay could see his breath, and after sitting still for so long, he had begun to feel the cold. He sat on top of a three-foot high stack of plywood sheets up on the second floor, with his M-16 laid across his lap and a big beam flashlight at his side. From up there he had a good view of the driveway leading to the mansion, and a thin sliver of moon provided just enough light to see the vague outlines of anything that moved down below. Mac, due to relieve Clay about now, was sound asleep nearby on the bare plywood of the second floor, snoring slightly with each inward breath.

An old pickup truck, that had cruised by the entrance to Fairview a quarter hour ago, reappeared coming from the opposite direction. It slowed, inching past the driveway, and then disappeared down the road. Clay watched intently. He couldn't be absolutely sure, but it looked like the same truck as before. In any event, the driver seemed to be checking out the entrance to Fairview. Clay's suspicions were confirmed when the pickup reappeared, slowed, and turned into the driveway. It's headlights suddenly blinked off. Here we go, Clay thought, as he felt a rush of adrenaline.

"Mac!" Clay called out. "Wake up. Quick. Somebody's coming. Mac!"

By the time the truck pulled to a stop below them, Mac was awake and had taken up a position behind a stack of 2x8s they'd be using for roof rafters tomorrow. They watched as two bearded men jumped out of their truck, jabbering to each other in hushed tones. Clay couldn't make out what they were saying, but what they were here for became clear enough when they pulled five-gallon gasoline cans from the truck bed and started toward the mansion.

"Oh no you don't," Clay growled as he flicked on his big beam flashlight, throwing a cone of bright light to reveal a stark, bug-eyed look of total shock on the bearded faces. "Halt, or I'll shoot!"

The gas cans hit the ground as the two men wheeled and sprinted to the truck. Clay fired a couple rounds in the air to scare them, then plugged one of the gas cans. The five gallon can exploded, spitting flaming gasoline skyward and setting fire to the truck's hood.

"Hah," Mac laughed. "That got their attention, Clay." Clay was about to answer when he saw one of them reach in the passenger side door. Suddenly muzzle flashes spit out of the darkness down below and splinters of wood went flying as the gunman raked the second floor. Clay and Mac hunkered down behind cover during the burst of semi-automatic gunfire. An AK-47, Clay guessed, by the sound of it.

"These guys aren't amateurs," Clay yelled as they returned fire, peppering the truck. Clay saw the bright spikes of muzzle flashes from two AK-47s now and ducked down behind the plywood pile again just ahead of bullets ripping into the wood. He felt a sharp sting in his neck. "Two shooters now, Mac," Clay called out, then touched the spot. He felt the end of a small splinter sticking out and grabbing hold, pulled it out. "One at the tailgate, and one on the far side of the bed." Another burst of gunfire from below raked the second floor framing.

"Don't seem to know they're not welcome," Mac yelled. "I think they're planning on sticking around."

"How about we light up their life, Mac? Let's see if we can't hit the truck's gas tank. What do you say? On three?"

"Roger that. Where the hell is it?"

"Don't know. Didn't see any saddle tanks, so it's got to be somewhere under the bed. Ready? One, two, three!" Both Clay and Mac lifted their M-16s and began spraying the truck bed, which suddenly erupted into a ball of flames with a boom and whoosh. Bloodcurdling screams followed the flash as searing flames engulfed the two shooters. Clay and Mac stayed hunkered down, waiting for more gunfire, as the roiling flames engulfed the truck and lit up the night.

"You okay, Mac?" Clay said, standing up. He was silhouetted in the bright light of the burning truck.

"Yeah. Guess those guys won't be in any shape for their seventy-two virgins though."

"Bastards. At least they got a taste of hell before they checked out."

"Guess we'd better call the Fire Department."

"And the cops."

Twenty minutes later, the Augusta County Fire Department was on the scene, in time to extinguish what remained of a fire that had almost burned itself out. The smell of burned flesh hung in the air, an unwelcome reminder that the stakes had just ratcheted up a few notches. A sheriff's deputy showed up about the same time and on being shown the grim scene with two twisted, partly charred bodies, he immediately put in calls to headquarters in Verona and to the coroner's office. An hour later, Clay and Mac were seated in Clay's truck with the radio and the heater going. An unmarked county police cruiser pulled to a stop nearby and a plain clothes cop got out.

"Oh damn," Clay grumbled. "It's Armstrong again."

Det. Armstrong huddled with the sheriff's deputy before turning to look over at Clay's truck. Then he made a beeline for the driver's side and Clay, seeing him coming, rolled down his window. At least the bastard will have to talk up to me, Clay thought.

"It would be you, Cantrell, wouldn't it?"

"Of all the flatfoots in all the counties of this world, you had to walk into mine, eh Armstrong?" Clay answered. Mac stiffled a laugh.

"Hey, dipstick, in case you haven't noticed, it's one a.m. and I got dragged out of bed to come all the way out here to investigate your damn barbecue. So what was it? You piss off your coolie laborers or something?"

"Funny. Genuine wit, Armstrong. If you'd been doing your job, maybe you'd have caught those two terrorists before they had a chance to shoot up my job site."

"Terrorists? Don't make me laugh, Cantrell."

"Hey it's true," Mac shot back from the passenger side.

"Take a look at the bodies, Armstrong. They're not burned so bad you can't tell they're not from around here. One of them is still holding his AK-47. Don't tell me you really think they were just out hunting deer and mistook my building for a big-assed buck. Even you can't be that stupid."

"You're a real boatload of laughs, Cantrell. What makes you think these guys would even bother with the likes of you?"

"Well now, that I can prove. Don't you remember that black flag somebody spray painted inside? Come on, Mac. Give me a hand digging those sheets of painted plywood out of the burn pile. They're states' evidence now."

* * * *

Two days later, at eight in the morning, the roar of the helicopter's turbine engine startled Susan right out of a sound sleep. She sat bolt upright in bed. Wide-eyed, she looked out the window and right into the cockpit of the black Hughes 500 helicopter, now hovering outside the bedroom window at Clay's mill house. The chopper pilot laughed as she instinctively pulled the covers up over her chest, then waved before he side slipped his chopper and landed in the driveway.

"What the hell was that?" Clay groaned as he finally rose up to consciousness.

"A big black helicopter! Clay, it was right outside our window! That man was looking right in!" Susan exclaimed.

Clay was sitting up when the banging on the door started. "Who the hell is this guy?" Clay grumbled as he pulled on a pair of pants and headed downstairs. The banging continued as Clay sleepily negotiated the stairs and didn't stop until he bellowed "All right, I'm coming, dammit."

Clay yanked the door open and found himself face to face with a tall red-haired man about his own size and age dressed in a flight suit. *He* was smiling broadly.

"Morning sir," he said cheerfully. "Sorry to drop in on you and the missus like this. You must be Clay Cantrell. The Clay Cantrell who's been drawin' crazy Arabs like flies lately."

"Jeez. So what are you, the cavalry?" Clay asked with irritation.

"Might say so. Yes sir. I'm agent Bunker Hill. Special section, Homeland Security."

Clay grunted a laugh. "Bunker, I guess you'll want to come in. I assume Homeland Security can wait until I've brewed some coffee before you tell me what this is all about."

"Yes sir, that would be most fine."

"Susan," Clay called out on the way to the kitchen with Agent Hill close behind. "Get dressed, we've got company. Bunker Hill is here."

"What?"

Ten minutes later, Clay and Susan sat side-by-side, elbows resting on an antique white porcelain enamel kitchen table, sipping coffee and looking expectantly at Agent Hill. For his part he sat sideways blowing on his steaming coffee mug. Still grinning.

"Well now, here we all are," he said finally. "I suppose I'm a tad early, but when I got word about those two you and your partner terminated the other night, I just had to rush right down here and connect some dots."

"How did you find out about that so quickly?"

"Well sir, we are very interconnected these days. Very interconnected. And when two Hamas fighters turn up dead on our soil, computers beep, blink, flash, and do all sorts of things to get our attention. Especially when the guys aren't even supposed to be here."

"Hamas, hunh?"

"Yes, luckily you didn't barbecue them so badly we couldn't pull some fingerprints. A couple of real unsavory types. You're lucky you got the drop on them, instead of vice versa, if you know what I mean."

"Yeah well...."

"You got a look at two of them that night of the big pileup on I-64. Think they are they the same two you saw kill Weiss?"

"The fog was thick as pea soup, cars flying all over the place, wrecks on fire. I really didn't get close enough to those guys to be able to ID them. I yelled and they took off. If I'd gotten there a little sooner..." Clay said regretfully, feeling a pang of guilt again.

"It's not likely you'd have stopped them. It's obvious they had him marked for the kill. If you'd gotten there sooner, they might have gone after you too."

Susan tensed on hearing that.

"Did Weiss say anything to you? Anything at all? It may be very important. It might even help us find out why he was killed."

"Nothing more than I've already told the cops a million times. He told me to find someplace called Blake's Hill."

Surprise swept across Bunker's face. "Hah! Grandfather strikes again!" he exclaimed. Clay and Susan exchanged puzzled looks.

"Like a lot of things, it's all in the way you look at it. Blakes Hill isn't a place, it's a person. My father to be exact. My grandfather never could resist a joke, so when father came along, he lumbered him with the name Blakes. The house was on Blake's Hill, you see. My father kept that family tradition alive by naming me Bunker, and my twin brother Boot--I was born first, and Dad always said my brother got the 'boot' for being born second. My mother drew the line with my sister though." Hill chuckled. "She absolutely refused to let him name her 'Ant Hill.' She said that the poor girl someday would be an Aunt Hill, and that Dad would just have to wait until then."

Clay almost spit out the coffee he'd been drinking.

"So what did he name her then?" Susan asked, trying desperately to keep a straight face.

"Dad knew when he was beat--he agreed to Jane. She's the only one of us who got off easy."

When he finally stopped laughing, Clay asked, "So what's the connection. Why would Weiss tell me to find your father?"

"I really don't know. I was hoping you were holding back something else Weiss said. They were friends and they worked together on one of Dad's cases back in World War II."

"World War II? What was your father doing back then?"

"He was an FBI agent. He never talked much about his work, I guess he mostly wanted to forget about it. Weiss visited the house when I was growing up, and for some reason the two of them kept in touch. About all I know is that the case he and Weiss worked had to do with a process for manufacturing synthetic gasoline.

"Nazi Germany had few domestic sources of oil," he continued, "they desperately needed gasoline for their war machine--planes, tanks, and trucks. They had plenty of coal, though, and before the war they developed a way of turning the coal into gasoline. The process was expensive and not efficient, but better than nothing. So they were trying to steal a secret formula we developed. Almost got it too, from what Dad said."

"So why don't you ask your father about it?"

"First place, that's pretty thin. I mean the two of them have been out of action for a long time. And my father wouldn't be much help now anyway. Whatever he might know, if he knows anything about Weiss, is locked inside his head. Doctors say he's got Alzheimer's. Or some kind of dementia anyway."

"Oh I'm sorry."

"Thanks. Not much anybody can do about it. He's 96. He lived a long and fruitful life. It's only been recently that the dementia has been taking over. He's in and out now." Bunker paused and looked out a window overlooking the millpond. "His doctor says it's only going to get worse. It's bad enough now. Sometimes he knows me, but most times not. That hurt a lot at first, but I'm getting used to it."

"There has got to be a link of some kind between them," Susan offered. "Maybe if you talked to him about it."

"You're welcome to try, but I can't see that getting you anywhere. His lucid moments are getting rarer these days. And the Weiss case was a long time ago, way back when Dad was just starting out at the bureau."

"We could try," Susan said. "Is he in a nursing home?"

"As a matter of fact, yes. He checked himself into one last month, after the doc gave him the bad news. It's right here in Staunton. Sunnyvale. I'll call and ask them to let you see him, if you want. Then if you find out anything, call me at this number, day or night," he said, handing Clay his card. "Meantime, I'll dig up whatever background I can on Weiss and that case he and Dad worked. But I don't think we'll find much."

As if to change the subject, Bunker paused and looked around at the deliberately antique-style of Clay's kitchen. "This is quite a place you've got here, Clay. I don't think I've ever seen anything like it before."

"Clay and his friend Mac completely restored this old mill by themselves," Susan said proudly. "Everything works just like it used to, the water wheel, conveyors, even the grindstones."

"Really? That must've been a heckofva job."

"It was that," Clay answered with a grin. "What we couldn't salvage, we re-created from scratch using the same woods, sometimes even using old hand tools. I've always loved working with wood."

"I bet," Bunker said, impressed, then joked, "You've got a resurrection obsession, eh?"

Clay laughed, then looked away for a moment. "Maybe. Mac and I committed a lot of destruction while we were in Afghanistan. Don't get me wrong. It was war, so you had damn well better be good at it. But after we quit the Rangers, rebuilding this place was something we really needed to do. Kind of restored the balance."

4

SIGNS OF THE TIMES

The All Islamic Friendship Center occupied the top floor above a strip mall in Bailey's Crossroads, an area south of downtown Washington, DC. The location was no coincidence. Bailey's Crossroads was heavily populated by Muslim immigrants and embassy workers from many different Islamic countries. The "friendship" center was a warren of small offices and two larger conference rooms, one of which was now being used to view a videotape on a large flat screen monitor. A dozen olive skinned men of fairly obvious Middle Eastern descent surrounded three sides of a large conference table. They were about evenly divided between those with traditional full beards and those who were clean shaven, though all were dressed impeccably in western clothes and exuded an air of tailored respectability.

Imam Abu Habib Abdullah Moktar, one of the clean shaven men, sat at the head of the long table facing the monitor. He smiled as the TV camera zoomed in on a tight shot of him and the attractive blond television reporter, Brandi Holloway, as she smiled and tipped the handheld microphone toward him.

"Islam is a peaceful religion," he heard himself say in answer to her loaded question about Islamic terrorists bent on jihad against the West. "It is the fundamentalist extremists who misinterpret Islamic scriptures, and in their zealotry distort them to suit their violent designs."

"But hasn't your All Islamic Friendship Center stated a goal of promoting Islamic Shariah Law here in the United States?" Brandi insisted in her best imitation of a hard-hitting reporter.

Moktar smiled benignly as the TV camera zoomed in on his face again. "You must understand that there are over six million people of the Muslim faith living in the United States today. Here in Bailey's Crossroads, for example, our Islamic brothers and sisters make up the majority of the population. Why should we be forbidden to live under our own laws, laws set down centuries ago as part of our religious faith? Surely you can see that this is nothing new. For centuries Americans have lived with laws and rules of conduct derived from their Christian heritage. Why should it be any different for Muslims? Shouldn't we be free to practice our religion too?"

"This country was founded on religious freedom," Brandi countered in an effort to show off her knowledge of history and political correctness. In fact, she served him up just the whiffle ball he wanted from her.

"And that is all that we ask. To practice our faith, to be true to our religion, and live in peace in this great land."

"Thank you Imam Moktar. This is Brandi Holloway for station WKYZ TV reporting from Bailey's Crossroads."

As the screen went blank, all eyes turned toward Imam Moktar. He adopted a humble, almost penitent smile in return. "Allah Akbar," he said with conviction. Those around the table answered in unison, "Allah Akbar!"

"Do you see now how we shall carry out Allah's will and defeat the Great Satan? It is so simple. What you saw is a perfect example of our 'stealth' jihad in action. We must present ourselves as peace-loving innocents, play on their sympathies, while we lay the foundation for what is to come. That allows us to take full advantage of their fundamental weakness, their slavish devotion to religious toleration, while we spread our faith and place our people in positions where they can do us the most good.

"This will not happen overnight, or perhaps not even in our lifetimes. But in the name of Allah, we must persevere. This jihad for the supremacy of Islam against the infidels has been fought for centuries, and now, praise be Allah, we have our foot upon the neck of the Great Satan. Our brothers in far away lands have sown the seeds of hatred, fear, and confusion, that we might bring the world to the altar before Allah. We must not let this opportunity slip from our grasp."

Moktar turned to recognize his assistant, who had entered the room and now stood waiting respectfully at the door, not wanting to interrupt.

"What is it, Uman?"

"The call from Qatar."

"I'll be right there. Ask him to hold, please." And to those at the table: "Please excuse me."

Moktar closed the door to his small office and picked up the telephone receiver laying out of its cradle on his desk.

"This is Moktar. I was hoping to hear from you. Have you decided on my request for funding for our new outreach campaign?"

"Yes," the high-pitched nasal voice responded. "I have drafted the check and will have it sent to you by courier. We were very pleased with your interview. But not with the way you have been dealing with our friend."

Moktar looked pained. "Understand, please, that I cannot always control the ones you send."

"Then pass along our displeasure. Their methods of dealing with him are getting nowhere. And attracting more attention than anything else."

"It is my understanding he has just been lucky so far. You should know they are very angry."

"Listen, it is likely he doesn't know anything, but we are giving him every reason to be suspicious. That is what's wrong. Tossing bombs and killing people is not always the best answer. Sometimes you must use more subtle methods, no?"

"It has served our purposes well enough in the past--," Moktar argued.

"Yes, well times have changed, don't you agree? We have another way of finding out what he knows. So tell them to turn their attention back to what they were sent for in the first place. If we need to take care of things their way later on, there will be time enough for that. Peace be with you."

The line went dead with a click. Moktar put the receiver back in its cradle and stared thoughtfully at the far wall. They will not like this, he thought.

*　　　*　　　*　　　*

Clay and Susan followed a rotund, middle-aged nurse wearing a white uniform and an eternal smile down a long, antiseptic corridor at the Sunnyvale Home. She pushed open the door to Room 314, revealing a withered, frail old man propped up in his hospital bed, staring vacantly out the small room's single window. His ninety-six years had taken their toll. His face was drawn, his skin sallow and draped loosely over his boney frame. But his eyes were almost strangely clear and sharp, peering as they did out of his deepened eye sockets, and he retained a full head of white hair that was long and unkempt, giving him a sullen, yet wild appearance that reminded Clay of a trapped animal. The bed took up most the room, leaving barely space enough for the sparse furnishings--a nightstand at the head of the bed and two chairs along the wall opposite the bed--much less the three visitors.

"Mr. Hill, you have visitors," the nurse announced loudly without breaking her smile. "These nice people are here to see you."

Blakes turned only part way toward them, his mouth opened slightly as if to speak, but he didn't respond. The nurse turned to Clay and Susan and smiled apologetically. "Today may not be one of his better days."

"Thank you nurse. We'll stay awhile," Susan said.

Shortly after she left, Blakes looked over at Clay and Susan with those sharp eyes. "Do I know you?"

"No. We're friends of your son, Bunker."

"Bunker?"

"Yes, your son."

"Oh, that Bunker. Yes, I swear I'll tan his hide if he's skipped school again. He's a regular hell raiser, that boy. That why you're here? Are you his teacher?" he asked in a quavering voice as he looked over Susan.

Clay muttered to Susan, "Oh boy."

"No Mr. Hill," Susan answered, "We're his friends. He said you might be able to tell us about Weiss."

"Nothing to tell. He's an old coot." Blakes eyed Susan. "But you're very pretty. Are you sure Bunker isn't in trouble?"

"No, not at all, Mr. Hill," Clay interjected. "Bunker said that you and Weiss worked a case together. Sometime before Pearl Harbor. 1940 or maybe 1941. Something to do with synthetic gasoline."

Blakes looked away, as if remembering. "That was a long time ago. So long ago...." He looked back at Clay, his gaze sharpening, but still he didn't say anything for a moment. "Treacherous times then. Spies and fifth columnists everywhere, couldn't tell the players without a scorecard. Are you a player?"

"No, Mr. Hill, I'm not. I don't really know Weiss, but he told me to get in touch with you. Your son thought it might have something to do with that case."

"Is Ben all right? Why didn't he come himself? He was supposed to..." Blakes drifted off to a vacant stare.

"No, he's not." Clay hesitated, wondering whether he should deliver the bad news or try to dance around it. It might better have come from Bunker, if he had to be told at all. But it seemed Blakes had already guessed the truth.

"Ben was a good man. He loved this country. He risked his neck more than once to defend it. He didn't have to, but he did it. What happened?"

"Two Arab terrorists, at least I think they were terrorists, stabbed him a week ago. I chased them off, but it was too late. He was-- His last words to me were, 'Find Blakes Hill.' But I haven't a clue why, unless you can shine some light on this. Was he working on something with you?"

It was as if something clicked inside Blakes's head. Suddenly he was an FBI agent again, sifting through the possibilities of a puzzling case. "That's all he said?"

Clay nodded.

"Are you FBI?" Blakes asked.

"No."

"CIA?"

"Nope. Civilian now. Ex-Army Ranger. I happened to witness the stabbing and tried to help."

Blakes ignored him. "1940--We were sitting on the fence," he said resolutely. "Nothing was what it seemed to be. Britain and France desperately needed us, but we were supposed to be neutral, and Nazi Germany did everything it could to keep us out of the war. The country was crawling with spies and fifth columnists, and they were waging politics like war.

"You didn't know what to believe. Hitler said he didn't want to conquer the world, he just wanted his 'Lebensraum.' Half the country said we should stay out of the war, claimed that the British wanted nothing more than to trick us into fighting on their side, like they did in World War I. And half the country saw Hitler for what he was, a lying fanatic, and believed we'd better help out the British and the French, because once Hitler swallowed them up, we'd be next. It didn't take a genius to see what would happen if Hitler got control of the British and French navies. But listening to the propaganda machines was like looking into a funhouse mirror. Big fat lies actually seemed like they could be true, and the truth, well the truth looked all wobbly and uncertain. Confuse and conquer."

"Sounds like today."

"Some, I suppose. Duplicity knows no age, sonny. But a monster was on our doorstep back then."

"Okay. But where does the synthetic gasoline project fit in?"

Blakes looked away and thought for a moment. "I don't know," he said matter-of-factly. Then he seemed distracted by a noise out in the hallway.

"But Bunker said you and Weiss worked on--"

"Bunker?" Hill looked momentarily confused. "Why didn't Bunker come to see me?"

"No, he couldn't come today, Mr. Hill. He told me about the synthetic gasoline case--"

"Please, I'm tired. I want to rest. Maybe you can come tomorrow and we'll talk then."

Clay and Susan promised they would return and closed the door behind them. As they pulled out of the Sunnyvale parking lot, Clay said, "Wonder why he shut down like that?"

"Must be a bad memory in there," Susan answered.

"Maybe. Could be he knows something he didn't want to tell us about. Or maybe the dementia kicked in. I don't know that we're ever going to get anything out of him. Bunker might be right."

"He was pretty sharp for a bit. I think we should keep trying."

She was right of course. Weiss's last words had deliberately pointed them in this direction. Clay couldn't ignore that. And at this point, they really didn't have anywhere else to look. "Jimmy might be able to help. He knows a lot about World War II history and can probably get him talking, if we bring him along. "

They were quiet for a few minutes, until Susan noticed Clay looking up at his rearview mirror for the third time. "Clay, what's the matter?"

"I do believe we're being followed."

"Oh no," Susan said nervously as she turned around to look back.

"It's that white Camero two cars back. He's been on us since we left Sunnyvale."

"Do you think it's those terrorists, Clay?"

"Don't know Susan. But I think we can lose them at that light up ahead." Clay began deliberately slowing down and, it being just one lane in each direction, the cars behind had no choice but to slow down as well. The light turned yellow as Clay approached the intersection. Clay counted out five seconds to himself. On five he hit the gas and accelerated into a left turn as the light changed to red. The car in front of the Camaro hit his brakes, forcing those behind to stop as well. Meanwhile Clay sped up the residential street and out of sight.

"There, up ahead, that's the ticket," Clay said as he slowed shortly after rounding a curve.

"Clay, what are you stopping for? He'll catch us."

"See that hedge? I'm going to back into the driveway and wait until Camaro guy goes by. I want to get behind him to get his plate number."

"Clay. Shouldn't we let the police handle this?"

"We don't even know if he really is tailing us," Clay said as he backed far enough into the driveway to be concealed by the hedge. "See, Susan, just like a cop hiding behind a billboard. Trust me, there's nothing to worry about."

"Yes dear," she droned.

They waited for more than five minutes but the Camaro didn't show and Clay, feeling a little foolish, had to admit he had been wrong. But he told himself that after all that had happened, being overly cautious was probably a good thing.

*　　*　　*　　*

As Clay and Susan drove away from Sunnyvale, Blakes stared blankly at the window, reliving that day in Washington, DC, back in the spring of 1940, when he first met Weiss.

It seemed like it was only yesterday, that warm sunny April afternoon when the air was sweet with the promise of spring, the last of the pink blossoms still clinging to the cherry trees along the walkways of the National Mall....

Twenty-two-year-old Blakes Hill and his partner, Ed Johnson--older and the senior agent--walked with a third man, Benjamin Weiss, alongside the Reflecting Pool. The sight of the Washington Monument's white marble obelisk rising above them in the distance still managed to stir feelings of awe and patriotism in Blakes. He imagined that eventually, if he stayed in Washington, he would take it for granted, but for now, a year into his newfound career in the FBI, it was all still new and exciting.

He couldn't believe how lucky he had been to land the job. Raised on a farm in rural Madison County, Virginia, during the Depression and the years of uncertainty after it, he had been the first of his family to attend college. Two years ago, as Hitler's rampages began to destabilize Europe, the FBI started a recruiting drive to deal with an expected rise in foreign espionage activity. And now, here Blakes was in Washington, DC, strolling among the monuments to America's great presidents. The thrill lasted only a moment, though, because his Washington was entirely different from the one tourists milling about the Reflecting Pool saw.

Which was why Blakes and Johnson were meeting Weiss. All three men wore the wide lapel suits in style then, with their pants hitched up to their bellybuttons. Blakes and Johnson wore their hair slicked down and brushed straight back. Johnson, perhaps affecting a gangster look, wore a black fedora hat; Blakes, a brown trilby pushed back somewhat on his head. Weiss was hatless, his longish brown hair fluttering in the light breeze. Weiss's face, marked by sharp features, bushy eyebrows, and black-rimmed glasses, had a troubled look as he spoke.

"I do not know what to do, gentlemen. I have no proof, only suspicions that she might be spying for the Nazis. You must understand that my project has been classified secret because gasoline shortages might develop, if war ever comes." He spoke with a slight German accent, but his English was otherwise excellent for a recent immigrant.

"Can you tell us what you are working on," Johnson asked.

"I'm not supposed to now, but not so long ago there were only a few people who would even bother to listen," he said with an ironic grin. "And you must understand why it would be of such importance to the Nazis, so I will tell you.

"We are researching processes for making synthetic gasoline from coal and other materials. Because the Nazis have such limited supplies of oil, our work is of special interest to them. That hellish blitzkrieg of theirs in Poland--the planes, tanks, vehicles that made it possible--absolutely depend on gasoline and diesel fuel. But after Poland, many of Germany's overseas sources of oil were cut off."

"It's possible to make gasoline from coal?" Blakes asked with a tone of disbelief.

"Oh yes. It's not only possible, it is already being done."

"I had no idea. How can you turn a lump of coal into gasoline?"

"You must understand that both coal and gasoline are what we call hydrocarbons--compounds of carbon and hydrogen. Coal is made of carbon and a little hydrogen, while gasoline contains carbon and a lot of hydrogen. So the problem is simply one of attaching more hydrogen molecules to the carbon in coal, which as it happens also turns the coal into a liquid. German scientists discovered the Fischer-Tropsch process for converting coal to oil in 1925. That helped Germany, because even though that process is expensive, Germany does have lots of coal.

"But *we* are working on an entirely new process that is highly efficient and does not rely on coal. What that is, I cannot tell you, but I assure you it would be of great importance to the Nazis, and they would stop at nothing to get it."

Agent Johnson, who up to this point had been giving Weiss a stony look of disbelief, interjected impatiently, "Okay, you think your lab assistant might be a spy. Why not just fire her?"

Weiss took a deep breath. He had expected that, and now responded in a firm voice, his bushy eyebrows raised emphatically. "With only my suspicions? That would be doing what the Nazis are doing. My assistant is a German-born, naturalized American citizen. My wife and I are German-born naturalized citizens too. We came to America to be free of such persecutions, and most assuredly to not commit them ourselves."

"Those are only rumors--." Johnson stopped himself.

"Rumors? About the Nazis? I am very sorry, but you don't know what you are talking about. Those gangs of Nazi Storm Troopers! My neighbor Franz, he had been a baker all his life, like his father before him, and those animals attacked his little bakery, beat him senseless and broke everything, because," Weiss stopped and drew in a breath, "Because he was a Jew!

"That was 1935. We thought he must have done something wrong, that it couldn't happen to us. Then one night in 1936, my wife and I were walking home after a movie. Those animals! Ten of them began following us, taunting us for being Jews. We kept walking, trying to ignore them. Then one of them grabbed hold of my Helena, knocked her to the ground and began kicking her in the head. Poor Helena lost sight in one eye and all of her front teeth. I tried to fight them, but they beat me unconscious. Broke three ribs." He struggled to continue with the painful memories. "The animals. Beating us senseless wasn't enough. They urinated on us and left us lying in the gutter.

"Those were outrages, not rumors, Mr. Johnson," Weiss hissed indignantly. "My Helena and I were lucky to get out of Germany when we did. We came to America to escape that kind of thing, to live in a democracy. No, I will not be a party to it."

An awkward silence followed. Johnson's face had twisted into a tight-lipped grimace, but he held his tongue. Blakes stared at the old man in stunned silence for a moment. The hatred and the wanton brutality was beyond anything he had experienced. Newspaper stories had alluded to such things from time to time, but Germany was so far away. To suddenly come face-to-face with a victim of Nazi brutality made it inescapably real, starkly repugnant. Blakes was overcome by a confusing mix of sympathy for the man and anger at the brutality he had suffered. Blithely unaware of his partner at that moment, he blurted out, "But what about Father Coughlin here--"

Weiss's gaze leapt from Johnson to the young Blakes. "That devil in priest's clothing? This wouldn't be a democracy if even that man didn't have a right to speak. But he goes too far. He attacks President Roosevelt and, ach!, that ridiculous lie that Jewish bankers financed the communists in the Russian Revolution. He is trying, he *is* inciting hatred against Jews like me, and in that he is no better than the Nazis.

"And I'll tell you something else that should be plain as the nose on your face. Coughlin's gang is a fifth column for the Nazis here in America. They will say anything to keep us out of the war against Germany. Hitler doesn't want to fight us just yet. He wants Europe first. Look at how he attacked Finland. Mark my words, that's just the beginning. Hitler and his cronies must be stopped."

"Yes, but isn't it Europe's war?" Blakes countered, repeating what he had read in the newspapers and what many people had been saying for the past few years.

With the interview obviously going astray, an annoyed Johnson pulled out his notebook and demanded, "What is your lab assistant's name? We'll check her out."

"Marla, Marla Schumann."

Jarred back to the business at hand, Blakes gave Weiss his card. "Meantime, call us if you see her doing anything you think is suspicious."

Late that afternoon, on a stakeout on DC's north side, Blakes slouched in the passenger seat of their parked black, '38 Plymouth sedan, idly watching a shadow slowly edging toward them as the sun moved behind a three-story building up the street. Johnson, smoking a freshly lighted Lucky Strike, seemed irritated and exhaled a cloud of smoke through tightly pursed lips. He flicked the cigarette ash out the open driver's side window with his left hand and returned the cigarette to the corner of his mouth. His right hand rested on the Plymouth's steering wheel, ready to pull out and pursue at a moment's notice, but they weren't likely to be going anywhere. After four hours of watching people coming and going from the union hall a few doors down and across the street, Blakes was pretty sure this stakeout would turn out to be a bust.

The lead had been pretty thin to start with. An anonymous informant reported seeing a clerk from the German embassy entering that hall a few times about this time of day, and each time the suspect had left for the embassy with a package under his arm. According to the FBI's files, Local 435 of the Amalgamated Freight Haulers Brotherhood had been infiltrated by communists in the early 1930s and now was little more than a communist front.

What is going on here? Blakes wondered. Germany and the Soviet Union used to be mortal enemies. But they have been uneasy allies ever since signing the Non Aggression Pact last year. Had Local 435 become a conduit for getting stolen American secrets into German hands? Right now it looked more like the FBI had been fed bum information. Blakes and Johnson had been on this stakeout every afternoon for nearly a week now without a sign of the German courier.

"Looks like another no-show," Blakes offered, "it's almost five."

"Yeah, maybe," Johnson grumbled without even looking over at his partner. Johnson had been all business--distant, more than anything--ever since the meeting with Weiss. Blakes finally decided he had to say something.

"What's eating you, Johnson?"

Johnson seemed agitated by the question and didn't say anything at first. He took a deep drag on his Lucky Strike. "I hate it when people talk about Germany that way. Especially those people," he grumbled with a mix of anger and exhaled smoke. The response surprised Blakes.

"You mean Jews?"

"Yeah, and all those other people trying to drag us into another war. Like those idiots right there," he said pointing at a storefront on their side of the street. Just two doors beyond where they were parked, the store display windows were emblazoned with slogans calling on Congress to institute the draft and begin preparations for war. For the past hour, a man had been standing on the sidewalk out front, passing out leaflets and collecting signatures on a petition. The passersby had not always been receptive.

In fact, Blakes already had seen him shoved roughly twice. Passions were running high these days and for Blakes the prospect of his being yanked out of the bureau for a year of military service, much less actual combat, made him uncomfortable. To be sure, no one knew if American intervention--a polite, more politic euphemism for war--would come, but he couldn't help feeling it was getting closer by the day. He would do his duty, but like a lot of people, only if he had to.

"Don't they know," Johnson growled, "that as soon as we have an army, our boys will be sent overseas and cut to pieces in a war we can't possibly win? Maybe you haven't heard what Mr. Lindbergh has been saying. He thinks we shouldn't be fighting the Germans. They're too powerful. We ought to be more like them. Look at their efficiency, their determination. They've recovered from the Depression--their economy is strong, and they've built an invincible military machine. What have we got? A lot of Roosevelt promises.

"You have to respect the Germans," he continued. "They did it on their own and they deserve to be proud of it." Johnson took a drag on his Lucky Strike and gave Blakes a steely look, exhaling a lungful of smoke for emphasis. "I'll tell you something else. There wouldn't be a war, if Britain and France had offered to help when the Germans were struggling after World War I. But no, Britain and

France did everything they could to humiliate them. That's how they started this war."

Was Hitler a savior or a madman? Johnson's vehemence startled Blakes, even though he'd heard those arguments before. The newspapers and radio stations had been hashing out the pros and cons of the war for a couple years now, but people seemed to be caught in limbo, not sure whether to fight or not, or even who the enemy was. Blakes knew how strong anti-war and anti-Semitic sentiment was in the Midwest and South. In the East, though, a lot of people seemed to favor helping Britain and France.

This was the first time Johnson had talked about politics, much less revealed such strong pro-German sentiment. Blakes had no stomach for a fight with his senior partner, though, so he kept his mouth shut and let Johnson vent. Nobody in America wanted this war, certainly Blakes didn't, but he couldn't help thinking Hitler seemed bent on making it unavoidable. How could America, anyone, stand by while Nazi Germany gobbled up countries like Poland and Finland? And if they let him get away with it, who would be next?

Blakes stared at the man passing out leaflets, trying to think of something to change the subject, when a dozen burly, bare-headed men wearing angry expressions marched past on the sidewalk at a determined clip.

"What the?" he uttered, half to himself, and then "Uh-oh" as the men surrounded the leafleteer.

One man yelled, "Get out of our neighborhood," before roughly shoving him to the ground.

Blakes was half out of the car when Johnson barked, "What do you think you're doing?"

"They'll kill that guy if we don't do something," he yelled back. The man on the ground cried out as his attackers stomped and kicked him.

"Jeez, Blakes, there's too many! We need backup." But with his partner already on the sidewalk, Johnson had no choice but to follow.

"FBI! Break it up," Blakes roared as he grabbed hold of one of the attackers. Before he knew it, the man wheeled and caught him on the jaw with a right cross, knocking him to the ground with the one shot. Johnson slammed into the attacker, throwing him down on top of Blakes. Blakes grabbed him in a choke hold from behind, held him on the ground, and kept yelling "FBI, FBI!" That's when a dozen or so thugs armed with clubs and baseball bats burst out of the store, turning the attack into a full scale riot between two gangs of opposite political passions.

Suddenly Blakes was surrounded by a forest of struggling legs and feet, kicking and jerking wildly in the melee. One booted foot struck a glancing blow to his jaw, but still Blakes clung to his prisoner. Two growling combatants fell in a heap on top of them, then rolled off and scrambled to their feet, trading punches as they did so.

Meanwhile, Johnson grabbed one of the attackers, just managing to duck under a mighty round house as he did so. Furious, the man yelled "Schweinehund" and pulled a revolver from his belt. Johnson grabbed his wrist, trying to push the gun down and swung at the man's face with his right. But the man was stronger than Johnson thought. A gunshot rang out and Johnson suddenly felt a stabbing pain in his thigh. Blood welled up from the wound. Johnson cried out in agony and fell to the ground.

The startling bang! of the gunshot might as well have been an alarm bell ending the melee. Rioters fled the scene in every direction, leaving a wounded Johnson, along with Blakes and his prisoner down on the sidewalk. A siren sounded in the distance, and though his prisoner struggled against the choke hold, Blakes wasn't about to let go.

Shopkeepers and customers from nearby stores filtered out now that the fight was over, and by the time the police arrived, someone had provided Johnson with a cloth to help stop the bleeding. The two policemen pushed their way through the gathering crowd, quickly handcuffed the prisoner, and called for an ambulance. By the man's accent, Blakes judged his prisoner to be a first generation German immigrant. Though the man refused to answer any questions about the attack, Blakes found a card in his wallet identifying him as a member in good standing of the pro-Nazi, German-American Bund. Johnson was in obvious pain as the white-clad medics finally lifted him onto a stretcher. Blakes went over to him to report what he'd found out.

"He wouldn't talk, Johnson, but we'll get the shooter. I'm betting they were all Ger--"

"I heard," Johnson interrupted and glared at him. "Don't you dare say another damn word," he growled as he disappeared into the ambulance.

Blakes smiled to himself as he climbed into their unmarked car and joined the exodus of police vehicles leaving the scene. It was time for him to write up his report, and he knew this one would raise his section chief's hackles, a thought that wiped the smile off his face. Johnson getting shot was definitely not FBI procedure, and it was Blakes's fault it had happened.

Stopped at a light on his way back to the FBI headquarters in the Department of Justice Building, he mulled over his options and came to the conclusion there really wasn't any way to cover it up. Any way he played it, he'd surely get a reprimand in his jacket for having got Johnson shot, even though he was only trying to stop a beating.

The light turned green and he was about to go when a newsboy started yelling"Extra!, extra! Germany invades Norway, Denmark." The car behind him honked impatiently as Blakes pulled over to the curb and waved to the newsboy, a gangly youth with a missing front tooth. Reaching across the passenger seat, Blakes handed the boy a nickel and then opened the folded copy of the Washington Ledger Star. The big, black headline across the top of the page proclaimed the shocking news. He hurriedly skimmed the first few paragraphs as a queasy, sinking feeling overcame him. "We're in for it now," he said to no one in particular.

5

FOXHAVEN

Clay and Mac got an early start for the drive to Conrad Nebel's estate, which was in rural Bath County, almost two hours south and west of Staunton. It was another bright, clear, fall day, and the leaves were approaching full color now, especially in the mountains to the west. A lingering chill hung in the air, giving a crisp, invigorating edge to the morning. A good day for getting things done, Clay thought to himself as he pulled his Vette out of his driveway. The cool air, morning coffee, and the anticipation of meeting a potential new client had him pumped up and ready to roll, but he knew better than to count on closing a deal on Fairvew. Today's meeting was a first step, a chance for Mac and him to show off the project and get a sense of how serious his client's interest was. Besides, these days he and Mac were under no pressure to clinch a deal. That, Clay decided, was a welcome change.

"Do you suppose Nebel has other things in mind for us? Besides Fairview?" Mac asked idly as Clay swung his Vette onto the southbound lanes of I-81 and merged with the onrushing traffic.

"Anything's possible. You mean he wants us to work on his other properties?"

"I guess so. That big black limo appeared out of nowhere," Mac replied.

"Fairview's been in the news a lot lately. We have George to thank for that. Maybe that's how Nebel got onto us."

"At least we know there's big money there. The limo, I mean."

"Might be rented," Clay joked, just to be difficult. "Could be we're meeting a guy living in a trailer."

"Not likely. Is your palm itching?"

"Nope. Not a bit." Clay turned to his superstitious partner and laughed. "It's too early for that, Mac. We haven't even met the guy."

About a half hour due south of Staunton, Clay exited I-81 at Bell's Crossroads and headed west into Bath County. The winding two-lane highway drove deep into the Allegheny Mountains, meandering through picturesque valleys, here and there sidling up to a shallow river or rushing stream, and up and over one mountain after another. Clay kept busy working the gear shift as the road roller coastered up and down increasingly steep mountain slopes and snaked through switchbacks and sharp curves. Mac gave up on trying to keep up with drifting radio stations and munched contentedly on a donut while taking in the countryside rushing by.

After a stretch of almost nothing but woods, they rolled down a long incline and into the village of Lime Springs. Just before hitting the downtown section, they passed by an historic resort complex, The Allegheny Mountain Resort, a massive brick edifice flanked by two five-story wings, all of it surrounded by manicured grounds and sprawling golf links. The sheer grandeur of it struck Clay as strangely out of place way out here in the sticks. But then the scenery and change of place--with all the civilized amenities you could ever want--was probably what that resort was all about.

"What do you think, Mac, would you and Rita be up for a week-end at The Resort sometime?" Clay said as they passed through the village and back out into the countryside. "I'll bet Susan would like it. Jimmy and Trisch would probably go for it too."

"Yeah, it might be fun. See what the other half has been living like," Mac joked.

"Hah! You're one of us now, mon."

Mac smiled to himself and muttered contentedly, "Yeah." The Confederate gold had done that.

Turning off the main road to head toward Thunder Mountain, they found themselves following winding country lanes snaking up steep inclines until, finally, they saw the modest blood red and black sign emblazoned with the word "Foxhaven" in old German-style lettering. They turned into a paved drive winding its way up onto a gently sloped ridge carpeted by a thick forest of hardwood and pine. Clay figured they must have gone three miles, passing increasingly threatening "No Trespassing" signs, before finally reaching the main gate, a massive stone archway with black wrought iron gates. A squad of enormous pine trees stood guard on either side of the edifice, casting a deep shadow over the entryway and the road before it. Clay impulsively stepped on the brakes and came to a stop outside the open gates.

"Should we knock?"

"I don't know. It seems kind of creepy, like Dracula lives here or something," Mac replied.

Clay laughed. "Yeah, I know what you mean. At least the sun is up," Clay said with a wry grin as he shoved the gearshift into first and rolled forward through the gateway. A quarter mile of gracefully curving roadway later, they came up a small rise and passed through a final gateway in a high stone wall. What greeted them was a looming, European-style mansion, a castle really, towering four stories above them. Flabbergasted, Clay almost ran off the side of the lane.

The behemoth had a bulbous looking circular tower with a cone shaped roof on the left, a Dutch style gambrel roofed section in the middle, and a steep-pitched gable-roofed wing on the right--each jutting outward from the straight, four-story high front wall of the mansion. The massive facade had a layered look, the tall first story being of a greenish cut stone, the second, red brick, but not as tall, and the shorter still third and fourth were clad in decorative shingles stained a traditional dark brown. Clay guessed the mansion had to be over twenty-five thousand square feet. The forest of chimneys poking the sky above the rooftops easily topped a hundred feet above the ground.

"Jeez," Mac breathed, "He knows how to make an impression, doesn't he?"

"Yeah, and this is just one of his houses." Clay looked at Mac. "I think we're underdressed for this meeting." They both had on dress shirts with ties under waist length dark brown leather jackets, their standard contractor-meets-client garb at this time of year. "But at least now we *know* he's got money."

"If he wants us to do any roof work, we're going to need bigger ladders."

Clay, still looking up at the imposing edifice, eased the Vette forward into a broad courtyard and followed the curving, cobblestone driveway around a trio of towering pine trees. He pulled up to a covered porch with a wide stairway leading up to the front entrance. As Clay and Mac got out, still dazed by the sheer size of Foxhaven, a butler appeared at the top of the steps and announced with a slight German accent, "This way gentlemen, if you please."

The butler turned to lead them through a heavy, ten-foot high arched door with thick, black wrought iron strap hinges extending horizontally almost all the way across it. The thud of the door closing echoed with a disconcerting finality in the wide, high ceilinged entryway.

Following the butler now, they entered a large circular room--an atrium open all the way up to an ornate skylight in the roof four stories above. Hung on this lower level walls were dark portraits in gaudy, gold gilt frames--stern faced men and women who, Clay supposed, were the long dead forebears of Conrad Nebel. To Clay's right, a wide Italian marble staircase led to the second and third floor balconies, and for a second Clay imagined he caught sight of a beautiful young woman looking down from the upper floor. But she had disappeared before the second half of his double take, if in fact she had been there at all. Straight ahead lay a short hallway with a vaulted twelve-foot-high ceiling and through it Clay saw what appeared to be an immense ballroom.

"Mr. Nebel's assistant, Mr. Krieger, is waiting to greet you this way, sir, in the Library," the butler announced with a faint displeasure when Clay began to veer toward the ballroom.

"Do people really live like this?" Mac whispered to Clay. "This baby has got your parents' house beat, partner."

"By a mile, Mac. I think we're looking at how those robber barons back in the 1800s and early 1900s used to live."

"Makes you feel really small."

Clay eyed his friend, a hulking 6-foot-5 and 260 pounds. "Mac," Clay deadpanned, "*you'll* never be small." Mac smiled as they followed the butler into the library.

Krieger, dressed informally in a sport coat with no tie, stood up to greet Clay and Mac from a leather chair at the far end of the library. Dark stained oak shelves, filled with leather bound books, rose from the floor to the high ceiling along one long wall of the library. On the opposite wall, tall curtained windows graced its entire length, admitting bright shafts of late morning sunlight. Dark oak paneling covered the walls at each end of the library up to about twelve feet. Above that, hung stuffed heads of wild game. Bear, elk, deer, mountain lion, a tusked boar, and even, appropriately, two snarling foxes, stared vacantly from the walls at each end.

"Mr. Conrad will join us in a moment," Krieger said, as all three took seats in the burgundy leather wing chairs grouped around a large, square coffee table. Made of polished ebony, the table top was inlaid with lighter-colored woods depicting a hunting scene, in which a magnificent wounded stag was being run to ground.

A momentary look of uncertainty crossed Krieger's face and then he asked tentatively, "I thought you would bring the plans today."

"Jeez," Clay exclaimed, feeling like an idiot. So amazed by the mansion's sheer size, he'd forgotten all about the plans. "They're out the car. I'll run out and get them."

"No need. Barkley can do that for you. Are they in the trunk? Will he need keys?" Krieger said with a self-satisfied smile.

"The cardboard tube with the plans is behind the passenger seat. The Corvette is unlocked."

"Would either of you like coffee?" Krieger asked. "Barkley can bring it after he gets the plans." Both Clay and Mac passed on the offer with thanks. Krieger nodded to Barkley and without a word the butler left to retrieve the plans. Clay's attention was just returning to the wild game heads--had Nebel shot them himself?--when the lord of the manor came in through a door at the other end of the library.

"Sorry for the delay, gentlemen," Conrad Nebel said breezily and with complete insincerity. He had been biding his time in his study, purposely waiting until Krieger had got them seated. A distinguished looking man of medium build, he was about sixty with a longish mane of wavy gray hair trending toward white, and a neatly trimmed Vandyke beard that had already arrived at that color. He had dressed informally, for him, in a brown tweed sport coat and dark pants. Instead of a tie, he wore a red and black silk ascot to complete the impression of a country gentleman.

As they shook hands, Clay smiled and looked him directly in the eyes. They were cold, expressionless blue, revealing nothing.

"Gentlemen, please sit. I'm anxious to get a look at what you have planned for Fairview."

"Well, as I told you over the phone, Mr. Nebel," Clay began, stalling for time while Barkley went out to the car, "the exterior will be virtually unchanged from the original. We've only made changes in the interior, changes we'd intended to make anyway."

"Your plans, sir," Barkley said, handing the tube to Clay after noiselessly entering the room.

"Thank you Barkley." Clay twisted the top off, pulled out the blueprints and spread them out on the coffee table, facing Conrad.

"We'll show you the exterior renderings first, and then I'll explain what we'll be doing on the interior--how it will differ from the original floor plan. This top one is the architect's rendering of the exterior, the front elevation." Clay let Conrad study the blueprint for a few moments, then moved it aside to reveal the rear view elevation.

"All this is as it was on the original?" Conrad asked idly.

"Yes, Mr. Nebel, we--"

"Please, let's not be so formal. Let's use first names here, if you don't mind."

Clay smiled. "Certainly, Conrad. Yes, it's virtually an exact replica. Fortunately we took lots of photographs of the original house before we started work on it. So, we had a good record for our architect to use in drawing up these plans."

One by one, Clay went through the plan views, while Conrad asked a few questions but otherwise showed no more than polite interest. Clay was fairly sure the man was playing his cards close to the vest, but couldn't be certain. There was always an element of the hunt in business dealings, but at the moment Clay wasn't sure whose head was going to wind up on the library wall.

"What do you think, Conrad?" Clay finally asked after presenting the last drawings. "Is Fairview something you'd be interested in?"

Conrad was still looking over the interior floor plan and didn't answer for a few moments. "And how many acres come with it?" he asked, looking up at Clay.

"Fifty. You might be able to get another hundred or so from a farm on the south side of the property, but you'd have to negotiate that separately with the owner. I don't know what his plans are, but if the price is right, you know."

"Yes, well--," Conrad paused thoughtfully and appeared to unconsciously drum his fingers on the armrest of his chair. "A very good presentation, Clay. Thank you. I am interested." He paused. "But I want to think it over. Perhaps then I might make an offer."

"That will be fine of course, Conrad. We'll be glad to hear from you. The price will depend, naturally, on what stage you would want to take possession, and whether you want to use C&H Construction to finish the job, if it's before that. I could give you some numbers--"

"I see," Conrad said, letting a knowing smile slip through his studied nonchalance. "I take it you would prefer to be the one finishing the job?"

"Yes, we're well into it and it's one of those special projects that we can take real pride in." That was a roll of the dice. On the one hand, Clay had to admit they wanted to do the work, on the other, Conrad would probably use that to shave thousands off what they could expect to get paid.

"I'm sure. Let me think about it. And I might send Krieger over to sound out that farmer about getting more property. A hundred and fifty acres would make a better setting, I think. Don't you?"

Clay's smile was a bit forced, but he nodded in agreement. The hundred acres would up the package price significantly and put pressure on Mac and him to lower their price.

Conrad straightened up a bit and looked past Clay, as if thinking it all over. Then he smiled and focused on Clay. "Krieger showed me the news reports about all that gold you found in the cave up in Highland County," Conrad said finally, as if to get off the subject of Fairview. "That must have been quite an adventure."

Clay and Mac both grinned. "Yes, it was," Clay answered, uncertain about the sharp turn in the conversation.

"And, forgive me, I don't mean to pry, but did it really turn out to be the $12 million they said? That's quite a find."

"We're waiting to hear. The coins haven't been formally evaluated yet. It all depends on the condition. If enough are at 'mint' condition, it could be substantially more."

Conrad smiled slyly. "Perhaps you'd like to buy Foxhaven then?"

"Hah! Who's selling whom here?" Clay responded with a grin. "It's definitely an impressive house, no doubt about it. But a bit more than I need, Conrad."

"Just a thought," he said returning the grin. "What about that man who set fire to Fairview? What's his name, Krieger? Buddy something?"

"George Kilgore. Buddy is his nickname."

"Was he a friend of yours, Clay?"

"No, definitely not." Conrad had obviously done his research. Clay leaned back and did his best to appear relaxed. This conversation was not going in the direction he wanted. But once the subject had been broached, Clay had no choice but to take control of it by explaining as best he could what had happened.

"George was a high school classmate, and back then we didn't get along. He wound up marrying an old girlfriend of mine, but I really didn't have anything to do with him after high school. Anyway, he got into drugs, became a dealer, and managed to hook one of our helpers out there on the Fairview job. He started using Nick, that was our guy, to run the drugs until something happened between them. George stabbed him to death. Unfortunately for me, George decided to pay me back for old grudges by making it look like I set Fairview on fire to get the insurance money, and that I killed Nick to keep him from telling the cops about what I was doing."

"Ah, I see," Conrad said thoughtfully. "Then you will be at his trial?"

"Yes. I'll have to testify in a week or so. Mainly to give evidence about his two attempts to kill me."

"Really? He tried to kill you? Twice?"

"First with a hit man," Clay said with irritation. He really didn't like dredging all this up, particularly in a business meeting, but since Conrad had asked. "Then with a personal visit to my home. The hit man wound up dead and George wound up in the hospital."

"I would say you are a survivor, Clay. And probably very lucky too."

Clay smiled and then turned at the sound of a door opening to his right. It opened only far enough for a young woman to poke her head in. “Oh, Uncle Conrad. I’m so sorry! I didn’t know you were meeting in here. I just wanted to get a book.”

Conrad turned in his seat. “Nonsense. We’ve finished. Come and get your book, my dear. And meet my two guests.” Conrad and Krieger, then Clay and Mac, stood to greet her.

The door swung open and Clay’s jaw dropped perceptibly for a split second before he regained himself. In walked a beautiful, blue-eyed blond, an archetypical German *fraulein*--young, lithe, and confident, maybe even a bit brash--yes, brash, Clay decided as she walked right up to him and held out her hand. There was still a bit of the perky schoolgirl in the way she carried herself, but her figure had already forged ahead into womanhood. Probably in her mid-twenties, she was dressed in designer jeans and a white blouse. Clay couldn’t help noticing the top two buttons of her blouse were undone and she smiled as his eyes wandered in that direction. She looked up at him, her tanned face beaming as she waited for him to take her hand.

“Maria, this is Clay Cantrell and this gentleman is his partner, Mac Harper. Clay, Mac, this is Princess Maria Theresa von Marburg, a distant cousin of mine. She is vacationing here before returning to Germany to complete her masters degree.”

“Princess?” Clay did not know whether he should kiss her hand or shake it. He judged by the devilish look in her eyes that she must have read his uncertainty and in an instant went with the modern-day handshake.

“Yes,” Conrad answered, watching Clay’s obvious interest in Maria with amusement. She was indeed a beauty. “She is a real princess, Clay. Her grandmother was a daughter of Kaiser Wilhelm II, the last monarch to reign over the German empire.”

“Oh, Conrad, please!” Maria exclaimed. “Germany is a democracy now. We have no kings and queens.” She smiled as Clay finally turned back to her and realized he was still holding her hand.

Clay flushed a bit as he released it and managed only, “I can’t say I’ve ever met a princess before.”

"Now Maria, you know it is an honor to belong to such an important family," Conrad scolded. "You should be proud of your heritage."

"Oh I am, Uncle Conrad, you know I am. But it is like jewelry, something you wear only on special occasions. Here in America it is much better to be a rock star, no?"

Conrad's scowl forced both Clay and Mac to stifle their laughter.

"Have you been here for long?" Clay asked to break the awkward moment. "Your English is very good." He wasn't lying, but he probably would have told her that even if she were spouting pidgin English. In fact she spoke with only the slightest trace of an accent, so far as he could tell.

"Oh thank you. I have studied it in school, of course, but using my English is one reason why I wanted to come to America."

Just then Barkley came into the library. "Excuse me, sir, but the call you've been expecting. Would you care to take it in the study, or should I tell them to call back later?"

"No Barkley, we're finished here for today. Clay, Mac, I don't mean to be rude, but I really must take this call. We'll meet again after I've had time to think over your project."

Clay extended his hand. "We do appreciate your interest, Conrad. You know how to reach us."

"Yes," he said with a slight smile. "If you don't have to go right away, I could leave you with Maria, here. Perhaps she would like to give you a tour," he said glancing at her. "Practice her English."

"Oh yes, Uncle. I'd like that."

"Very well. I'll leave you two now. Krieger, I'll need you on the other line."

Clay watched Conrad and Krieger pass under the two snarling foxes and out through the connecting door to Conrad's study. He turned back to Maria. She was already looking up at him.

"This is the library," she said with an impish schoolgirl look.

"So I gathered," Clay answered drolly. Then, trying to be serious, he continued, "Is this your first visit here?"

"Oh no. Uncle Conrad has been very good to me. I've been here several times, and at his other houses too. I have known him since I was a little girl."

"You like him a lot, I can tell," Clay offered.

"He is a dear man. He lets me stay as long as I want. But it's not just that. He's a very smart businessman too, he knows so many important people, and sometimes I think he gives away everything he makes to charity. He is always meeting people and helping to organize events. He's gotten tons and tons of awards for his good works, you know."

"No, I didn't. But he's obviously very successful. Does he have royal blood too?" Clay said, teasing.

Maria wrinkled her nose a bit. "His grandfather was an aristocrat. He came over here long ago, in the late 1890s I think, and made a fortune mining iron ore. Originally mines not far from here, as a matter of fact, and later around what you call the Great Lakes."

"What do you do way out here?" Mac asked in an effort to get into the conversation. Clay, for his part, was a bit annoyed at the interruption. The princess was an obvious source of background information on a potentially important client. She was also damned attractive.

"There is so much. I can ride horses. Swim in the lake and lie out in the sun in the summer. Ski in the winter. And parties. There are always parties here. Do you like parties, Clay?" she said, turning back to him.

"Oh sure."

"We are having our fall charity ball two weeks from this Saturday. For the Children's Hospital at Lexington. The ballroom will be overflowing with people. It will be such fun. Would you and Mac like to come? I can have Barkley mail you invitations."

"That would be nice," rolled off Clay's tongue. Mac smiled pleasantly.

"Wonderful! If I'm not being nosey, what do you and Mac do?"

"We renovate old houses. We were showing Conrad plans for one we're doing in Bell's Crossroads, south of Staunton."

"Oh," she giggled. "I thought you were talking about rebuilding that old burned out mansion."

"What old mansion?"

"There's one on another part of the estate. It is very big, and very ruined, but there is a pretty view from there. Would you like to see it? Perhaps you will decide to offer your services to rebuild the mansion. Do you ride?"

"Not unless it has at least two wheels."

"Very well, then we shall take the Gator? It has four, I'm quite good at driving it, and I know the way. It's only about a mile from here."

"Only" turned out to be a wild, bumpy ride along an old fire road cutting through the woods of the estate--with Clay and Mac hanging on for dear life and Maria laughing wildly the whole way. When she finally skidded to a stop, Clay and Mac eased themselves off the Gator and gawked at what was once a huge square block of a mansion--a castle really.

Made entirely of cut stone, with turrets, tall chimneys, and carved stone ornamentation, only about half of the castle remained standing. In the middle, the front wall had collapsed, leaving only part of the wide central tower in place and exposing sagging, blackened remnants of the second and third floors. A tower at the right corner of the building still stood, but the front of the left side was gone, crumbled into ruins and home now to a stand of mature maple trees with leaves turned to flaming yellows and oranges. The rest of the ruin was partly overgrown with the vines and underbrush, a jumble of colors, reds, yellows, browns, and greens, threatening to swallow up the whole.

Mac started laughing. "What do you think, Clay? Want to tackle this one?"

"Mac, I'd be dead before we got half of it back in shape." He turned to Maria. "What is this place?"

"It's the mansion that Conrad's grandfather built. There was a terrible fire in the 1940s, I'm told. Conrad's grandfather died in it, and Conrad's father was a boy when it happened. It is a very bad memory for them."

"Must be," Clay said, as much to himself as to Maria. "Why didn't they tear it down?"

"Conrad doesn't like to talk about it, but my mother told me his father wanted it left the way it was, as a memorial. A reminder of what happened to his father." She studied Clay's expression for a moment, perhaps looking for some sign he knew about the tragedy. Then she continued, "They built Foxhaven instead of restoring it."

"Where's that view you told us about, Maria? All I see is trees and a lot of underbrush." Mac said.

"Over that way. See the path?"

They didn't have to walk more than a few hundred feet before they came to an overlook with a stunning view of a wide lake stretching a half mile or so in every direction. Down a nearly straight drop of some two hundred feet, the sun dappled waters of the lake lapped slowly, rhythmically at the rocky shoreline below. The view was truly breathtaking, a pristine mountain paradise spread out before them, the trees aflame with fall colors and the only obvious sign of civilization being a seaplane bobbing at anchor a short distance out in the water.

Clay stepped out closer to the edge, a bald outcropping of rock that curved downward into a precipitous angle before disappearing into what must be a near vertical face somewhere below. "Hey, look, Mac. There's a dock down there. Over there, to your right. And they've even got a seaplane."

"Yes," Maria offered. "They still use that dock. Tunnels inside the cliff lead back up to here. Guests use them when they come by seaplane. And Conrad has taken me on trips from here." She laughed. "I used to have a crush on Eric, the pilot."

When they got back to the Gator, Clay couldn't help turning around to take a last look at the ruins. That's when he spotted a man about a hundred feet away looking at them from the rubble of the left side. They locked eyes briefly, and Clay could have sworn the man at first seemed startled. Then suddenly the stranger smiled and waved before disappearing into the underbrush.

"Do you know him," Clay asked Maria.

"Who? I don't see anybody."

"That man with a beard. He waved, but he's gone now."

"Oh, it's probably a groundskeeper. Sometimes they come out here and drink beer on their lunch hour. They're not supposed to, but they do."

The ride back took considerably longer because Clay insisted on driving. Then Maria walked with Clay and Mac to his car, chattering like a schoolgirl the whole way. As Clay settled into the driver's seat, she leaned down and asked as sweetly as she could, "Will you and Mac be coming to the ball? It will be such fun."

Clay looked at Mac, who answered with a noncommittal shrug. "Yes, we'll be there Maria."

Conrad, meanwhile, stood looking out a second floor window watching Clay and Mac drive off. He couldn't help a nagging twinge of jealous irritation at the sight of Maria smiling and waving to Clay with such girlish enthusiasm. She can be such an impetuous child, he thought, but she had never returned anything beyond simple familial gratitude for his attentions. He had hoped, and now he consoled himself with the thought that she was still quite young. She might yet see the advantages of the wealth and power he could offer her.

"What are you looking at?" came the reedy, irritated voice from across the large sitting room. "Nothing, Sir. Just watching my guests leave." Conrad turned to look at his father, Klaus Nebel, a withered, eighty-four-year-old man confined to a wheelchair. Graced with the Nebel family trait of a full head of hair, combed and neatly trimmed as always, but now white with age, the elder Nebel sat erect with aristocratic bearing despite his obvious infirmity. Dressed in a tweed jacket and red and black striped tie, he sat with a scotch plaid blanket covering his legs. As Klaus looked up at his son, his deeply wrinkled face seemed set permanently in a scowl, and the fingers of his right hand moved nervously on the wheelchair's armrest, as though he were trying to tap his fingers impatiently but no longer could.

"You should not have brought them here," the old man scolded.

"Sir," Conrad responded with the formality ingrained in his youth, "It may prove useful to have them close at hand."

"If you are wrong-- You cannot have forgotten where it can lead."

Forgotten? Conrad thought. Not possible. He had had it drummed into him, from birth he was certain, though he had no direct recollection of it. He just knew how Sir operated. "How could I forget," he answered with some irritation.

His father raised a boney finger as if to emphasize the point, "Those who forget history are condemned to repeat it," intoning the words with apparent great satisfaction.

"Sir, I won't forget. Haven't forgotten."

There was a moment of silence while the old man savored his small victory. They were becoming harder to come by these days. His son was chafing at the bit, he knew, but the boy--he was still a boy, always would be a mere boy in Klaus's mind--would never see things as clearly as he could. For his part, Conrad wanted to get back to the subject at hand.

"If they finally do succeed, we will have to move quickly, Sir."

Klaus directed a steely glare at his son. "You are dreaming. Such things cannot be. There are laws of physics which cannot be ignored, Conrad, you know that. They were wrong twenty years ago and they will be wrong again. You mark my words. They will fail again."

"Perhaps." Conrad felt his nerve slipping away like sand under his feet in a receding wave at the beach. He hated to argue with Sir. More to the point, he hated the way Sir treated him. But that was the order of things, the way it had always been. There were times when he wished the old man were dead, but then strangely, he always regretted the thought. He took a deep breath and steeled himself. Sir could be so obstinate sometimes.

"But if they do prove it works, it will turn the world upside down. Fortunes will be made and lost overnight, and we must be ready to protect what is ours, to capitalize on the transformation."

"Bah," the old man grumbled and dispensed his son with a wave of his withered hand. "They'll never do it."

6

LEADS

Blakes Hill's tiny room in Sunnyvale Nursing Home was dark except for the thin shaft of light from an outside security light slipping between the two incompletely drawn curtains. Blakes lay on his side, but he couldn't sleep.

He could see it like it was yesterday. The memory of driving past that weathered sign, "Welcome to Brownsville, Texas" flashed in his mind like the opening scene of a spool of film he knew would unwind whether he wanted to watch or not. He wished what he was remembering had been nothing more than a bad dream, but he knew it wasn't....

May, and it was already stinking hot in Brownsville. Blakes drove with the windows of the black '38 Plymouth wide open despite the dust--all the roads around Brownsville had turned to dust, and the lane leading to Alston Chemical's Brownsville research facility was no different. Even the weeds lining the roadway were covered with a thick coat of gray dust. Already. Third week in May. Christ, it wasn't even summer yet. Blakes drove slowly through the unmanned front gate without being stopped--security obviously was very lax here even though they were doing government research--and threaded his way through a rows of white, barracks-like, one-story wood frame buildings before pulling to a stop in front of Building 11. Benjamin Weiss popped out of the building's front door almost as soon as Blakes pulled up. He wasn't surprised. Weiss had made it sound pretty urgent.

"Thank you for coming," Weiss said perfunctorily as he climbed into the passenger seat. "Now can we please drive somewhere away from here?"

"No hello, how are you, after my driving a thousand miles?"

"Okay, hello. Now can we drive somewhere? I can't talk here."

Blakes obliged by pulling the floor mounted stick shift into reverse and backing up to turn around. Neither of them said anything until they passed through the front gate.

"So what's up, Mr. Weiss?"

"What's up, he asks me. The world is falling to pieces, I have a spy in my laboratory, and my country, my adopted country, this great country of the United States of America, wants me to keep my new discovery a secret."

"Is it your lab assistant? The spy?"

"Yes, yes, I am certain of it. I caught Marla looking in my desk three days ago. Just before I called you. She was looking for a key to the cabinet where I keep my notes on the new process. I'm sure of it."

"Why didn't you call the police?"

"I did. I called you."

"No, I mean. Just have her arrested."

"My research. I must protect that too. *You* can keep this quiet. We've found the formula for making gasoline from silica gel--which is made from sand! Don't you think the Germans would love to get their hands on that? Mussolini already controls Libya. All Hitler would have to do is get control of the Sahara and the Germans could make all the gasoline they want."

"She's your assistant. Wouldn't she already know everything she needs?"

"I can't be sure of course, but the process requires three separate stages, and she has been working only here, on the first stage. The research is compartmentalized, you see. The only way she could find out about the other two stages is from people working on them--or by stealing my notebook, which covers all three stages."

"If she's trying for your notebook, that means she didn't have any luck getting it from the others."

Blakes mulled over the situation. He could call the Bureau and within a day have a couple dozen agents on the case. If Weiss was wrong, Blakes would have egg on his face--again. If Weiss was right, cracking a dangerous German spy ring would be a big coup. Too big. Blakes would get shoved to the sidelines and his boss would take all the credit. He needed a way to flush out some more information before he called in the cavalry, and he thought now he knew how to do that. It was risky, but a chance worth taking.

"We checked on her after we saw you last spring, Mr. Weiss, but we didn't find anything. So as of right now, we can't arrest her. We don't have enough proof."

"Can't you take her in for questioning or something? Give her a scare to make her stop?"

"That won't work. She's already made the decision to be a spy, so she's probably not going to scare easily. Because she's the first link in the spy ring, she could run and hide until they find her a new assignment. Then we have nothing. No, until we find out who her contact is, we're better off leaving her where she is."

"But what if she gets my notebook. She could disappear with my discovery!"

"Let's give her a brass ring to grab. As soon as you can, tonight if possible, make up a fake notebook with just enough correct information to make it look real to Marla. You can fake some formulas and reference some processes that didn't work, can't you? Use the same kind of notebook as the real one and then leave the fake in the locked cabinet. Make the switch at night so she won't know."

"What do I do with the real one?"

"Take it home. Hide it in some safe place until she makes the grab. Then I'll follow her to her dead drop. Once I know where that is, I can call in backup for a stakeout on the dead drop. Since it's a fake, we'll follow it until we can roll up the entire ring."

"You know I could get into serious trouble taking that notebook home with me. Somebody might accuse me of stealing government secrets."

Blakes straightened up, looked directly at Weiss, and tried to sound completely confident. "Not with me here to back you up."

He was in fact taking a big risk by not reporting to the Bureau right away, and he was already under the gun for that incident up in DC when his partner got shot. But if his play worked, he'd come out looking a lot better than before.

"*Ja*, I do that tonight. Now take me into town, please, to the Woolworth's. Then drop me back at the lab."

"Woolworth's?"

"Yes, that's where I always get my notebooks."

Blakes laughed. "A secret powerful enough to help Germany conquer the world, and you keep it in a Woolworth's five-and-ten notebook?"

"You want I should engrave it somewhere? A notebook is a notebook."

At home that night, Weiss took the job of creating a convincing fake to heart. He used different pens and pencils and deliberately altered his handwriting to create the illusion of daily entries over a period of months. He salted the text with real formulas, but most in the second and third stage notes were credible fakes. He also made a point of inserting a few formulas he knew would blow up. That was particularly satisfying for him.

His labors left him exhausted by 2 a.m. when he finished, but he decided to switch the notebooks that very night. Why give Marla a chance to steal the real one?

The drive to the laboratory took only about fifteen minutes before he passed through the unguarded gate. Except for the circular pools of light spilling from the street lights, the compound was pitch dark. And dead quiet. He always got a small thrill being out very late at night. Everything looked so different at this hour when not a soul was to be seen anywhere. The aloneness allowed him the fleeting fantasy that the world was all his. That thought evaporated as he approached his lab at Building 11. A light was on inside.

Weiss saw it go off as he pulled up outside. Was it Marla? It had to be. The thought frightened him and made him angry at the same time. Had she already broken into the cabinet and stolen his notebook? Or had he arrived in time? There was a night watchman roaming around somewhere on the grounds, but Weiss knew that by the time he had found the man, Marla and his notebook, the real one, would be long gone. If only Blakes had arrested her today, he grumbled to himself as he got out of his car.

The door to Building 11 was unlocked. Someone was definitely there. His heart pounding, he went inside. He tried to make as little noise as possible, but the floorboards creaked under his feet with every step. He thought about not turning on the lights, but what was the advantage? Marla knew he--somebody--was here and keeping it dark would only give her an advantage.

Weiss stepped forward to the doorway leading to his office and deciding on the bold approach, flicked on the light. "Marla, I know you are in here," he called out.

The overhead light illuminated his office, confirming his worst fears. The door to his cabinet had been jimmied and stood open. He hurried over to it, hoping against hope that he'd got there in time, but his notebook was gone. He had no choice now but to try talking.

"Marla, I know you have it. Give it back now or you will be in serious trouble. The FBI knows about you and they will hunt you down." Weiss listened for a moment. No answer. Then he heard a scraping sound in the laboratory, like a stool being pushed sideways. He went down the hallway to the lab. Taking a deep breath, he pushed open the door ever so slowly, reached in, and flicked on the light. He could see about half the lab from where he stood. No Marla. He desperately wanted to back out and run, but he could not let the Nazis get his discovery. There was just too much at stake.

Weiss stepped into the lab and shut the door behind him. "Marla, I know--"

Marla stood up from behind a lab bench only five feet away. She wore an evil grin and pointed the .38 revolver directly at him. Turning pale, he tried desperately to think. His only chance was to convince her she had a fake notebook.

"You'll never get away with it, Marla." He raised the fake notebook up so she could see it. "I have the--" Marla's face twisted into a sneer as she pulled the trigger. He felt the bullet slam into his chest, knocking him backwards against the door. His knees buckled and his chest felt like it was on fire as he fell to the floor. Marla stepped over him and then roughly shoved him aside to open the lab door. She disappeared an instant later and Weiss, clutching his bloodied chest, knew he would never see her again. They had beaten him again, and that thought stung him almost as much as the burning in his chest.

The sight of his blood-soaked hand frightened him and he clapped it over the wound again to slow the bleeding. Woozy and getting weaker by the minute, Weiss felt like he might die right there. He refused to give up, though. It took all his strength, but he dragged himself, slowly, painfully to the outer office. The secretary's desk, and the cord for the telephone on her desk were a few feet away. Weiss rested for a minute, or maybe it was an hour, he had no way of knowing. He might have blacked out for a while, until the pain woke him up and he started inching forward again. Those last three feet were an agony, but somehow he made it. He barely had the strength to lift his arm to grasp the chord and pull the phone off the desk. It hit him on the head as it tumbled to the floor, the receiver off its hook. Weiss passed out.

Somewhere, miles away, Brownsville's night switchboard operator noticed a light come on her board. When she got no response to her request for a number to connect to, she hesitated and then called the police. Three hours later, Blakes Hill was roused from a deep sleep by the banging on his motel room door.

"What? What is it?" He fumbled for his watch on the nightstand and groaned. Five fifteen a.m.

"Mr. He-e-ill, there's a call for you'all in the office."

"Can't you just take a message?"

"No sah, 'fraid not. It's the po-lice. They're sayin' man in the hospital is demandin' you come see him raait now. Some-body called Mister Weiss. He's been shot."

The news hit Blakes like a slap in the face. He threw back the covers and jumped out of bed. "Get me directions to the hospital, and tell them I'll be there right away."

Though Blakes flashed his FBI credentials at a nurse's station on the second floor of Brownsville General Hospital, it didn't do him any good. The diminutive angel in white--she couldn't have been over five feet tall--adamantly refused to let him see Weiss. "Doctor's orders. No visitors!" She did pass along the information that Weiss had been operated on successfully, and that he was in serious but stable condition. Relieved to hear Weiss would live, Blakes couldn't shake the nagging feeling that all this was his fault. Was Marla the one who shot him? If so, none of this would have happened--if he'd arrested her when Weiss asked.

Blakes left the hospital and tracked down the two uniformed officers who had responded to the emergency call. They gave him what they knew, which wasn't much. Weiss had gone to his laboratory at about 2 a.m. and surprised someone, probably a burglar, in the laboratory. A locked cabinet had been broken into, but Weiss refused to talk about what had been taken or who the shooter was until he talked with FBI Agent Blakes Hill. He insisted they make the call to him. They'd done all they could. A detective on the day shift would follow up.

That was all Blakes needed to know. It had to be Marla, he thought, and she probably got the damned notebook too. Things couldn't get any more jacked up than this. He'd gotten an innocent man shot and nearly killed, and now the Germans had the formula for synthetic gasoline. And might win the war with it. Unless he got some answers quickly, Blakes thought, he might as well enlist in the Army right now.

Blakes drove out to the lab, hoping that Weiss had switched the notebooks before Marla shot him. The building was deserted and the front door unlocked when he arrived. Inside, the grim sight of Weiss's blood pooled by the secretary's desk momentarily stopped Blakes in his tracks. Clearly, Weiss could have bled out and died right there. Following the blood trail into the lab, he found a notebook on the floor. Was it the real one, or the fake?

Next stop was Marla's apartment, an upstairs studio in a private home. The landlady living downstairs was none too happy about being roused at 6:30 a.m. She reported hearing her tenant coming and going late last night and complained that the woman had cleared out without any notice. The police hadn't been there yet, so Blakes warned the lady to stay out of the room until detectives arrived. Meanwhile, he had first crack at it. But there wasn't much to see. The apartment had only one room, furnished with a bed, dresser, a small table, and a hot plate for cooking, plus a private bath. Marla had cleared out everything--the closet, drawers, and the bathroom medicine cabinet.

Too bad Marla was so thorough, he thought, as he tipped the oval metal trash can forward to look in it. It was empty too. "But she's not perfect," he said to himself. Off to one side on the floor, he spotted a small wad of crumpled orange-colored paper, as though it had been tossed at the trash can and missed. Smoothing it out, he discovered it was a ticket to the Trentino Bros. Traveling Circus. Blakes threw it back on the floor and wrote down the name in his pocket notebook.

On his way out, he interviewed the landlady, but the only useful information she offered was that Marla owned a car, a green '34 Dodge coupe. It was gone too.

Blakes found a seedy diner nearby, a converted railroad passenger car painted a dull green. Inside, a long counter ran lengthwise with a string of booths opposite. Using the pay phone, he got the Brownsville police to put out an APB on Marla Schumann and her car, and then headed for a booth in the very back. The shooting and lack of sleep had left him tired and feeling guilty about Weiss. It had been his call and he wasn't looking forward to facing the man. For that matter, headquarters wouldn't be happy about last night's screw up either. Just now, he couldn't imagine not being fired.

Blakes shoved aside a newspaper lying face down on the bench seat when he sat down. A short, dumpy waitress with bad makeup and a worse disposition took his order for coffee and scrambled eggs. She returned moments later with a mug of black coffee. At least she was quick. After medicating the coffee with a ton of sugar, he took a few sips and started feeling better. What he needed now, he decided, was something to take his mind off the case. Reaching for the newspaper by his side, he turned it over and immediately felt sick all over again. Huge black letters screamed the headline:

ALLIES EVACUATED FROM DUNKIRK!

With each sub headline below it, the news only got worse:

340,000 British, French, Belgian Troops Barely Escape Annihilation By Germans

-- 130,000 Others Dead, Wounded, Or Captured --

British PM Churchill Declares "We Shall Never Surrender!"

"My God," Blakes gasped as he tried to imagine tens of thousands of soldiers killed, wounded, or captured. Not even the image of the cornfields back home on the farm--hundreds of acres of rolling fields covered by legions of tall, waving corn stalks, one to a man--could equal it. Dunkirk was death and destruction on a scale beyond anything he could imagine.

"Hitler's gobbling up Europe. France will be next," he said to himself.

Suddenly the Atlantic did not seem so big, nor Europe so far away. We'll have to do something, Blakes thought. If Hitler conquers France and Britain, he won't be stopping there. America will be next.

Late that afternoon, the stubborn angel in white finally allowed Blakes in to see Weiss. They had him in a private room and the hospital bed had been cranked up so that he could sit up. Weiss was very pale, though he recognized Blakes.

"Mr. Weiss," he began apologetically, standing hat-in-hand by the side of the bed. "I'm so sorry. This was all my fault."

"Nonsense, Blakes. How could you know that she would be there last night? How could I have known? Believe me, if I had, I'd never have gone. That was bad luck. Right now I am feeling my good luck is that I am still alive."

"I'll say. I checked your laboratory last night. How did you manage to get all the way to that phone?"

"Very slowly, I'll tell you that," Weiss said, grimacing at the pain as he stifled a laugh.

"Was it Marla? Did she get the real notebook? I found this one at the lab," Blakes said holding it up.

"Yes, Marla shot me. I went to put the one you are holding in the cabinet, but she'd gotten there ahead of me. I guess she tried to hide when she saw me coming. My mistake was getting between her and the way out." He lowered his eyes. "She has the real one, and soon so will the Nazis," he added dejectedly.

"Not if we catch up with her first," Blakes said giving his best impression of being confident in the result. "I've put out an APB on her."

"I hope you get her. Hitler doesn't need any help from my discovery, the way the war is going now. Have you seen the newspaper? Dunkirk was a disaster. It makes me sick to think about it. Well, President Roosevelt will have to help the British now. He can't stall any longer. France is doomed and Britain will be next, unless we get into the war."

"Why does Hitler do it?" Blakes exclaimed, still shocked and confused by the sudden collapse of the Allied armies.

"Because he can! Don't you understand? Hitler is a fanatic. And he has the power now. He didn't always. He started out as a hateful pipsqueak, leading small gangs of other hateful pipsqueaks. They preyed on people's weaknesses with lies and propaganda, and when that didn't work they used intimidation and brute force to push aside those who opposed him. Hitler is clever and very determined, you have to give him that. Piece-by-piece he took complete control of the German government. While many good Germans either looked the other way or didn't take him seriously--or were too afraid to stand in his way--he established a totalitarian state.

"Totalitarianism. You understand that? Total control. Here the three branches of government counterbalance each other to prevent abuses of power. In Nazi Germany now, all power flows from a fanatical tyrant, Adolf Hitler. He has life and death power over all Germans--over everything--and he is not afraid to exercise it. In fact, he revels in it like every other fanatic before him. Mark my words. He will not stop, until he *is* stopped."

"You think America will fight?"

"I don't see how we can avoid it." Weiss grimaced as though hit by a stabbing pain. "But you can be sure President Roosevelt will avoid it as long as he can."

Blakes left the room thinking he wasn't doing any better than the French and the British. Nothing seemed to be going his way these days. He'd gotten two people shot, a German spy had stolen an important government secret, and Blakes didn't have the vaguest idea idea of where to look for her.

*　　*　　*　　*

The next day found Clay with Susan beside him in his Vette, driving back from Waynesboro toward Susan's townhouse in Staunton. They'd just spent an hour at the Volvo dealer ordering her new Volvo wagon. Clay had tried mightily to convince her she ought to get something sporty, that he would cover any extra cost, but she insisted on being practical. She needed the wagon for her real estate work, she said, because she often had to ferry whole families to and from houses for sale. And besides that, she felt safe in the car. Given what had happened recently, Clay had to concede the point.

Traffic on Richmond Road's four lanes was fairly heavy, but Clay couldn't help noticing a white Camry several cars back that seemed to be pacing them. Was it the same one from the other day at the nursing home? Deciding it was time to find out, Clay took a left turn at Fishersville, heading toward I-64.

"Clay, where are you going? This isn't the way," Susan insisted.

"Don't turn around, Susan, but I think the white Camry is back. I want to see if he's following us." Clay checked his rearview mirror after making the turn. Sure enough the Camry made the turn too, a good distance back, but there nevertheless.

"Clay, this is getting scary. What if it's those terrorists who killed Mr. Weiss?"

"Whoever they are, they get good marks for persistence. They're still back there. It's time we found out who they are," he said in a determined voice.

"Can't you lose them, like you did last time?"

"No Susan, this time we're going to try something different. This is going to be fun. Call Jimmy on your cell and see if he's free." By the time Clay drove onto I-64 heading west toward Staunton, Susan was talking with Jimmy.

"He's on his way home," Susan reported.

"Good. Ask him if he can meet us at the corner of East Beverley and Coalter Streets. Tell him to park at the corner on Beverley and watch for us. Keep the line open and we'll give him a heads up when we start up Coalter. After we pass by, tell him to wait until he sees the white Camry. Then pull in behind the guy and get the plate number."

As they came off the highway and back onto Richmond Road toward downtown Staunton, Susan asked, "Is he still there?"

"He sure is. He's definitely tailing us, Susan. No reason in the world for him to take the long way around to get here."

"Jimmy says he's in position, Clay."

Clay nodded and smiled at his side view mirror. "So's our Camry. We've got him this time," Clay declared. "Aren't cell phones great?"

The plan should have worked like a charm but, like all plans, there was a hitch. Jimmy waved at Susan as Clay's Vette went by. But he couldn't pull out right behind the Camry because two other cars were in back of it.

"Damn," Clay grumbled after Susan relayed the bad news from Jimmy. "Tell him we're going to stay on Coalter. Maybe the other cars will turn off."

Patience paid off sooner than Clay expected. One car turned off onto Frederick Street, and a short time after, the second car turned into Henly's Quick Stop.

"Jimmy's got it," Susan reported. "MZLM 273."

"Tell him to turn off as soon as he can. We'll meet him at Phil's Diner after we lose this guy." Turning to Susan, Clay said, "I really don't want him to know where you live, honey."

Now Clay went to work, turning left off Coalter into a residential neighborhood. The Camry suddenly became totally obvious despite trying to keep a discrete distance. Taking advantage of that, Clay turned a corner and hit the gas. A block up, he turned right at a four-way intersection and was gone before the Camry even figured out he had been dumped. Clay pushed it through three more turns before coming out on Augusta Street. From there he headed toward Phil's at a leisurely pace.

Jimmy already had a table when Clay and Susan walked into Phil's. They all ordered coffee while Clay called Lt. Youngblood and explained what had happened. Speculating there might be a connection with the Hamas attack at Fairview, he asked Youngblood to run the plate number. Meanwhile, Clay called Mac and asked him to meet with them at Phil's.

When Mac strolled in and sat down, he asked, "Did you get anything on the Camry?"

"Youngblood called back a little while ago," Clay replied. "It's registered to the Ali Bashkar Halal Meat Market up in Bailey's Crossroads. That's a suburb of DC. And get this. That neighborhood happens to have a big Muslim population."

"So it fits. What's next then?"

"Well, Youngblood can't do anything with it. DC is way out of his jurisdiction, and driving around in a Camry isn't a crime. No, I was thinking that maybe we should drive up there tomorrow and have a look around. Maybe we'll get something Bunker Hill can work with."

"Clay, that sounds like it might be dangerous," Susan warned.

"We're just going to do some surveillance. Can't get into any trouble doing that."

"You always say that."

Mac laughed. "Looks like the lady is getting to know you, Clay."

"Didn't take long, did it?" he replied with a big grin.

*   *   *   *

Two o'clock the next afternoon, Clay and Mac arrived at the dead center of Bailey's Crossroads, outside of Washington, DC. The neighborhood was a mix of high-rise apartment towers, retail shops, commercial buildings, and government offices. It was a racially mixed neighborhood, that was clear, but from what Clay had learned, there was no shortage of Muslims here. And of course, even at this time of day, the traffic was heavy. This was northern Virginia, after all.

Clay, at the wheel of his Vette, turned left and cruised up Hampton Boulevard, while Mac kept an eye out for street addresses. After a few minutes Mac spotted the Halal Meat Market in a two-story, suburban-style strip mall. Clay pulled into a parking spot across the street from it.

"Looks like this little mall has got Allah on its side, Mac. Besides the Ali Bashkar Halal Meat Market there's the Ali Cash Grocery, the Hookah Coffee Shop, Ibn Alwaite Book Shop, and something called the All Islamic Friendship Center. Whatever that is, it looks like it's got the whole second floor."

"What do you suppose a meat market has got to do with what's been going on down our way?"

"Mac, your guess is as good as mine. Might be an employee is connected to Hamas. Or maybe the store is really a front for a terrorist logistical cell. But either way, I can't figure why they killed Weiss. Or what they think he told me."

"I never did ask you. Did you get a look at the guy driving the white Camry?"

"Not really. Black hair, olive skin. Definitely Arab, but I only saw him sitting in the car. I doubt I could identify him."

"What are we looking for here then?"

"Don't know that either, Mac," he said giving his friend an apologetic shrug of his shoulders. Then he grinned. "But it's the only lead we've got. Maybe we'll stir something up."

Two massively boring hours on the stakeout passed before Clay suddenly sat up and nudged Mac. "Hey, it's the white Camry," he told Mac excitedly as the car pulled up to the meat market. Clay waited anxiously until the two men got out, but neither looked anything like the man who had been following him. Still, it was enough to keep Clay's hopes alive. So they stayed put, sitting and watching, as DC and Virginia taxi cab drivers streamed in and out of the Hookah

Coffee Shop. Otherwise, business appeared very slow at the meat market, and the other shops too.

With the late afternoon light fading, one-by-one the shops closed. None of the shopkeepers left by their front doors though, which seemed strange since the Camry had been left out front. Mac guessed they all could have used back doors, but something was not right. Meanwhile, with only the upstairs Friendship Center remaining open, Clay was about ready to give up and head for home. Then he did a double take.

"Looks like company's coming, Mac," Clay said idly.

"Oh yeah?"

"Two hajis. Big ones too, just came out of that Friendship Center. Coming right at us. Don't look too friendly." Clay rolled down his window as the thugs walked up and bracketed the Vette, one alongside Clay's door and one by Mac's.

"Evening," Clay called out as the two came up.

"What are you doing here?" the one on Clay's side growled. He half bent down to look at Clay.

"Oh, just taking a break."

"You've been parked out here all afternoon."

"It's a free country, last time I heard. And this is a public parking space."

"This is our neighborhood, smartass. Time for you to move on, if you know what's good for you."

Clay turned to Mac. "These guys don't seem too friendly, Mac," he said, taking hold of the door handle. He nodded to Mac, who moved his hand to his door handle. Clay's blood boiled as the thug dragged a key across the Vette's rear quarter panel. He shoved his door open hard, slamming it into the thug's knees and knocking him over. Mac's door flew open at the same time, sending the second man flying like a bowling pin.

Out of the car now, both Clay and Mac stood their ground when the thugs came flying back at them howling "Allah Akbar!" Stepping aside at the last instant, Clay landed a solid punch to the charging

Muslim's head, putting him face first on the ground. But only for a moment. The thug charged Clay again and this time drove him back against the Vette. Clay struggled to get his breath before bringing both hands, clenched together, down on the man's back. With the Muslim down on all fours, Clay finished him with a flying drop kick to the head. The man hit the pavement hard.

Clay was about to help Mac when he spotted a dozen more menacing bad guys, armed with baseball bats and sticks, coming out of the Friendship Center.

"Mac!" Clay shouted. "Better finish him quick. Their cavalry is coming!" Clay jumped into the Vette while Mac loosed a hard left to the Muslim's gut, doubling him over. A pile driver uppercut with his strong right sent the man stumbling backwards and onto his backside. There he sat with a dazed look as the Vette roared to life and Mac jumped in.

Clay put the pedal to the metal, left ten feet of burned rubber, and was halfway down the block before the pack of angry Muslims had even gotten close. One raged something in Arabic and threw his baseball bat. It spun in a high arcing, but totally futile, attempt to strike the infidels. Clay's Vette was already long gone when, seconds later, the bat clattered ineffectually to the pavement.

* * * *

Early in the morning three days afterward, Clay, Mac, Jimmy, Lt. Youngblood, and Bunker Hill sat drinking coffee around a nicked up oak table in a meeting room at Staunton Police Headquarters. It was a miserable morning as fall mornings go, raining cats and dogs with blustery winds blowing sheets of rain against the room's one large window. Bunker Hill had begun reporting on his questioning of the Halal Meat Market owner, Razzaq Ali Bashkar.

"He's lying of course, but he said two employees had permission to drive the store's Camry to Staunton to check it out. He claimed they were scouting out possible locations for a new store and had no idea they were following you, Clay."

"That's bull."

"Of course it is. He got a little flustered when I pointed out there aren't many Muslims in Staunton. Then he backpedaled and said he wasn't planning on another Halal Meat Market. He said it's going to be an adult movie rental store."

"You're joking," Clay exclaimed between guffaws from around the table.

"God's honest truth. He claimed he needs the money. He said he'd clean up supplying sex tapes to decadent westerners. But the store had to be far away from his mosque, so word wouldn't get back and sully *his* reputation."

"Well, Staunton would never let him do that. People would be up in arms," Mac offered. "Do you think he's tied somehow to the Weiss murder? Or to those two Hamas terrorists we smoked at Fairview?"

"I wouldn't put it past him, but we don't have any proof of a connection. He's an Egyptian emigre, but he's legal and has his green card. From what we've learned so far, I think he's just a go-between for the man who's really running the show, an imam named Moktar at that All Islamic Friendship Center. Moktar's been active in pushing Muslim causes here in the U.S. of A., and he's been making a lot of calls to Qatar."

"Causes?" Jimmy asked. "You mean like time off in the workplace for Muslims so they can pray to Mecca?"

"Yes, that too. Federal recognition of Muslim holy days, stuff like that. The big one is propagandizing for recognition of Shariah Law."

"What the heck is Shariah Law?" Youngblood asked.

"It's an all-encompassing legal code written in the seventh century," Bunker answered. "The code is based on the Koran and other sacred Islamic texts."

"We saw it in Afghanistan," Clay added. "Those Taliban fighters would enforce it in villages they captured. Really crazy, fanatical stuff.

They'd cut off people's hands for robbery and stone women for adultery. Execute nonbelievers. It's ridiculous to think Shariah Law would work here," Clay grumbled. "We've already got a legal system that works just fine. Besides, he came to this country from wherever. He's the one who should change, not us."

"I agree with you Clay," Bunker continued, "but it's politics and politics is never simple. We've got millions of practicing Muslims in this country, and you'd be surprised at how many were born here. There are lots of legit activities for promoting the Muslim faith, and it's definitely gaining devoted followers here.

"Remember our country was founded on religious freedom. Muslims have every right to practice their religion, unless it conflicts with the law of the land. Ever since 9-11 there's been a problem though, because our government has focused on fighting the Islamic radicals, the terrorists. The great majority of Muslims are peace loving and not at all radical. But to paraphrase Mao, they are the sea in which the radicals swim."

"What's that mean?" Lt. Youngblood asked Bunker.

"The millions of moderate Muslims provide cover--unwittingly or not--and a certain amount of sympathy, as fellow Muslim brethren, for the radical fundamentalists. And as faithful members of the Muslim community, they can be intimidated by the radicals into helping--or at least keeping quiet."

"How can they get away with that?" Youngblood asked.

"Fear of being denounced as an apostate--a nonbeliever--by the radicals," Bunker continued. It is a key weapon for keeping would-be reformers and critics among the moderate Muslims in line. Under Islamic law, being an apostate is punishable by death."

"But where is all the violence coming from?" Jimmy asked. "I wouldn't begin to know what to tell students in my history class. It's not like the West has supported any Crusades against Islam in the last seven hundred years, and Jeez, we've spent gazillions on their oil. And now Muslim terrorists have even turned on their own inside Muslim countries. But what they say in the newspapers, Islam is supposed to be a peaceful religion based on reason and enlightenment."

Bunker hesitated a moment, wondering how much he could tell them about the threat assessments he'd seen. "And would like us to believe. To understand what is *really* going on, you have to realize there is a fundamental schism over Shariah--Islamic--Law in the Muslim world. Islamic moderates and reformers recognize as relevant only parts of Shariah Law, which means literally 'the path.' For them it is a private matter, accepted as a guide for personal conduct.

"Muslim supremacists--Islamists, those radical fundamentalists--are ideologues. They follow the dictates of Shariah Law as it was originally written. They believe in its rigid, compulsory system regulating everything in their society--the political, legal, social, economic, and military spheres, as well as the religious aspects of life. It's religious totalitarianism.

"Islamists believe Muslims everywhere must work to establish Shariah Law. In fact, Shariah Law commands it, and that all Muslims must conduct *jihad*--religious war--until all unbelievers everywhere accept Islamic law. Muslim supremacists want to reestablish the seventh century Muslim caliphate, a theocratic, totalitarian state based on Islamic law. Worldwide."

"You're joking," Jimmy said, looking aghast. "They can't really believe that their *jihad,* terrorist acts like flying planes into the twin towers and setting off car bombs, horrible as they are, will make us accept being governed by a caliphate. That's stupid."

"True, but Islamists take two different approaches to *jihad,"* Bunker continued. "Both groups of radical fundamentalists believe in violent *jihad* to achieve the supremacy of Islam, but differ in the timing. The most radical of them--al Qaida, the Taliban, Hezbollah, Hamas--are waging a violent war right now by terrorist acts and military ops to force all nonbelievers to accept Shariah's totalitarian society. Other fundamentalists engage in the more insidious *dawa,* what's called stealth *jihad.* These Islamists work from within, to establish the movement here and in other countries, to get their people in positions of influence, to co-opt our leaders, and to circulate propaganda. It's cultural subversion to promote Shariah. They believe they are preparing the way for violent *jihad* and the ultimate triumph of Islam at a later date."

"What are you saying?" Jimmy asked. "That this stealth *jihad* is nothing more than a fifth column for Muslims who want to set up a theocracy here in our country?"

"And throughout the world, Jimmy. Shariah Law teaches that the faithful must continue *jihad* until infidels everywhere have accepted Islam."

"But how can a bunch of fanatics expect to take over the world?" Clay exclaimed.

"Look what happened in Egypt."

"You mean Morsi?"

"Yes, Morsi and the Muslim Brotherhood very nearly succeeded in establishing Egypt as an Islamist state. They got control of a democratic government and started ramming through Islamic law. Until protesters took to the streets."

"Well, that's Egypt."

"Don't you know Islamist groups have been established here in this country for decades already? With the support and generous financial backing of certain Arabs--very devout and very wealthy Muslims--some have established front organizations to advance their primary goal--stealth *jihad* and the eventual establishment of Shariah law here.

"And since 9-11, while keeping up a shooting war with al Qaida, our government has fallen all over itself to deny the terrorists' violent *jihad* has any precedent in Muslim religion. Our leaders have been promoting the idea that al Qaida and other violent terrorists have 'hijacked' the Muslim religion for their own ends. At bottom, it's a policy of benign neglect, a well-intentioned effort to help prevent a popular backlash against nonradical Muslims. But, in effect, the government has blindsided itself to the very real schism between radicals and moderates in the Muslim world, and to the fundamentalists' strategy of stealth jihad, which is doing what it can to exploit our civil liberties and religious freedoms to destroy our culture from within."

"I'll tell you, Bunker," Youngblood said, sitting up as though getting ready to leave the room, "that's some pretty scary stuff. I mean, it's all possible. It even kind of fits as an explanation for what's been going on with Muslims. But what I don't see, is what it has to do with us. I mean the stuff you've been talking about is way outside my jurisdiction."

"True enough, lieutenant, except that this guy over here," Bunker said pointing at Clay, "has been getting a lot of attention from crazy Muslims lately. I can't help thinking that *something* is going on and that we'd better figure out what it is, sooner rather than later. We're dealing with very nasty people."

7
HOT ON THE TRAIL

Blustery winds whipped brightly colored leaves from the trees and buffeted Clay, Susan, Mac, and Jimmy as they walked up to the front entrance to Sunnyvale after their meeting with Bunker. The nurse at the information desk shunted them to a waiting area while Blakes was being examined by his doctor. With their coats off and seated in the antiseptic lounge, the four friends inevitably turned their attention to Blakes and his memories.

"He's kind of stuck on Weiss and that synthetic gasoline project back in 1940," Clay told Jimmy. "I wish we could fast forward him, because I don't see how that story is going to help us with what got Weiss killed."

"I don't want to be a drag on this, Clay, but I'd like to hear about what he remembers. World War II history was a special interest of mine when I was in college. Most people don't realize that oil was Nazi Germany's Achilles heel. Domestic oil production was far below what they needed for their war machine, and the lure of Russian oilfields became a big part of Hitler's decision to attack the Soviet Union in 1941.

"When that failed," Jimmy continued, "the Nazis had no choice but to make it synthetically from coal. Germany had plenty of coal, so toward the end of the war they were making millions of gallons of gasoline that way. Until," he said with a grin, "the Allies started bombing the hell out of synthetic fuel plants. By 1945, they'd cut the output of aviation gas alone by ninety percent."

"There's more than one way to win a war," Mac observed.

"Yeah, you're not much of a threat if you can't get your planes off the ground, or keep your tanks and subs running," Clay added.

"The fate of the whole world hung on keeping the Germans from filling up their gas tanks," Jimmy said. "It just goes to show how critical oil is to modern war machines, heck, to modern society. We need the energy from oil to make it run."

The dowdy nurse in white with an eternal smile appeared and led them to Blakes's small room, where they had to stand practically shoulder to shoulder. Clay took the lead and introduced everybody.

"Mr. Hill, I'm Clay. We spoke last week. This is Susan, and that's my friend Mac. And this fellow is also a good friend of ours, Jimmy. He knows a lot about World War II. Last time we talked about Mr. Weiss's synthetic gasoline project. Do you remember me?"

"I remember her," Blakes said as he defensively pulled the covers up to his chin. "She's very pretty. Bunker's lucky to have her as his teacher."

"That's very nice of you to say," Susan answered with a smile. "But I'm not a teacher. He is," she said pointing at Jimmy. "He teaches history."

"Is Bunker getting good grades?"

"Bunker is a friend of mine," Jimmy replied. "But he's not my student. Bunker is all grown up and finished with school. He's an agent for Homeland Security."

Susan stepped closer to the bed. "You were going to tell us about Weiss and his synthetic gasoline project. Do you remember anything about that case now, Mr. Hill?"

"That's the trouble, sweetie, I can remember it like it was yesterday."

"Will you tell me about it?"

"Okay." The blanket moved down an inch or two and Blakes seemed to relax. "Ben came to us, my partner and me, because he suspected his lab assistant was a German spy. That was 1940, just before we got into World War II. Ben was working on a secret project for the government. He was a Jew who'd been persecuted by the Nazis, so he definitely didn't want to do anything to help them."

Slowly, in a sometimes quavering voice, Blakes recounted the story of his trip to Brownsville. "I felt terrible," Blakes admitted afterward. "You have to understand, I was just starting out with the bureau. I'd gotten Ben shot--I felt plenty guilty about that--and let German spies get hold of an important secret. I caught hell for that, I can tell you, and a bunch of pointless all night stakeouts back in DC as punishment."

"What was it like in Washington then?" Jimmy asked. "You are talking about the summer of 1940, right?"

"Yes. After Dunkirk, France surrendered to the Nazis. It was a hell of a soup. When the Nazis started their blitzkrieg attacks back in '39, most people here wanted us to stay out of it. Officially we were neutral, and at that point we couldn't have done much anyway. But plenty of people were arguing about it. There were antiwar protests, big rallies staged by America First to keep us out of the war. A lot like it was in the Sixties with all those protests over Vietnam. Politicians and propagandists denounced anything that smacked of 'intervening' in Europe--that's what they called it. Intervening. They wanted America to stay neutral while Hitler's armies just rolled over Europe. Charles Lindbergh was the antiwar poster boy, but a lot of people figured he was nothing more than a stooge for the Nazis.

"Worse yet, Hitler and Stalin had signed a pact. They played us like a fiddle--doing everything they could to keep us out of the war. The British worked just as hard to get us into it, because they were desperate for our help. It was the war of words before the fighting war. And until 1940, when the Nazis kicked the British off the Continent and France surrendered, President Roosevelt just sat on his hands. Yep, nineteen-forty, that's when attitudes really started to change.

"A lot of people suddenly realized we could be next, that America *had* no choice but to get ready for war. Even though it was an election year, President Roosevelt finally came out for the draft and war preparedness. He caught a lot of flack for that. And Wendell Wilkie, Roosevelt's opponent, he took even more. Roosevelt tarred him as a stalking horse for big business, and Hitler made things worse by saying he'd welcome Wilkie as president. Poor Wilkie," Blakes chuckled. "At campaign rallies people threw rotten eggs, vegetables, you name it at him. Got so bad the New York Times carried a box score on what was tossed at him.

"France's surrender changed a lot of minds, all right," he continued. "I remember it wasn't long after that I finally got out of the dog house at the bureau. That September, the local police in Bigelow, Tennessee, called to say they had found Marla's car. My boss sent me down to investigate, I suppose figuring it would be a dead end and I couldn't possibly mess up."

Blakes kept on talking, but Clay could tell from his eyes he was back in 1940.

"I can still see that old green Dodge coup sitting there, looking like it had hurtled off the road and belly flopped into the heavy brush..."

Bigelow, Tennessee, in 1940 rated only a small dot on Blakes's Esso roadmap, being nothing more than a tiny hamlet nestled on a bend in the Clinch River. The county's lone lawman, Sheriff Ronald P. Jefferson, stood on the edge of an embankment, watching Agent Blakes Hill work his way down into the gully where the green Dodge coupe had come to rest. A stocky, middle-aged man, Sheriff Jefferson wore a khaki uniform, his blond hair slicked down and combed straight back under his flat brimmed campaign hat. A .38-caliber revolver hung in a black leather holster on his right hip. He worked a plug of chewing tobacco for a moment, then leaned forward to spit a wad of brown goo onto the ground.

"Ain't goin' to find nothing," he called out. "We done already checked."

"I know sheriff," Blakes called back. "But I've got to look anyway. For my report."

"Keys was in it when we found it. You want 'em to open the trunk?" When Blakes turned and nodded yes, Sheriff Jefferson tossed them underhand, watching them sail in a lazy arc out and down to Blakes's outstretched hand.

The sheriff is right, of course, Blakes thought as he pulled open the driver's side door and peered in. Marla and her handler are smart. They'd have cleared out everything incriminating before pushing the car over the embankment. And they had. He found nothing at all in the glove compartment, under the seats, or in the trunk. They'd even erased their footprints and tire tracks up above, where they pushed the car off the dirt road and into the gully. Struggling back up the steep embankment, he decided his only hope was canvassing the village shops to see if anybody recognized Marla's picture. Winded by the time he got near the top, he gratefully accepted the sheriff's outstretched helping hand.

"Find anythin'?"

"Nope."

"Told yah."

"Yeah, well--"

"Suppose now I can have Earl winch it outta there?"

"Sure."

Blakes rode back to Bigelow with the sheriff. There wasn't much to the town, only a Main Street with stores on both sides for about three blocks, and a scattering of homes on the side streets. In a town this small, any stranger would have stuck out like a sore thumb. After an hour or so, Blakes realized he'd struck out again--nobody recognized the picture of Marla or remembered any other strangers. Marla's handler probably had dumped the car in the dead of night. Stymied, Blakes decided to break for lunch. He couldn't think on an empty stomach, he was sure of that.

Two big picture windows flanked the double doors at Hy's Hometown Restaurant, and as Blakes walked up, he saw a man in a white uniform taking a small poster out of the left-hand window. Though it was only about the size of a standard sheet of paper, the poster's bright colors caught Blakes's eye. A circus ring with roaring lions dominated the center and across the top in large print were the words "Circus Is In Town." At the bottom he just had time to read "Traveling Circus" before the sign disappeared along with the man in white.

"Well, I'll be. Could that be the connection?" he wondered out loud.

The restaurant's spring-loaded screen door slapped shut behind him as he stepped into a large room with square tables under red and white checked table cloths, a counter on the left, and pinball machines in the back. Black ceiling fans spun slowly in the midday heat, stirring up just enough breeze to rustle the sticky, brown fly strips hanging from the ceiling. Sheriff Jefferson put down a sandwich thick with ham and waved to Blakes from the counter. "Set yurself over here, Blakes. Any luck?"

"Nope. Nobody's seen her. But when I came in, that guy behind the counter took down a circus poster. Was there a circus here not long ago? I need to know the name."

"Who, Hy?" Sheriff Jefferson said pointing at the man in white. "Say Hy, can we get a look at that poster you took down?"

"What for, Ron? You're too late. Circus already left Knoxville."

"I swear, always an argument with you, Hy. Why can't you just let us see the poster?"

"It's all dirty. I just put it in the garbage," Hy complained. "Got grease on it."

"Well take it out for Chrissake and bring it here!"

Hy dredged it out as ordered and brought it over, dangling it between two fingertips. "Don't get it on my nice clean countertop, hear?" Sheriff Jefferson accommodated by swinging around on his seat to keep the poster from dirtying the counter.

"Says here, it was in Knoxville August seventh to the twenty-first. He's right, you missed it. They left over a week ago."

"Okay, but there's something about that circus' name, Trentino Brothers." Blakes was getting excited now. He pulled out his notebook and flipped through the pages. "Hah! That's the name on a circus ticket I found in Marla's apartment. How long has it been since you found her car abandoned out there?"

"About a week, I reckon."

"That fits then. I'd bet my eye teeth she's connected to that circus somehow. Does it say where it's headed next?"

"Nope, never do. But mah friend over there at Knoxville Pee-Dee might could help. Circus like that has to register their i-tinerary with the city, case there's any complaints after they move on."

Blakes was already up out of his seat. "How about we do that now, sheriff?"

"Sit down, sonny. Ain't nothing can't wait until I've finished my lunch. Seein' as how Hy helped you out with that sign, ya'll could give him some business too."

A blue-plate special and an hour later, Blakes had in hand the Trentino Brothers' Traveling Circus itinerary for the entire season. The following afternoon found him in Roanoke, Virginia, sitting in the parking area outside the fairgrounds on a warm, sunny September day. He knew all too well that this lead was really thin, but it was all he had. A traveling circus *could* be an ideal cover for making contact with agents across all the states in which it operated. But short of actually finding Marla, Blakes didn't know what else he could do to prove that. And then there were the problems of finding out who her handler was, identifying the rest of the spy ring, and getting Weiss's notebook back.

Blakes couldn't help feeling out of place strolling down the crowded circus midway. All the people around him were smiling, having a good time--trying, for a few hours, to escape the misery in the world around them. And what was he doing? Looking for Nazi spies and an attempted murderer. Was it his job, or the times that made him feel so out of place? *Both,* he decided.

Blakes bought an Italian ice soaked with orange syrup and forced a half smile as he wandered along the midway, casually eyeing the circus people working the concessions. On his second go around, he spotted the barker at the shooting gallery watching him. Blakes continued on nonchalantly, pretending he hadn't picked up on it. But a while later, he came back to the shooting gallery.

This time, he walked up to the counter, put down a nickel, and hit five of the moving targets with his five shots. The barker wasn't at all pleased as he called out, "We have a winner here! Five shots for a nickel. Win a prize!" Then he leaned in conspiratorially, and in a low voice grumbled, "What are you, some kind of Lone Ranger? Pick any prize on the second shelf, mister."

Blakes smirked, then looked down at the little girl who had pushed up to the counter. She had her eyes glued on the stuffed toy prizes. "Which one do you want?" he asked with an amused smile.

"Oh please, mister," she said in her small voice, "the bunny rabbit!"

"One bunny rabbit coming right up," Blakes answered. "You heard the lady. The rabbit."

Blakes wrestled with his next move while the barker retrieved the rabbit. He'd covered the midway and hadn't seen anybody even resembling Marla. He had her picture, but showing it to the wrong person would tip his hand. Then she'd disappear again. But he really wanted to see the barker's reaction to the picture.

He flashed Marla's picture as the barker handed the little girl the stuffed pink rabbit. "Ever seen this woman before?" Blakes read the momentary surprise in the barker's eyes. He knew the man had lied when he answered, "No. Never seen her before."

"Gee, thanks mister," the little girl chirped excitedly. She cuddled the rabbit and then ran off.

Blakes smiled to himself as he walked away. Sure, he'd made the little girl happy. He liked that. But that split second look on the barker's face was what counted, and it spoke volumes. Marla was here. He was sure of that now, but the nagging problem was where? The only places left to check were the big tent and the circus trailers beyond the midway.

Blakes picked a front row seat under the big top, to check out the performers and, he had to admit, so he wouldn't miss any of the show. Side flaps on the tent had been opened for air circulation, but it was still hot under the canvas dome and musty animal smells from the previous performance lingered. There was only one ring--this was no big city three-ring operation--with bleacher seats up twelve rows all around, but they had a full house and Blakes could feel the excitement in the air. *He* was excited too--he hadn't been to the circus since he was a boy.

He wasn't disappointed. Clowns and a funny slapstick routine started the show, then came a caravan of five dancing elephants, sequined acrobats flying overhead in death defying leaps and spins between high trapezes, a magic act and fire-eater, prancing trained horses, more clowns, and finally four snarling, trained lions he remembered scared him to death as a boy.

That's when he saw her. Marla, big as life, held the hoop the lions jumped through when the trainer cracked the whip. She wore a sequined, gold body suit and her long dark hair was piled high on top of her head in a regal looking hairdo. Femme fatale, Blakes thought. She had a nice body for a would-be murderess and spy.

From where she stood on the ring's far side, he was too far away to be noticed, so Blakes knew he'd have the advantage of surprise. His best shot would be to make the arrest after the next show. He'd catch her coming out of the tent, or if too many other performers were around, he'd follow her to her trailer. He knew circus people could be a tight knit bunch and might defend her. That Nazi spies could be among them only added to the risk.

The final act, a comedy routine with clowns and a rickety old tin lizzie, brought the house down and for a few moments of laughter Blakes forgot all about Marla, Weiss's discovery, and the war in

Europe. As the ring emptied and the house lights came up, it took Blakes a moment to return to reality. He stood up to leave, but then lights dimmed, a curtain opened, and a parade of the performers led by the prancing horses spilled into the ring. Around the ring they marched, smiling and waving as the audience stood and applauded enthusiastically. Blakes joined in the reverie until he saw Marla coming toward him. She was looking right at him, and he knew she had made him. It pained him, but he kept smiling and applauding as she strode by. How had she recognized him? Did she see him that day at Weiss's lab? Or had he jacked things up again by showing her picture?

Not that that really mattered now. He had to act fast or he'd lose her again. While Marla was finishing her circuit of the ring, he hurried out and around back of the big top. A knot of performers in costume milled about, looking much less larger than life outside the ring. But no Marla. Blakes rushed toward the circus trailers, finally spotting her as she ducked into an alleyway between them. He darted into the alleyway, passing the first few trailers before seeing her up ahead. She turned around and smiled at him, a galling look of unconcern for Blakes as he sprinted toward her. Then something hit him on the head, hard. Blakes's world suddenly went black.

He came to in a small storage room lighted by only a shaft of light coming through a rectangular vent high up on the wall. He had no idea how long he'd been out. His head hurt like hell and he lay on the floor, bound hand and foot and gagged for good measure. Struggling against the ropes proved useless. Two men argued somewhere nearby, but Blakes could barely make out the muffled voices. He thought he heard "FBI" and "What are we going to do?" but little else.

That was enough, though, to know the trouble he'd fallen into. The thought he had screwed up again stung him anew, then the realization they would probably kill him washed over Blakes. Now in a cold sweat, he beat himself up--he should have called local cops for backup, shouldn't have shown Marla's picture. All that was pointless, though. What really mattered now was getting untied. But the ropes refused to yield.

Light streamed into the room as a door swung open. Two men wearing hoods walked in. One was very big, probably a weightlifter, while the other was smaller and obviously older. The big man put his foot on Blakes's chest while the small man slipped Blakes's wallet back into his pocket. Gone for a moment, the small man came back holding a hypodermic. Blakes watched in horror as a tiny jet of liquid squirted from its tip. The small man wore an evil grin as he announced with a German accent, "This won't hurt a bit, Herr Hill."

Fighting for his life now, Blakes cried out into the gag and desperately tried to roll away, but the more he writhed the harder the big man's foot pressed down on his chest. Wide-eyed with terror, Blakes saw the needle coming closer and closer. He felt the sting of it in his shoulder. The burning lasted only a few moments before he blacked out again.

Sometime later, hours, maybe days--he had no way of knowing--the cool night air slowly brought Blakes back to consciousness. The soft glow of the full moon was the first thing he saw while climbing out of the haze clouding his brain. He blinked several times. Gradually, the dark shadowy outlines of the trees around him and the starry sky above came into focus. He was conscious of lying on his back on what he thought was grass. He had a splitting headache and without thinking, put his hand to his head. Only then did he realize he wasn't tied up any longer. Why, he wondered, did they dump him out here? Had they shot him with some kind of truth drug and found out what they wanted to know? Did they even need to?

Blakes rolled over on his side in an attempt to stand up and bumped into something lying next to him. Propping himself up on one elbow, he looked at a woman's motionless form. Had she been drugged too? He shook her, but there was no response. Instinctively, he touched her neck. Her skin was cold and there was no pulse.

He sat up and examined her in the moon's silvery half light. That's when he noticed the dark stain smearing the front of her dress.

Without thinking, he touched it. It was wet, cold, distressing to him now. She had been stabbed twice, maybe three times in the gut and left to bleed out next to him. A cold, brutal death. Some of her blood had soaked into the side of his shirt and the upper part of his pants. He picked up the bloody knife lying right there between them.

Blakes was horrified. In his young life, he'd never seen a corpse before and to come face to face with death like this, alone, confused, and in the dark, made it doubly shocking. Every living soul must make that dismal, disturbing discovery at some time or other--to see for oneself the death we hear is lurking out there for us all. We may know it in our minds, as Blakes had, but it is still a shock when we first see it, in a stark, lifeless corpse. Such an unwelcome reminder of what lies ahead.

He threw down the knife, suddenly afraid of the thought that he might have done that to Marla. He struggled against the fog clouding his brain. What had happened here? He tried to stand up, but he was too woozy and fell back on his butt. Vaguely, he heard a car drive up somewhere close by. Was it help, or had the German come back to give him another shot?

Two flashlight beams came to rest on his face.

"Don't you do anything stupid, mister. You're under arrest."

Blakes felt his arms being pulled behind his back. The two policemen lifted him to his feet, but he was still too weak to walk, so one on each arm, they dragged him to the patrol car. The ride from the park to the Roanoke Police Station lasted only a few minutes. He was booked on suspicion of murder and thrown into a cell.

"Have you ever seen a corpse, missy?" Blakes asked Susan. Clay, Mac, and Jimmy had drawn closer to the hospital bed, but she was closest to him.

"Yes," she said quietly. "Both my mother and my father. But that was at their funeral services. I didn't wake up next to them in the dark, like you did."

"How about you, sonny?" he asked glancing at Clay.

"Yes, too often," Clay answered after a moment. The old man obviously did not remember that he had seen Weiss murdered not so long ago, and Clay saw no point in bringing up the deaths of friends and foe in Afghanistan.

"Took me a day before my head cleared and I figured out they'd set me up for Marla's murder. They were probably afraid of the heat if they'd killed me, and I guess they figured Marla was just excess baggage anyway. I spent two days in the jail before we straightened that mess out. It was a stretch in the first place, me being an FBI agent, but those local cops weren't letting me go until they'd dotted the eyes and crossed the tees. Sheriff Jefferson back there in Bigelow helped by telling them I'd been out there, but my shoulder was my ace in the hole. I still had a needle puncture mark on my shoulder."

"I got chewed out royally again when I finally got back to DC. But nobody had to tell me those Germans were serious. Deadly serious."

Blakes fell silent for a moment, as if remembering that time many years ago. "I'm tired," he said finally. "I don't want to think about this any more today. Please go away."

* * * *

Prof. Wentworth could barely contain his excitement as he checked the clipboard that Valerie, his dish of a lab assistant, had handed him in his private office at the laboratory in Loudon County. He eagerly raised and lowered the top page, comparing the previous day's readings with today's.

"Only a few more hours to go," he said distractedly.

"Yes, and this time it looks like you'll have your Nobel Prize, you selfish bastard."

"Valerie, *please!*" he complained angrily. "Not now. When we are so close. Heat output and helium formation right where they should be. If this continues for a few more hours, we will have it. Why can't you just shut up for once?"

"Why couldn't you keep your fly zipped up?" she snapped back at him.

"You wanted it too. And I told you up front I'd never leave Anita."

"Yeah, well, I was the one who had to get the abortion."

"That's what trying to *screw* your way to a Ph.D. got you," he sneered.

"Bastard!"

"I'm sorry," he quickly apologized. "I shouldn't have said that. Look, Valerie, when this proves out, it's going to change things. You know it as well as I do. Really change things. I'll give you credit for your work and you'll be able to write your own ticket after that."

"You say that now. We'll see what happens when you start getting mobbed by reporters."

"Oh, for Christ's sake. Here, take the clipboard and tell Dan I'd like to see him in my office."

Dan Forrest, in his early fifties, married with three grown children, was the one assistant Prof. Wentworth could always rely on. Dan was smart, but not brilliant, and more importantly he was very loyal. He seemed to have accepted the fact that his career at Babcock depended on Prof. Wentworth. There was no resentment there, and the professor always felt he could safely open up to him.

Prof. Wentworth smiled broadly when Dan came in and sat in the hot seat, the chair in front of his desk. At six-six, Dan was a skinny beanpole of a man with a prominent nose and a monk-like bald spot on top of his head. He beamed right back at his boss.

"It's looking very, very good, Dan. Valerie showed me the latest readings. I think we'll have it this time, and soon. Finally, we've hit the right combination. I can feel it in my bones. The reaction is self-sustaining, it's stable, and it's pumping out heat."

"Yes. Heat output has been really strong, stronger than I thought it would be, and holding steady. We couldn't ask for any better performance. But don't forget, we have to measure degradation of the catalyst. It could be substantial, and if it is being consumed, that could account for some of the heat."

"Do you really think it is?"

"Well, no. It's possible, that's all. We shouldn't get too excited until we've checked the results six ways to Sunday, that's all."

"Yes, yes, Dan. In my head I know you're right. But I just can't keep all this bottled up. Doing good science is like having good sex! It excites you all over and makes you feel all powerful."

Dan laughed. "You're on a tear all right."

"Just think how this will change the world!" Prof. Wentworth exclaimed, his eyes glazing over. "And if we handle this correctly, we are going to become very, very wealthy indeed." His excitement got the better of him and he started talking faster and faster. "We will have to tear this experiment apart, examine everything microscopically, and then build a new device to be sure we can duplicate our findings. Then we have to start doubling the run time, and doubling that again, testing for any limits to the reaction. But we must be careful about keeping this quiet too. A discovery of this magnitude could make some people very angry."

* * * *

Moktar sat in his office at the All Islamic Friendship Center in Bailey's Crossroads pretending to be busy with paperwork. Ever since those two, Clay Cantrell and Mac Harper, had shown up outside the Center, he had been under surveillance of one sort or another. He was followed wherever he went now. He was certain the Center's phones had been tapped and for all he knew, they were watching him through telescopes from one of the apartments across the street. This kind of attention was oppressive to him. He realized it was dangerous as well, but at the moment what he wanted most was to make a move, show them he could outwit them anytime he wanted. And now he had enough of a reason to do just that.

Moktar looked at this watch. Eight o'clock. Time to get going. It was raining hard and dark enough now. He slid open his desk drawer and removed one of the many pre-paid cell phones it contained. He smiled as he dialed the number.

"Hello. Yes, it is time to pick up the children. It is raining here. Fifteen minutes? That will be fine. Thank you."

He opened the bottom desk drawer and withdrew a paper bag containing a fake black beard and black rimmed glasses. So obvious, an amused Moktar thought to himself, yet so effective. He waited for five minutes, then removed a black raincoat from the closet and shut the door to his office on his way out. He went to the far end of the corridor running the full length of the Center and turned down a stairwell leading to the ground level storage room behind the Hookah Coffee Shop. There he sat down in a chair thoughtfully provided by the coffee shop owner.

Some minutes later one of the many cabs streaming in and out of the Hookah Coffee Shop parking lot pulled up and parked. A man in a black raincoat and wearing a full black beard and black rimmed glasses got out, ordered a cup of coffee and asked to use the rest-room.

Moktar smiled when the man came into the storage room and greeted him. Without the beards, they didn't look very much alike, but they were about the same height and weight and on a dark night with the beard and glasses, Moktar doubted anyone would have noticed, even close up. He gave his double a hug, picked up the coffee on the way out and gave the cabbie, also one of his followers, the address of the safe house.

He laughed with the cabbie at having fooled the Americans yet again. Nevertheless, they would not take any chances on being followed. The cabbie made a number of unnecessary turns and once even doubled back before pulling up at the safe house, a two-story walkup located in a mixed neighborhood. Moktar knocked and was admitted almost immediately.

"So good to see you well, Habib," Moktar said warmly. "Are the others here? I have news."

"Yes, Moktar. We have been hoping you would come. Has the order been given?"

"Not yet. They are sending reinforcements. Six more, I was told. Yes, that will delay the attack, but it is still very much alive. We are all praying to Allah for your success."

"That is good, Moktar. I have told my brothers the attack must take priority, but it has been hard. They want revenge for the killing of Ashar and Fazz."

"I know, I know. I feel it too. But we must wait. We cannot afford to attract any more attention until after the attack. American agents are watching me constantly now and it won't be long, I fear, before they find this place. I think tonight we should talk about moving to another location, perhaps even split your men up into two or three groups. They will be less obvious that way."

"Allah's will is our command," Habib said solemnly.

8

LOST IN THE FUN HOUSE

(WITH APOLOGIES TO JOHN BARTH)

Another warm Indian summer afternoon was coming to a close at Clay's mill house, the lowering sun casting lengthening shadows across the millpond. Clay and Susan relaxed on the patio next to the pond, between them a small round table laden with several empty beer bottles and a basket of Virginia grown peanuts. Susan leaned forward at the table, digging her polished fingernails into the soft brown husk of a peanut, while Clay tipped his chair back against the mill's stone wall towering above them. The stone--solid, permanent--felt cool against his broad shoulders and the back of his head. Clay took a sip of his Belgian ale, a locally brewed craft beer, and for a moment watched a flotilla of fallen orange and gold leaves floating idly on the glass calm water. He loved this spot, especially like this in the late afternoons. It was so peaceful. The world at large could be going to hell, but here he could always count on being able to clear his head to think. The beer helped too.

"You know, Susan, that was some pretty scary stuff Bunker told us about. Makes me wonder all the more about why Weiss was killed.

"Know what else," he said after a long pause, "we're spinning our wheels with Mr. Hill. I can't see any connection between these stories he's telling and Weiss's murder, unless there are some closet Nazis dressed as renegade Muslims running around on the loose."

"Is that what's been going on?" Susan asked idly, distracted for the moment by digging the two peanuts out of the surrounding husk. She popped both in her mouth and followed with a sip of beer.

"I haven't a clue. I'm not even sure Mr. Hill ever knew there was a connection. But he sure likes you. Man's got good taste in women."

"Clay!"

"Don't worry, I'm not being jealous, honey. I'm thinking that maybe we give Jimmy another shot at jogging something loose. If he doesn't get anywhere, then you should take the point. You could be our ace in the hole."

"Maybe we have to let those memories of his unwind until he finally gets to the part we're looking for."

"We don't have much choice. Those guys at Halal Meat Market know they're being watched now, so unless they make a stupid mistake, we probably won't get anything more out of them."

"What do you think they're up to?"

"I don't know that either. It must be something big, an attack of some kind, for them to be so worried about what Weiss might have said to me. And it must be getting close to happening. I wish Weiss had been able to tell me more. Might have made the flack we've been getting worthwhile."

"Couldn't they just be reacting to having the existence of their spy ring exposed?"

"No, they're up to something. They'd have made a lot less noise if they'd just disappeared into the woodwork."

"Or if they'd scared you enough to keep quiet."

"Yeah, well, they got more than they bargained for there. I doubt it will stop them from whatever it is they've got planned, though."

"I still think Mr. Hill holds the key to this. Weiss must have told him something about what he knew."

"Well, yes, but I think that was before the Alzheimer's hit him. It seems to have scrambled everything."

"That's such a horrible disease. He's so lucid sometimes. Then he gets confused and seems to fall to pieces."

"That confusion is a big part of the problem with Alzheimer's, isn't it?"

"Yes, I think so." She stared off at the millpond thoughtfully. "Clay, what if that happens to us?"

"What? Alzheimer's? It's way too early for either one of us to be worrying about that." Clay took a sip of beer and knew exactly what to say next. "Besides, I'll never forget you, Susan."

Susan looked over at him and smiled, then a devilish look crossed her face. "You say that now. Maybe we should get married right away, before you forget."

Clay tipped his chair forward and rested his beer bottle on the table. "That's okay with me. But I'm thinking that until we figure out what's going on, we shouldn't do anything that will attract attention, especially to you. You know, keep a low profile for now."

"So a June wedding would be okay with you?"

"Of course, sweetheart." Clever girl, he thought, but apart from a twinge of regret at having his male independence corralled, he had to admit that he wanted it too. "Whatever day you think best. Just wait a bit before we go public."

That was exactly what she had wanted to hear. She started to get up to give him a big, wet kiss, but then she heard a car coming up the gravel drive. "Who's that, Clay?"

"I think it's Jimmy. It's his car anyway. Wonder what he's doing here. Did he say anything to you?"

"No, and I haven't heard anything from Trisch either." Then she planted the big wet kiss on a grinning Clay.

When Jimmy finally made his way to the patio, Susan was sitting on Clay's lap and both were grinning like Cheshire cats. Clay had his arm around Susan's waist while she had wrapped hers around his neck. Jimmy took it all in with the look of a man making the best of a bad situation. "Hi. Hope I'm not interrupting. I have good news and bad news," he announced, halfheartedly glossing over the fact he'd walked in on an unexplained moment of intimacy. "Which would you like to hear first?"

"The good news," Clay and Susan chimed in simultaneously.

"You're a million bucks richer, Clay. That's the first payment on the gold coins that have been sold so far. Each of us got a million deposited electronically in our accounts as of this morning. I thought you would want to know."

"Well, thank you very much. That *is* good news. I feel like a million bucks right now," he said with a laugh. "Guess I'm ready for the bad news?"

"I was wondering," an embarrassed Jimmy said weakly, "if I could stay here for the night. Trisch and I had a big fight. She threw me out."

"Jimmy, that's awful," Susan cried out sympathetically as she slipped from Clay's lap and sat at her own chair. "Of course you can. That's okay with you, Clay, isn't it?"

"Sure. I'd better get us some beers and then you can tell us all about it."

With a beer in hand, Jimmy proceeded to unburden himself. "Trisch's mother," Jimmy began angrily, "has always had it in for me. Before we got married, she told Trisch I'd never amount to anything, that our kids would starve to death on a teacher's salary. She's never been anything but a rude, complaining bitch to me. But oh, now that I have money, she's telling Trisch she needs a new car, Christ, she's even insisting I buy her a new house. Trisch can't say no to the woman."

"Maybe you should pay up, Jimmy," Clay offered apologetically. "Familial greed can be tough to deal with."

"If it was just her, maybe. But she's leading the charge! I haven't heard from my in-laws in years--Trisch's mother's got two brothers and a sister. Now the bitch is lobbying for them too. The ink isn't even dry on the damn check and these people are beating down my door to get at my money."

"Poor Trisch," Susan said. "It's her mother, Jimmy."

"I know," Jimmy vented. "But I blew a cork when Trisch told me. We had a knock down, drag out fight after that. Then she threw me out."

"You've got to get this patched up," Susan said sternly. "Think of your children. They must be really upset too."

"*They are.* They were home from school and heard the whole thing," Jimmy replied with an anguished look. Then an evil grin crossed his face, and he added, "Maybe I should buy her mother a total dump with a bunch of junk cars abandoned on the lot."

"A redneck paradise, hunh?" Clay said. "That might be satisfying, Jimmy, but it's not going to solve the problem. If you want to do something nasty like that, maybe you should offer to give her the cash to buy her dream house. Then you tell her she can keep it all, or share it whatever way she wants with her brothers and sister."

"Clay, that's evil," Susan complained.

"It's only a suggestion. Sure, it puts the shoe on her foot, but it might also get her off Jimmy's back."

"Don't listen to him, Jimmy" Susan said dismissively. "You stay the night. Tomorrow Rita and I will have a talk with Trisch."

The talking lasted all day, and Susan's real estate negotiating skills had a lot to do with putting things in perspective. In the end, Jimmy had to agree to a house and car for his mother-in-law, and twenty-thousand-dollar lump sum payments to her siblings--a small price for domestic peace, arrived at once Susan got Jimmy to stop thinking in terms of a high school teacher's salary and to start thinking like a millionaire. For her part, Trisch agreed she would say "No" to any further demands from her relatives, barring dire emergencies. Jimmy was relieved to be home again, and Clay was glad that peace and tranquility had returned to his little corner of the world. "Money," he grumbled to Susan, "isn't always the blessing it's cracked up to be."

The following day found Clay, Susan, Mac, and Jimmy back at the Sunnyvale Nursing Home. Jimmy led the effort to unlock the secret of Weiss's murder from Blakes Hill's all-too addled mind. Jimmy tried to start out where they'd left off the last time, but before he knew it, Blakes veered off his story again.

"You said something about spies and espionage before," Jimmy began.

"Yes, we were the center of a lot of attention back then. America didn't have much of a military, but we had the industry and the resources to produce the weapons and munitions everybody needed. So Washington was crawling with spies and fifth columnists. The Soviets get the prize for that. Their spies had wormed their way into important government posts in Washington, whether FDR knew it or not. Everybody thought Senator Dies and Joe McCarthy were nuts, and McCarthy overplayed his hand for sure, but secret documents declassified in the '90s proved that Alger Hiss was a Soviet spy and that he had plenty of company in the US Government." Blakes was obviously getting excited about remembering those times.

"How about German spies, like the ones you were following? They must have been pretty active here," Jimmy asked in an effort to get Blakes back on track.

"They tried, but they weren't as successful as the Soviets. Hoover did a good job of clamping down on them by the time war started. But even so, we knew there had to be more of them out there. There was a lot of sympathy here for the Nazis and their anti-Semitism in the late 1930s. That pro-Nazi group, German-American Bund, had a big following--"

"That's really interesting, Mr. Hill, but what about Mr. Weiss?" Clay broke in, trying to at least get Hill's thoughts going in the right direction.

"Don't interrupt me, sonny," Blakes said with obvious irritation. "Now I lost my train of thought. Where was I?"

Clay bit his tongue. Susan looked at him and then offered, "You were going to tell us about the raid on the circus at Staunton. To catch the German spy who stole Weiss's notebook."

"I was?" He looked momentarily confused, then fell silent for a moment. He looked toward the door, his attention apparently diverted by the sound of a janitor mopping the floor outside his room. He seemed to grow agitated. "It was another big mess, I remember that." Blakes gaze went from Susan to Clay to Jimmy and back to Susan again. "You're very pretty. What's your name?"

"Susan."

"Oh. I thought you were someone I knew," he said fingering the edge of his blanket nervously.

"Maybe that's enough for today," Susan said soothingly and looked at the others. "We could come back tomorrow and talk with you some more."

"Yes, that would be nice. I need to sleep now. I get so tired."

Clay and company left with Susan leading the way, but Blakes didn't sleep. The memory of that night would not let him.

Over seventy years had passed since the Trentino Brothers Circus raid, but it was his first big raid, and he remembered now how jazzed he had been. After all, his lead had brought about the raid. He had nearly paid for it with his life, but the raid was going to bust the case wide open. He could feel it in his bones, he was that sure....

The pre-raid briefing to the two dozen agents assembled inside the County courthouse in Staunton had been short and to the point. The raid would commence at 11 p.m., one hour after the circus had closed for the night. The circus people would be in their trailers, and Gypsy Hill Park would otherwise be deserted. Anyone resisting arrest or trying to escape would be presumed to be a spy, so lethal force was authorized if necessary.

About half the force, including Blakes, was to move in through the front entrance and fan out to round up the circus crew. Any runners would flee into the waiting arms of other agents positioned on both sides of the circus compound. Lake Tam, in the back, would block any escape in that direction. The plan seemed simple enough.

The FBI raiders filed out a back door to a narrow, dimly lighted alleyway where four black sedans waited. An earlier rainstorm had left the cobblestone pavement slick and puddled, and cooled the evening air. Fog was settling in as the two dozen agents clambered into the cars and slammed the car doors shut. Blakes and another rookie climbed up to their assigned spots on the running boards of the lead car, like firemen preparing to ride to an alarm. Blakes hooked his arm around the doorpost and looked down at his partner, Ed Johnson, sitting inside. Johnson took a drag on his Lucky Strike and grumbled sarcastically, "Blakes, try not to fall off, hear?" Even now, the sarcasm and the snickering from Johnson and the agent next to him made Blakes cringe.

Blakes tightened his grip as the lead car jerked forward and turned right onto Augusta Street, the centrifugal force tugging him outward, away from the car. This was fun. He looked back at the other three cars now spilling out of the alley, each with two agents riding the running boards. A real strike force, he thought and smiled, just like the old days during Prohibition that he'd read about as a kid. Swift justice on the move. He swelled with pride. This was why he'd gotten into law enforcement.

Cruising at thirty miles an hour, with the car's engine roaring, its gears whining happily, and the wind buffeting his face, Blakes let himself be caught up in the momentum of the moment. They were going to catch a bunch of Nazi spies, thanks to his work tracking them down. And for now, at least, he could forget about the mistakes he'd made getting to this point.

The raiders made no attempt at a stealthy approach. The cars roared into Staunton's Gypsy Hill Park from the Churchville Avenue side, climbed over the hill, and coasted down to the field where the circus had set up. One-by-one the cars bumped over a curb and onto the oval of the dirt race track that encircled the circus compound. Two cars, one with Blakes aboard, veered off to the right to cover the circus' front entrance, while the other two went left and followed the oval track to take up positions outside the circus. They quickly disappeared into the foggy darkness.

Before Blakes knew it, they had come to a stop before the wide, arched "Trentino Bros. Circus" sign at the entrance to the circus grounds. Blakes and his opposite on the other running board hopped off, looking for signs of trouble. But to Blakes's great disappointment, everything appeared to be dead quiet. Only one man, bare to the waist, noticed their arrival, and he quickly melted into the fog-shrouded shadows inside the circus grounds.

"Stick with me, Blakes. And stay out of trouble," Agent Johnson barked as he came up alongside. Blakes bit his tongue, knowing this was not the time for a smart comeback. Then it occurred to him that his partner might be jazzed too.

The strike force proceeded in pairs to sweep the compound, their chrome-tubed Eveready flashlights throwing shafts of light this way and that. They quickly probed shuttered concession stands, empty tents, equipment trailers, animal cages, and cargo vans at the front of the compound. Then, when the sweep finally reached the circus living quarters, the misty night gave way to pandemonium. Rousted from their trailers, the circus people howled protests and hurled curses at the agents while being herded to the big top for questioning. Johnson, meanwhile led Blakes to a large trailer at the edge of the compound. A sign alongside the door promised "The Buck Stops Here" and another above it said simply, in big letters and fanciful typeface, "Ringmaster."

"Must be the head honcho," Johnson said as he bounded up the three steps to a small landing and pounded on the door. "FBI," he called out. "Open up!"

Ringmaster Antonio Trentino, an imperious man with a portly body and a coiffed mane of jet black hair, answered the door with a large dinner napkin tucked into his shirt collar and a dollop of tomato sauce still clinging to his double chin. "What sir, is the meaning of this intrusion!" he demanded.

"FBI," Johnson retorted. "We have some questions we want to ask you. Please come with us to the big top."

"I will not! You have no right to--"

"Yes we do. Now, either come with us peaceably or we'll cuff you and carry you there. It's your choice Mr. Trentino." Blakes studied the look on Trentino's face as the ringmaster mulled it over. Without a doubt, it had been a long time since anybody had carried the plus-sized ringmaster anywhere. Equally certain was that he was no happier about the prospect than Blakes, who would have had to take part in that dubious enterprise.

Fortunately, Trentino caved. "Let me get my shoes on," he said sullenly. Blakes breathed a sigh of relief.

Being led down the midway toward the big top, Trentino was denying everything, even that Marla had ever worked for him. Blakes couldn't believe his ears. Trentino was putting on a real performance. All he needed was his megaphone.

Blakes was about to add to Johnson's "That's bunk!" when he saw the shadowy figure of a smallish man disappear into the raised entrance of a large tent on the midway. A swirl of fog followed the man into the pitch dark entryway. "What's that over there?" he called out and pointed at the tent.

"What's what?" Johnson responded.

"Somebody ducked in there. What's in that tent?" Blakes said, grabbing hold of Trentino's arm.

"That's the fun house. Nobody's in there. It's closed up for the night."

"I saw him," Blakes exclaimed. "We should go after the guy."

"Don't get your knickers all twisted," Johnson grumbled. "We'll come back for him, once we get Mr. Trentino here to the big top."

"No! He'll be gone by then. He's got the same build as that German who gave me the shot back in Roanoke. I'll bet it's the same guy!"

"Must be a million guys with a small build."

"I know, I know. But this one tried to duck out of sight when he saw us coming."

"All right. See if you can catch up with him in there, but you'll have to go it alone while I deliver Mr. Trentino. Just don't take any chances, Blakes. Wait for backup, if you need it."

Blakes turned to the ringmaster. "Is there any way to put the lights on?"

"The barker's box on the landing," the ringmaster reported glumly. "Under the counter." Moments later, Blakes fumbled with the switch and strings of lights outside the tent blazed blurry in the foggy night. Inside, there seemed to be nothing more than a vague glow of light, but he decided not to worry about that. He turned and rushed into the fun house, where black painted walls forced him into a dimly lighted, narrowing hallway that turned sharply first right, and then left, like a maze. This must be how Alice felt, Blakes thought, when she fell through the rabbit hole.

Inside, he stopped to get his bearings. There was just enough light that he didn't need any help from his flashlight. The muffled sounds of whirring motors--was it fans?--nearly obscured the sound of someone moving up ahead. That must be the German, he thought, and lurched forward. He wanted to run, but couldn't see far enough ahead to chance it. So he walked quickly, sliding one hand on the wall to guide himself.

He felt the carpeting under his feet give ever so slightly. Suddenly, a beach-ball-sized, upside down clown head swung down directly in front of him, almost nose to nose.

Blakes nearly jumped out of his skin as a manic laugh came over a speaker above him and the clown head bobbed up and down on its springy neck. He just had time to swallow his heart when the monstrosity retracted into the darkness above. Thankful that wasn't the German jumping out at him, Blakes took it as a warning and pulled out his .38 revolver.

"Not my idea of fun," he muttered grimly, as he started edging down the hallway again. But it was too late to turn back now.

He rounded a corner and found himself staring down another, very long corridor, with open doorways getting smaller and smaller in the distance. Is this tent really that big? he wondered. Far off, one last door, was closed. He managed two steps forward before bumping smack into a solid wall. Running his hand over the surface, he suddenly realized that the "long hallway" was nothing more than an image painted with a perspective to make it seem like a hallway, when in fact it was a wall. That hyena laughing blared out of a loudspeaker while Blakes rubbed his nose. Reaching to his right, he found an opening and ducked through it.

Turning yet another corner, he confronted two huge, glowing, multicolored spirals apparently spinning in opposite directions, with a moving concave wall of brightly colored splotches behind it. Trying to follow the motions, Blakes felt himself losing his balance, feeling like he had fallen off of a merry-go-round. As soon as he touched the wall to steady himself, the laughing started again. The wall being solid on the other side as well meant he had no choice but to back out of the dead end and turn the other way.

Blakes next found himself in a hall of fun house mirrors. Right before him was a wild and wavy image of himself, fat above the neck and below the knees, and weirdly skinny in between. The now constant laughing assaulted his ears--Blakes wanted to put a round into that damned speaker, but he couldn't see anything to shoot. Moving into the hall, he passed between mirrors that first made him appear tall and skinny, then ones that made him short and fat. Next, he came upon four images of himself, smiling stupidly. This hallway opened up into a room of full-length mirrors ringing him, and the infernal laughing only got louder. In the middle of the room, Blakes saw full-length images of himself repeated a dozen times.

Something, instinct maybe, made him turn around. His jaw dropped. There stood a dozen images of the small, dark-haired man pointing a German Luger at him. Blakes ducked and rolled, firing six shots and shattering six mirrors without hitting the German. The image, and the mysterious man, had vanished.

Scrambling to his feet, he ran through the broken glass and into a short hallway. This one dead-ended in a closet-sized room with rectangular black and white tiles covering the floor and a doorway on the opposite side. The tiles were laid in concentric circles and appeared to drop down into a black hole in the floor.

"Oh no, you're not going to fool me this time," he growled, stepping toward the doorway opposite him. The hyena laughing started again after one step and with his second step, Blakes fell feet first into the all-too-real hole, a soft canvas tube, a chute actually, that deposited him outside onto a cushioned mattress. The humiliation lasted only a second. As he sat up, he saw the German disappear into the shadows, the fog closing in around him.

"Stop. FBI!" Blakes yelled out. Jumping off the mattress, he broke into a run. He briefly gained enough on his quarry that he could see him, then lost him again in the foggy darkness. The German had heard his footfalls and started running too.

Blakes could hear his fellow agents calling out to one another in the fog somewhere behind him. "Who's that shouting?" one yelled. Blakes shouted back to him, "Over here. Suspect is on the run!"

"Maybe heading toward Thornrose!" Blakes yelled and then stopped to listen. He could hear the man's footfalls veering to the right, apparently onto Thornrose St. "Taking Thornrose," he yelled to what he assumed would be his backup. He broke into a run again, pouring on the coals and gaining enough to again see the German's shadowy form cutting through the fog. Blakes's gun was in his right hand, but he wanted the guy alive, so he held off taking a shot. That only left the problem of what to do if the German took a shot at him.

They topped a hill about three blocks from the park and were running alongside a low stone wall surrounding the Thornrose Cemetery. Blakes was breathing hard, but he was getting closer. Suddenly, the man looked back, and then vaulted the cemetery wall. That was not what Blakes wanted to see. All those gravestones will give him plenty of cover, he thought.

"Where the hell's my backup? They must have heard me," he muttered in frustration between gasps for air. But he couldn't wait for them to catch up, and now he worried the German might escape. Jumping the wall, he stopped and fired at the receding shadow, but the German never lost a step. Running again--mercifully, it was a steep downhill slope--Blakes wove between headstones and blockish vaults the size of small houses.

He lost sight of the German in a grove of big oaks, and beyond it, stopped to listen for the sound of him running. Nothing, not a sound. Blakes cursed while his chest heaved. They were on grass now, soft, silent damp grass, and up ahead the terrain sloped uphill again. The vaults, obelisks, and other Victorian monuments on the far slope blocked his view. The German could be hiding behind any one of them. Or was he long gone?

It was nothing more than a vague feeling of danger, but he thought that the German had picked a perfect spot for an ambush. Blakes was in the bottom of the bowl-like depression. The bottom extended about thirty level feet ahead, with nothing but widely spaced stones no more than a couple feet wide and three or four feet high. They'd do for cover if the shooting started, but not by much. Beyond that, on the uphill slope, he could see the eerie shadows of the big vaults and statuary. He listened again, and heard nothing, not even the sound of his fellow agents running up Thornrose Street. Where are those guys?

Thanks to the wet grass, his feet were damp and uncomfortably clammy, a discomfort that, along with the thought the German might already be long gone, convinced him to take a chance on moving forward. Ducking down, Blakes ran a winding serpentine route between the low gravestones. He tripped on one of those small rectangular grave markers that only protrude three or four inches above ground--almost fell flat on his face--but stumbled to a recovery and kept weaving between the stones. He made it almost all the way across the bottom of the bowl before the first shots rang out.

Blakes reacted instantly, diving for cover behind one of the upright gravestones. The German had turned the tables, and a single shot slammed into the gravestone Blakes hid behind. Another shot ricocheted off the top of the gravestone when he peeked around one side to get a fix on where the gunfire was coming from. Just before he pulled back behind the stone, he saw the muzzle flash coming from alongside a tall white obelisk halfway up the hill, one of a forest of big monuments there.

He's got plenty of cover, Blakes thought, as he hugged the three-foot-high stone protecting him, wracking his brains for some way out of this jam. He could try moving sideways. The rows of stones were about three feet apart. That would be risky, but better than retreating backward to the next row, about ten feet of nothing but grass in that direction. The German was far enough up the slope that he'd have a clean shot either way.

"Damn, where is the cavalry? I can't wait forever. I need help, *now,*" Blakes muttered to himself. A couple more guns and we could outflank the German, he thought. At least pin him down. But now he's got the high ground. He can plink away at me, maybe get a lucky shot in, or just disappear into the night.

None of the options were appealing. He poked his head out the other side of the stone. A shot rang out and sent up a spray of dirt as it rammed into the grass beside the headstone protecting him. He exhaled in frustration. Still there, he thought. Angry now, he yelled out. "Hey Johnson, where the hell are you?"

Another shot ricocheted off the gravestone. That was a mistake, he thought. Then it hit him. The German may have me in his sights, but he can't see any more in this fog than I can. He smiled. Yes, it was a ridiculous idea, but Uncle Warren might just come in handy here.

Old Uncle Warren had entertained the young Blakes and his brothers for hours by throwing his voice. Sure, he had puppets, but he could make anything seem like it was talking--a chair, a tree, whatever. You could never see his lips move, and he could make his voice sound like different people too.

Blakes knew his lips moving didn't matter at all now. The German couldn't see him behind the gravestone anyway. The important thing was that he hear the conversation Blakes was about to make up. The trick would be to make his voice sound different, and far enough away from where he actually was.

It will work, it has to work, he told himself, and silently thanked his uncle for having taught him the trick to ventriloquism. Blakes tightened his abdominals, curled his tongue back in his mouth, and began talking loudly.

"Hey, Blakes, where are you?" seemed to come in a deep voice from off to his left.

"I'm over here," Blakes said in his normal voice. "The German is over by the obelisk up the hillside."

"I see it," responded the deep voice. "George is coming up on your right."

"George can you see where I am?" Blakes said in his voice.

"Ya'll think I'm blind?" Blakes stumbled a bit with *blind,* "b's" being one of the harder sounds to throw.

"How about if you work your way around to his right. I'll cover you."

"Think ya'll can shoot straight enough to make him duck?" came the reply.

"Ha-ha! Just get moving, will you?" With that Blakes fired off three shots at the obelisk and ducked back behind the gravestone. The German didn't fire a shot, which made Blakes wonder if he was still there. He pulled a handkerchief from his coat pocket. Tying it to the end of his .38, he eased it out on one side of the gravestone where it could be seen. Still nothing.

Blakes was about to stand up and make a run for the next row of gravestones when Agent Johnson's voice broke the silence. "What, are you planning to surrender or something?"

Startled, Blakes turned around and saw his partner approach with two fellow agents. The cavalry was already laughing at the rookie.

"Where the hell were you guys when I needed you," a red-faced Blakes managed to sputter at last. "He had me pinned down."

"Pinned down? He ain't there now, that's for sure. And what was all that talkin' we heard on the way down here? You sure you didn't make all this up?"

"The hell--awh, forget it. How about we fan out and see if we can catch up with him?"

A half hour later Agent Johnson and a crestfallen Blakes were assigned to help search the German's trailer, a dilapidated wood-sided job with a curved roof and splashy circus scenes painted on the sides--dramatic high wire acts and trapeze daredevils painted to look like they were about to fly out at you. Blakes and Johnson climbed the stairs at the trailer's front end and found two other agents inside, already at work tearing the place apart. The two reminded Blakes of the comic strip characters Mutt and Jeff.

"We're looking for codebooks, microfilm, letters, anything tying him to the spy ring," the mustached taller of the two--Mutt's look-alike--reported while rummaging through an open bureau drawer.

"My bet is he was too smart to keep any of that stuff in here," the smaller round-headed "Jeff" added. Jeff was bald as a cucumber like the comic strip character, but he was clean shaven. No mutton chops. "We found some account books in his desk. Seems like he was the circus business agent or something. One of you should check them. How about if the other helps us tear this place apart. We've got to be sure he didn't have a hidey-hole in here."

Johnson went over to the desk and opened one of the ledgers, flipping idly through the pages. "This looks like your kind of work, Blakes. You're good at this stuff."

The scutwork again, Blakes thought, then sat down at the desk, resigned to his fate--page after page of town names with figures on the gross take broken down into categories by ticket sales. He pushed this accounting of regular circus performances aside and opened a second, smaller book, a ledger for special shows, mainly charity affairs--on behalf of orphanages, church groups, hospitals, you name it. He was no forensic accountant, but Trentino Brothers made a good profit on these shows, even after the charity got its cut. The ledger contained some fifty special performances, one to a page, and as Blakes leafed through it, he came across only seven that were not public events. In all of those, the circus had no gate, being paid instead with a hefty lump sum check.

"Find anything?" Johnson asked as he pulled a suitcase out from under the German's bunk bed.

"Maybe. I don't know," Blakes answered as he began writing down the names of the groups sponsoring the paid special performances. "They do a fair number of charity performances that seem legit. A few others aren't open to the public though, and the circus gets a check from a sponsor, instead of making money on the gate. Maybe this is how the Nazis funnel them the money needed to run the spy ring."

"You mean they don't even give the performances? Why would they keep a record of it then?" Johnson asked.

"They're Germans, that's why," Mutt called out from the wardrobe he was leaning into, apparently looking for secret compartments. "They keep records of everything."

"I'll bet they even pay taxes on that money," Jeff chimed in sarcastically.

"We probably should check these out," Blakes said, holding up his notebook. "One's not too far away. Barton Yates Children's Hospital. They supposedly sponsored the most recent special show, and they're just south of here, in Lynchburg. Looks like they have one every year."

The "we" quickly became Blakes alone ("It's your lead, Blakes, so you ought to follow it up.") The next morning found him in Lynchburg, an hour south of Staunton, shaking hands with the administrator of the children's hospital. Mr. Sidney Black was a fit-looking, middle-aged man wearing a charcoal gray pinstripe suit and burgundy tie. He seemed more than a little amused at being interviewed by the FBI, but so far as Blakes could tell, he was completely forthcoming.

"I can assure you, Agent Hill, that the Trentino Brothers Circus did indeed put on a special performance for the children. No question about it. They do it for us every year. Set up their big top right out there on the grounds," he said, pointing out a window to his left. Blakes's spirits sank as his theory went down in flames.

"You can't imagine what a wonderful event it is for the children," Mr. Black continued. "Some of them are so sick, to see them excited and laughing, even for just a few hours, is such a blessing. And our doctors think it helps them in their recovery too."

"Yes, I'm sure," Blakes said darkly. Reaching now, he asked, "The shows, they're strictly for the children. Not open to the public?"

"Oh no, that would not be possible. Many of the children are in wheelchairs, some on gurneys even. We only allow hospital staff and parents to accompany the children."

"Then you use hospital funds to pay for the performance?"

"Yes. Well, not directly. We've established a separate fund for performances like these. A lot of it comes from the parents of the children we've helped. They sometimes wish to make donations in their child's memory. That fund is one of the options we offer them."

"And you make the payment to--?"

"The circus business agent. Mr. Hans Mueller."

"Dark hair, dark eyes, medium build, about 5'7"?

Mr. Black thought for a moment. "Yes, I think that would describe Hans."

"Hans? Do you know him outside your dealings with the circus?" Blakes felt his pulse quicken perceptibly. This lead might still be alive.

"Well, no. I'd say it's more I know of him."

"How so?"

"Well, he is a doctor. He practiced in Germany before emigrating here. But he's made no effort to get his license to practice here. I don't know why. Something awful must have happened. He seems content to stay with the circus, to be a part of something that makes people smile and laugh."

"He told you that?"

"No, his brother did. I do know his brother, you see."

"His brother lives here in Lynchburg?"

"No, west of here in the mountains. His brother, Neil, works as the gamekeeper on an estate out there. The Cliffs. I know him because we treated his son. A very sad case. Cancer. An awful thing for a ten-year-old boy to die of, and it took him so slowly. Neil spent a lot of time here, just to be with him."

"Do you have an address for Mr. Mueller? Neil, I mean." Blakes could barely contain his excitement. Hans Mueller was on the run and it was a fair bet he'd head for the hills--specifically his brother's house.

"I think so. I'll have my secretary dig it up for you."

Blakes's heart was pounding while he waited.

9

THE CHARITY BALL

Clay handed the valet the keys to his Vette and watched Susan as she walked around from the passenger side to the walkway where he stood. She wore a svelte-looking black, sleeved ballroom gown with a wide V-shaped top, revealing the soft white skin of her shoulders and neck, before plunging tantalizingly southward, without actually revealing anything beyond what could be called moderately suggestive. She smiled with satisfaction at the look in Clay's eyes as she approached and took his arm. For her part, Susan thought Clay cut an impressive figure dressed to the nines in a formal tux, with the massive Foxhaven mansion looming four stories high behind him as a backdrop. Mac in his tux, and Rita in a soft peach sleeveless silk gown, caught up with them seconds later.

"Where's Jimmy?" Mac asked.

"I thought he was with you," Clay responded, looking back toward the side lawn where the cars were being parked. Even he had been surprised at the lavish display of gleaming wealth on wheels over there--Bentleys, Rolls Royces (three Silver Clouds), Ferraris,

Mercedes sedans, and a smattering of Cadillacs and Lincolns. Clay couldn't help feeling his '67 Vette was a little outclassed.

"Here they come," Susan announced as Jimmy and Trisch approached, Trisch in a low cut white strapless gown and Jimmy in a tux with a red cummerbund. Trisch had described it disdainfully as "neon red."

"Clay," Jimmy breathed in a hushed voice as he came up alongside. "I had no idea. This place is huge! It's a castle for chrissake."

"Wait till you see inside," Clay said with a grin. Soon after, the ten-foot-high arched entryway swallowed them four abreast, with Jimmy and Trisch right behind. In the four-story-high circular atrium, it was all Trisch could do to stop Jimmy from outright gushing, her elbow jabs barely keeping under control Jimmy's amazement at the naked display of awesome wealth.

A river of tuxes and flowing ballroom gowns gathered before them at the arched hallway leading to the ballroom, and then cascaded through the portal to an eddy of hundreds of lavishly dressed partiers in the ballroom proper. The human current transported Clay and company into what was a world beyond their imagining.

"My God, Clay, did he steal this from the Versailles palace or something?" Jimmy gushed in a low voice and then winced at the poke from Trisch's elbow. The hall, exuding old world opulence, stretched out before them for perhaps a hundred feet by fifty feet wide, with walls painted in a muted green and trimmed with ornately carved beige moldings and gold fixtures. The hall's drapery and all the furniture were done in bold red fabrics, a gay counterpoint to the more formal elegance of the room. Wide, arched windows on the right side rose twelve feet high, only to be surmounted by another row of arched windows above them, culminating in a vaulted, ornately painted ceiling. Between the arches, along the length of that wall, hung tall rectangular mirrors in gold frames, and above them, at the level of the second tier of windows, were dark, oval portraits of, Clay presumed, more of Conrad's unsmiling forebears. The left side of the hall mirrored the two-tiered arched format, except the lower archways opened into furnished nooks decorated in that bold red fabric, and above them, in the second tier, the archways formed second story boxes, much like those seen at opera houses and concert halls. About midway along the left wall, a wide marble staircase curved down from the upper level to the dance floor. Two rows of massive chandeliers, ten in all, provided light and reflected in the parqueted floor, a checkerboard pattern of large squares of dark brown cherry alternating with yellowish oak. Round tables draped with red tablecloths lined either side of the hall for about half its length, the rest being left open for dancing. A twenty-piece band at the far end of the hall provided soft music, while waiters in white coattails artfully balanced trays of champagne glasses while circulating among the guests. Barely a minute passed before Clay and company had drinks in hand, a testament to the waiters' efficiency.

"Do you see those three over there?" Jimmy asked casually, making a discreet effort to avoid Trisch's elbow. "That's our Senator Jenkins talking to, I think, the publisher of the Washington Record. What are they doing all the way down here?"

"Same thing we are," Mac answered, "enjoying the not-so-free champagne in the biggest damn room I've ever seen that wasn't a sports arena."

"I see at least three people I've catered parties for," Rita announced. "That one in the middle is Dan Atwell, CEO of Connect Digital. He's talking to Laura Ashwood, the movie actress. Where's her hubby," Rita asked surveying the room. "He's so handsome."

"Where's the Pope?" Mac joked. "I don't see the Pope. You mean he forgot to invite the Pope?"

"Scheduling conflicts," Clay responded. "But that's Congressman Rollings over there getting an earful from Gen. Howe. Jeez, I haven't seen his mug for years."

"Hardass Howe?" Mac asked. "Where?"

"On your right, next to those two Arabs. Casually, Mac. Don't make it too obvious, otherwise he might remember us."

"He can't do anything to us now, can he?"

"What are you two going on about?" Susan interrupted.

"Nothing, honey. I'll tell you later, when old Hardass isn't around. One thing's for sure, though, Mac, our client is definitely well connected."

"Speaking of which," Mac said leaning closer to Clay, "here he comes now."

Conrad, smiling, proud and aristocratically erect with Princess Maria on his arm, breezed past several of his guests on his way to where Clay and company were standing. Clay and Maria exchanged glances as she and Conrad approached, a fact not lost upon Conrad. Or Susan.

"Clay," Conrad said with perfect aplomb, "so glad you and your friends could come. I'm sure you remember my cousin, Princess Maria Theresa von Marburg," he said with a twinge of irony. "My dear, you remember Clay Cantrell."

Clay most certainly did remember her, but not as the vision of blossoming feminine beauty who stood before him now, her blond hair pulled expertly into a French twist and wearing a royal blue strapless gown that hugged her fine figure to her waist and then flared out into a flowing satin skirt. But it was the exquisite diamond necklace that left him momentarily speechless. Clay nodded to her and then turned to Susan. "Conrad, Maria, this is my fiancee, Susan Stratton." Susan reached out to shake Conrad's hand only to be surprised by his courtly bow and a kiss on the hand. She barely suppressed a giggle and then recovered, managing a nonchalant, "Pleased to meet you Mr. Nebel. Princess Maria."

While Clay continued the introductions, and Conrad bowed and kissed the hands of Rita and Trisch as well, Susan greeted Maria.

"A princess, really?" Susan asked politely.

"Oh, it is nothing. A family heritage. We are a democracy in Germany now. Conrad makes so much of it, but what good is it? Only at parties like this one."

"So those would be the family jewels, so to speak," Susan said, nodding at Maria's necklace, a shimmering, golf-ball-sized diamond at its center, with smaller diamonds and rubies surrounding it.

Maria gave a surprised, girlish laugh. "This old thing? Yes--"

"You'll be happy to know, Clay," Conrad said, interrupting Maria, "that Krieger has talked with the owner of that hundred acre parcel adjoining Fairview, and he's willing to discuss terms. If we can agree on price, that certainly would make Fairview an attractive package, wouldn't you say?"

"Of course, Conrad. It would be money well spent."

"You certainly know how to put on a party," Rita said after an awkward pause in the conversation. "An impressive place, and a top notch guest list. I've catered for four of the people I see here," she paused looking around.

"Oh, you are a caterer?" he asked politely.

"Yes, but nothing as exotic as this!" she exclaimed with a laugh.

"It's all for charity, you know," he said modestly. "That's my work, I guess. To use what advantages I've been blessed with to help others--sick children, the homeless, wounded veterans--and to encourage others to help as well."

"He's built hospitals, schools, libraries, and I don't know what all else," Maria chimed in enthusiastically.

"Not all on my own, Maria dear. I'm fortunate to have a knack for meeting people and focusing their attention on the needy, and on projects with merit."

"Have you gotten involved with historic preservation?" Jimmy asked.

"Jimmy teaches history at Staunton High School," Clay added by way of explanation.

"Oh, I see," Conrad said. "Yes, I've helped with a few right here in Virginia. In fact, we are trying to raise money to preserve the Anna Marie Robinson Moses house near Staunton. You know her, the famous folk artist, Grandma Moses." He turned to look at Krieger, who had come up alongside him. "Yes, Krieger, what is it?"

"Sir, Senator Barton is waiting to see you in the library."

"Oh, thank you, Krieger. Clay, it was a pleasure meeting your friends. Enjoy the party. I have some arm twisting to do. The Senator is opposing a bill I would very much like to see passed in this session of Congress."

"Guess he's got some clout," Clay said once Conrad and Krieger were out of earshot.

"He's got quite a reputation," Jimmy said, "according to the magazine articles I've read. International business tycoon, philanthropist, jet setter. He's never been married, has he Maria?"

"No. Many have tried. Uncle Conrad is married to his good works, I think."

"Maybe he's waiting for you, dear," Rita said with a motherly smile to cover the hand grenade she'd tossed. Susan cracked a small smile. "He'd be quite a catch."

"I hardly think so," Maria answered defensively, becoming a bit agitated. "He's always been wonderfully kind to me, but I don't think of him in that way."

"Of course not," Clay offered by way of support. Meanwhile the band struck up a tune and the dance floor began to fill up.

"What a nice song," Maria said, sensing an opportunity for escape. "I haven't danced all night, and Uncle Conrad is off on another of his projects. Would you be good enough to ask me, Clay?" She smiled sweetly at him. For his part, Clay turned to Susan and shrugged his shoulders in a show of innocence.

"Oh, go ahead, Clay," she said with a twisted smile.

Out on the dance floor, Clay was awash in the contrary hot blooded currents coursing through his brain. Susan was beautiful, his bride to be, his friend and lover now. And right there across the room. He wanted to be faithful. He knew he should be. But Maria was a beautiful, tempting young woman, still part brash, flirty girl, but very much matured now. Her perfume was subtly sweet and it took the better part of his will power to hold her at a discreet few inches away. She had gotten to him, and he wasn't used to dealing with having to say no. It made him angry and confused. And hot.

She looked up at him. "Is that what you are really here for? To sell Uncle Conrad that estate?"

"Yes. What else do you think?"

"Oh, nothing," she said and smiled sweetly as the song ended.

Sometime later, Conrad returned to the ballroom, his business with Senator Barton concluded in his favor. He had sealed the deal with a handshake and a check for a twenty thousand dollar donation to the Senator's reelection campaign. Flushed with that success, Conrad stood almost unnoticed with Krieger at the fringe of the party, content for the moment to watch the sea of guests enjoying themselves. Across the ballroom, a slim, young-looking Chinese man with white hair noticed Conrad and Krieger, smiled, and raised his glass in a salute. Conrad and Krieger both returned the gesture.

"He could become a problem," Krieger said after casually turning his back to him. "Why did you invite him?"

"Krieger, Krieger" Conrad said under his smile. "I think he already is. How many times must I tell you, 'Keep your friends close, and your enemies closer."

"Yes, but why bring him here?"

"What better place? He's paid $5,000 to charity for a ticket, so we can watch him," he said with an amused laugh.

The guests on the dance floor drew his attention. "Ah, I see my lovely fourth cousin has corralled the handsome Clay Cantrell." Almost reflexively, with the eyes and instincts of a hawk, he surveyed the room and, finding Susan, calculated an advantage in her irritated expression. "You'll have to excuse me, Krieger. I've been neglecting my guests. A host's duty is never done."

Conrad sidled up to Susan, who was standing along the sidelines of the dance floor with Mac. Mac had likewise been deserted by Rita for a young rake.

"I see my lovely Maria...," Conrad began and then feigned hesitancy before continuing. "She is very beautiful, but so young and headstrong, you know. Do you trust him?" he asked with an out of character, greasy smile. Susan looked at him closely, inquisitively, then nodded. The band struck up a waltz and seizing the opening, he asked graciously, "Would you allow me to ask you to dance?"

Susan brightened and smiled as he led her onto the dance floor. Conrad was an excellent dancer and whether he knew it or not, he managed to lead her to where Clay could see them dancing. Susan took that opportunity to give Clay a haughty smile and a dagger or two when Maria was turned the other way.

When the song ended, Conrad and Maria joined Clay's group at a table. After a moment of awkward silence, Rita spoke up. "Conrad, did you say Maria was your cousin?"

"Yes, a fourth cousin," he said with a trace of stiffness. Then he thought better of it, deciding instead to use the opportunity to needle Maria a bit. "I've watched you grow up, haven't I, Maria? You were just this tall the first time I laid eyes on you, and now look at you. You are *almost* grown up."

"Uncle Conrad!" she complained and wrinkled her nose at him, like a little girl. A moment later the band struck up a new song. Conrad gave her an avuncular smile.

"Come now, Maria. Don't be angry with me. Let me make it up to you with a dance."

When they had gone, Trisch said, "They make quite a couple."

"I'll say," Susan added with a telling look at Clay.

"I think I'd better ask you to dance, honey."

"Good move," Rita said, getting a round of grins at the table as Clay and Susan got up to dance.

"Hey Jimmy, did you notice Krieger talking to those two Arab types," Mac asked moments later, hoping to change the subject. "He was going at it pretty hot and heavy from what I could see, and now the three of them have disappeared."

"Nice try, big fellah," Rita said sarcastically. "Are you going to ask me to dance, or should I go dance with that young buck again?"

"Rita, they're about to serve dinner!" He took in her scowl for a moment, then caved. "Oh, all right. Let's dance."

"That's historic!" Jimmy exclaimed. "Mac passed up food to dance with his wife. I can't believe it."

*　　　*　　　*　　　*

At the Fairview job site two days later, Clay and Mac sat eating lunch on the open tailgate of Mac's Ford pickup--Italian combo subs dripping with oil and vinegar, Clay's favorite. Mac, of course, needed two to fill the void. The bright, clear day--Indian summer still--and the yellows, reds, and browns of the foliage on the distant slopes only highlighted the stunning view of the mountains to the west. Better still, so far as Clay and Mac were concerned, was the sight of the mansion, now fully closed in with sheathing, the roof deck on, and windows and doors in place. There was still lots to do, but now it could rain or snow and it wouldn't really matter. The house was weathertight.

"Did you call your brother William?" Mac asked, having finished his second sub. William, a successful venture capitalist, had access to all sorts of background information on businesses and industries around the world, and more importantly, on the people who ran them.

"Yes, he called last night with a pretty complete rundown. Maria was right. Conrad's grandfather, Gerhard Nebel, was a German aristocrat who came here in 1889 and started an iron mining company. His first mine was somewhere on the estate and when that played out, he bought into iron mines up around the Great Lakes. Gerhard built up quite a fortune. He, and all the Nebels since, have held dual German and American citizenships.

"Gerhard's son Klaus is Conrad's father. Klaus continued running the business after Gerhard died in a fire in 1941, and eventually diversified into oil, building up a really profitable tanker fleet in the '60s. Klaus is in his eighties and Conrad runs the company now.

Conrad finished taking the company out of mining and into the oil shipping business. He's got a reputation as an astute businessman with serious ties to Saudi Arabia, Qatar, and Kuwait, as well as with bigwigs in Washington, London, and Berlin."

"Phew! I guess he can afford Fairview, Clay."

"The word on Conrad is that there have been rough patches on his watch, but he always seems to be a half step ahead of disaster. Conrad has founded various charitable groups and has a hand in many others, we know that, and he makes hefty political contributions at both the state and federal levels. Oh yeah, he's also a patron of the arts. In short, he's probably a good candidate for *Time's* Man of the Year."

"I guess the oil business connection explains why Krieger got into it with those two Arabs the other night. I wondered about that."

"I did too, Mac. Seemed sort of out of place, so I asked William to check out Krieger as well."

"And?"

"Not much. William turned up a news report from 1993. Krieger was implicated in an illegal arms shipment aboard a cargo ship seized in the Adriatic. The arms were intended for Bosnian Muslims fighting Serbian rebels."

"Did he do any jail time?"

"Nope. The Clinton administration had been secretly supplying arms to the Muslims and when the 1995 Dayton Agreement ended the conflict, the charges against Krieger disappeared."

"Lucky guy."

"I'll say. He apparently hooked up with Conrad in the late 1990s and has been clean ever since."

"You don't suppose he's doing a little arms dealing on the side, do you? You know, using those oil tankers to ferry the stuff around to Mideast hot spots without the Nebels knowing? Maybe building up a retirement fund for himself?"

"That's not something William would be able to find out. But, you know, I'll bet Bunker Hill could." A sly grin crossed Clay's face. "I suppose I could ask Maria. Ask her out on a date and see if she knows anything."

"Clay, that's just asking for more trouble. Susan was none too pleased with you after--"

"I know, I know," Clay said holding up his hands in surrender. His cell phone interrupted any further reassurances. The phone conversation was brief, but when Clay closed his flip phone, his face was ashen.

"Clay, what's the matter? Who was that?"

"The county district attorney. Apparently George's defense counsel has come up with a new witness, a guy who is challenging my alibi for the night Nick was murdered."

"I don't believe it. How could--"

"I know. It's got to be bullshit. But it looks like I'll find out Thursday at George's trial for murdering Nick. I'm still supposed to testify for the prosecution."

*　　　*　　　*　　　*

Maria's bedroom suite at Foxhaven overlooked a rear courtyard and gardens three floors below. She had, as she always did on her visits here, this large bedroom with canopied bed, a private bath, and a sitting room. Decorating the sitting room was a huge fireplace faced with blue ceramic tile and surrounded by a carved limestone mantelpiece decorated with images of winged cherubs, lilies, and acanthus leaves. Above the fireplace, a large oblong mirror with a thick gold leaf frame hung horizontally, spanning nearly the entire width of the mantel. As a young girl, Maria often thought of it as a portal to herself, but she had no time for such childish thoughts now. She had seen the two Qatari men arrive in their long white limousine moments ago and hurried up to her room so quickly she was nearly out of breath. She went directly to the left side of the mantel and pushed the figure of a cherub upward. There was a slight scraping sound of wood against wood as a narrow section of wall, outlined by picture molding, suddenly swung inward to reveal a secret passageway.

As a young girl, Maria had learned about the secret passageways running throughout the mansion like wormholes inside its thick walls. Frederika, a former maid at Foxhaven, had shown her the entryway and cautioned her to never use the passageways except as a means of emergency escape, the kind of extra measure of safety only the very wealthy could afford, or even want to have. Being inquisitive and a child of privilege, Maria naturally explored the passageways many times during her visits to Foxhaven. She knew not only how to reach the passageway overlooking the library but also kept a small flashlight in her antique writing desk for just that purpose. She had the light in hand as she stepped into the passageway. The secret door closed automatically behind her.

Maria always felt a little claustrophobic inside the dark and dusty passageway. Here and there small shafts of light pierced the darkness, the result of peepholes for spying on the living spaces outside the secret passageways. Maria kept her flashlight aimed low at the long stairway she was negotiating carefully, one step at a time. The rough inside walls of plaster and lath on either side were close here, and the narrow stairs squeaked unless you stayed to one side and tread lightly. The last step, where her stairway joined a larger passageway on the first floor, creaked so loudly now that she had to avoid it altogether, by turning sideways and throwing her leg out to meet the floor at the bottom.

Negotiating the steps slowly had taken all the patience she could muster. She knew she had to hurry if she was to find out what the Qataries were up to, so she charged into the main passageway with long strides, quickly passing by other side passages from various rooms of the mansion's first floor. She was getting close now and in her impatience she nearly bumped into an old chair covered with cobwebs, a seat probably used long ago by someone to spy on the first floor servants. Maria stopped to catch her breath and compose herself. She didn't have far to go now and not making any sound that could be heard in the library was paramount. Getting caught could prove fatal.

She was about to turn into a side passage leading to the library when she heard a scraping sound, that of another secret door opening, coming from a side passage on her right. She froze. Her heart started to pound and her mind raced. What should she do? Somebody was coming. Had she been found out? How could they have known?

She had to do something quickly, but she was trapped. The sound of approaching footsteps came from that right-hand passageway. Maria flicked off her flashlight and began backpedaling into the passageway she had come from. She could only hope that whoever belonged to those footsteps was not looking for her, and had taken a shortcut to the library instead. Her hand brushed the old chair, which hadn't moved in years. She knelt down on the far side of it and made herself as small as she could.

Maria held her breath as the footfalls came closer and closer. A flashlight beam bounced on the walls at the junction of passages up ahead. Someone was obviously in a hurry. Maria crossed her fingers and watched anxiously.

Krieger's shadowy figure appeared at the junction and stopped, shining his flashlight first straight ahead and then to his right. Maria trembled. Krieger, she knew, was a most dangerous man. Was he looking for her, or just unsure which way to turn? Maria felt she would explode if she held her breath any longer, but she didn't dare breathe now. If Krieger turned his flashlight down her passageway, she'd be caught and probably as good as dead. She willed him the directions. Straight ahead was the ladder to the upper peephole over the library. To the right was the passage to a closet off the library, the way Krieger probably needed to go. Turn right, she thought desperately, turn right, now!

Krieger turned right and disappeared down that passage. Maria exhaled as quietly as she could, then gave in to short panting breaths while her body recovered from oxygen privation and a dose of cold, stark fear. On her feet again, she flicked on her flashlight and swiftly, silently turned left into the passageway leading to the library peephole. She came up to the tall ladder leading to a landing and a peephole twelve feet above. She shined her flashlight on the wood rungs. Several new pieces of one-by-three lumber had been nailed to the two-by-fours forming the vertical rails of the ladder.

Those weren't there before, Maria thought. Someone else has been using this peephole. That thought gave her a start and she cast a worried look up at the landing. But no one appeared to be up there now, so she went up. From there she could see the two snarling foxes mounted on the opposite library wall and had a clear view of Krieger and the two Qatari oil sheiks sitting across from him. She turned her head to put her ear closer to the peephole. Krieger was doing his best to calm the obviously anxious Qataris.

"You must know what this...this low energy nuclear reaction, will do to us if it is ever developed," said the obviously well-fed Qatari named Sa'id. His olive-skinned, round face appeared all the rounder for his jet black mustache and beard, trimmed around his mouth to form a near perfect "O." He continued almost breathlessly, "The world already has too much oil--who will want our oil when these L-E-N-R powered generators can create electricity without needing any? Or are made small enough to power a car or heat a house? You should worry too. Conrad's tankers will sit empty in port until their bottoms rust out. Then where will you be?"

"Sa'id, please. Remember back in the '80s, when it was called Cold Fusion? Remember all the fuss? Everyone thought cold fusion was going to save the world, and look what happened. It became a mockery, a scientific embarrassment of the first order. Even today, the media won't give any play to LENR because they got burned by the cold fusion mess. And meanwhile the demand for oil has only increased."

"Yes, but the scientists kept on experimenting, didn't they? Now they know it is real, have proved it. They've successfully explained why these "weak" nuclear reactions can actually produce energy without really consuming anything. Don't you see how that is going to change the world? What it will do to us in the Mideast? What have we got but oil and sand? If the market for oil dries up, we'll have to go back to riding camels from one water hole to the next."

"Relax, Sa'id. Take a deep breath. Yes, they've proved it can be done, but only in small scale laboratory experiments. It could be years before they find the right combination of heat and catalysts. Then they have to develop the technology to make the kinds of LENR generators you are talking about."

"But they are getting close? Your source said--"

"Yes, she says so. But they have been 'close' before. They blew up the lab only a few weeks ago. Remember, those scientists only have a theory. They don't yet fully understand what is happening. It's not a nuclear reaction as we understand it today, and yet it isn't a chemical reaction either."

"Enough talk! We cannot risk an unexpected discovery. Al'yasir wants you to take care of the problem now."

"Me?" he said with a surprised laugh. "You forget, Sa'id, that kind of action is your department. I am but a go-between here, never directly involved in anything. That is how we survive to be of service again another day."

"And make your blood money," the second Qatari said sarcastically.

"You have little room to talk when it comes to blood money. You have used that puddle of oil you sit on often enough to bleed this country dry. Not that I mind that very much."

"Very well. We will see if our Palestinian brothers will lend us some additional fighters. We will need more men. The destruction of the laboratory must be complete," Sa'id said.

"Bring a whole army, if you like. But it's your operation."

"That will not be necessary, but we will want to use the lake again. We'll be bringing them in by seaplane from one of our tankers."

Krieger gave an exasperated sigh. "Very well. The transit fee for your men will be the same per man as last time. You will arrange for transport from the lake. I assume they will be heading for the safe house in Fairfax?”

10

THE WITNESS

The Augusta County Circuit Court in downtown Staunton was a windowless mausoleum of justice lighted only by the harsh, ceiling-mounted fluorescent lights. Relieving that brash light were the pale oak paneling surrounding the room, a light gray paint on the walls above that, a smattering of stately portraits, and a bland-colored Berber carpet whose sound absorbing qualities helped give the proceedings a properly hushed tone. Small clusters of interested parties had scattered themselves about in the dozen or more rows of churchlike, high-backed oak benches that took up two-thirds of the courtroom. Susan, Mac, and Rita sat in the front.

A low, gated oak partition stretched across the room in front of them, separating them and the other spectators from that part of the courtroom where justice is meted out. Just beyond that partition were the tables for the defense and prosecution. The jury box, peopled with twelve jurors presumed to be good and true, hugged the wall on the right. The judge's bench, a dais made of the same light oak used elsewhere in the courtroom, dominated the center of this judicial stage, indeed the entire courtroom.

The black robed judge, a dark-complexioned black man with close-cropped salt-and-pepper colored hair, looked down impatiently at something the court clerk had just handed him. To the right of the judge, lower down, was the witness stand, filled at this moment by an uncomfortable looking Clay. It was Clay's second day on the stand, the first as a prosecution witness against George, and now re-called as a hostile witness for the defense. Rusty Womack, the tall, wispy looking defense attorney with a bushy crop of brown hair and thick, black-rimmed glasses, was doing everything he could to make Clay as uncomfortable as possible.

"Isn't it true, Mr. Cantrell, that you never liked George, Mr. Kilgore?" Womack intoned in a loud, accusatorial voice. Clay, obviously getting irritated by the browbeating, barely held his temper in check.

"You've got it bass ackwards, counselor," Clay said after taking a deep breath. His comment prompted a wave of snickering in the courtroom, a double rap of the judge's gavel, and a reprimand from him. Clay continued, "It was George who hated me. Until he tried to frame me for Nick's murder, I really didn't think about him at all."

Womack paced back and forth in front of the witness chair, pretending to think that over. "But you don't deny that you and your friends started stalking my client?"

"No, I don't." Clay wanted to say more, that they had uncovered good reason to be suspicious of George, and that Det. Armstrong had only wanted to pin the murder on Clay because he and Armstrong hated each other. But Clay bit his lip, heeding the prosecutor's warning about saying too much during questioning by George's lawyer.

"Or that you and your friend broke into that house up on Dogwood Road?"

"That's not true. The front door was unlocked and George's girlfriend was passed out on the couch."

Since he wasn't making much headway on that line, Womack appeared to decide to take a new tack. In fact, he'd planned it all along.

"Let's go back to the evening of the murder. You testified you went for a joyride up to Highland County, and were gone from about 6 p.m. to just after 9. Is that true?"

"Yes, that's correct. It was a nice evening for a drive, and I wanted to check out the lay of the land up there, where we thought the treasure would be. Mac and I knocked off work at five. I had dinner and then left for the drive."

"You testified you were driving your Corvette, is that correct?"

"Yes."

"And you didn't stop anywhere along the way? You don't have any witnesses to prove where you were until returning to Staunton at 9 p.m.?"

"Yes, to both questions."

Womack resumed pacing back and forth. "The police established Nick was murdered at about 7 p.m. You *say* you were well outside of Staunton by then. Correct? Where would that put you, at seven, I mean?"

"An hour after I left? That would put me about at McDowell. That's where I turned south."

"That's what you say."

"Objection!" Prosecutor Tony Berelli shouted. A suave looking, dark-haired, clean shaven man of Italian descent, he jumped to his feet. "Your honor, the witness has answered the question. Mr. Womack is badgering the witness."

"Sustained. I'll allow you leeway, Mr. Womack, but your job here is to elicit testimony, not give it."

"Yes your honor. That is exactly what I intend to do." Womack turned to Clay, "You're excused." Then to the judge, "Your honor, if it please the court, I'd like to call my next witness, Mr. Fayaq Khan."

Prosecutor Berelli jumped to his feet once again. "Your honor, I object. Mr. Womack is grandstanding. So far as I can see, he's been hiding this witness so that we couldn't question him or verify his testimony. There can't be any other reason for waiting until late yesterday to let us know he planned to put this mystery man on the stand today."

"That's not true," Womack protested. "He only came to our attention the day before yesterday. We had to find out if he had anything relevant first. We delivered notice to the prosecutor's office as soon as we could."

"All right, Mr. Womack, I'll allow it. But this had better not be a stunt."

"Yes, your honor. I call Mr. Fayaq Khan to the stand."

Khan was an olive-skinned, intense-looking young man in his early twenties. Dressed casually in a green long sleeve dress shirt and tan slacks, he had the look of a student. After taking his oath he sat down in the witness chair, adjusted his silver wire rimmed glasses, and looked directly at Womack.

"Mr. Khan," Womack began in his friendliest tone, "Please tell the court, are you an American citizen?"

"No sir, I am Pakistani. I have two uncles here in America and I'm here on a student visa. I am studying to learn electronics. I live with my uncle here in Staunton."

"You are here legally then?"

"Oh, yes sir. I am very legal."

"Would you tell the court what you saw on the evening of July 22 at approximately 7:30 p.m.?"

"Yes sir. I saw that man, Clay Cantrell," he said without hesitation and pointed directly at Clay. Clay turned to Berelli and whispered in an angry voice, "The bastard's lying."

"And what was he driving?"

"He was driving his pickup truck on Frederick Street. I know because it had C&H Construction on the door and he almost hit me as I was crossing the street. Also, I recognized him. I've seen him around town before."

Womack turned to the judge. "Your honor," he belted out, "since the prosecution has yet to find a witness who puts my client at the scene, and we now have a witness who saw Mr. Cantrell in town a mere half hour after the murder, I move for dismissal of the murder one charge against my client. I also stipulate that charges be brought against Mr. Cantrell for the murder of Nick Davis. Remember, the bloody knife was found in his truck!"

There was a collective gasp from the audience at sheer audacity of Womack's motions. Berelli, went livid with anger and yelled over Womack, "You honor this is ridiculous. Defense has no foundation for this!"

The judge meanwhile banged away with his gavel demanding order in the court. "Mr. Berelli, shut your mouth now! Not another word until I call on you. Same goes for you, Mr. Womack." The judge gnashed his teeth while sorting through the mess just dumped in his lap. "All right. Mr. Womack, I don't know whether you planned this stunt or not, but you'd better be able to convince me that you didn't know about this witness until two days ago. I'll give you a few days to come up with something convincing, then I'll rule on your motion. Mr. Berelli, since it's Thursday, I'm adjourning this case until next Wednesday at 9 a.m. That should give you time to plan your cross examination of Mr. Khan here. Court *is* adjourned."

The judge stood, turned, and left the court with a flurry of his black robe. Briefcases slapped shut, and before being led out to the holding cell by the bailiff, defendant George Kilgore turned toward Clay to mouth "Hah, hah!" at him. Clay only managed a half step toward George before Berelli grabbed him by the arm and growled, "Don't even think it, Clay! I want to talk to you in my office right now."

Following Berelli past the gated partition, Clay paused to speak to a distressed looking Susan. "Don't worry, honey, we'll get this mess straightened out. Berelli wants me in his office but it shouldn't take long. Wait for me out in the hallway, okay?" He looked over at Mac. "I think we may have some work to do." Mac smiled.

Minutes later Clay took a seat across from Berelli, who stood behind his mahogany desk, leaning forward with both palms down flat on the desk. "I'm serious, Clay. You do nothing. You don't get anywhere near Mr. Khan. If you do, I'll have you locked up, understand?"

Clay didn't like it at all, but he nodded in agreement.

"Kilgore is guilty as hell, I know that, Clay. This new witness has got to be bogus, but it means now we've got to go back over everything. Take some time this weekend and think about that drive you took. See if you can remember anything more. Maybe somebody you know saw you leaving town. Your Corvette is pretty distinctive. I'll have Det. Armstrong run out to McDowell to see if anybody remembers seeing a dark blue Corvette. It's a long shot, I know, but we're going to have to attack Khan's story one way or another, and every bit of evidence helps."

"Armstrong? He won't do squat. That guy's had it in for me from day one. I'm as good as cooked, if you're going to rely on him to investigate," Clay snarled. "And I hope we're not forgetting that bastard George broke into my house and tried to kill me."

"Clay, it's Armstrong's case. He's the investigating officer. And no, I'm not forgetting about George attacking you. But my big concern here is making sure the murder one charge sticks. Attempted murder is a lot less serious. Maybe not to you, but to the court it is. And I don't want to see you charged with Nick's murder."

"They wouldn't--"

"That's what Womack is asking to the court to do, Clay. We've got to make damn sure he doesn't get away with that. We've got to prove in court that you weren't lying, or that the new witness is. If we can't, Womack has a shot putting that murder on you."

Leaving Berelli's office, Clay wrestled with the incredible possibility that he could again be charged with a murder he didn't commit. Anger and confusion roiled his stomach. How could something so obviously false be made true? George had been caught in Clay's house trying to kill him, and police had found both the gasoline can and the makings for a crude time-delay fuse in George's car that night. George obviously planned to torch Clay's mill house after murdering him--with the same type of fuse he'd used to set Fairview on fire after killing Nick. And yet, now that someone *claimed* to see Clay driving his truck in Staunton that same night, suddenly Clay was at risk of once again being charged with Nick's murder. And George could walk away scot-free.

What worried Clay was Berelli's comment that Clay's story would have to be proved in court. How do you prove something that is already true? Clay knew, as Susan and Mac knew, that he had no reason to murder Nick. Yet Det. Armstrong had been able to conjure up the story that Nick had caught Clay in the act of torching Fairview for the insurance money, supposedly leaving Clay no choice but to kill him. In court, without a witness, it seemed to Clay his word was worth nothing. Suddenly, he's presumed to be lying, based on someone else's lie, and a motive for murder can be pinned on him based on nothing more than sheer speculation and circumstantial evidence.

That damned bloody knife, Clay thought. If only he'd locked his truck, George wouldn't have been able to plant it there. Well, too late now for that, he told himself. But I'll be damned if I'm going to let George get away with framing me.

Later that day, Clay, Mac, and Jimmy took a table at the Ratskeller to talk over what to do next. Angela--one of the twins tending bar there and a long-time friend of Clay's--brought them three frosty mugs of beer. Finally back in familiar surroundings, Clay, for the first time in several hours, started to relax. His anger and confusion over the day's events did not disappear entirely though. The thought that George might get away with murdering Nick and that he, Clay, might be charged instead was just too massive.

"Thanks, Angela," Clay said.

"This round is on the house, Clay. I heard what happened today at the trial. Nobody believes that guy is for real."

Clay smiled. "Now how do I get you seated on the jury?" Angela laughed and headed back to the bar. Jimmy, meanwhile, drank a slug of beer and turned to Clay.

"What did the prosecutor say after the bomb dropped?"

"That they're going to leave no stone unturned. And Armstrong's going to be the lead investigator. Hah, some chance I'll have."

"This whole thing seems so bogus," Jimmy said. "Especially with everything else that's happened since that pileup on Afton Mountain. You don't suppose they're connected, do you?"

"Well, the guy is Pakistani," Mac offered. "What do you want to bet he's a Muslim?"

"It's definitely a change in their style of attack," Clay added. "I'd sure like to know if, all of a sudden, he's come into a large sum of money." Mac and Jimmy laughed at that.

"You can bet Armstrong won't be digging that deep," Mac said. "Maybe we should check out the guy ourselves."

"I can't. Prosecutor says he'll throw me in jail, if I even go near Khan. But he didn't say anything about you, Mac. Jimmy, you've got school to deal with, but I'll bet I can get Lt. Youngblood to help Mac out with a little background research."

"Sounds like a plan," Mac answered.

Lt. Youngblood wasn't happy about it when Clay called and asked him to find out what he could about Fayaq Khan, but he came through. He found addresses for both of Khan's uncles, the technical school where he was taking classes, and the mosque he had belonged to. Youngblood hinted that there had been some trouble at the mosque, and that they ought to check that out first, since Det. Armstrong or his partner would probably question the uncles first. Mac might get first crack at a good lead.

Late next morning, Mac pulled up in front of the Alliance Mosque on Charlottesville's south side. The mosque was a spare looking one-story building, at one time probably a doctor's office, Mac guessed, with a faux stone exterior and double glass doors in front. Inside, Mac found a janitor and asked directions to the mosque's imam.

A momentary look of surprise crossed Imam Aadil Hasan's face when he turned from his computer screen and saw the hulking form of Mac filling the doorway to his office. He recovered, then with a pleasant smile asked, “Can I help you with something?”

“Sorry to disturb you, sir. Would you be imam to a young fellow named Fayaq Khan? I was wondering if you wouldn’t mind talking with me about him.”

Imam Hasan’s face hardened. Turning completely around to face Mac, he remained seated in his office chair. “Are you from the police? The FBI perhaps?” he asked with an effusive politeness.

“No sir. I’m just a private citizen. You see, Khan has testified in court that he saw a friend of mine at a time and place where we know my friend wasn’t. That testimony may get the real murderer off and my friend charged with killing the victim.” Mac paused. “Which I swear to you he did not do.”

Imam Hasan looked away for a long moment, thinking. Then, a decision made, he looked up at Mac. “I do not give out information about members of my mosque,” he said firmly. But a moment later the corner of his mouth moved up into the slightest of smiles. “But since Fayaq is no longer welcome at this mosque, I will talk with you about him.”

“Thank you, Imam--“ Mac gave him a confused look.

“Imam Aadil Hasan.”

“Thank you, I appreciate your willingness to talk about him. Can you tell me why he is no longer in your mosque?”

“Yes, he was asked to leave because of his radicalism. He has fallen in with fundamentalists who preach violence and strict adherence to Shariah Law. Are you familiar with Shariah Law, Mr.--”

“Harper, Mac Harper. Yes, I know a little about it. Strict rules of conduct written in the Seventh Century, I think.”

“Yes, that’s correct. Those texts are part of our sacred writings, but for moderate Muslims like me, and my followers here at the mosque, we look only to those parts of Shariah Law that can give us guidance in our personal conduct. We do not believe, as the radicals do, that Shariah Law should become the law of the land, that women should be stoned to death for adultery, that thieves should have their hands cut off, or that anyone who does not believe in Allah should be killed. In a sense, we look at much of the ancient Shariah Law as you do the more violent scriptures of your Old Testament. Words and thoughts appropriate to another time."

"That's a relief," Mac said with a wry grin.

"Yes, the radicals among us feed on political and social discontent. They use Shariah Law as a means of legitimizing murder, justification for desecrating churches and monuments, and advancing religious exclusivity--putting Islam above all else. We, I, cannot abide by that. I have built friendships with many Jewish and Christian leaders here in Charlottesville, and I will not tolerate anyone attempting to spread fundamentalist radicalism in this congregation."

"And that is what Fayaq was doing?"

"Yes, he approached several of my younger followers and tried to convince them to go with him to a mosque near Washington. He filled their heads with radical nonsense, cajoled, and even threatened some of them. Told them they were infidels for ignoring the will of Allah."

"Do you know where that mosque was?"

"Yes. Bailey's Crossroads."

A smile crossed Mac's face. "Would the imam's name be Moktar, by any chance?"

"Why yes, how did you know?"

"We had a run in with some of his followers too. Thank you Imam Hasan, for speaking so frankly with me."

"This is a critical time for all Islam, I think, Mr. Harper. Radical fundamentalists are vicious in their attacks on anyone who does not agree with them, Muslim or otherwise. We moderates are going to need all the friends we can get."

The smile on Mac's face lasted all the way out to the mosque parking lot. They now had a solid lead tying the witness to those Muslims in Bailey's Crossroads. Bunker probably could help them make the connection stand up in court, and that might be enough to begin to undermine Fayaq's testimony.

Driving through Charlottesville's side streets on his way back to I-64, Mac spotted Susan's new Volvo turning into traffic up ahead. Or was it? What would she be doing over here, Mac wondered. Speeding up to close with the Volvo--they were both heading east on the 250 Bypass now--Mac got close enough to read her license plate, SUZ 5520. It was Susan's car all right, and the woman driving had Susan's dark, shoulder-length hair. Thinking he would stop and tell her the good news about Fayaq when she got to her destination, Mac backed off and kept pace with the Volvo.

Soon after, they crossed Free Bridge and headed up the hill to Pantops. As they crested the hill, Susan's blinker suddenly signaled a left turn. "What the--?" Mac said out loud as Susan pulled into a motel parking lot. Mac, initially stalled by oncoming traffic, finally made the left. He followed the parking lot as Susan had, heading toward the rooms in the back. That's when he saw Susan--he was sure it was her now--already out of her car and walking quickly to a first floor room. The door opened almost immediately and she disappeared inside.

"Awh, Jeez," Mac groaned and his gut twisted. He didn't want to believe what he had just seen. But he'd gotten a good look at the woman as she crossed the parking lot. It was Susan, no doubt about it. There must be some explanation, Mac thought, but what would she be doing way over here, in the middle of the day, going into a motel room? What else but--

Mac waited about fifteen minutes, but by then he'd seen more than he ever wanted to. He pulled out of the motel lot wondering what he should do. He definitely didn't want to be the one to break the news to Clay that the love of his life, his fiancee yet, was doing a nooner with some guy. Especially considering everything else Clay was going through now. He told himself it wasn't any of his business, but that didn't wash either. He and Clay had been friends far too long for Mac to sit back and let him be made a fool.

As usual when he couldn't figure out what to do, Mac decided to call Rita. He dug his cell phone out of his pocket and speed dialed her.

"Hi. No, I'm just now heading out of Charlottesville. Rita, honey, you're not going to believe what I just saw. Susan is in Charlottesville. I saw her going into a motel room...I know it's none of my business. Except Clay is a friend and she shouldn't be cheating on him...Yes I'm sure it was her...Well, if you want to call Clay and ask him where he thinks Susan is, fine, go ahead. But I'm telling you, I saw Susan...Call me back, okay? And don't tell him!"

Mac answered his cell phone on the second ring. "Hi...He said she's out with a client showing houses? See, what did I tell you? That was Susan I saw...No I don't want to get in the middle of it..." Mac exhaled. Exasperated, he said, "Maybe you're right Rita...Okay. I won't say anything. But it doesn't seem right."

Mac begged off Clay's invitation to join Susan and him for beers at the Ratskeller that evening. He was sure Clay would know something was bugging him, and if Clay asked, Mac worried he might tell him.

By the next day, Mac had come to terms with not saying anything, so he went with Clay and Susan to see Blakes. Susan led the way into the room, and the old man immediately perked up at the sight of her, even managed a momentary smile.

"Hello, Mr. Hill," Susan said with a big, patronizing smile in return, as though she were talking to a child. "Do you remember me? I'm Susan."

"Yes. Yes, I remember you. I wondered what happened to you. I thought maybe you weren't coming any more."

"Oh, we thought you might need a rest. You seemed sort of tired when you were about to tell us what happened at the circus."

"Nothing to tell there. Our man got away. The big raid was almost a complete waste."

"Almost? What do you mean by that?"

"Heh, yeah. I found a lead. Made me look good. I really needed that after making a couple of rookie mistakes." Blakes proceeded to tell her the story of finding out that the spy, Hans Mueller, had a brother who was the gamekeeper on a Bath County estate. "I figured a guy on the run would probably hole up with his brother, especially one who lived out in the boonies. It just fell into my lap. I get lucky that way sometimes. Kind of like a pretty lady, like you, showing up in my room."

Susan stifled a laugh and shot a glance at Clay, who *was* laughing. "Thank you Mr. Hill. You're very kind. But can you tell me what happened next? Did you catch the spy, Mr. Mueller?"

"No, honey, we found him, but you couldn't say we caught him."

"My partner and I drove up there to Hacketsville, in Bath County."

The breezy spring day came back to Blakes so clearly he could almost smell the crisp, clean air. The trees had sprouted young, vivid green leaves and puffy white clouds sailed languidly across the bright blue sky....

Johnson had gotten a search warrant for the house and premises of one Neil Mueller, brother of that fugitive spy. A winding country road, more up than any other direction, took them well beyond the hamlet of Hacketsville and up into the mountains, with their Plymouth in second gear much of the way. They finally turned off the country road and followed Mueller's rutted driveway to the house, a rustic stone cottage with a large barn behind it.

Johnson took the search warrant out of his pocket as the two walked onto the porch. The place seemed deserted, so Blakes peeked in a window. He looked over at Johnson and shook his head no. Johnson moved to one side of the front door, while Blakes stepped directly in front. Johnson glared at him, then shoved him over to the opposite side. Then he knocked hard.

"FBI!" he shouted. "Open up. We have a search--"

Suddenly all hell broke loose. A shotgun blast drowned out Johnson's voice and exploded through the wood door, spewing chunks of splintered wood past them. The first blast was still ringing in Blakes's ears when he heard the click of the pump action and a second shot shredded what remained of the door. Johnson fired three rapid shots from his .38. Blakes heard someone running toward the back of the house.

Johnson signaled him to cover the back. Blakes was jazzed now, his heart pounding as he sprinted around back. He got there in time to see a man on a motorcycle erupt from the barn, spin through a 270-degree turn on the dirt, and take off down a dirt road leading into the woods behind the house. Then he heard another shotgun blast inside the house.

Blakes ran up the steps to a small rear porch and tore at the door, but it was locked. Somehow his .38 had found its way into his right hand. He took a step back and angrily blasted the door with three shots before it submitted and fell open. With his gun upraised, Blakes crossed the mud room and stopped alongside the doorway to the kitchen. He took a deep breath. He had no idea where Johnson was, or the shooter for that matter. He chanced a quick look into the kitchen. Nothing. He could hear someone moving slowly somewhere inside the house, but who was it?

"Johnson! I'm in," he yelled and then sprinted across the kitchen to the doorway opening onto the dining room. "Clear in the kitchen."

"I think he's upstairs, Blakes. Cover me."

Blakes darted through the dining room to the living room where Johnson, .38 raised high, was starting up the stairs. From where he now stood, Blakes could see the stairway and part of the second floor hallway, the straight run of stairs being open to the living room. Johnson was about halfway up when Blakes saw the shooter's legs appear near the head of the stairs, where Johnson couldn't see him. Blakes took two steps closer to get a better shot, aimed just as the shotgun barrel swung toward him, and fired two shots. The shooter doubled over and fell forward onto the stairs, firing one final blast that ripped out part of the railing. The shooter tumbled down the stairs right into Johnson's waiting arms, already stone dead.

"Special delivery," Blakes cracked.

"I would have liked to ask him a few questions," Johnson replied sourly.

"You're never happy with anything I do, are you, Johnson?"

"Yeah, well, now that you mention it, if I had to choose between him or me, I'd be glad it was him. Thanks, partner." Johnson was already fishing in the dead man's pockets as he said it. "Be nice to know who he is. Do you know what Hans looked like?"

"Basically, yes. That looks like him."

"That's what his driver's license says too."

"Then that must have been his brother Neil who took off like a bat out of hell on a motorcycle."

"And probably has the notebook now. Which way was he headed, Blakes?"

"I don't know. There's a dirt road out back that runs into the woods."

"If it's Neil, he's the estate's gamekeeper. So he's probably going to hole up in some cave only he knows about."

"Great, we'll never find him or the notebook then."

"Maybe, maybe not. He's got to make contact with the next link in the ring sooner or later. Maybe Neil's boss can tell us something that'll lead us to that link. Let's take a look around here first, and then go up to the main house. The estate manager should know something. Any idea how to get there?"

"Sure. Just continue on that road we came up."

An hour later, Johnson drove through an imposing gateway and continued on the estate driveway for about a mile before stopping at the first structure they saw, a two-story stone gatehouse. They stood to either side of the door while Johnson knocked, but this time the door simply swung open, revealing a short, barrel-shaped man with brown hair and a generous handlebar mustache. Endowed with the meaty shoulders, chest, and the thick arms of a real bruiser, Gerhard von Richter, the estate manager, had a heavy German accent and a decidedly unhelpful attitude.

"Vut can I tell you?" he said after closely examining their IDs. "He cout be anyvhere. Zhere ist over a tausand acres out zere. It vud take an army to find him daire."

"Does he have any other relatives? Any friends in the area?" Johnson asked.

"Nein. Maybe, but I don't know."

"Can we talk to the owner? Maybe Mueller will try to contact someone on the estate. We should talk with the staff. It's very important we find Mueller."

"Zie owner does not vant you traipsing around hiss property, zhank you very much. Das ist verboten! But I vill ask him aboot qvestioning die laute. Peeple. You go avay now. I give you zee number, you call to me tomorrow."

"We'll leave when we're good and ready, Mr. Richter," Johnson answered angrily. "You have a telephone in there, don't you? I need to call the State Police to report the shooting at Mueller's house."

"Ja, you can use my phone for dat."

Blakes and Johnson drove back to Mueller's house and met with the State Police while the crime scene was investigated and Hans' body was removed. Then they drove down off the mountain, heading about a half hour south to a blue collar factory town called Trustlow, which had grown up on both sides of a swift running river. They found rooms for the night and when they called the next morning, Richter told them in no uncertain terms, fractured though the words might be, that the owner did not want to talk with them.

"Vee are hafing ein eevent here and you are not velcome. Das ist alles. Gut bye."

Johnson fumed, and forgetting his affinity for things German, slammed down the phone. "He says bugger off. They're having an event. Let's drive back up there and shove our badges down their throats. I want to talk to the help about Mueller."

Passing through the first gate, they stopped at the gamekeeper's cottage, but it was still very much deserted. Mueller obviously had not risked returning during the night. Driving onto the estate, they were greeted by a barricade at the estate manager's house. A banner attached high up on poles and stretching over the roadway announced, "Welcome Brothers of the German-American Bund." Manning the barricade were two dozen stout looking German-American thugs, standing with arms folded across their chest and faces set in steely expressions of grim determination. One of them walked forward, leaned down to look in the open driver's side window, then laid a beefy hand on the door. He looked Johnson directly in the eyes and sneered.

"You are not allowed. Dis is private party. Turn around and go avay."

Johnson turned to look at Blakes. "You know, I think maybe you were right about Krauts being nothing but a bunch of butt-headed assholes." He jammed the Plymouth into reverse. After backing away a safe distance, he did a quick K-turn and disappeared down the road.

Blakes and Johnson spent the rest of the afternoon canvassing every house in and around Hacketsville, knocking on doors, flashing their badges, and asking the locals about Mueller and anyone else they might know who worked at the estate. Blakes was surprised by the chilly reception they received at virtually every house. It was eerie. Either everyone's been bought off, he told Johnson, or they've all been frightened into not saying anything. Given what he'd seen at the gatehouse, he was pretty sure they'd been scared silent.

But somebody always has a beef, and it's just a matter of pounding the pavement until you find them. They finally did late that afternoon. The house was a rundown cottage, badly in need of paint and repairs, but there was a little flower garden in front of the porch and the small yard appeared to be well kept. An old black woman, white haired and looking as though she was shriveling up inside her old, worn, pale blue dress, sat in a rocking chair on the front porch snapping the stems off green beans and dropping them into an old pot laid at her feet.

When Blakes and Johnson showed their badges and stated their business, she stiffened, complaining in a frail, bitter voice, "About damn time ya'll did sompin' about dem Nazi goons up dere."

"Yes mam," Blakes answered, taking the lead. Johnson shook his head and muttered, "Oh boy."

"I swear, dem people been gettin' away wif murder up der for tooo long. Dey runnin' everything round here like it's dey's own damn kingdom. Dey's lord and masters and we's nothin' but trash to kick around anytime dey's feels like it."

"Do you know anybody here in town that works up there, mame?"

"One time or other, ain't nobody who hasn't," she answered curtly. "'Cept me, I hadda good job. I was cook for Judge Barton Elroy. Didn't need nothing to do with dem damn Nazis. Judge, he was a good man. Worked for him 'til I got too weak to stand long nuff to cook hiss dinner.

"I tell you about dem Nazis. My Jed, he my husband." She rocked back and forth a moment lost in thought. "He dun passed near ten year ago now. He worked up dere. Was a stable hand, you know, taking care o' da horses. Well, one day he took Jed Junior--we's call him JJ--wif him to da stable. JJ dint know no better. He's playing wit dis really fine huntin' dog. Was runnin' loose in da stable whiles Jed is bringin' a horse out of his stall. Da stick JJ throwd landed right at duh horse's feets and duh dog, he jumps in dere to git it. Dat poor horse wus so skeered, he dun reared up and kicked dat poor dog right crosst da barn.

"Da masser heard dat dog's yelpin' and come a runnin', seen what's happen, and he starts ascreamin' at Jud cause it be his favor-it hound. Masser, he be likkered up like olways. Jed, he was apologizin' like crazy, but masser, he won't pay no 'tention, he so mad 'cause his dog's leg be broke real bad.

"Den he's grab little JJ's arm, JJ warn't but ten, an' he screams 'eye for an eye' an' gits some his big goons to hold Jed. Jed he be cryin' and pleadin' to let JJ alone. Do whatever they hafta to him, not da boy. But da massar, he say no. He make 'em hold JJ down and dey's hit hiss little leg with a bat agin and agin til it broke real good. Den day lets Jed take him home."

"I'm sorry, mame, that's terrible. Couldn't you get him arrested?"

"Da masser? You kiddin'? I told Judge Elroy all abouts hit, an' he say he terrible sorry, but cain't nuttin' be done. Masser gots too many friends in high places, ya' know, and no witness to prove it. Just be Jed's word agin da masser's.

"Here he come now," she said pointing a boney finger at a young black man coming up the driveway as a car drove off. In his early twenties, he dragged his left leg, and his left foot was turned inward at an odd angle, but otherwise he was a strapping young man. "JJ, dese men be FB-eye. Dey be investigatin' da masser's peeples."

"Did he tell you anything?" Susan asked. The question seemed to bring Blakes back from his reverie. He looked at Clay for a moment and then back to Susan. "He sure did. Turned out he knew lots of ways to sneak in and out of that estate, despite his bum leg, and he'd even seen some Nazis in uniform up there. He offered to show us, if we wanted, but we figured we'd better get a search warrant and go in the front door."

"It was dark by the time we left Hacketsville, heading back to Trustlow for the night. The road was really winding, I guess because it was alongside a river. It was too dark to see though. One thing for sure, a truck was following us. Johnson picked up on it. The truck laid back until we got way out in the middle of nowhere, then it came right up behind us. Johnson hit the gas, but the road was so windy, we couldn't put any distance between us and the truck. The first time the truck hit our rear end, it slammed me back into the seat. Johnson started yelling at me, 'Shoot the sonofabitch! Shoot the sonofabitch!' I tried leaning out my window, but I couldn't get a clean shot what with the curves in the road, so I shot out our rear window and kept firing."

Blakes took a breath. "I hit one of his headlights. I guess that made him pretty mad, 'cause he really wacked us the next time.

Johnson screamed 'I can't hold it' and all of a sudden we're rolling down an embankment. Crash. Bang. The noise was deafening. One second I'm falling onto the ceiling, the next I'm banging into Johnson, then I'm coming down headfirst on the seat--the whole world was spinning around and around. We were like flies in a bottle and somebody was shaking the hell out of it. Then there was this big splash and I was slammed down in my seat. Water, ice cold water, started pouring in through the windows and before we knew it the car was filling up. Really scary. But we were lucky. The river wasn't very deep there, and once our heads stopped spinning, we got out and made it to the riverbank. Johnson and I both were banged up some, but we managed to walk to a house that had a phone."

"You were lucky the car landed right side up. You could have drowned." Clay said. Remembering his own bout with a rampaging truck, he thanked his lucky stars his encounter hadn't ended the same way.

"That's right," Blakes answered grimly.

"That big estate. It was up in Bath County. But you never did say. Did it have a name?" Clay asked, his suspicions aroused.

Blakes studied Clay for a moment, before glancing at the doorway of his room. Then his mouth betrayed the faintest of smiles. "Yes. It was called "The Cliffs."

"Oh," Clay said, obviously disappointed. He had been sure the name was going to be Foxhaven.

A nurse appeared at the door to Blakes's room. "Sorry folks. You'll have to leave for a while. It's time for Mr. Hill's bath. You can wait in the lounge area, if you like, until we're done here."

"That's all right," Clay answered. "It's late and we should be going. We'll come back another day." In fact, Clay wanted to get Jimmy started on finding out what he could about that estate Blakes mentioned, The Cliffs. It was becoming such a focus of the old man's story that Clay was convinced there had to be a lead there.

It was still light when Bunker's helicopter landed at Clay's mill house, the chopper's rotor wash sending a blizzard of fallen leaves flying in every direction. By the time Bunker finished shutting down the chopper's turbine engine and the rotor was coming to a stop, Clay and Mac had walked up from the mill house to greet him. Still in his flight suit, Bunker jumped down from the cockpit and gave both a knuckle bump by way of a hello.

"I'm parched," Bunker said with a grin. "You wouldn't happen to have a beer handy, would you?"

"You'll have to come inside for that," Clay answered with a laugh. "Then maybe you'll tell us what's so all-fired important that you had to fly down here to tell us."

Minutes later all three had beers in hand. Both Clay and Mac were seated at the kitchen table, while Bunker stood, leaning back against the kitchen counter.

"Hard day at the office, guys. I needed to get out of Dodge for a breather. Some people jog. Some meditate hanging upside down. I fly my bird to relieve the tension. But anyway, I did some digging, and I do have some news about Weiss's murder.

"First," Bunker continued, "you should know that Weiss lived up in DC in the same Bailey's Crossroads neighborhood as that Halal Meat Market you fellows stirred up."

"Well, I'll be," Clay breathed. "Small world."

"Yeah. He'd lived there since he retired in the early '70s. His neighborhood didn't used to be so heavily Muslim, but they kind of filled in around him. Apparently he got along okay with them. Everybody we talked to spoke well of him. His next-door neighbor, Khalid Qasam, was a Muslim, and a close friend."

"Was?"

"Yup. Murdered a couple of weeks before Weiss. Got his throat slit and bled out in an alleyway near a restaurant where he worked nights. Police put it down to a random killing, maybe a small time drug deal gone bad, but Weiss didn't buy it. He knew Khalid and he was angry and upset, from what neighbors said. He tried pushing the police to investigate further and when they put him off, he started going around asking questions himself."

"Maybe that's what got him killed," Mac speculated. "Maybe that guy Khalid was in with the wrong people. They heard about Weiss asking questions and decided to put a stop to it."

"That could be what happened," Bunker conceded, "but so far we haven't been able to dig up any connection between Khalid and anybody remotely radical--or even suspicious. He was a devout Muslim, had no leanings toward fundamentalism, and no interest in drugs. He was just a hardworking citizen who worked days in a lab and nights at the restaurant, and not much else. What gets a man like that killed? Maybe he really was in the wrong place at the wrong time, but I'll keep digging."

The sound of a car rolling up Clay's gravel drive interrupted Bunker's train of thought. "Looks like you've got company coming."

"Probably Jimmy," Clay said. "He did some research for us on an estate called The Cliffs. Your father told us about it. Ever heard of it?"

"Sounds vaguely familiar, but I don't remember why."

"What connection to Weiss it has, I don't know, but it was the estate up in Bath County that he and his partner chased that Nazi spy to."

"Hi guys," Jimmy said as he walked into Clay's kitchen and went straight to the refrigerator to grab a beer.

"Jimmy," Clay said by way of introductions, "This is Bunker, Mr. Hill's son. Bunker, this is our friend Jimmy."

"Oh yes," Jimmy said. "The son he doesn't remember."

"That would be me, and I'm not laughing."

"Sorry."

"That's all right. I'm learning to live with it."

"So Jimmy, you said you found something for us," Clay said.

"That estate you asked about, The Cliffs, had a big mansion on it that burned down June 25, 1941."

"Really!"

"Yes, and get this. It was owned by a man named Gerhard Nebel, who died in the fire. Is he any relation to Conrad?"

"Must be," Clay answered without hesitating. "When Mac and I first visited Foxhaven, Maria took us on a little side trip to a burned out mansion a mile or so away from Conrad's mansion. She said it had burned down in the 1940s and that Conrad's grandfather had died in that fire." He thought a moment. "Well, now we're getting somewhere."

"We're getting a lot of puzzle pieces that don't quite fit, I'd say," Bunker complained. "In the first place, who is this Conrad Nebel and how do you know him?"

"Conrad is a client," Clay answered. "He's thinking about buying Fairview, the mansion that Mac and I are rebuilding."

"And Maria, is she his daughter?"

"No, a cousin. Princess Maria something or other," Clay said.

"Princess Maria Theresa von Marburg," Jimmy added.

Bunker unzipped a top pocket of his flight suit and pulled out a notebook and pen. "I'll see what I can find on both of them, if there is anything to find." After he finished writing, he looked at Clay. "So far as you know, there is no connection between this Conrad and Weiss?"

"So far, not a thing from what your father has told us, Bunker. This link between the two estates is the first time he's given us anything that could possibly be connected with today. He seems to be leading up to something, but who knows what that is. We'll keep talking to him, but he either can't or won't jump ahead in his story. He's telling it his way and there's no changing his mind."

"Sounds like Dad."

"We've got another piece that doesn't fit too," Mac added. "Don't forget to tell Bunker about the witness, Clay."

"Wish I could forget! Back this summer, a drug addict high school classmate of mine--who hated my guts, by the way--tried to pin a murder on me. He's also the guy who burned down Fairview. Well, he's on trial now for the murder and his lawyer introduced a surprise witness who says he saw me driving my truck in town a half hour after the murder. It's a lie. I was out in McDowell joyriding in my Corvette, but I don't have any witnesses to prove that."

"We're trying to find some way to prove the guy is lying," Mac said. "I talked with his former Imam. He said this Fayaq Khan was told to leave the mosque for trying to radicalize some of the younger members."

"A radical Muslim, eh? Interesting." Bunker wrote Fayaq's name in his notebook.

"If Mac here can't come up with something, I'm liable to be framed for that murder," Clay grumbled.

"Really?"

"Yes, *really*, Bunker. So if you can find out something on the guy, I'd really appreciate it. Meantime, I'm getting kind of curious about that burned-out mansion. I know it's probably nothing, but that day Maria showed it to us, I saw a suspicious looking character out there. Maria said he was probably one of the groundskeepers, but now I'm not so sure. He seemed pretty startled when he spotted me looking at him. It's just a hunch, but something may be going on out there.

"My brother William did some checking," Clay continued, "and found out Conrad's assistant, Gerhard Krieger, was involved in an illegal arms deal back in the '90s. Maybe Krieger has a sideshow operation going on out at the old mansion. I think it's time Mac and I did a sneak and peek recon mission out there. What do you say, Mac?"

"I'm with you partner."

"Clay, that's not a good idea," Bunker scolded. "You may be getting in over your head."

"They've got to catch us first," Mac said with a grin.

11

THE SNEAK & PEEK

"Oh, Clay, it's beautiful," Susan gushed as he pulled his Vette into the drop-off space for valet parking at the Allegheny Mountain Resort at Lime Springs. The U-shaped, five-story resort hotel offered up an imposing spectacle of luxury against the looming, forested backdrop of the Allegheny Mountains. The two outward reaching wings forming the sides of the U gave the impression of welcoming arms reaching out to incoming guests. Between those wings lay lush green lawns, gardens, three fountains, and waterfalls joining a string of small ponds. Clay handed his keys to the uniformed valet along with a scratch-preventing ten-dollar tip. A bellhop loaded Clay and Susan's luggage onto a cart and followed them into a grand main lobby to register.

Their third floor suite came complete with a lavishly furnished sitting room, a balcony overlooking the gardens below, a bedroom significantly larger than the sprawling king sized bed, and a vintage-style tiled bath with his and her sinks. The wallpaper throughout the suite was a soft pastel blue with a white floral design, while the colors in oriental style carpets were predominately bold red in the sitting room and pale gold in the bedroom.

"What do you think, Susan?" Clay asked with a bit of a self-satisfied smile, after the bellhop left with another of Clay's ten-spots."I've been successfully bribed," she answered coyly and draped herself on him, her arms around his neck. "It's fantastic. You and Mac can go play soldiers tomorrow, so long as I get you the day after."

"You drive a hard bargain, my dear," he said, giving her a kiss. "Suppose we make sure the bed is up to snuff."

"Oh yes," she giggled and kissed him hungrily. "Can't be too careful in these five-star hotels."

With Susan dangling from his neck and his arms around her waist, he lifted her off the floor and walked her into the bedroom. He paused for one last kiss before lowering her backwards onto the bed. She squirmed quickly up to the pillows, and Clay was climbing onto the bed with her when someone knocked at the door.

"Awh, Jeez," Clay groaned and his head dropped disconsolately onto the pillow. "They can't be here already. I thought we had a big head start on them."

"You're the man of the house," Susan said laughing at Clay's agonizing, "You answer the door. I have to fix my hair." She gave him a playful shove to roll him out of bed.

"The things I do for love," he said with mock suffering. Then he made a quick grab at Susan's ticklish waist. She convulsed and let out a scream mixed with girlish laughter and a scolding "Clay!"

"Are we interrupting something?" Jimmy asked tentatively when Clay finally answered the door.

"Hi guys. No, Susan just saw a mouse or something."

"Yeah, right. Should we come back later, or can we come in?"

Clay stepped back and waved Jimmy, Trisch, Mac, and Rita into the sitting room. Susan came out to grins and some good-natured ribbing from Jimmy.

"So, everybody happy with the accommodations?" Clay asked. Mac and Rita smiled and nodded. Trisch turned to Jimmy and scowled, "He had to book the Presidential Suite. It's going to cost us a fortune!"

"Hey, we're millionaires. We can afford it, hon."

"Okay, no dissention in the ranks," Clay joked. "Jimmy, did you bring the maps, I hope?"

"Yes, got them right here," he said pulling two maps from a large manila envelope and unfolding them on the mahogany coffee table. "He's got a helluva lot of property, I can tell you that. It's like five miles on the short side and ten on the long, according to this tax map."

"Mac, you and Clay are going to have a long walk tomorrow," Rita chided.

"That's all right. I need to stretch my legs. Besides, the lake is only about seven miles in, if we approach from the east boundary."

"And what exactly is a 'sneak and peek'?" Trisch asked.

"Reconnaissance," Mac answered smartly. "You get in, take a look around, and get out without being detected. Part of your basic Ranger training."

"Yup. And it looks like the lake is the best approach," Clay confirmed, turning the Geological Survey topographic map toward himself. "This dirt road runs along his property line," he said running his finger over the map, "and we can hide Jimmy's Jeep somewhere on the other side of the road. That way, if anybody from Foxhaven does spot it, they'll think we're poaching on somebody else's property. We could try walking around the lake, but the closer we get to the ruins, the closer we are to Foxhaven, and the more likely somebody could spot us. I like swimming across it at night better. That's the last place they'd expect anybody to come in from, and it'll give us a chance to check out that dock we saw. Maria said there is a way up to the ruins from there. A tunnel or something.

"Is everybody clear on what we are doing tomorrow?" Clay saw all their heads nodding in the affirmative. "Just to be absolutely safe, we don't talk about any of this in public, okay? Conrad has lots of friends around here, I'm sure. I don't know that it is anything like what Blakes described with his grandfather, but let's not take any chances. We're good friends, here to relax together for a few days. If anybody asks where Mac and I disappeared to, we're the fly fishermen in this group, and we're spending tomorrow on our own, fishing the trout streams hereabouts."

Next morning, Clay and Mac loaded backpacks and fishing gear into Jimmy's Jeep, joked a bit with the valet about getting lost trying to find some good fishing spots, and headed west toward Foxhaven. The sun was already high in the sky when they pulled into a rutted old fire road to hide Jimmy's jeep. The sun's warmth felt good as they unloaded the jeep, though it would likely get downright cold in deep ravines, and surely would after sundown tonight. For that, they'd packed some extra clothes along with their other gear.

After donning their backpacks, they set off almost due west, bushwhacking their way down a steep incline and into Conrad's huge estate. A light breeze stirred the shriveled brown oak leaves clinging stubbornly to the branches high above them. It being late October and high up in the mountains, most the trees had already shed their leaves, but oak leaves were often the last to drop, and in sheltered spots some would hang on until the new growth of next spring. The underbrush, thorny blackberry and raspberry thickets nearest the road, gave way to rhododendron and mountain laurel, here and there in thick clusters that tore at their clothing. They crossed a small stream at the bottom of the ravine and worked their way up the next ridge.

"You know, if we get caught," Mac said finally, "it could kill any possible deal with Conrad to buy Fairview. Hate to lose a prospect with so much money," he said, starting to breathe heavily.

"Yeah," Clay said laughing. "But then we don't really need the money anymore, do we? We can afford to wait for another prospect. For my money though, it's Krieger who is dirty. So, if we opened

Conrad's eyes to what is going on, he'd be happy with us, right? And if Conrad is up to no good, we're not going to get a sale anyway."

"Do you suppose they patrol these woods? You know, to keep out poachers and trespassers like us," Mac said as they came up on a big grove of tall pine trees. The underbrush thinned out and the going became easier.

"Way out here? Probably not. At least not where they aren't any roads. We'd better be careful when we get close to the lake though."

"Yeah, especially if they really are up to something fishy."

There weren't any roads for the next hour, just steep ridges and plenty of underbrush to make the going tough. As Clay and Mac were discovering, out there you didn't need fences or guards for protection. The rugged terrain did a fine job of discouraging trespassers. Then, finally, they topped a ridge that gave them a view of the lake. Clay pulled out a pair of binoculars, and after checking the sun's position so the glass lenses wouldn't reflect a flash of sunlight, he slowly swept the cliff, the boat dock at it's base, and the ruins, which were partly visible at the top of the cliff.

"Here, take a look, Mac. That dock runs right into a tunnel in the face of the cliff. There must be a way to get up to the mansion from there."

"Must be," Mac agreed as he homed in on it. "That cliff has to be 200 feet high. Most of it looks like it's straight up. And it must run a half mile on either side of the ruins. If that tunnel doesn't give us a way up, we'll have a long swim and a long walk after."

"Check out that seaplane, Mac. Make sure there's nobody in it, will you."

"Nope. Looks empty."

"Good. We can swim to that tonight and hide between the pontoons until we're sure it's safe to go to the dock."

"Looks pretty deserted over there. Oops! Three guys in nothing but underpants just came out of the tunnel."

"What do they look like?"

"You mean are they hajis? Two of 'em are, got black beards and hair. One of 'em is white as a sheet though."

"Let me see," Clay said, taking the binoculars back. "When you're right, you're right, Mac. Pure vanilla, except, wait, I've seen that tattoo before in Afghanistan. A crescent moon with a star. Sonofabitch, Mac, I'll bet Vanilla's fought with the Taliban."

"You're joking."

"See for yourself. Nope, sorry, too late, they jumped in the water."

Clay and Mac eventually reached a partly overgrown fire road following the lake shore and then burrowed into a thicket of brush at the water's edge. The brush gave them good protective cover while also allowing a view of the dock.

When the three terrorists finished their swim and disappeared into the tunnel, Clay and Mac broke out lunch, MREs, the Army's version of trail food.

"You know," Mac said after consuming two of them, "I'll never understand why they make them so small."

"Didn't know you were going to join up, Mac. You're probably the hungriest man in the world."

"You think?"

"We could ask Rita. Bet she'll back me up," he said with a grin. Then he looked up. "I hear a plane, Mac. We'd better lay low and be invisible, in case he makes a pass over the lake."

The noise of the plane's engine got steadily closer, then they heard a splash and a whooshing sound as this second seaplane streaked along the water toward the dock. Clay sat up and peered through a break in the underbrush as the seaplane taxied up to the dock. His jaw tightened. Three more Arabs climbed out and scrambled up onto the dock. The three men he had seen earlier, apparently their comrades, came out to greet them with bear hugs and backslapping. The seaplane took off for parts unknown.

Convinced now that they really were on to something, Clay and Mac hunkered down to wait for nightfall. They were definitely going in to check out that tunnel, but clearly it was a bigger hornet's nest than they had expected.

As night fell, they stripped and began pulling on wetsuits. They'd packed closed circuit underwater rebreathers, chest mounted units good for four hours at shallow depths, guaranteeing plenty of leeway for the long swim back. Clay attached a tiny dive light to his weight belt, so that Mac would be able to follow him in the darkness. Once they reached the seaplane, he'd kill the light and they'd have to wing it for the hundred feet to the dock. They planned to come up under it, get their bearings and then submerge again for the final underwater leg into the tunnel. It was anybody's guess what was going on in there, but Clay wasn't about to leave without finding out.

Clay took a couple of breaths through his rebreather's mouthpiece, then he whispered, "Ready to get wet?" Mac nodded. Clay crawled out onto the rocky shoreline without making a sound. He looked up at the crystal clear sky, a million stars winking at him from heavens above. The waning moon provided a faint light for them to see by. He couldn't have asked for better conditions, he thought, as he slithered into the water and sank beneath the surface.

The only light now was a wavering glow up at the surface. Otherwise the deep, inky blackness surrounded him, and as he turned to wait for Mac, only his regular breaths broke the eerie silence. Floating upright about five feet below the surface, he could feel very cold water around his legs, while closer to the surface, it was still relatively warm from the day's sunshine. He heard Mac entering the water and remembered to turn on the small flashlight. The light was weak, but Mac soon came up alongside him. Clay poked his head above water, drew a bead on the seaplane, a faint apparition in the soft light, and headed for it.

Both men were in good shape, but a half-mile swim underwater is still a workout. Both were breathing hard when they surfaced at the seaplane. Hanging onto the pontoon struts, they rested for five minutes before submerging again to swim for the dock. Clay bumped his head on a crossbar as he surfaced under the dock, and was rubbing it when Mac surfaced alongside him.

"You okay?" Mac whispered.

"Banged my head. I'll live. There's a light on over a doorway back there at the end of the tunnel. Let's stay close to the dock and ease on in with our heads above water. If anybody comes out to the dock, we duck under it, okay?" Mac nodded.

Clay gently pulled himself post by post to the far end of the tunnel. Mac stayed close behind and the two barely stirred a ripple. Clay carefully crawled up a ladder attached to the dock to check out the doorway. Back down in the water again, Clay whispered, "Nobody home. Let's ditch the rebreathers and take a look inside."

They spent several minutes unhitching the units and strapping them to a crosspiece under the dock. Then Clay went up the ladder and stepped quickly and quietly as he could over to the doorway. It led into another tunnel, also cut into solid rock, jogging this way and that, as though following a vein of ore. Up ahead, water dripped relentlessly from the rocky ceiling into puddles--plip, plip, plip echoed in the tunnel--and a raised walkway of wooden slats ran down the middle of the tunnel. Clay could hear muffled voices from somewhere far off, and about fifty feet in, a stairway led upwards. Was that the way up to the ruins? The tunnel's rock walls gave them no place to hide until they reached the stairs, but they'd have to chance it. He signaled Mac to come up onto the dock.

Looking like black suited aliens in their wetsuits, Clay and Mac tiptoed as fast as they dared to the stairway. This tunnel seemed to be honeycombed with side passages, and though it was impossible to be sure, it sounded as though voices were coming from the tunnel not too far ahead. With Mac close behind, Clay started up the wooden stairway carefully, testing each step to make sure it wasn't going to creak. They were nearly at the top when Clay and Mac froze at the sound of someone walking in the tunnel below. They dared not move for fear of making a sound, even though they were out in plain sight.

Down below in the tunnel, the man dubbed "Vanilla" appeared, then slowed as he reached the stairs. Clay held his breath and stared at the top of Vanilla's head, desperately hoping he would not look up. If Vanilla did, they'd be toast. What seemed like forever finally passed and Vanilla continued on his way toward the dock. Moments later, Clay and Mac broke into relieved, toothy grins at the sound of trickling water as Vanilla relieved himself off the dock.

Clay and Mac hurried up the stairs and into yet another old mine tunnel. This one seemed to parallel the one below, and when they rounded a bend, Clay came to a sudden halt. He heard the voices clearly now and to his left there was a large open gallery in the tunnel wall overlooking a large, brightly lighted room below. Clay crept up to the opening and peered down. All six of the Muslims were seated around a large table in the middle, field stripping and cleaning their guns. Clay's eyes widened as he recognized AK-47s, M-16s, and semiautomatic pistols littering the table. Bunk beds and foot lockers occupied the walls. Clay couldn't make out what the men were saying, but it sounded like an Arabic dialect.

Ducked down until past the gallery, Clay and Mac continued on, following the up sloping passageway. Single bulb electric lights blazed against the darkness every twenty feet or so, fed by a single wire attached to the ceiling. Here and there, side tunnels veered laterally. They ignored all of them until they came upon one with an old wooden door sitting half open. A new padlock hung in the hasp.

Clay tapped Mac on the shoulder and with hand signals, pointed the way for him to follow. Clay twisted the small underwater flashlight into the on position and led the way for about thirty yards until they entered a large room. Plastic tarps covered what appeared to be several big piles of wooden crates. Clay lifted a tarp and his eyes widened on seeing the crate's stenciled markings.

"Mac!" he exclaimed in a horse whisper. "M-16s! Look at all of them." Clay could hardly contain himself as he went to the next tarp. "RPGs!" And the next. "Ammo!"

"Krieger must have been running guns all along," Mac whispered back. "This is where he's stashing it until he makes a deal."

"Yeah, and then he flies the shipment out by seaplane to one of Conrad's tankers. Slick operation." Clay thought for a moment. "I wonder how many more of these arms caches he's got squirreled away down here. This place is honeycombed with tunnels."

The two went back to the main tunnel. It wasn't long before they found another passageway blocked by a decrepit old wooden door, secured by a rusty padlock that looked as old as the door. Without really knowing why, Clay tugged at the padlock, perhaps hoping it would give way because of old age. It didn't, but the screws holding the hasp to the old wooden door seemed to give a bit. He pulled, twisted, then twisted the opposite direction until the screws finally pulled free of the rotted wood. Clay grinned at Mac as he opened the old door enough to enter. The tunnel led to another room serving as a munitions dump. Except this one was like stepping into another time.

"Swastikas, Mac. Look at these crates. What the heck is a Karabiner 98K? The crates they're in look like they are probably rifles." Clay turned his flashlight on another stack of crates and brushed off a thick coat of dust. "Maschinenpistole 35. Must be some kind of automatic. Look at all of this. Some of these boxes must date back to World War I. Incredible. There's enough stuff here to equip a small army."

"Maybe Conrad's granddad was in the arms trading business too," Mac whispered.

"Could be. Or he was planning to help Hitler when der Fuhrer finally got around to invading the East Coast."

"Now that's spooky."

"Let's see what else we can find here. I'd still like to get up into the ruins."

As they left, Clay made sure to reinsert the hasp screws into their holes to cover the fact they'd broken in. They followed the main tunnel past three or four more apparent storage rooms with locked doors until they came to a dead end. A wooden stairway wove back and forth in a vertical shaft, disappearing into the darkness above. "Nowhere to go but up," Clay whispered as he started up the stairway. They covered what probably amounted to two or three stories before reaching the top landing and what appeared to be nothing but a bare wall. Clay shined his mini flashlight on the wall.

A crack outlined a large four-foot-wide, eight-foot-high panel, but nothing else. Impulsively, Clay pushed on one side and the panel started to swing on a center axis. He pushed harder and the panel swung completely open, revealing an old cabinet on the opposite side and an opening wide enough for them to slip through. Clay turned and grinned at Mac. "Now it's secret passages. This place is a real trip!"

They stepped through the doorway into a long corridor of what probably once served as the mansion's basement kitchen and servants' quarters. A thick coat of dust covered everything in sight, except for a well-worn path on the floor that led to their left, up the kitchen corridor. Clay swung the doorway closed.

Following the track, they passed a servants' eating area with a large empty table, broken and overturned chairs, and a glass partition with all the panes broken out. Next came the kitchen with its hulking cast iron stoves and ovens. Tables were overturned, chairs broken, and windows smashed. Pots, pans, and utensils were strewn everywhere, and in the next room, it appeared all the mansion's dishware had been smashed on the floor. A food pantry on the opposite side had been similarly ransacked long ago and left to rot. And it all had been left as it was to gather an ever thickening blanket of dust.

"The fire was up in the living quarters, right?" Clay whispered to Mac.

"Yeah, that's what I thought."

"I've never seen firemen do this kind of damage. Looks like somebody deliberately ransacked the place. Weird."

"I wonder what really happened here, Clay."

"Me too," Clay muttered half to himself as he pushed through a doorway. Mac saw him suddenly tip forward and grabbed Clay's arm just in time, saving him from taking a header into oblivion. Beyond that door lay a dark pit where a chunk of the mansion's three floors had collapsed into some sort of a sub basement. With Mac still holding his arm, Clay leaned forward and looked upward to see the starry sky above and the ragged outlines of the broken first, second, and third floors above him.

"That was close. Thanks, Mac. Looks like that's where the house got the worst of the fire. We should have turned back there," he said, pointing the flashlight a few feet back, where the well-worn track went up a narrow staircase.

Beyond the stairs, the track headed straight out of the mansion. To their right, the floors above were sagging, and the walls and ceilings had all been seared black by the fire. To their left was the gaping hole of collapsed walls, floors, and roof--a quarter of the huge mansion gone, now lost in the cratered subbasement. Clay and Mac followed the track out of the mansion, across a rubble strewn porch, and into the overgrown front yard. They stopped and turned to look at the ruins. The weak moonlight draped the shattered building in eerie shadows, conspiring with the gnarled walls and sagging roofs to give it the appearance of being haunted. Given what they'd seen in the tunnels below it, Clay decided, it must be.

A path led them past the spot where Clay had seen the suspicious-looking man, then looped out to the fire road Maria had driven to show them the mansion. They were out on the fire road when Mac heard it, the sound of a small engine off in the distance breaking the nighttime silence. "What's that?" he whispered.

"Sounds like the Gator's coming this way. I'm pretty sure it's not Maria, so we'd better get out of sight."

"That's easy. Just take ten steps in any direction."

"We'd better find someplace outside. We don't want to leave tracks in that dust inside."

"Okay, where do you think?"

"The front porch. Let's get down behind the far end. Unless somebody is looking for us, they won't go there."

With the Gator fast approaching, Clay and Mac hunkered down in the brush at the far end of the stone porch. The porch floor stood five feet above ground level, with the marble railing above that. Clay figured the railing would effectively screen the tops of their heads and allow them to check out anybody stepping onto the porch. But to do so, they would have to remain in an awkward, half squatting position.

The two waited anxiously as the Gator stopped and the engine died. Then they heard footsteps and the sound of somebody pushing through the underbrush. Clay and Mac sank down to nose level behind the porch and waited for a look at the new arrival. Suddenly the man, still out of sight, stopped in his tracks. Clay and Mac exchanged worried looks. Had they been seen? Nearly a minute passed and not a sound. What was he doing, Clay wondered. Another minute passed and finally, the footsteps restarted on the path to the porch. Meanwhile the muscles in both Clay's and Mac's legs began to burn, hunkered halfway down as they were.

Nothing more than a shadowy figure at first, the man finally climbed up onto the porch. Clay and Mac saw it at the same time. Turning face-to-face, they silently mouthed "Krieger!" Perhaps sensing he was being watched, Krieger stopped in the middle of the porch, turning slowly first in one direction, then another, as if trying to locate the peering eyes by radar.

Mac's leg muscles burned furiously now and he could not stand the awkward position any longer. Waiting until Krieger turned the other way, Mac slowly lowered himself down until his knees touched the ground and took the weight off his legs. But as he did so, the weight of one knee snapped a small twig lying on the ground. Krieger, his instincts already aroused, reached down and un-holstered his sidearm, a Glock, and took a step in their direction. Clay's leg muscles were screaming too, but he dared not move while Krieger was facing his way. Krieger looked toward the front of the porch, then took another step toward Clay and Mac. He was close enough now that his feet were in plain view.

Clay was sure they'd had it, but then a voice came over Krieger's two-way radio. Krieger turned away as he answered it, pacing back toward the mansion's front door. Clay desperately felt the ground for twigs as he lowered himself down and stifled a sigh of relief. Krieger's conversation was clipped and brief--"Ja, ja, I can do that." Distracted by the call, he forgot all about the snapping twig and disappeared inside the ruins. Clay and Mac waited until they heard him thumping down the steps to the kitchen before standing up.

"Looks like Krieger's the one," Clay said as he and Mac rubbed the knots out of their leg muscles. And I'll bet I know where he's going. Let's go find out what he's going to tell them."

"Easy, Clay. We don't want to bump into him going down there. He's the one with the gun, and six friends with a bunch more."

"Good point," he answered with a grin.

They gave Krieger a good head start before heading into the ruins. They had to stop and listen at every turn in the path because of the other possibility, that they'd run smack into Krieger coming out. At the secret passage, Clay swung it open part way and listened for Krieger coming back up, but heard nothing. They'd be dead meat if anybody caught them on the stairs, but they had to chance it. Finally, down and in the long main tunnel, Clay breathed easier. There they at least had half a chance to duck into a side passage if they heard someone coming.

When Clay and Mac got to the gallery and peered down into the room below, Krieger was standing at the head of the table. Vanilla was sitting on his right.

"You have all the papers now that you will need for your cover. You'll be fine, unless you do something stupid. Listen to Muhammad here. He's made the transit before and knows what to do if some emergency should come up. Mainly, keep your heads. Do not panic.

"You will leave shortly in one of the motor launches tied up at the dock. Muhammad will steer you to the far end of the lake. A van will meet you there and take you to your safe house outside Washington. We will retrieve the launch tomorrow. Now I think Muhammad has a few things to say.

"My brothers," Vanilla began in English as he stood to address them. "Praise Allah. We begin our journey's final leg to strike at the heart of the Great Satan. We must succeed. You five men have been chosen to join me because you have fought for Allah's glory and can speak at least passable English. From now on, we speak English even amongst ourselves. We must do everything to avoid arousing suspicion, so be as natural as you can. So far as the infidels are concerned, you are just cashiers in one of their convenience stores." That drew laughter from the assembled terrorists, and silent grins from Clay and Mac.

"I must be serious now. What glory awaits us? We will deliver death and destruction upon what is but a small part of the Great Satan's body. It will be a pin prick, what his generals like to call a surgical strike. We will draw the blood of six American infidels, show them our wrath before we put them to death. We will celebrate Allah's glory in the destruction we will wreak upon them. But know too that we will be slitting the throat of Satan's future. And that is why we must succeed.

"How often has the Great Satan invaded our lands, soiled our women, spread his blasphemy, killed and maimed our own? The infidels deserve to die. All infidels deserve to die. The Koran tells us that. Why? Because the glory of Allah cannot exist where there are unbelievers. So long as there are unbelievers, his glory is not complete. Praise Allah!" Krieger stood stern-faced and silent as the others shouted back, "Praise Allah." Vanilla had them fired up now, and he raised his voice as he continued preaching his doomsday message.

"I was not born to Islam, but through my studies I came to know the truth. It was inevitable, as it is for anyone who embarks on the path to the righteousness that is Islam. I know of the disillusionment, degradation, the disgust which the culture of the Great Satan breeds. Infidels, all of them. Jihad in Allah's name is our duty, and our dream, a caliphate spreading our holy Islamic law over all the world--here too, even. Death to anyone who opposes us, death to all infidels! ”

The others shouted back, “Death to all infidels!”

“Our brother Ayatollah Khomeini has preached, ‘Islam says: Whatever good there is exists thanks to the sword and in the shadow of the sword! People cannot be made obedient except with the sword! The sword is the key to Paradise, which can be opened only for Holy Warriors!

“That will be our reward. Our mission is clear. Our strength is in Allah’s will. It is time we go.”

When Vanilla led the terrorist squad out, Clay and Mac backed away from the gallery and ducked deep into a side passage. After a long delay, they heard a motorboat engine fire up and then rumble at idle as the boat headed out onto the lake. Minutes later, Krieger passed by in the main tunnel on his way up to the ruins.

That was their cue to head back to the deserted dock. Then came the long, uneventful underwater swim back, and for Mac, anyway, a welcome return to their supply of MREs. After changing into their clothes, they hiked up over the first ridge in the dark, then waited for daybreak before continuing on.

Back at the hotel later that morning, everyone gathered in Clay and Susan’s room. The always thoughtful Rita had already ordered food. Though Clay and Mac had only begun working on their sandwiches, Jimmy couldn’t stand the suspense any longer. “So what did you guys see out there?”

“A lot,” Clay said while wolfing down his sandwich. “We saw six damn terrorists leaving for some kind of attack somewhere here in the states. And Krieger, Conrad’s assistant was there to give them a sendoff. It looks like he’s got a sideline smuggling Muslim terrorists in and out of the country. Plus, he’s doing some arms smuggling too.”

Mac swallowed, then added, “There’s tunnels, old mine shafts--running all around in the cliffs under that ruined mansion I told you about, Rita, even one tunnel going up into it. Krieger damn near caught us while we were sneaking around up there."

"We've got to clue Bunker in on this," Clay said, "but the thing I can't figure is whether Conrad knows about this or not."

"A man like him?" Susan said. "Why would someone with all that money and prestige, who does all that charitable work, ever get involved in something like smuggling terrorists?"

"That may be the sixty-four dollar question here, Susan," Clay replied.

"We could try to arrange a meeting with Conrad," Mac offered, "and kind of talk around the subject of Krieger. See how Conrad reacts."

"Yeah, I suppose, but how do we make sure Krieger is out of the room. Those two are joined at the hip, from what I've seen."

"Which might just answer your question right there," Jimmy offered.

"True, but that's still a guess. We *know* Krieger is dirty. We could dump that in Bunker's lap and see what he comes up with. He's sure to want to know about what we saw.

"That would be the smart thing to do," Jimmy said, "but I'll bet you're not going to let it go at that."

Clay smiled. "Right you are, Jimmy. I'd like to know a little more about Conrad and I just had an idea. Mac, suppose we call Conrad and arrange a meeting to talk about Fairview. Say we want to discuss any concerns he might have about buying it. You know, talk things over to see if we can reach a deal."

"I hope you're not planning on giving away the candy store, Clay."

"No, I might dangle a $20K discount in front of him, but only if it becomes necessary to get a meeting. What I'm hoping is that the princess will be there, and that I can come up with an excuse to talk with her alone. If anybody knows Conrad, it's her."

"I don't think that's a good idea, Clay," Mac countered, remembering the looks that passed between them. Susan didn't either, but she didn't say anything. "Why don't you at least wait until we've talked to Bunker?"

12

REVENGE, SERVED COLD

Susan sat on the edge of Blakes's bed, smiling pleasantly at him. He'd remembered her right away, had even said "Hi, Susan." A good sign, but Clay still wondered if this morning would again be wasted on the old man's ramblings. Blakes had come up with one important lead, though, the name of Gerhardt's estate. Clay had no doubt that there was more to The Cliffs fire than ever made it into the newspaper articles Jimmy had dug up. And that somehow it was connected to what they'd seen out there the other day.

Blakes, in his exasperatingly plodding way, was now getting close to that event and might finally tell all. Clay wanted Susan to try prodding him about it, but she insisted that they let Blakes tell it in his own way. Clay relented, in part because Bunker had called. He had information for them and would be flying in this afternoon. So even if Blakes shut down without giving them anything definite, things were finally moving in the right direction. Clay could only hope that whatever those terrorists had planned was still weeks away.

"They pulled us back to Washington," Blakes answered sullenly when Susan asked what happened after he and Johnson had been run off the road that night seventy-three years ago. His eyes appeared to glaze over as he remembered that day.

"Chief Carswell was mad as hell. We got a real chewing out, but that didn't stop me...."

Sitting with Johnson outside the office, the young Blakes fidgeted nervously, even though he knew full well that's exactly what Section Chief Carswell wanted. He felt like he'd been thrown back into school and sent to the principal's office. Johnson sat there impassively awaiting their fate, seemingly more interested in the cute blond secretary who, having seen this routine played out before, totally ignored them and went about typing up some report or other. Blakes swallowed hard when her intercom finally buzzed and she waved them into the Chief's office.

Chief Carswell was a bulldog of a man, thick, broad-chested and big-bellied, his jowly face sagging with middle age. He stood behind his desk, a standard, government issue, wood desk and swivel chair made of golden oak, his two coal black eyes glaring at the two agents as they walked in. Blakes, in the rear, closed the door behind them. Carswell's jowls jiggled when he got mad, and Blakes noticed they were jiggling like crazy now.

"Sit down, both of you. Johnson, you don't have any excuse at all. You're supposed to know better. You start freelancing and this is what happens. Agents get hurt or killed. You know I don't like it when my agents get hurt."

"Yes, Chief, I understand completely," Johnson answered contritely, hoping that might end this session quickly. But it was not to be.

"Good. But that's only part of the mess you two have made. You've really stepped in it, do you know that?"

"What do you mean, chief?" Johnson asked. The same question ran through Blakes's mind, but he was taking a back seat to Johnson on this, even though he'd chased down the lead that got them into trouble.

"We've got procedures for operating in the field, Johnson. Before you start flashing your badge at local judges for search warrants, you're supposed to check in here. You wound up stepping on some mighty well connected toes, boys, and the director's getting flack from some important people on the Hill. He doesn't like that, and now I'm getting flack from him."

"We were on the trail of a German spy, Chief. He'd already rab-bited on us once, with stolen classified papers that could really help the Nazis. So we thought we had to move fast. And it was just a house out in the boondocks. How could that have any blowback?" Johnson asked plaintively.

"Didn't you know that house was on an estate?"

"What, The Cliffs? No, not at the time. We knew his brother was a gamekeeper there, but all we had was an address. That's what we used for the warrant, and a judge approved it. It's all in our report."

"Yeah, well, you should have checked with us first. We'd have set you straight. Gerhard Nebel is a major contributor to the campaigns of senators and congressmen. I can't go into details, but he's helped our government's friends more than once with some shady arms deals. He's answered the call, so he gets a pass. I'm telling you in no uncertain terms to back off. There will be no more search warrants for any part of his estate."

"What if Mueller gets the notebooks to the Nazis?" Blakes blurted out. He couldn't believe what he was hearing. "How do we catch this guy if we can't even get onto the estate? We can't prove it, but we have that unconfirmed report of some Nazis in uniform showing up there."

"Settle down, Hill. I made note of it, but as I said, Nebel has done some work for our government and that could well be part of it. If Mueller's brother turns up somewhere off the estate, then we'll arrest him and squeeze him for what he knows about Nebel."

Blakes's face flushed red with anger. He had been chasing that notebook for weeks now, had been frustrated, drugged, and shot at. He couldn't let go now, after all that. "But Chief--"

"That's it, end of discussion! You two are officially off the case. Take a few days off and report back to me next week. I don't want to hear any more about this."

Blakes said nothing to Johnson, but the next day he was back in Bath County sneaking onto The Cliffs property with JJ, the crippled black man he'd talked with in Hacketsville. He knew he'd be fired if Chief Carswell found out, because he was way out of bounds on this. But he'd been through too much to stop now. The key lay somewhere inside that estate, and proving Mueller's brother was there would give Blakes some leverage.

JJ lead the way sneaking onto the estate, limping along at a surprisingly good pace, a lot faster than Blakes thought possible. They followed what appeared to be a deer path in the general direction of the mansion itself.

"So, now will you tell me what it is you're going to show me?" Blakes asked between breaths.

"You'll see, in jus a little bit. We almost there. Jus over that rise, we can see from dere."

JJ wasn't lying. They topped the ridge and through gaps between the trees lay a sweeping panoramic view of a big lake, a towering cliff on the far side, and what Hill was certain was a castle perched on top. A hundred feet or so of lawns and gardens gently sloped down from the mansion to the precipitous edge. JJ handed Blakes a well-worn set of binoculars.

"They old, but they work good," JJ said proudly. "Judge Elroy give me dem, so's I could hunt deer wif 'em. Judge, he looked after me, 'cause he felt sorry for me on account of my leg. Made me learn to read and write, yes siree. Said if a man caint walk right, he got to have some smarts if he's goin' to earn a living."

Blakes nodded and focused the binoculars on the mansion, a rococo-style, three-story stone edifice with castlelike turrets at each end. Blakes couldn't believe his eyes. The place was huge, at once truly impressive and repulsively grandiose, especially considering that it could be a Nazi haven. A series of stone arches occupied the middle third of the building, providing shelter for a porch. Blakes homed in on a table centered in the middle of an archway. Two men dressed in white suits were being served a sumptuous lunch. Blakes had hoped to see Mueller's brother, but he didn't recognize either man.

JJ taped Blakes on the shoulder. "Look over to the left some. Over where da trees is thin. See all dem tents?" Blakes swung over that way and saw what JJ was talking about--an encampment of about three dozen or so tents and a few Nazi flags fluttering in the breeze. "Told you dey was Nazis up here."

"Well, that's the German-American Bund, JJ. Not real Nazis. My partner and I ran into a bunch of them over by the estate manager's house. They're holding a rally here."

"Bull. I seen real Nazis up dere. Army officers, what dey call Wehrmacht. I seen der patch, dat black cross. Dey fly in and land in one of dem planes lands on water."

"My boss says Mr. Nebel sometimes does secret work for our government, some kind of business dealings maybe."

"I'll show you his bizness," JJ said angrily. "Foller me." With JJ leading the way, they headed down a steep slope toward the lake. Once they reached a rutted dirt track running alongside the lake, JJ turned to stay parallel with it but well back under the cover of the trees and brush. They went about as far as halfway along the lake until they were almost directly across from the mansion.

"We gots to be extra careful now. Don't want to let masser's guards see us. See over dere, jus off the road we bin followin'? That be the entrance to a mine. Dey's got a big iron gate in front, locked up tight. But dey didn't put nothing on dee air shaft. Dats how weez gettin' in."

"Gettin in? What for, JJ?" Blakes didn't like the idea of crawling into an old mine, much less getting caught in there by Nebel's men.

"You see. Foller me."

JJ limped up the slope and into a narrow ravine, a dry creek bed that probably served as a wash during heavy rains. Big boulders bumped up against each other so that in places the ravine seemed impassible, but JJ, twisting this way and that, always found a way through. Finally they came to a cleft in the rock.

"In here," JJ said, pointing to the narrow opening. "Gots to go on your hands and knees."

"JJ, I don't know about this."

"Jes follar me."

Blakes's one consolation was that with JJ in the lead, JJ wound up with the cobwebs in his face. Blakes didn't even want to think about the spiders, or snakes that also must be in here, but after ten feet or so, it was so dark he couldn't see anything anyway. He was just following the sound of JJ scraping along this twisting, rocky tunnel, breathing hard and here and there issuing advice on which way to turn. Blakes was beginning to get really scared. They were going deeper and deeper into the pitch blackness, with no end in sight and a passageway that was getting smaller and smaller. Too small now to even turn around to get back out. Finally, JJ stopped, and after a moment struck a match.

"Weez here, Mr. Blakes. Deys some crates 'bout four feet down. Once't I gets inside I'll light us a torch." Blakes was in no position to argue, so he waited until the sudden flare of light hurt his eyes and made him turn away for a moment. Then he too squirted out of the air shaft.

What Blakes saw, in the flickering light of the torch the Germans had thoughtfully supplied, left him speechless. They were in a large open gallery cut into the solid rock, a room filled to the ceiling with stacks of long crates, all of them marked with Nazi swastikas. Most likely rifles, Blakes guessed. And there standing in the middle of it all, smiling proudly, was JJ.

"See? I told yah. Dey's four rooms like dis one. Dey got rifles, machine guns, mortars, eben uniforms. I know, 'cause I watched 'em practicing with all dat stuff down by de dam at da end of da lake. Here, I show you da other rooms."

Blakes was flabbergasted. This mine was nothing but a huge cache of small arms, enough to equip a small army. What was Nebel planning to do with all of it? Start a revolution? He could be selling it, simply storing it here for transshipment to say, South America. A rebellion in the banana republics always seemed to be in the offing anyway. But then why would he store it here?

No, more likely Nebel was doing just what JJ said--using the equipment for practice by his German American Bund friends. Maybe to arm them someday. Like maybe when Hitler finally got around to attacking the U.S. That thought sent a shiver of fear down Blakes's spine. So did the realization there wasn't anything he could do. Nebel had powerful friends. Powerful enough that Blakes probably would never be able to get a warrant to have this mine searched. And even if he did, Nebel likely would hear about it soon enough to have the stuff moved. Who knew how many other mine shafts he had around here, or if they weren't already full of more arms and ammunition.

Much as he hated the thought of crawling back out that tunnel, he'd seen enough and told JJ it was time to go. Again surrounded by total darkness, with only the sounds of JJ ahead of him, Blakes struggled with the notion that there really were people in the world like Nebel, totally unscrupulous, smiling at you one day and plotting your overthrow the next.

Why would a man as rich as Nebel do such a thing? Power? Money? He already had plenty of both. Or was he a patriotic Nazi living a lie here in the US? When Blakes finally crawled out into the daylight, he still didn't have an answer to that question, much less what he could do to keep the Nazis from getting that notebook. If, that is, it hadn't already found its way into their hands.

Blakes smiled at the memory of a report he saw years after the war. He knew Susan thought he was smiling at her, and decided that letting her think that would be for the best. During the 1950s, a friend of Weiss's in the West German government came across a file on Weiss's synthetic gasoline project. It had been prepared by the Abwehr, the Nazis's foreign intelligence division, and Weiss had his friend send a copy to Blakes. The report revealed a Nazi agent named Detter had arranged with Nebel to use his German spy ring in the U.S. to obtain the formula from Weiss's lab. The last report in the file stated that Nebel had the notebook in his possession, but had quadrupled the price to $10 million American, which was to be deposited into his Swiss bank account.

On orders from the German government, Detter twice attempted to negotiate a lower price, but Nebel refused to budge. American FBI agents had uncovered parts of his operation, and he was being forced to use valuable political capital, not to mention cash, to keep the FBI at bay. A final communique had been sent in code to Detter, reluctantly agreeing to pay the required price, but nothing was ever heard from him again.

Blakes smiled again at Susan. He knew what had happened, and that Susan and her friends would want to know too. But something was holding him back. He was tired, he told himself, and wanted to think. He shooed them off, asking that they come back tomorrow. He could see that Clay was angry--no frustrated--but knew Clay would get over it. Clay was smart, Blakes could tell, but still had a few things to learn. Blakes smiled at Clay as he left the room.

Soon after, Clay held the door of his Vette open for Susan to climb in, and looked over at Mac. "Do you want to meet us at the mill house? Bunker will be there about four. Bring Rita and we'll do dinner there, once we find out what Bunker has to say." Mac gave him a thumbs up and then drove off.

Climbing into his Vette, Clay turned to Susan and teased, "You can come too, if you want."

"Need help with the dinner?" she answered with a feigned sweet innocence.

Clay laughed. "That too."

"You don't really think I'm going to let you guys out of my sight when we're this close to finding out what the heck is going on," she replied.

"I have to admit, you've done a great job of getting the old man talking. He said a lot today, and he sure confirmed that Nebel's granddad was working for the Nazis. I wonder what made Nebel turn against the US? He had to have made a fortune here. Blakes did make sense of that old cache of Nazi weapons Mac and I saw in the tunnel, though." Clay paused thoughtfully, then started the engine and pulled out of the nursing home parking lot. "I keep getting the feeling he's holding back something else though. And I don't know why."

"I know what you mean. I've had that feeling too. But who knows what that is."

"Maybe he'll tell us tomorrow, but I don't know what good it'll do. I mean everything he's told us so far is seventy-odd years old and hasn't got a damn thing to do with Muslim terrorists."

"Well, there's the connection with why Weiss got killed, isn't there?"

"I suppose. But what if we're looking at two different, unrelated cases? Same guy, but completely different incidents."

"With the grandfather and grandson, two members of the same wealthy family, possibly--probably--involved? What are the chances of that, Clay?"

"Good point. I hope Bunker can shed some light on this when we see him."

"I've got an idea, Clay. Suppose we ask Bunker to stay over. He could come with us when we see his father tomorrow. Blakes might tell him whatever it is he's holding back."

"Positively brilliant, Susan! I knew there was a reason why I'm marrying you." He reached over, put his arm around her. She rested her head on his shoulder, smiling.

By the time Bunker's chopper arrived with a roar, Mac and Rita were already at the mill house. Jimmy, still at school, planned to arrive later with Trisch at dinnertime. Bunker didn't need to be told where the beer was and having found one of Clay's favorites, a Vienna Lager, to his liking, he grabbed that and inspected the standing rib roast occupying a lower shelf of the fridge.

"That beautiful hunk of beef I see in the fridge, would that be for dinner?"

"No, we're going to feed that to the squirrels, Bunker. What do you think?" Clay joked.

"I'm going to have to stop by more often, if that's what you're putting on the table."

"That's the bribe, Bunker," Clay said with a grin. "We're hoping it'll convince you to spill the beans on Conrad and Krieger. Find out anything?"

"Yes indeedy, I most certainly did. I can't tell you everything, classified stuff, you know, but since your holding out that roast, I guess I'll have to divulge some of it, eh?

"Okay, here we go. Conrad and Krieger have been flying just beneath the radar for a while now. I think you already know Conrad's got a big fleet of oil tankers, and controls the family fortune. He's got friends in high places here, and in the Mideast, especially Qatar. Some of those friends are very shady. He and Krieger have done some work for our CIA, Britain's MI6, and Germany's BND, mostly supplying arms to the rebel groups de jour who are in favor with the west. But not always, and that's raised some eyebrows from time-to-time.

"I got nothing back from BND on your German princess, so either they're holding out or she's clean. That fire at the Cliffs is a different matter. There's something there, but I can't get at it. It's been buried for a long time, and I'm not sure there is any record of what really happened."

Clay smiled broadly. "We may be able to help you with that. Or rather your father may. Susan had him talking again today and he's getting close to telling that story. He almost did today, but something held him back. He said he was tired, but I don't think that's it. Susan came up with a way to pry it loose though. She suggested you stay over tonight and come with us when we see him tomorrow. How about it? Can they do without you up there in DC for a day?"

"Sure, I can arrange that. Question is, will he even recognize me?"

"He's been pretty lucid the last couple of times we've seen him," Susan replied. "I think you ought to try."

"Okay, now that's settled," Clay said, "We've got some news for you, Bunker."

"Uh-oh."

"Yeah, I think what we saw is going to raise more eyebrows, Bunker. Mac and I did a sneak and peek recon at the Foxhaven estate. We found a really extensive tunnel complex inside the bluff under the ruins of The Cliffs. You won't believe what's going on there."

"Try me."

"Well, for starters, we overheard Krieger giving directions to six Muslim terrorists being shipped to a safe house somewhere up in the DC area. One of them, a white guy we call 'Vanilla,' gave them a pep talk before they left. They're definitely here to spill American blood, but he didn't give any details on the where or when. The only hint I got was that they were going to 'slit the throat of Great Satan's future,' if that means anything to you."

"Jesus, Clay."

"Yeah. And we found arms caches in those tunnels too. One big one of modern-day stuff, and one with crates marked with Nazi swastikas. From what your Dad told us today, he saw a big stash in yet another old mine shaft way back in 1941. He thought maybe Conrad's granddad, Gerhard, was training German-American Bund members for the day when Hitler decided to attack the US."

"He never told me anything about that. How'd you get him to open up?"

"The miracle of Susan. The pretty woman has the power to melt a heart of stone, or make an old man smile," Clay said with a laugh.

"Clay! Be serious."

"But I am, honey."

Next morning, Susan led the way into Blakes's room as usual, but this time with Bunker right behind her.

"Hi Blakes," Susan said cheerily as she entered the room. "Look who I've brought to see you today." Blakes looked momentarily confused at the sight of his son, then surprised as he seemed to recognize him. Clay saw the look of relief in Bunker's face. Not knowing whether he'd be remembered had to be hard on the man.

"Bunker, where have you been? It's been so long, boy. Why haven't you come to see me?" Blakes's voice cracked a bit as he spoke. Bunker replied with a slightly pained smile, but decided to say nothing about his recent visits.

"Work. You know, Dad." He put his hand on his father's frail shoulder. "I missed you too. Are they treating you okay here?"

"The food stinks. The nurses are all cold fishes. But she's nice," Blakes said pointing to Susan. Clay and Susan exchanged amused looks.

"Yes, she is. She said you told her about sneaking into that estate back in 1941. How come you never told me about that?"

Blakes said nothing for a moment, thinking it over. "I'm sorry son. You have to understand that I never talked about it because I'm ashamed of what I did. I was young, green, and just plain mad that Nebel was going to get away with helping the Nazis. I went outside the Bureau, and that was wrong. You've got to realize I spent thirty-five years working on the side of the law, catching bad guys. I won't say I never bent any rules to do that, but I didn't do anything like what I did to Nebel again. I should've found another way. I couldn't see how, though, and if anybody had found out, they could've locked me up and thrown away the key. "

"What did you do, Dad?" Bunker asked plaintively.

"I was back up in DC after sneaking onto that estate. I told Susan about that yesterday. Nebel had used his contacts on the Hill to have my partner and I pulled off the case. I didn't know for sure how dirty Nebel was until years later, but I knew he was a closet Nazi and that he was up to no good."

Blakes fell silent for a moment, thinking back to that time....

Agent Johnson lived in a modest bungalow outside DC on the Maryland side. Blakes had parked himself in an easy chair in the sparsely furnished living room Monday evening, soon after returning from his escapades with JJ. Both he and Johnson were still officially on Chief Carswell's enforced "vacation." Johnson returned from the kitchen with two cold, long-necked bottles of beer and stuck one in Blakes's hand.

"Okay, Blakes, what's so all-fired important?"

"You remember JJ, don't you?"

"Sure. The gimpy colored boy. What of it?"

"Do you remember he offered to show us what was going on up there at The Cliffs? Well, I took him up on it."

"You're kidding. That was risky as hell, Blakes. If Carswell finds out, you're goose is cooked. He'll fire you on the spot."

"Yeah, it was damn risky, but wait till you hear what I saw. Gerhard Nebel has a damn castle up there, overlooking a big lake. From what JJ said, he's seen Nazi army officers being flown in by seaplane."

"You believe him? He's just a kid, with a legit axe to grind against Nebel."

"That's not all. JJ and I sneaked into an old mine by the lake. There are four big rooms in it stuffed with crates of small arms, all the crates marked with swastikas. He's got enough to equip a small army. JJ says he's seen those German-American Bund thugs practicing with the equipment out there in the woods."

"Jeez."

"Yeah, Gerhard has to be a goddamned closet Nazi. That notebook we've been chasing might already be gone." The thought made Blakes's blood boil. "But all those crates of Nazi weapons got me thinking. He really could equip a small army, Johnson. I think he's got it stockpiled so that when Hitler finishes with Europe and attacks the US, he'll have an army of German-American traitors ready to help out der Fuhrer any way he can."

"Blakes, that's crazy."

"Sure it's crazy. But it fits. We've got to do something to stop him, I just don't know what."

"Hey, look Blakes. You're my partner and all, but when the master speaks, I listen. Read my lips. We...are...off...the...case, remember?"

"Yeah but this is new information. Carswell's got to change his mind once we tell him what I saw."

"What's with this *we* crap? I like my job, Blakes. What you've got, yeah, that could be what Nebel is up to, but the Bureau knows about his arms smuggling. What Nebel's got is a lot of clout, enough to make you and your suspicions disappear, permanently."

"All right," Blakes said angrily. "If you don't want to get involved, I'll do it myself."

"Don't be a damn fool, Blakes. You're a smart kid. You could go places in the Bureau, but you've got to play the game. There's no way you can nail Nebel now, not without being fired for insubordination."

Blakes face reddened and he slammed his beer bottle down on the coffee table. The worst part was he knew Johnson was right. He either had to shut up, or take it to the bureau and get fired. But he couldn't let go. Too much had already happened. Blakes stood up to leave.

"Think about it, Blakes," Johnson almost pleaded as Blakes stomped out the door without looking back. "Why throw yourself into the fire, when you know Nebel will get away with it anyway?"

Blakes climbed into his '38 Desoto coupe. He sat there fuming for a minute, before starting it. What the hell should he do? Johnson was right. He'd sacrifice his job and in the end, Nebel wouldn't be touched. But he couldn't shake it. The frustration twisted his guts--there *had* to be something he could do.

Blakes started the car, then fiddled with the radio dial in the middle of the dash until he found a station playing an old Jimmy and Tommy Dorsey Orchestra tune, *Chasing Shadows.* That's appropriate, Blakes thought grimly as he shoved the floor shift into first and pulled out into traffic without looking. Screeching tires and a honking horn woke Blakes to the car that had almost plowed into him. Blakes cringed, then yelled out his open window, "Awh, blow it out your ear!" as he stomped on the gas.

Blakes drove aimlessly around Washington, angry and frustrated. The driving helped him think though. Somewhere in the capitol district he came to the obvious conclusion that basically he'd been outgunned by Nebel. That was it, he decided. A guy like Nebel could lie and do just about anything he wanted, because he had the firepower--money, connections, reputation, and lots of people to do his dirty work. He had Blakes outgunned. He even outgunned the FBI, hard as that was for Blakes to swallow. Or at least Nebel had rendered it impotent.

What do I have? Blakes wondered. If I make a move, I won't have a partner or even a job, much less the resources of the FBI behind me. It's just me. All I've got are some shreds of evidence. Information that's worth nothing to me, because I can't use it!

Then another Jimmy Dorsey hit came on the radio, *Pennies From Heaven.* Blakes, driving on Constitution Avenue toward the Capitol, reached forward and turned up the volume. He was just getting into the melody when the announcer broke into the song.

"We interrupt this broadcast for an important news flash. Germany has invaded the Soviet Union across a broad front. I repeat, Germany has broken it's Non-Aggression Pact with the USSR and launched a massive invasion of its former ally. Hitler has committed thousands of tanks, planes, and artillery pieces to the attack. A White House spokesman said that Hitler's decision to go to war on two fronts can only help relieve the pressure on Britain. President Roosevelt is expected to offer the USSR all possible aid in repulsing the invasion."

Blakes's mouth was still wide open with amazement when the stationed returned to *Pennies From Heaven.* "I don't believe it," Blakes said out loud. "Now the commies are going to be our friends! That sure turns the tables."

And in that moment of sheer surprise, as the shock waves of a major upheaval in world affairs washed across him, it hit him. Blakes suddenly knew exactly what to do about Nebel the Nazi. The communists, he knew, will be desperate to hit back at the Germans. Any German. You didn't have to look very far in Washington these days to find a communist, and by God he knew where to find a big fat Kraut target for them. All of a sudden his shreds of evidence might turn the trick, if he talked to the right people. And he didn't need the Bureau to pull it off.

Blakes hit the gas and flew by the Capitol, heading toward his house. He knew just whom to contact and how to do it on the sly. He'd been listening to enough tapes of the man's phone conversations to know he was a firebrand and that he had plenty of friends in the unions. A bunch of commie union thugs ought to do the job just fine. They'd need a pretty big mob to back down the Bund, but once they did, they could tear that castle apart looking for the notebook. They'd be doing their bit for mother Russia by depriving Hitler of a new source of gasoline.

It was well past eleven and pitch dark when Blakes finally spotted Arkady Polaski walking toward him on Thirty-sixth St. in Northeast DC. Blakes took a deep breath. What he was about to do was way out of bounds, illegal even, but if Arkady went for it, Nebel was going to get a real kick in the butt.

"You're late," Blakes growled, trying to take control. Arkady, a big-boned bruiser with thick lips, a pug nose, and a deep voice, was having none of that.

"So? You contacted me, remember? My meeting ran late because we had lots to talk about. I suppose you heard the news too...Is that why you called? To tell me we are allies now and the FBI will no longer be spying on me?"

"You're a real piece of work, Arkady, know that?" Blakes said in a comradely way. "Yes, I called you, and yes, it looks like we're both going to be fighting the Nazis. Look, I have some important information I think you'll want. This is only by way of suggestion, it's not official, but it could benefit us both."

"Go on."

"I happen to have information about a Nazi spy, a very wealthy man, who very likely has possession of a critical secret, a process for making synthetic gasoline, that the Nazis want very badly. You know they will need huge amounts of gasoline to press their invasion of your country, Arkady. The man is very powerful. Our hands at the FBI are tied. But you have friends--you will need a couple hundred--who could take matters in their own hands."

"A couple hundred! You want us to start a war?"

"No, but it may come to that. Your men must be well armed. We will soon be allies, Arkady, that is certain, and whatever happens the FBI will look the other way. They will have to, or own up to looking the other way when a Nazi was in our midst."

"This isn't official then?"

"No Arkady, it isn't. But I swear to you, I've seen with my own eyes a man who I know had possession of the notebook describing the process escape onto the Nazi's estate. We tried to question the Nazi about his employee, but he has about a hundred German American Bund members guarding the entrance. His friends in Congress made my boss tell me to back off."

"How do you know he is a Nazi?"

"Arkady, he's got a hundred or so wannabe Nazis on his estate with German flags fluttering in the breeze. I've seen with my own eyes a huge stockpile of Nazi small arms, enough to equip a small army, and I have a witness who has secretly watched those wannabes practicing with those weapons. It doesn't get much clearer than that."

"I want to talk to my people. Shall we meet tomorrow? I would call, but you know, Blakes, these days you never know who's listening."

"Okay, tomorrow then. And one more thing, Arkady. I want to go along with you, as a private citizen." Arkady gave him a long look.

"It's your neck, Mister FBI."

Late afternoon two days later, a dozen heavy trucks, borrowed surreptitiously by members of Local 435 of the Amalgamated Freight Haulers Union, snaked up the access road toward the gatehouse guarding the entrance to The Cliffs estate. Blakes sat up front in the lead truck with Arkady, worried about how this would play out, but hoping for the best. On the one hand, he was amazed at how quickly Arkady had assembled nearly two hundred armed men, on the other, a bit scared by how easy it had been.

He'd had a look at Arkady's army. They were a tough-looking bunch, probably veterans of attacks by strikebreakers and company cops. Most were armed with hunting rifles or pistols, the rest with baseball bats and clubs. They'd do fine if it came to a fight, but Blakes was hoping the outnumbered Nazis would cave and give up once they saw what they were up against.

Apparently, they'd caught Nebel by surprise. There were only four burly looking men at the gate. One ran into the estate manager's house, while the other three tried to hold up the convoy. Surrounded by ten beefy communists with rifles, the Bund wannabes decided to head for the hills. With that, the convoy headed up the road to the mansion.

What they couldn't know was that the telephone in The Cliffs was now ringing off the hook. The butler answered and seconds later rushed to inform Gerhard that a small army of thugs approached by the main road. They didn't have much time, so Detter, the middleman for the Nazi Abwehr, ran to the nearby Bund encampment and ordered the men to take up positions inside the mansion. Weapons and ammunition, he told them, were being brought up from the basement. Gerhard, meanwhile ordered his wife, his fifteen-year-old son, Klaus, and the women servants to be ready to escape by the secret passage to the dock below. Gerhard went to his gun cabinet in the study and grabbed a hunting rifle. Then he poured himself a glass of brandy.

The convoy came to a halt in line a few hundred feet from the mansion itself. In truth, Arkady and the others were awestruck at the imposing edifice. The turreted stone mansion was three stories high with tall windows, carved stone ornamentation, and tall chimneys poking at the sky. Rifle barrels protruded from not a few of the windows. The communists began dismounting from the trucks, milling about, muttering in amazement that anyone would squander so much on such a grandiose house.

Blakes turned to Arkady. “Shouldn’t you have the trucks pull alongside each other up on the lawn. Your men can use them for cover if the shooting starts,” Blakes said quietly, nodding at the rifle barrels aimed their way. Arkady passed the word and the trucks quickly jockeyed into position. Blakes stepped forward with a megaphone and called out to the mansion.

“You in there. We’re here for that notebook Neil Mueller brought onto this estate. That’s stolen U.S. government property. Bring it out and no one will be harmed.” Blakes didn’t think it wise to say anything about confiscating the arms cache. One thing at a time.

With the trucks now arrayed before the back of the mansion and Arkady’s men huddled around them, a tense stand-off dragged on for several minutes, each side taking the other’s measure. Blakes heard the rattling of cases of bottles behind the trucks, but it didn’t register. He focused on making another attempt at talking to Nebel’s people.

“I repeat,” he bellowed. “The notebook is stolen property of the US government. Neil Mueller, I know you are in there. Come out with the notebook now!”

“Get off my property now,” Gerhard Nebel yelled out his study window, which faced the semicircle of trucks. His voice was slurred and tinged with alcoholic rage. “Do you hear me? I am ordering you off my property. If you do not leave, I will kill you.”

Blakes raised his megaphone again. This time he saw Gerhard in his study window raise his rifle.

“Throw down your weapons and bring out the notebook--” Alarmed, Blakes saw Gerhard draw a bead on him and ducked just as the Nazi fired. The bullet smashed harmlessly into the grill of a truck, but Blakes got the message--and got the hell out of the line of fire. So did everybody else. Gunfire erupted from the mansion's windows, and was answered by a hail of bullets from around the trucks. The crackle of rifle fire and sound of shattering glass rang in Blakes' ears as he ducked in behind the truck for cover. He deliberately had not brought a weapon, though he regretted that decision now.

He noticed the boxes of bottles on the ground behind the trucks. Men were laughing as they lighted the rags hanging limply from the tops of the gasoline filled bottles. Blakes' heart sank. This was already out of control, and there was nothing he could do now. Of course, he should have known. Communists wouldn't hesitate to resort to Molotov cocktails. The men sprinted off to the sides of the trucks and with mighty heaves tossed the lighted bottles of gasoline at the windows. The first two fell short, but the next wave of four men risked getting closer and managed to get a couple through a broken window. One of Arkady's men was shot in the back and fell to the ground. Flames erupted inside the mansion.

Blakes saw Arkady and one of the men talking heatedly, while Arkady pointed at the study window where Gerhard was firing. A moment later the truck careened toward the mansion. The driver jumped clear before it bumped up the low steps onto a stone patio and crashed into the double French doors of Gerhard's study. A bright flash flared inside followed by angry roar of exploding dynamite. Huge chunks of rock from the back wall of the mansion rained down on the lawns and gardens and smoke belched from the gaping hole created by the blast. A part of all three floors and the roof collapsed into the basement levels below.

Blakes scrambled over to Arkady. "My God, Arkady! What have you done!"

"Your dirty work, Blakes. Your dirty work," he sneered.

"Jesus, you didn't have to--" The mansion was now fully engulfed in flames and smoke, a wrecked and burning funeral pyre for anyone still inside. Men of the Bund could be seen fleeing into the woods, while the communists laughed heartily and let them go.

"What, did you really think he was going to bring your precious notebook out and just give it to you? This is war, Blakes, and we won this battle. We came prepared for it, and you saw. They started shooting first. And I tell you this. If that notebook is in that hellhole, it will not be helping those stinking Nazis."

"Do you think your man made the phone call we talked about?"

"Yes, Mister FBI, the call was made at the exact time from my telephone, and by now your people have sent your brother agents speeding this way. And, yes, they will know where to look for at least one cache of Nazi weapons. No doubt they will go over what's left of that castle with a fine-tooth comb, if I know your J. Edgar Hoover. They will not like what they find, I'm sure, about the very respectable Gerhard Nebel.

"Then we'd better get going. Things could get very complicated if they find us here."

"A shame we won't get to see the headline--*Soviets Win Big Victory In First Battle Against Nazi's US Invasion*." He laughed heartily at that.

Blakes seemed to come back from his reverie as he reached out to touch Bunker' arm.

"That phone call did the trick. I knew Arkady's line was tapped, and it couldn't have been an hour after we cleared out that the first FBI teams arrived and sealed off the estate. They didn't even call in fire trucks. They just let that mansion burn itself out. Then they cleared out the munitions from that mine shaft, but looked no further. The newspapers got fed puff pieces on Nebel's tragic death in an accidental fire. Covered up the whole thing."

"Not a good day for the government, I suppose," Bunker responded.

"No, and not for me either, son. It was all so confusing. Those were really strange times, what with Hitler smashing the hell out of Europe. That cover-up was a black mark against the Bureau, as far as I was concerned, but considering what was happening, that made it easier to accept. I hated going outside the Bureau like that.

"Awh, Dad, you did the right thing. It's never easy."

"I know that, Bunker. I'd probably do it again, if I had to." He smiled weakly at Bunker. "I'm tired, son. Can you come again tomorrow? We can talk some more." He really was tired. He'd never told anyone about what happened at the Cliffs, other than Weiss, and it was a struggle to do so now. But as before, he really had no choice.

"You know I want to, Dad, but I've got to fly back to DC today. Duty calls. I'll be back in a few days. We'll talk then, okay?" Blakes nodded and smiled wearily as Bunker, Susan, Clay, and Mac filed out of the room.

Minutes later all four stood around Mac's Lexus in the parking lot, talking. Clay, Susan, and Mac all seemed energized, trying to assimilate what they'd heard. Bunker seemed distracted, distant.

"Do you suppose this is what Weiss wanted us to know about when he told me to 'Find Blakes Hill?'" Clay wondered. "That was some story about Nebel's grandfather."

"It's sure got me wondering about Conrad Nebel," Bunker replied. "Maybe double dealing runs in the family genes."

"Skipped a generation, though, from the looks of it. Conrad's father is clean, isn't he?" Mac asked.

"Nothing that I've heard. Maybe he was just better at not getting caught. I'll check into it when I get back to DC. Klaus Nebel, right?"

"Yes, Klaus," Susan replied. "I can't believe that Conrad would do such a thing. With all that money and power, why would he even want to?"

"More money, maybe--just plain greed. That and the kicks of getting away with it. Like Bunker said, it may run in the family."

"I still don't see how Weiss got mixed up in this," Mac said.

"I wondered about that too," Clay replied. "Maybe Blakes will tell Bunker. *He's* got the best chance of getting it out of him." He gave Bunker a friendly nudge on the shoulder. "Is something the matter, Bunker? You're Dad really seemed to open up to you today."

"Yeah, he did," Bunker replied sadly. "It's just that it's so hard to see him and know that next time he may not know me. Or anybody."

"All you can do, Bunker, is make the most of the time you've got with him."

"I keep telling myself that." He forced a smiled and the four then got into their respective vehicles. They drove off with no idea that Blakes had been watching them from his room. He sat upright on the bed, his feet dangling over the edge, rubbing his chin as though lost in thought. He had been careful to sit well back from the window, so he wouldn't be seen.

13

LOVE AND WAR

Surrounded by thousands of books filling tall, built-in bookcases on three sides of his study, Conrad leaned back in his desk chair, the telephone to his ear, admiring the crisp orderliness of his gleaming mahogany desktop. The deep reddish brown wood was inlaid with a central starburst--compass points actually--alternating rays made of pale, almost white maple and stark black ebony veneers, and all of it was overlaid by a thick sheet of glass. The design resonated in him, it was at once the world and his destiny. Little else enjoyed the luxury of being on that desktop: a marble pen holder and two pictures in gold gilt frames--one of his deceased mother, the larger of the two, and the other of Princess Maria as a smiling teenager. Everything else had its place in a drawer or in the hands of his servants.

"Yes, Valerie, that is very good news. But I must ask, you're sure that they achieved a fully functioning device? No more false starting, no explosions?" He smiled broadly. "And what is the estimated service life of this device?... Indefinite?" His brow wrinkled with some concern. "Come now, Valerie, let's be practical. There has never been anything that produces energy without being refueled. All right, well, let's say a year and be safe." He put his hand to the back of his head, gently massaging his neck. "Now, just so I'm sure, I have to ask you again. You have a copy of all the necessary drawings, formulas, and specifications? This is very important. We must have everything necessary to duplicate it, to build a working model. No, now I told you, you cannot be involved with that. Just deliver the plans and you can disappear with more money than you ever dreamed possible.So give everything to Krieger when he arrives. Do not hold anything back. Our friend will not pay for promises, and he can be singularly vicious when angered."

Conrad nodded his head. "You will be very, very rich, Valerie, that I promise. I'm going to make the call to the money man personally, as soon as I hang up."

Minutes later, Conrad's call went through to the Qatari embassy in Washington, DC.

"Please connect me with Sa'id...Sa'id, this is Conrad. I'm calling to invite you to the ball. You'll pass the word along? Yes, I've received word that it's definitely on now." He smiled and hung up.

It was risky making that call. There would be no turning back now. But Conrad had waited as long as he could stand for this moment--ever since meeting Valerie at a Symposium of Concerned Scientists. At last, the time had come. He stood up and turned to look out the window, then threw back his shoulders. He swelled with pride. One has to take risks, he thought, but--my God--the rewards!

This would be the biggest deal he had ever attempted, worth probably trillions of dollars ultimately, the deal of the century! It all rode on deception and timing, and it was dangerous, but this was how family fortunes were made. All the pieces had fallen into place, and he, Conrad Nebel, would be the big, big winner in this game. The only shame was that his role as mastermind would never be known outside the family, beyond whispers of suspicion of course.

The prospect of reaping his huge reward steeled him for breaking the news to Sir. His father would not be happy, would rail against it, but would be powerless to stop it. In some ways, defying Sir meant more to Conrad than even the money, a primal satisfaction at having complete control at last. To be master.

He mounted the staircase on his way to Sir's suite with determined steps and gave only a perfunctory knock before barging into the outer room. Sir, seated as usual in his wheelchair at the window overlooking the grounds, scowled at Conrad's sudden intrusion.

"Sir, I have news," Conrad said with a smile, the more so for having noticed his father's irritation. "Wentworth has succeeded at last. His lab assistant tells me the LENR device reliably produces heat without refueling for a year or more."

"Bah! Such things are not possible. And if they were, everyone would be building the contraptions. What good will that do you?"

"That's where you are wrong, Sir. *I* have a way of beating the Chinese at their own game. My spy!" Conrad announced with great satisfaction. "Very soon they will eagerly agree to pay me a fortune for my copy of the device specifications. I'm going to hold out for a trillion dollars, plus ten percent of the gross from licensing and manufacture of the equipment."

"Why should they do that?"

"Because," Conrad revealed with great satisfaction, "*I* will have the only copy of that information."

"Here?" A sudden fright caused his voice to quaver.

"Yes, Krieger will bring it to me. It's much too valuable to be left anywhere else."

"You fool! Have you forgotten what happened to your grandfather? Do you want to bring that down on us again?"

"That will not happen. *I will not let it*," he said with a touch of bravado.

*   *   *   *

Early afternoon found Mac in Harrisonburg, knocking on the door of Fayaq Khan's other uncle, Azziz, whom the police had been unable to contact for an interview. It seemed like a desperate ploy at this point, but Mac would do anything to help Clay. With the trial scheduled to resume in three days, conventional wisdom might have said that the man had skipped town to avoid a police interview, so that the false testimony against Clay would stay alive. Why else would he leave his convenience store shuttered with no word as to his whereabouts? Meanwhile, Khan's other uncle, the one in Staunton, continued to back Khan's story to the hilt. Mac was about to give up when he spotted a neighbor across the street watering his flower garden. Mac went over to him.

"Excuse me, I'm trying to get in touch with Mr. Khan. Do you know when he'll be back?"

"Maybe never." The middle-aged black man continued with the watering.

"What?"

"I heard a commotion over there a few nights ago. Then I saw him leave with two strangers. Haven't seen him since."

"Strangers? Could they have been friends? Maybe his nephew Fayaq Khan was one of them."

"No, I'd know Fayaq. It wasn't him, and I know Azziz wouldn't go away with him anyway."

"Why's that?"

"I know Azziz. He is my neighbor, but he is also a member of my mosque here in Harrisonburg and a good friend. We talked all the time. Azziz is very unhappy with Fayaq because the boy has turned to radicalism. The last straw was when Fayaq went to Yemen to fight with the militants there."

"He did? When was that?"

"Last summer. June, July, around then."

"Really. That's very interesting. Thank you, sir, you've been very helpful."

"I don't know what I did, but I am happy to help. I only wish Azziz would come home. I worry about him disappearing like that."

"You might want to tell the police what you saw. It may be nothing. I hope it is, for his sake, but...."

Mac was heading back toward the interstate and the half hour ride home to Staunton when he spotted Susan's Volvo up ahead.

"Awh, Susan. Not again."

She was three cars ahead after turning onto Route 11 heading south. This time Mac entertained no thoughts of catching up and telling her the good news. He followed until she turned into a motel on the south edge of town, as he knew she would. Then he worked his way back to I-81 south.

He felt terrible about what this would do to Clay. His friend was ass over tea kettle in love with the woman, but the worst part about it was that Mac couldn't avoid telling Clay any longer. He couldn't rationalize it away as a one shot slip-up, and he knew damn well it wasn't Clay she was seeing in that motel room.

He called Clay on the way back to Staunton, relaying the good news that Fayaq may have been in Yemen when he supposedly saw Clay driving around in his truck that night. He said nothing about seeing Susan at a motel. Clay immediately put in a call to Bunker asking for confirmation that Fayaq had been out of the country during July, when the murder occurred. It really came down to when, and whether Fayaq had travelled using his own passport.

Mac decided what to do about Susan while returning to Staunton. It made him sick to his stomach, but he saw no way out. He had to tell Clay, and the sooner he got it over with the better. Instead of going home, he headed directly to the mill house. He only hoped he'd get there before Susan arrived, so that he'd have a chance to catch Clay alone.

Mac pulled up alongside the mill at four-thirty and to his relief, there was no sign of Susan's car. Mac let himself in, but Clay was nowhere to be seen. Then he spotted the open door to the stairway leading down to the floors below. The next floor down, where the grain hoppers and grindstones were located, was empty too. Mac continued down to the bottom level, where the shaft for the waterwheel came in and power was transferred to the floor above by a tangle of large wooden gears and shafts. Mac called out, "Clay, are you here?"

"Over here, Mac," Clay replied as he stood up from behind the idled main shaft of the water wheel. "Just checking my traps. It's getting cold out and the field mice are looking for places to bed down for winter."

Clay practically beamed as he climbed out from behind the shaft. "You'll never guess what, Mac. Bunker called back. Fayaq was out of the country from the beginning of June to the middle of August. Nick was murdered in the third week of July, so I'm in the clear. The prosecutor says when the trial resumes, he's going to get Fayaq back on the stand and then crucify him in front of Womack. He says he's going to prosecute Fayaq for perjury too."

"He damn well should. That's great news, Clay. I'll bet you're relieved."

"Yeah, man. Having something like that hanging over you really grinds you down. Anyway, it's finally over. Susan and I are going out to celebrate tonight. Do you and Rita want to come along?"

"No, we'll pass on that. So where is Susan?"

"Out showing a client houses."

"Was that up in Harrisonburg?"

"I don't know, why?"

"Clay, I didn't want to have to tell you this..." Mac stumbled and fell silent for a moment. "Jeez, this is hard...Clay, you're not going to believe this. I didn't at first, but I've seen Susan going into a motel room twice now. Once in Charlottesville, and then today up in Harrisonburg."

Thunderstruck, Clay was speechless for a moment. "What are you saying, Mac?" he asked plaintively.

"I know you really care for her, Clay--God, I hate this--Clay, I think she's doing some guy on the side. Two-timing you. Maybe it's a client she's seeing."

"I don't believe you, Mac. Why...?" Clay's life lately had been nothing short of a roller coaster ride, and what Mac told him pulled the rug out. Then his face reddened and he growled angrily. "You're either mistaken, or just making this up. I don't know why you'd do that, but--"

"I'm not making this up, Clay. And it's no mistake. It was her Volvo I followed to a motel, twice. Same color, same license plate. Everything. The first time, I saw her get out and walk to the room. I waited for fifteen minutes, and she didn't come back out. Maybe she *was* in there getting a client to sign a contract. I really wish it was that. Once maybe, but twice?"

Clay stared at Mac, unsure what to think. He and Mac had been friends for so many years, he couldn't believe Mac would do anything to stab him in the back. But Susan? How could she do something like that? He was going to marry her, for Christ's sake. His gut twisted. She was a beautiful woman after all, and she would have plenty of opportunities for an affair if she wanted. But God, how could she?"

"I'm sorry man," Mac said mournfully. "I really didn't want to say anything, but I didn't want you to be blindsided either."

"Mac, I think you'd better go. I want to talk to Susan alone when she gets here." Mac didn't argue. This was the last place he wanted to be.

Clay was not a man to be caught in emotional crosscurrents. He knew well enough that life could not be all black and white, but for him, action was the key. Decide, pick one path, move forward. But right now he didn't know what he should do. No way seemed forward.

Susan didn't arrive until late and it was almost dark when she walked into the kitchen, where Clay sat drinking his fifth beer. He answered her cheery "Hi, hon" with a vacant stare and took another swig of beer.

"How did it go today? Did Mac find anything out?" she asked, suddenly worried that the news had not been good.

"He sure did. Good news and bad."

"What?"

"Turns out that lying kid was out of the country when Nick was murdered. Bunker checked and found out he was in Yemen. So I'm off the hook."

"Oh, Clay, that's wonderful," Susan gushed. She wanted to kiss him, but he was acting so strangely that she held back.

"That's not all. Were you up in Harrisonburg today?" he asked pointedly.

"What? What's this about, Clay?" His tone hurt and confused her. Clay was a different person, and she didn't know why.

"I said," he spit the words out angrily, "Were you up in Harrisonburg today?"

"No, Clay, of course not! Why the third degree?" She was frightened and angry all at once. Something was really wrong.

"That's funny. Mac says he saw you when he was up there this afternoon. He followed you to that motel you went to."

"I what! Now wait just a minute. I don't know who Mac saw, but *it was not me!*"

"Where were you then, Susan?" he droned like a prosecutor.

"This afternoon? Waiting to show a client a listing. But he never showed." Getting angry now at Clay's attitude, Susan's face tightened.

"Mac says he saw you going into a motel in Charlottesville too."

"I did not! Clay, do you really think I'm having an affair with somebody? My God, I love you. We're going to be married. How can you think that of me?"

"Mac wouldn't lie."

"Neither would I, Clay," she yelled, fuming now. "You're going to have to make up your mind, Clay. If you can't believe me, then maybe we should call off the engagement."

Her anger, and her threat startled Clay. There was a time when he could have walked away from any woman, but she meant too much to him now. What he wanted was for this problem to go away, because he didn't know what he should do. Or what he could do. There was no way to prove, or disprove what Mac had said. He didn't want to believe any of it, yet there was that dagger of nagging doubt.

"No, I don't want that."

"Well," she replied indignantly, "that's so nice of you." She could see he'd been drinking, and that made her even madder. "I'll tell you what I don't want. I don't want to be here with you tonight. I'm going home."

With that, she stormed out, slamming the door behind her. Clay sat there for a long time staring at the doorway leading out of his kitchen. Then he finished his beer, and had another. And others, until he was so drunk he fell asleep at the kitchen table.

* * * *

The innocent-looking white step van turned into the Halston Technological Park about 3 p.m. that same day. Dozens of those delivery vans entered and left the park all week long, though this one bore no company name or logo. Scrupulously observing the twenty-five-mile-per-hour speed limit on the wide, tree-lined boulevard leading into the park, the driver signaled a left turn onto the access road leading to the Babcock Chemical Co. laboratory. Then he turned to say something into the open doorway to van's cargo area.

Vanilla smiled and pulled down his black ski mask. As one, the ten other terrorists pulled down their masks. It was finally going to happen. Nothing could stop them now. They had practiced this hundreds of times during the long months of preparation, yet the air in the step van was electric with the tension. Vanilla and his Hamas brethren nervously checked their AK-47s. Moments later the van came to a stop and the driver gave the signal as he too pulled a black ski mask over his head.

Spilling out of the van, eight of the terrorists stormed into the building with Vanilla in the lead. Two remained out front, while another two sprinted around the back and to cover the rear exit. Their timing was perfect. They had the entire lab staff inside.

Prof. Wentworth and Dan were discussing their patent application when they heard the screams and breaking glass in the laboratory proper. Alarmed, Wentworth had only time enough to stand up from his desk before the black masked terrorist appeared in his office door.

"What the hell is the meaning of this?" Wentworth cried out. The sneering face behind the mask scared the hell out of him but said nothing. Instead the terrorist barged into the office and waved his submachine gun barrel, shooing them out into the hallway.

"Dan, we'd better do what he wants."

"I'm not arguing with that," Dan said, pointing at the gun barrel.

The terrorist marched them into the lab, poking the gun barrel into Wentworth's back. Wentworth was horrified. Valerie sat on the floor, crying and wiping blood from her nose. Babeesh and another lab assistant, Joseph, stood against the back wall, guarded by a terrorist. One terrorist operated a small video camera as Wentworth was marched into the lab.

"Valerie, what happened?"

"He hit me," she sobbed. "I didn't do anything. He hit me."

"Shut up!" an obviously agitated Vanilla shouted. "All of you, get up against that wall, now!." The man with the camera moved off to an angle to capture both Vanilla and his captives in the shot. When the cameraman was in position, it seemed Vanilla began talking more for the camera than his prisoners.

"Allah akbar! You Godless infidels are now prisoners of the Islamic State of Iraq and the Levant. We have confiscated this place in the name of the all-powerful and all-knowing Allah, our lord and master. For your sins of disbelieving Allah and conspiring to oppose his will, you shall be executed here and now."

"Ridiculous. This is America! You can't do this!" Prof. Wentworth cried out. Valerie sobbed loudly.

"Silence, infidels!" The barrel of his AK 47 came up. Oblivious, Valerie kept on crying. Prof. Wentworth stepped forward from the wall as the terrorist pulled the trigger, spraying Valerie with a blizzard of bullets. She loosed a bloodcurdling scream before toppling over face first onto the floor. The cameraman stepped forward to get a closeup of her bloodied corpse, and then panned to capture the terrified looks on the prisoner's faces.

"Please! Ouh, please, in the name of God, please don't do this!" Babeesh cried out.

Vanilla pointed at him and another of the terrorists stepped forward. With a powerful roundhouse swing, he smashed his gun butt into Babeesh's jaw, sending him flying.

"He's got a wife and three children--" Wentworth shouted. He too was smashed in the face with the gun butt.

Vanilla turned to another of the grinning terrorists, who were so obviously enjoying this complete domination of the hated, cowering Americans. "Get the explosives from the truck and start setting the charges," Vanilla ordered. "Gather up all the files and paperwork you can find. They must be burned first. Do you hear that infidels? You and your satanic works will be wiped off the face of this earth! Allah commands it!" Pointing to the sobbing Babeesh, he commanded, "He will be first!"

The terrorist who had hit Babeesh reached down and grabbed him by the hair and pulled the poor man to his knees. Babeesh shook uncontrollably as the cameraman stepped in close to record his sufferings. Vanilla calmly pulled out his .45-caliber sidearm and touched its barrel to Babeesh's forehead.

"In the name of all that is great in Allah, I condemn you all to death as infidels." With that he began to torture the whimpering Babeesh by lightly dragging the gun barrel around to various parts of his face, stopping for a moment in each place, as though trying to decide where and when to fire, and by his sneering smile, thoroughly enjoying his victim's abject fear. Finally, he let the gun barrel linger on Babeesh's left eye. Sheer terror contorted poor Babeesh's face for an instant before Vanilla squeezed the trigger. Babeesh's head jerked back at the loud bang. Blood and brains splattered onto Wentworth and the other prisoners.

"You bastard," Dan yelled as he wiped the blood from his face.

Vanilla pointed at him and yelled, "You, you're next. Down on your knees, infidel!"

While the cameraman zoomed in, a terrorist drove his gun butt into Dan's stomach, doubling him over. The terrorist then grabbed his hair, drove him to his knees, and then held his head up so that the cameraman could get a close-up of his face. Dan grimaced, shouted "Screw you!" and spit onto the lens. The gun butt crashed into Dan's head, knocking him unconscious. While the cameraman wiped the spittle from his lens, Vanilla shot the unconscious Dan in the head. The video would have to do with one less execution.

With the cameraman now filming again, Vanilla unsheathed a long bladed knife and pointed to Prof. Wentworth. "Allah has commanded that you shall be punished in a way that will demonstrate to all how we will deal with your crimes against Islam." He waved his free hand and the gun wielding terrorist grabbed Prof. Wentworth, dragging him to a lab bench. Vanilla swept the surface clear and helped pull the struggling Wentworth up onto the bench so that his head hung over the edge....

Late that afternoon, Moktar gently placed the receiver in its cradle at the All Islamic Friendship Center and with a broad smile looked up at the dozen or so of his followers crowded into his office.

"Allah Akbar! It is done. A complete success!" Then he grinned. "Film at eleven." That drew roars of laughter.

"Were any of ours lost?" a bearded follower asked Moktar when the laughter subsided.

"No, they are all safe. They are on their way south now, and will remain there in hiding for a time. They may be needed to deal with our friend." He smiled again. "The laboratory was completely demolished by the explosives. On its way out, our van passed by the police and fire trucks heading to the scene. The infidel fools were in such a hurry to get there, they never noticed it."

They again broke out laughing and, swelled by the victory, they exchanged gleeful smiles. Moktar let them savor the moment, then asked to be left alone to make the call to Qatar. He wanted to deliver the good news personally.

*   *   *   *

The sun was setting when Bunker's helicopter landed in an open space at the Halston Technological Park. The computer alert he'd received an hour earlier was still fresh in his mind. That was a moment he wouldn't soon forget. When the location of the terrorist attack popped up on his computer screen, Bunker suddenly realized his mistake. Embarrassed, angry, saddened, he was sure now that he probably could have prevented the attack, if only he'd taken notice of where Weiss's murdered neighbor worked--the victim had been a lab assistant in that lab at Halston. Weiss had worked for Babcock Chemical until his retirement and probably got wind of something from his neighbor that made him suspicious. And probably got him killed.

Weiss's neighbor was a Muslim. Bunker speculated now that the terrorists had tried to pressure the neighbor into helping. When he refused, they killed him. One thing was certain, the terrorists were rolling up the entire research operation. On the flight over from DC, he'd received an update from his office. The Babcock Chemical VP in charge of the Halston lab never made it into work today. They found him brutally murdered at his suburban New Jersey home at two o'clock that afternoon. His throat had been slit and he'd been left to bleed out. His wife had been murdered too.

These were not nice people Bunker was dealing with, and the sight of the smoldering remains of the laboratory building only confirmed their determination. Fire trucks, police vehicles, and the coroner's van were still on the scene when Bunker walked up to the FBI agent in charge of the crime scene and flashed his ID.

The explosions had reduced the large, one-story brick building to a heap of rubble and debris. Only a few sections of wall remained standing, stubble here and there no more than a few feet high. Rubble had been blown outward in a fifty foot radius.

"Jesus, what a mess," Bunker groaned. "Did anybody survive?"

"Nobody got out of that alive. The M.E. is still picking body parts out of the wreckage. Terrorists, for sure. We found a white van they used ditched alongside the road a few miles away. The lab boys are going over it, but from what I've heard so far, it's super clean. These guys knew what they were doing."

"I don't suppose you know what kind of research went on here?"

"We're checking. Looks like the terrorists burned all the files before they blew the place up. So far, all we've got from people in the surrounding buildings is that it was some kind of energy research. Very hush-hush. Nobody was allowed to talk about it."

"I suppose you know the Babcock Chemical VP in charge of this project was found murdered today," Bunker said.

"No, I didn't."

"Yeah, these guys were really thorough. There's nothing on this project at the headquarters in New Jersey, and nothing in the VP's house. So whatever they were working on has been lost. At least for now. If you come up with anything, I'd appreciate a heads up."

"We'll find out. And sooner or later we'll catch the bastards who did this."

"Let's hope so."

*   *   *   *

From her bedroom window early the next morning, Maria spotted a long, white limousine pulling up in front of Foxhaven. Thinking it was the Qatari oil sheik, she decided to risk another visit to the secret passage. Something was afoot, she could feel it in the air. Uncle Conrad had seemed like a changed man at dinner last night. He was practically celebrating. She pushed the carved cherub on her fireplace mantel upwards and disappeared into the secret passageway. She had just reached the peephole over the library when Conrad led his visitors in. What she saw surprised her.

Conrad, followed closely by Krieger, took seats on the couch with their backs to her. Two well-dressed Chinese men, one older and the other middle aged, took seats opposite them. What were they doing here? she wondered.

"Too bad about your man getting killed yesterday. Was he able to pass along anything at all?" Conrad asked, though he already knew the answer.

"We would not be here," the middle-aged Chinaman replied stiffly, keeping his anger in check, "if he had. But then you know that. Probably even knew it *would* happen." He did not add that the Pakistani's price would have been far lower, had they not insisted on waiting until the device had been fully tested.

Conrad shrugged and raised his palms upward, feigning innocence. "I sometimes hear things," he admitted, "but too often it is not enough to know what is going to happen, much less when and to whom.

"As it happens," he continued coyly, "that which you seek has by chance fallen into my lap. I am not a disagreeable man, Quan Lee. I think we can arrive at an equitable agreement. Wentworth's LENR device will solve China's energy problems for centuries to come, and unlike your friend, I can offer you exclusive control of the discovery. It will make you and your country very rich. Think how that will change your country's position with regard to the United States, what it will do for the prestige of the Communist Party. Not many people in our history have had the opportunity to so quickly and directly alter the course of their country's, the world's future. What I ask in return is but a small price to pay."

The two Chinese men looked at each other. "What is your price?" the older man asked.

"My price," Conrad said, looking directly into the eyes of the older Chinese man with as pleasant a smile as he could muster, "is $500 billion up front, $500 billion on acceptance, plus ten percent of the gross profit from licensing and manufacture of the devices."

"Your price is perhaps overly ambitious but not beyond the realm of possibility, Mr. Nebel, if the device works as well as you say."

"It does, and I think you already know that. As a gesture of faith, I am willing to turn over to you everything you need to re-create Wentworth's device. In return, I ask that your government deposit $500 billion in my Swiss bank account, before I give you the plans. The balance will come due within six months of the successful operation of the device."

"And if it can't be made to operate?"

"Then I shall return your $500 billion and move on to the next bidder. You see," Conrad said, exuding as much confidence as he possibly could, "I know the device works, and what it would be worth to the country that can successfully market it."

"I think $250 billion and five percent of gross profits is more likely to gain my government's approval."

"I'm sure of that Hwang Ho. But the price is $1 trillion US dollars, $500 billion up front, and *ten* percent. Take it or leave it."

"Perhaps you would consider payment in U.S. Treasury bonds."

"Is that an attempt at inscrutable oriental humor?"

"Not entirely," Hwang Ho said with a sly grin. "But no matter. I will pass along your demands to my government. We should have an answer for you in a few days, but I trust you will allow us to extend that, if it becomes necessary. We are talking a *trillion*."

"My preference is to deal with your government, Hwang Ho, so long as it does not become clear to me that your people are stalling. And I should emphasize the importance of secrecy. My Qatari and Iranian friends and their people want very much to maintain the primacy of oil and their lucrative place in the scheme of things, not to mention using it as a lever against the rest of the world. They would be very, very angry if they found out they had been used by you, I can assure you of that, Hwang Ho."

"At you, I should say," Quan Lee said with a knowing smile.

"Should they find that out, they would soon discover your role in it as well. Might I suggest that it would be to our mutual benefit, if they remained in the dark? Later, you could publicize the discovery as the work of your intrepid Chinese scientists."

Hwang Ho smiled at the thought.

Soon after seeing the Chinese off, Conrad and Krieger returned to the library in very good spirits.

"Let's have a brandy to celebrate, Krieger. A toast to a successful venture. They will try haggling some more, but they will pay my price in the end." He retrieved a bottle of brandy from a cupboard, poured two glasses, and handed one to Krieger. They clinked glasses.

"Here's to the Chinaman's deep pockets." After taking a healthy swallow, Conrad looked around, assessing the possibilities. "That file is not so large. Where do you think I should hide it?"

Krieger coughed but managed to swallow. "You haven't got it locked up in the safe?"

"Nonsense, Krieger. That's the first place they'd look. No, it's in the file drawer of my desk. Hiding in plain sight, as they say." He said it with great satisfaction, enjoying his moment of bravado. Risk piled on risk. The excitement of this game was infectious.

"Conrad, please, that might just be the second place they look."

"Possibly. But they'd have to get to my study first. And..." Conrad laughed, "I filed it out of alphabetical order."

"Really, Conrad. People have been murdered for what's in that file. It should be under an armed guard. At least hide it somewhere safe. Just don't forget where you put it."

"I'll think about it." His mouth turned up in a sly grin. "I suppose we can always use our guests for protection, without telling them what they're protecting, of course."

"Dangerous, Conrad. Very dangerous."

Conrad grinned like a Cheshire cat.

Making her way back to her bedroom, Maria knew she had to do something quickly, but what?

14

JUSTICE, THE PRINCESS, & THE LION'S DEN

Clay was knotting his tie, getting ready for court at nine a.m. when he heard a car pull to a stop in the driveway and a moment later, a loud knock. To his surprise, Conrad's driver greeted him when he opened the door.

"Princess Maria sends her compliments, Mr. Cantrell. She asked that I give you this, and wait for a reply." With that he handed Clay an envelope.

The note read: *My dear Clay. Please accept my apologies for offering this invitation with such short notice, but I should be very pleased if you, Susan, and your friends Mac and Jimmy and their wives would attend a little surprise party I am arranging for Uncle Conrad the day after tomorrow. Dinner and dancing, formal attire. I don't expect more than a hundred will attend. Festivities begin at six o'clock sharp. You would make me so very happy if you would all join us!*

Maria

Clay smiled as he read the note. This is a piece of luck, he thought, especially since Conrad hadn't responded to his request for a meeting about purchasing Fairview--itself just an excuse to ask Maria about Conrad.

"Please tell Maria we will be there," Clay said to Conrad's driver.

At 8:45 that morning Clay walked into the Augusta County Circuit courtroom and took a seat next to Mac and Rita. He felt a sudden pang when he entered the courtroom and did not see Susan there. Three days had passed since their argument, and it seemed there was no end in sight. When he sat down, Rita just gave him a shrug of her shoulders. Mac sat sullenly on Rita's other side.

A long fifteen minutes later, the black robed judge took his seat on the dais, Khan retook the witness stand, and his testimony started anew. Defense attorney Womack had no further questions and turned Khan over to Prosecutor Berelli for cross-examination. Berelli shot Clay a sly glance as he stood to begin his cross, then spent a moment directly in front of Khan pretending to refer to his notes. Then he smiled at Khan, showing rather more teeth than a friendly gesture would warrant.

"Fayaq, Mr. Khan, your legal name is Fayaq Khan, is that correct?"

"Yes sir," he answered with a slightly puzzled look.

"Just to refresh my memory, Mr. Khan, you testified that you are here on a student visa. So you have a passport, is that correct?"

"Of course. I am here legally."

"Do you have it with you?"

"No, I don't carry it with me all the time."

"But you have it somewhere. Can you remember when you last saw it?"

"Exactly?"

"No. Approximately will do."

"Maybe a week ago."

"So you could produce it, if necessary?"

"Oh, yes sir. I am completely legal."

"Good. Then let me make sure I have all my facts straight, Mr. Khan. You testified last week that you saw Mr. Cantrell driving his pickup truck--*in Staunton on Frederick Street*--at about 7:30 p.m., the night of the murder. Is that correct?"

"Yes sir. That's what I said."

"And you further stated that you remembered because he almost hit you?"

"Right. That's when I saw the C&H Construction logo on the truck door," Khan said, trying to bolster his testimony.

"I see. And would you please tell the court exactly where you were at 7:30 p.m. that evening of July 22."

"I told you," Khan said with some agitation. Something was afoot and he couldn't imagine what. He decided to pump up his testimony a bit more. "I was crossing Frederick Street. Okay, so I was in the middle of the block. Is that a crime?" Defense attorney Womack silently mouthed "Don't," but it was too late.

"Well, yes, actually, that is, Mr. Khan. But what I meant was, which country were you in?"

Khan went wide-eyed with shock and his mouth hung open for a moment before he managed, "What do you mean? Here. The United States, of course."

"Is that your sworn testimony, Mr. Khan? Remember you are under oath and that you are giving evidence in a murder trial. You can and will be prosecuted for perjury if you do not tell the truth."

Womack jumped to his feet. "I object, your honor. Prosecutor Berelli is badgering the witness."

"Mr. Prosecutor," the judge intoned as he leaned forward with a scowl directed at Berelli, "Do you have some foundation for this line of questioning?"

"Yes, your honor, I do. If the court will bear with me for a moment more, it will become crystal clear."

"Very well. Overruled. Witness will answer the question."

"Yes, that is my testimony," Khan said weakly.

"Isn't it true that you were, in fact, in Yemen in June, July, and August?"

"No!" Khan protested.

"Your honor," Berelli said holding up a document, "this is a notarized electronic copy of Mr. Khan's passport, obtained from the State Department. It proves he was out of the country from June through mid-August."

Womack jumped to his feet. "Your honor, I object!"

"Counsel, approach the bench," the judge snapped. "Let me see the document, Mr. Berelli." The judge looked it over and handed it to Womack. "Looks genuine, counselor. Your witness is lying."

"Your honor," Womack pleaded defensively, "I had no idea. We checked his story. The uncle he lives with backed his story."

"Yes, he did," Berelli said smugly, "but his other uncle has suddenly disappeared. Maybe we should ask Mr. Khan what happened to him. As I understand it, that uncle was unhappy about Mr. Khan's radical ideas--"

"Mr. Berelli, this is not the time for such speculation," the judge interrupted with irritation.

"Your honor," Berelli replied insistently, "at the very least, I would like this witness's testimony stricken from the record. And I ask the court to arrest him on suspicion of perjury."

"Your honor!" Womack protested.

"Sit down, both of you. Now, in light of this evidence, it is clear that the witness has lied about seeing Mr. Cantrell on the night in question. So, I am ordering that his testimony be stricken from the record. Jury is ordered to disregard Mr. Khan's entire testimony. Bailiff, I want Mr. Khan arrested on suspicion of perjury."

A wild-eyed Khan bolted out of the witness chair and charged right through the bailiff's arms, almost knocking him over. The judge bellowed, "Stop that man!" as Khan sprinted to the low wooden partition and laid on both hands to vault over it. In the same instant, both Clay and Mac stood up from their front row seats and stepped forward, a solid wall of muscle that caught Khan in mid-flight and slammed him to the ground. Mac put his size twelve foot on Khan's back, restraining the still struggling liar until the bailiff could cuff him and drag him out of the courtroom.

The judge banged his gavel through the entire altercation, demanding "Order in the Court!" to no avail, until at last the big oak exit doors slammed shut behind the still-struggling Khan. "Mr. Womack," he asked finally, "does the defense have any further witnesses?"

"No sir," a visibly embarrassed Womack answered. "Defense rests."

"Very well. We'll begin closing arguments now. And let's keep it on point, gentlemen. I've seen enough theatrics for one day."

Clay turned to Mac and Rita and whispered, "Let's get out of here now." As they stood to leave, Clay saw George look over from the defense table. Clay smiled and George quickly turned away, the proverbial shoe being back on his foot.

* * * *

The following evening found Clay and company at Foxhaven for Conrad's surprise party.

Susan had sweated Clay, but finally agreed to go with him, if only to keep up outward appearances. They were both still angry with each other, but had, by that unspoken communication between lovers in a quarrel, set upon a simmering course of outward calm, punctuated by the occasional public slight, barely perceptible to all but those who knew them well. Susan, for her part, had on the blue dress she had worn for the dinner at Clay's parents' estate, the night they had announced their engagement. The fact was not lost on Clay, but he said nothing.

True to her word, Princess Maria kept the guest list to under a hundred friends and associates of Conrad's. By partitioning off part of the grand ballroom, she managed to counter a feeling of emptiness so "small" a gathering might have otherwise engendered. Engineering the "surprise" aspect of this supposedly intimate gathering of Conrad's friends was all but impossible though. Even in so large an estate, the arrival of so many people could hardly have been kept secret with Conrad still on the grounds. Maria had no choice but to arrange a creative suspension of disbelief by one and all.

Conrad was ordered confined to his study while the guests arrived. Once everyone had been seated in the ballroom, the curtains were drawn and the lights turned out for a full minute. Then by pre-arrangement, Conrad made a deliberately noisy entrance to the ball-room, whereupon the lights came on and everyone yelled surprise! Conrad had, of course, been told in no uncertain terms by Maria herself that he was to express complete surprise, which he did, much to the amusement of all, including himself. Who, after all, does not like to be the center of attention, and at this particular time, Conrad had more than enough reason to want to celebrate with his friends.

Maria was radiant in her strapless white sequined gown, the lush, soft skin of her bare shoulders competing for attention with her extravagant diamond necklace. She danced with Conrad, sat with him at his table, and generally gave him her full attention and outward affection. She was only biding her time, though. She had to do everything possible to avoid arousing suspicion, but it was absolutely imperative that she get five minutes alone with Clay. A full hour had passed before Sen. Jenkins's dowdy wife, Mandy, insisted Conrad should dance with her, thus freeing Maria to do likewise with Clay. Needless to say, that did not sit well with Susan, but she did not protest.

Fortunately for Maria's purposes, the band played a slow dance, allowing her to get close enough to whisper in his ear, "Clay, this is serious. I absolutely must talk with you alone. There are things you should know about. After this dance, meet me on the South porch." She smiled, then feigned a laugh, as though Clay had made some witty remark.

"What's wrong, Maria? Why the secrecy?"

"Don't look so serious, Clay. Smile. I can't tell you here. Just meet me on the South porch. Please Clay."

"Okay, Maria, but I don't know where it is."

"Oh," she said with some embarrassment. "You wouldn't, would you? Just go through the archway to the left of the stairs." She gently tugged him into turning to face it while they continued dancing. "There, see it? Follow that hallway to the other side of the mansion and go out the French doors to the patio. I'll meet you there."

A moment later the song ended. She gave him a little curtsy and, for the benefit of those around them, thanked him for the dance. Clay returned to the table but didn't sit down. He leaned down and put his arm around Susan's shoulders and spoke in a low voice. Mac and Rita gave him a puzzled look.

"Something's going on, Susan. Maria needs to tell me something important in private. I'll be on the South Porch and will come back soon as I find out what." Susan gave him an angry look. He answered with a shrug, and then walked off toward the archway.

Softly lighted by the glow spilling from the mansion windows and small spotlights in the gardens, Foxhaven's South Porch was a broad half circle of beautifully veined marble tiles, bordered on its curving outside edge by a carved limestone railing. A wide stairway of marble led down a few feet to a long rectangular garden of shrubs and flower beds, now populated by the remains of a few fall blooming varieties. The garden had been laid atop the roof of a long, eighteen stall garage, which opened out lower down the terraced slope at the back of the mansion.

When Clay walked out onto the porch, he saw Maria standing by the railing, looking expectantly in his direction. They were alone, and she had her arms crossed against the chill night air. She smiled up at him as he approached.

"Clay, I am so relieved," she said putting a hand on his arm. "I thought you weren't coming."

"You said it was important."

"It is, Clay. I have to tell you something. I'm not who you think I am. I'm Conrad's cousin, but that is not the reason I'm here."

"What do you mean, Maria?"

"I know about your friend Bunker," she said matter-of-factly. I know he checked on Conrad and me for you."

"How in the hell did you find that out? From Conrad?"

"No, I've been recruited by German intelligence--BND. Uncle Conrad is suspected of having supplied weapons for a terrorist attack on a nightclub in Hamburg in 2008. They think he and Krieger have been smuggling arms and explosives to Hamas terrorists for some time now."

"Jeez. I wanted to ask you about Conrad. I know Krieger is dirty. I saw him with some terrorists in the tunnels under The Cliffs."

"How did you--" Just then the French doors opened and another couple strolled out onto the porch, taking up a spot far enough away to be out of earshot. Maria looked up at Clay. "Clay, put your arms around me. I can't let them suspect anything."

Clay drew her close to him. Her soft touch and the subtle smell of her perfume aroused him. He couldn't help wondering where this was going on a couple of different levels.

"Clay, are you working for the FBI? The CIA?"

"What? No, Maria. Something's going on and I'm trying to find out what it is. I had run-ins with terrorists, then all of a sudden Krieger shows up, and then I find out he's got something going on with terrorists out there in those tunnels. I thought maybe he was doing it on his own, but now you tell me Conrad's in this too."

"As soon as you can Clay, you've got to get word to your friend Bunker. Tell him something big is about to happen. Uncle Conrad somehow got hold of plans for some kind of device, he called it L-E-N-R, that produces energy. And somebody has been killed, I think. A Professor Wentworth. I don't know any more about it, except this. I overheard Uncle Conrad trying to sell those plans to the Chinese for $1 trillion and ten percent of the profits."

"A trillion dollars!" Clay said out loud. "What the hell is it?"

"Ssssh! Yes, Clay, a trillion and the Chinese are actually considering it, so it must be a very important discovery. But I don't have a clue about what it is."

"I'll try to contact Bunker after the party, as soon as we get back in cell phone range."

"For obvious reasons, I can't use the telephone here, and it's hard for me to come up with excuses to get off the estate. So, I've got to rely on you. Now listen to me, Clay. Conrad has a file with the plans for the device in his desk drawer. From what I heard, it is now the only copy. I don't know how he did it, but I think Uncle Conrad arranged that somehow. Or at least knew about it. I was hoping you would be an FBI agent, because my people, and yours too, will want it as evidence for a case against Uncle Conrad."

"Is the drawer locked?"

"I don't think so. Uncle Conrad told Krieger he put it in there--out of alphabetical order so that it would be hard to find."

"I could try to get it."

"Clay, that's too risky. If he finds out you took it, he will have Krieger hunt you down. Krieger is not a man to be fooled with. From what I was told, he does all Uncle Conrad's, what you call 'wet work.'" She pulled him a little closer. Clay was trying to think, and her being so close didn't make it any easier to concentrate.

"Where's his desk? If I can get in there, I could take pictures of the file with my cell phone, then put the file back where I found it. At least we'll have proof he has it."

"But if someone catches you--"

"I'll take Mac along with me. Between the two of us, we can take care of anybody Conrad throws up against us. Can you keep Conrad busy for a while?"

"Of course. But he is not the only one you have to worry about. What about Krieger? The servants? If someone sees you, they could alert Uncle Conrad. And you have Susan and your friends to think about too."

"I know, I know," he said to reassure her. His mind was racing as he took it all in. Conrad was definitely dirty too. But what was it that he'd gotten hold of that could be worth $1 trillion to the Chinese?

And what had happened to this Prof. Wentworth? While he was running down the possibilities, he did not notice Susan start to open the French doors to the porch, then stop and abruptly turn back to the ballroom.

"Look, Maria, I don't want to lose the chance to find out what's in that file. Those plans could be really important all by themselves, but if he stole them, you're right, the FBI will want them as evidence."

"Clay. If you take them, he'll find out. I don't want anything to happen to you," Maria said earnestly.

Clay was a little surprised by her pleading tone, but then he knew she had feelings for him. And though he didn't want to admit it, especially now with her soft, warm body against him, he felt the same way. But he had to concentrate now. He and Mac were going after those files, he was sure of that.

"Don't worry, Maria. Mac and I will be all right. I'll copy the plans with my cell phone and put them back. Try to keep Conrad busy, but if anybody comes into the study, I'll tell them I needed some privacy for an important phone call or something. Now tell me where Conrad's study is."

"Oh, Clay. I wish you would just get a message to your friend Bunker." She hugged him tighter, but she told him what he needed to know.

"We'll be all right, Maria. You'll see. You just do your best to keep Conrad busy."

"Be careful, Clay." She looked up at him, then slipped her hand behind his head and pulled him into a kiss. Swept up in the moment, he pulled her tight against him and kissed her back. When finally she stepped back from him, she gave him a last look and hurried back to the ballroom. Clay watched her go, then wiped his lips.

"Mac," Clay said in a low voice when he returned to their table, "I need your help." He looked at Susan, her face set in an angry scowl. "It's important, honey."

"I'll bet it is," she answered sarcastically.

"Susan, please don't be mad. I'll explain it all when we get back. Come on, Mac."

Though it took a concerted effort, Clay forced himself to walk at a normal pace and to appear as nonchalant as possible. Once they'd left the ballroom, Clay began explaining to Mac in hushed voice what his plan was and why. They walked through the four-story high atrium, passing under the scowling faces of Nebel family members long dead, and followed a hallway to the library. Clay stopped at the first door immediately after the library and tried the knob. He breathed a sigh of relief when it turned freely. "We're in," he said conspiratorially to Mac and opened the door.

"Mac, how about staying by the door. Give me a signal if you hear anybody coming," Clay said, closing the door behind him. "If we get surprised, we say we wanted some privacy to make an important phone call."

Mac gave him a thumbs up. "Do you know where to look?" Mac asked as he scanned all the bookshelves. You're not going to tell me he hid it in a book are you?"

Clay grunted a laugh. "Maria told me he put it in his desk drawer." He sat in Conrad's chair and began opening the drawers. "Worth a trillion and he just stuck it in a drawer. Pretty ballsy, or maybe just plain stupid, if you ask me." In fact, the drawers didn't even have locks. Clay found the file drawer on the lower left side, slid it open, and began riffling through the files.

"You know Susan's pissed at you," Mac said in a loud whisper as Clay concentrated on the file drawer. "Where were you, anyway?"

"Out on the South Porch, where I said. Why?" He had thumbed through about half the drawer and found nothing but estate paperwork. Had Conrad moved the file?

"You were gone for a while. So she went out to get you. She came back, saying she couldn't find you. But she was really mad. Wouldn't say why."

Clay looked up from the drawer, remembering holding Maria. And the kiss. Had Susan seen that? He could explain it, but he was sure

Susan wouldn't listen. And now he felt guilty enough that he couldn't blame her in the least. Mac brought him back to reality.

"Hey! Are you going to find that file or not?"

"Yeah. It's gotta be in this drawer someplace." He walked through several more files, lifting them part way up and then opening them just enough to get an idea of what they contained. "Wait. This looks like the one. Chemical formulas, drawings...Ever heard of Babcock Chemical, Mac?...Hah! There's Prof. Wentworth's name. We've got it!" he exclaimed in a hushed voice.

"Well, start snapping those pictures, Clay. Let's not wait around for somebody to catch us in here."

Clay grinned and pulled out his flip phone. Activating the camera, he moved the phone up and down until he got the full page in the view screen. Pressing the button to take the shot, he then flipped to the next page. Clay estimated there were about thirty pages in the file.

"This is going to take a while, Mac. Let me know if you hear anybody coming." Clay made a point of taking an extra shot of that first page. He wanted part of that starburst inlay on Conrad's desk in the shot. That distinctive design would help prove where the file had been found.

Out in the ballroom, Krieger could be seen approaching the table where Conrad sat, engaged in what looked like, to those who noticed, an intimate conversation with Princess Maria. He seemed to be truly having the time of his life. Already whispers were beginning to circulate that perhaps the old man had finally caught her fancy.

"Conrad, sir," Krieger said deferentially, "I don't mean to interrupt, but could I have a word in private? Something important has come up."

"Important? Yes. Maria, darling, will you excuse me a moment?"

"But Conrad, what shall I do all alone here?" she protested. Maria did not like the idea of letting go of Conrad while Clay and Mac were still in the study, but she couldn't make too big a fuss. And for all she knew, it really was a business matter.

Krieger drew the unsuspecting Conrad out of earshot. "Conrad, have you not noticed that our friends, Clay and Mac, are nowhere to be seen?" Conrad's pleasant smile disappeared and he turned to scan the room. Krieger was right. It was as if a bolt of electricity had shot through him.

"You don't suppose...?"

"How could they know, Conrad? It may be nothing, but I think we must make sure."

"Come with me. Let's check the study right now."

Clay still had two pages to go when Mac said in a low voice, "I hear someone coming. Better hurry up!"

Mac, who had the door open a crack to look out into the hallway, closed it gently and then moved to the other side, so that he'd be behind the door when it opened. He leaned back against the bookshelves and balled his fists.

Clay meanwhile worked as fast as he could, but he was having trouble with the last page. It was a large, folded diagram of the device, and Clay had to take several frames to get it all in. The footsteps were very close now, and Clay could hear voices. It was Conrad. They'd be dead if he found out.

Clay took the last shot, closed his phone, and put it down on the desk while he fumbled with refolding the drawing. Finally, he shoved the papers back into the file folder, closed it, and with his phone in the same hand, turned to slip the file back into the spot he'd marked. That's when he spotted the study door begin to open.

Hurrying to get the file into the drawer, Clay accidentally let the phone slip and fall between the files to the bottom of the drawer. With the door opening, Clay had no choice but to leave his phone. Instead, he slid the drawer closed and got up in one smooth motion. By the time the study door opened far enough for Conrad and Krieger to see, Clay was leaning casually alongside of the desk.

"Hi, Conrad. Nice office you have here."

"Thank you. This is my *private* office, Clay."

"Oh, I needed to talk with Mac there--he's right behind you--in private. So I guess we wandered into the right room."

Conrad and Krieger both turned to look at Mac, who, with folded arms, gave them a smile and a little wave of hello.

"And what would you be talking about in here that you couldn't say out in the hallway?"

"Susan, you know, my fiancee. We're having a fight. I just needed to be somewhere with my friend here. Get some advice on what to do. You know how women can be, Conrad. Relentless."

"Perhaps. Next time use the library." Conrad could barely contain himself. "Now why don't you two rejoin the party. I have some business to conduct with Krieger here. We'll be out in a bit."

Conrad waited until the door closed behind Clay and Mac before rushing over to the desk.

"Thank God!" he gushed with relief. "It's still here, Krieger." He pulled out the file and flipped the pages. "Yes, yes, it's all still here."

"Now will you put that damn file in the safe, Conrad?"

"All right. Let's go do it now. Then we have to decide what to do about our friends. I don't believe for a minute he was doing anything *but* looking for this," he growled and held up the file.

"Do you suppose he's working for the Chinese?"

"Maybe. You checked him out. He's not working for the American government, is he?

"No, but he might be freelancing for somebody. We probably should do something about him."

"Drastic?"

"That was my thought. And soon," Krieger snapped.

"Well, him first. Then the others."

Clay and Mac did their best to appear nonchalant as they walked back to their table. Clay sat down next to Susan, who turned to glare at him. Jimmy spoke up first.

"Where have you guys been? What's going on?"

"A lot," Clay said and motioned to everyone to huddle closer. "Look, the Princess is working for Germany's spy agency. Apparently

Conrad and Krieger have been doing some gun running. Charity of a different sort. She told me that, and the fact that Conrad has a stolen file that he's trying to sell to the Chinese for, get this, $1 trillion!"

"You're kidding," Jimmy gasped. Susan, for her part, was awash in confusion. She didn't know what to believe.

"Wish I was. Maria told me that Conrad hid it in his desk, so Mac and I went to his study, and I used my cell phone to take pictures of all the pages."

"Good going."

"Not quite. Conrad and Krieger came in just as I finished. The phone slipped out of my hand and fell into the file drawer. There wasn't time to fish it out. I don't think Conrad knows for sure what I was doing, but you can bet he's suspicious. I think I've worn out our welcome here. Like maybe we should leave now."

Conrad and Krieger came back to the ballroom as Clay and company were filing out. Conrad touched Maria's shoulder.

"I see our friends are leaving. Did they say good night?"

"No, they just got up and left. I do hope nothing is the matter."

"I think Clay and Susan are having a fight. At least that's what he told me."

"Oh, I see." She didn't dare ask how he had come upon that information. She smiled up at Conrad. "Well, *we* are still here. And I haven't danced in ages." Conrad smiled warmly. She was such a beautiful flower. Krieger, meanwhile left the ballroom.

Susan said nothing, was resolutely silent as the friends walked out to where their cars were parked. Clay guessed she was mad as hell, but what worried him was that he didn't know how much she had seen. The night air was cool and a fog had settled in, so it took a bit of wandering to find where the cars were parked among the fifty lined up on the mansion's side lawn. Even so, Susan never said a word, and Clay thought that was probably for the best. It was going to be a long ride home, and he knew that would be his best chance to smooth things over. Just how much he would own up to was another matter. He was still as confused about that now as when he and Maria had kissed.

As Clay opened the door to his Vette for Susan, he said over the roof to Mac, "Will you call Bunker and fill him in as soon as you get bars?"

"Okay, Clay," Mac said before disappearing into his Lexus.

The thump of Clay's driver side door closing was as good as the bell for the start of round one with Susan. They were alone now, and what remained of the public show of togetherness came to a screeching halt. As Mac and Jimmy pulled out of the parking area, Susan turned to Clay, her face drawn into an angry grimace.

"What's going on between you and Maria?" she blurted out, venting a flood of emotions--anger, hurt, and indignation at having been accused of what she'd seen Clay doing. Clay said nothing, waiting for a further tirade but it didn't come.

"Nothing, Susan. I told you. She's spying on Conrad for Germany's spy agency. I just found out all this tonight. She wanted me to get a message to Bunker about this LENR thing that Conrad's got hold of."

"Clay, don't lie to me. I saw you with her out there." Susan's anger and frustration got the better of her and she started crying.

"Awh, Susan, honey. Please. This is all a terrible mistake. She was explaining what was going on with Conrad when another couple came out onto the porch. She asked me to hold her so that it would look like we wanted to be alone, well, for you know. But it was an act, so she could tell me about Conrad. Honest."

"I saw you with her, Clay. How could you do that to me? Don't you know how that hurt me? We're going to be married, Clay, and there you are with that girl, *that princess*. Like I'm nothing," she sobbed.

A woman's tears are a bitter medicine for all but the most heartless of men. Clay was not used to feeling as though he had let anyone down, much less Susan. But he had, and he knew it. Not because he'd embraced Maria, but because of that kiss. No, it hadn't been his idea, but he was very much there in that impulsive moment. He regretted it, but if Susan hadn't seen it, then he wasn't about to bring it up. He had already hurt her enough.

"Susan, you are everything to me. Please, honey, believe me. I love you, not her. What you saw there was an act. A stupid act!" There was more truth to that than he intended, but he meant it sincerely, and she could see it in his eyes. Impulsively, they both reached out for each other to embrace. He held her tightly in his arms and kissed her, then held her until she stopped crying.

"I don't want to lose you," he told her at last, then, "Are you okay now?" She nodded yes, gave a little, embarrassed laugh and wiped away her tears as she settled back into her seat.

"I think we have to do something about that gear shift, Clay," she kidded softly.

"Mac and I'll rip it out tomorrow," he replied with an apologetic smile and, relieved that things had been at least partly smoothed over, started the engine. Moments later they passed by the fog-shrouded mansion and headed out the main gate. Clay didn't notice the open door to the bay in Conrad's garage, nor did he hear the engine of the big Mercedes sedan roar to life.

"Fog's pretty thick around here. Looks like it's getting worse," Clay said as he tried raising and lowering his headlights. With about thirty feet of visibility, he had no trouble while driving at the slow speeds on the estate driveway. That winding mountain road would be another problem, though, with its posted speed limit of forty-five. Clay knew he'd have to do better than twenty-five there, but with so little traffic on it, he wasn't worried. Leaving Conrad's driveway, Clay turned left and headed down the mountain at thirty. A half-minute later, the black Mercedes also turned left and sped off into the fog.

Clay approached a hairpin turn he remembered from past trips to Foxhaven when he spotted headlights coming up fast behind him.

"We've got company, Susan. I don't like the looks of this. He's moving pretty fast."

"Not again, Clay!"

"I hope not, Susan. But if it's who I think it is, these people like to run you off the road. And this is definitely the place to do it."

"You're scaring me, Clay."

"Sorry, honey," he said as he sped up to forty through a tight set of S-curves after the hairpin. The Mercedes receded into the fog, but only for a moment. Coming out of the curves, the car began catching up again. "Hang on tight, Susan," Clay said and downshifted, heading downhill into another tight hairpin turn. The Vette, being much lower to the ground, whipped through the turn flat. Clay accelerated out of it and gained ground as the Mercedes fishtailed around the curve. Clay grinned as the Mercedes' headlights wobbled this way and that in his rearview mirror.

On a clear night, Clay knew that Mercedes was no match for his Corvette. He had a big edge over it in power, speed, cornering, and braking. It was the damned fog in front of him that was keeping it close. Barreling downhill at forty-five and fifty, he barely had time to react to turns that he could hardly see coming, and there were lots of them on this road. His salvation, if there was to be one, was what he could remember from having traveled this road before.

Like this downhill stretch now. He remembered it because it was really steep, going on for a mile or so of fairly gentle curves before ending in two really tight hairpins, first to the right, then the left. And there was a big sign on the right for a runaway truck ramp just before that first hairpin. If he could see that, he'd be okay. Clay picked up speed, hitting fifty-five through the curves, slicing through the fog so fast now he could barely see the road ahead. Susan hung on to the armrest for dear life.

Clay's eyes flicked up to the rearview mirror and back to the road. The Mercedes was clearly losing ground about halfway through the curves, fishtailing on the damp pavement. Then, suddenly, it was gone. Clay hit the brakes, coming to a stop on a narrow shoulder, waiting for some sign of the Mercedes. Then he popped the Vette into reverse and turned around in his seat.

"Clay!" Susan cried out in disbelief. "You're not really going back there, are you?"

"Looks that way, honey. I'd like to see who was coming after us."

"I thought the getting away part was the important thing here."

"It was. Is. But I'm kind of curious, you know." His one concession to sanity at this point was to switch over to the left lane, in case anybody should come downhill. Backing around a last curve, he pulled up alongside the black Mercedes. It had run up an embankment and hit a tree. He backed up a little farther and then turned so that his headlights illuminated the wrecked car. The driver's side door hung wide open and a man dangled unconscious, half in and half out, suspended by his seat belt.

"I do believe that's Krieger, Susan."

"Since he was obviously trying to run us off the road, I think we should just go. And quickly."

"When you're right, you're right, dear. He has a lot more friends around here than we do."

Clay drove straight to the mill house, Susan having agreed to spend the night with him. For his part, he no longer believed she was seeing someone else on the side. There had been something fishy about that from the beginning, and the way she had reacted to *his* indiscretion convinced him that while Mac obviously believed he'd seen Susan, it had to be someone else. They were still en route to Staunton when Susan's cell phone rang--she had that ring tone emulating old-fashioned telephone bells--and Mac reported Bunker would be flying down tomorrow at lunch time.

"I suppose he expects me to provide the lunch," Clay commented loud enough for Mac to hear.

"Mac said 'Me too,'" Susan reported. Still on the phone, she broke into a smile. "Yes, Mac, tell Rita we're friends again. And don't come over too early tomorrow morning, okay?"

Ten o'clock the next morning, Clay and Susan had finished breakfast when her phone rang. It wasn't Mac, however. Instead, it was the County Prosecutor's Office calling them with a heads up.

Apparently the jury had sent word that they'd reached decisions on all but the last count against George Kilgore and would soon be ready for reading their verdict. Clay and Susan would have to hurry if they wanted to be there for it.

They were out of the house and on the road to town like they'd been shot out of a cannon.

Mac and Rita met them on the steps to the County Courthouse and the four found seats in the front row, a courtroom being one place most people have little desire to sit up front. Prosecutor Berelli saw them arrive and just had time to ask Clay to meet with him after the reading of the verdict. The court clerk then called out, "All rise," as the judge swept through his private doorway and climbed up to his dais. He waited patiently as the jury filed in and took their seats.

"Mr. foreman," the judge asked in stentorian tones, "has the jury reached a verdict?"

"Yes sir, your honor, we have."

Clay watched George nervously fidgeting at the defense table as the clerk walked the paper with the jury's written verdict over to the judge. The judge opened the folded sheet and read from it:

"On the count of conspiracy to distribute narcotics, guilty.

"On the count of arson in the first degree, guilty.

"On the count of attempted murder, guilty

"On the count of murder in the first degree, guilty. Mr. Kilgore, you are going to jail for a long time. Your sentencing hearing will be in two weeks. Bailiff, take the defendant into custody."

Clay watched George stand, his head hung down, and then turn to look back in his direction. Clay barely smiled and slowly, lightly, clapped his hands in applause. The bailiff took hold of George and led him off to the holding cell.

"There is some justice in the world," Clay said, "and that's one guy who deserves a good dose of it." Clay got up from his seat and approached the prosecutor. "Things got a little shaky for a while there, but you got a nice win."

Berelli smiled. "The wheels of justice triumph again. Thanks to you and your friend Mac there."

"More him than me. And I'll tell you, he's pulled my butt out of the fire more than once."

"I thought you'd want to know," Berelli said in a more serious vein, "That Khan's missing uncle has turned up. Dead. The coroner up in Harrisonburg says he'd been stabbed multiple times and then his throat was slit. A particularly cold-blooded murder was how he put it. Given the trouble you've been having with radical Muslims lately, we've reported it to Homeland Security. It might be connected somehow."

It was, but how would not become apparent for some time.

15

THE MISSION

"So, are you getting frequent flyer miles for all these trips you're making down here?" Clay asked between bites of his ham and Swiss on rye, slathered with yellow mustard. The early November day--dank, cloudy, gray--had forced Susan to turn on the kitchen's overhead light at the mill house, even though it was midday. An occasional gust of wind rattled the windows, and the two old cast iron radiators in the kitchen gurgled happily as the heat came on again.

"No, but I'm getting fat on all this good food Susan here has been feeding me," Bunker replied, abandoning his sandwich for another run at his potato salad. "This is really great, Susan. Do you have an extra gallon I can take back with me?"

"Clay'll never part with it. He loves it too."

"Guess I'll have to keep coming back then."

"That's okay," Clay added. "Especially if you've got some news."

"Tons of it, Clay. Tons. Things are coming together." Bunker kept them in suspense while he finished his sandwich and cleaned the last of the potato salad from his plate. Then he leaned back in his chair with beer in hand.

"Where to begin? I guess at the beginning. I don't have all the pieces yet, but I know at least part of the story about Weiss's murder. His next-door neighbor, it turns out, worked in a research lab. He was a Muslim who got himself brutally murdered in what police said was a mugging or drug deal gone bad. Weiss apparently didn't believe that. That much I knew, but why was Weiss so worked up? Nothing my father had said to you shed any light, and frankly I thought Weiss was upset just because the man was his neighbor.

"So, suddenly two presumed Muslim terrorists chase and murder Weiss in that chain reaction pileup, which you happen to witness, Clay. Okay, now you're in the picture, and crazy Arabs start buzzing around you, until you roast two of them.

"Now it's become pretty clear we're dealing with some kind of Muslim fundamentalist underground here in the good old US of A. That fellow Moktar is connected, though I'm not entirely sure how yet. We've bugged his office, and phone records show he's made pretty regular overseas calls to Qatar. We're working on the who.

"So they're up to something, they think maybe you know more than you do, and they try to scare you into shutting up. That doesn't work, in fact it costs them, and suddenly they disappear. And *that's* not like them. Maybe they figured out you really don't know that much, or that you can't interfere with their operation. Or maybe the time of their attack was getting close enough that it couldn't be stopped, even if you knew something important."

"We still don't know what it is that they're setting up, Bunker," Mac interjected.

"Unfortunately I do, and it's already happened. A few days ago they attacked a Babcock Chemical Company laboratory up in Loudon County, executed everybody working there, burned all the paperwork, and then blew up the building. They even murdered the Babcock exec who oversaw the lab and he was up in New Jersey. The worst part of this is that as soon as I heard about the attack, I realized the connection between Weiss and his neighbor's murder. Weiss is a retired Babcock research chemist, and the neighbor worked at the Babcock lab that the terrorists attacked. The lab guy must have said something to Weiss before he was murdered. If I'd put that together sooner, I might have headed off the attack."

"Bunker, hindsight is twenty-twenty, and you know it," Clay said. "You can't kick yourself for that."

"That's what I'm getting paid for, Clay. I'm supposed to see these things coming. Stop them before they can happen."

"Well, okay. What do you make of what Mac told you about last night?"

"Now we know that Conrad and Krieger are involved with radical Muslims. He's obviously not a Muslim, but from what you told me about The Cliffs, he's definitely helping them. At the very least with logistical help, maybe even supplying them with arms, that kind of thing. Probably making lots of money too.

"But his trying to peddle that LENR file is a real puzzler. The video of the Muslim attack on the lab is about to hit the Internet. We did everything we could to downplay the attack in the news media, and we got the internet people to hold off airing the video. But Al Jazeera got hold of it and now it's going viral. It's really gory, barbaric stuff. They beheaded Dr. Wentworth and showed closeups of the other executions too.

"What's strange is the terrorists brag about having destroyed Wentworth's sinful work on orders from Allah. Removed it from the face of the earth. Then their compadre, Conrad Nebel, winds up with a copy of it that he's trying to sell to the Chinese. The only possible explanation is that he's double dealing. Somehow he's gotten the LENR device specifications and sold out the Muslims."

"A trillion plus," Clay interjected, "would be lots of motivation."

"Did Maria give you any names of the Chinese men Conrad talked with?" Bunker asked.

"No, things were kind of rushed."

"I guess we'll have to tap the phones of every Chinese man who's gotten anywhere near Conrad for the past three months."

"So what is this LENR?" Susan asked. "Why is it worth so much money?"

"I can tell you about that," Mac interjected.

"You can?" Susan said with surprise.

"That he can," Clay confirmed. "He and I started getting *Popular Science, Discover,* and magazines like that when we were in high school. Lot's of cool, futuristic science stuff. I gave up on that a long time ago, but he still gets 'em every month. Mr. Science here is how I keep up with our future."

"Give me a break, Clay," Mac said with a grin. "I like reading about the stuff."

"Yeah, so, what's LENR?" Clay countered.

"Susan, did your science teacher in high school ever talk about that cold fusion experiment back in the '80s?" Made self-conscious by the sudden attention, Mac started out a bit haltingly, them warmed to his subject. "Two scientists out in Utah, Fleischman and Pons. They claimed to have fused hydrogen atoms, creating excess heat by the nuclear reaction. And they said it happened at room temperature. That was a big deal. Until then, scientists thought fusion could only take place under conditions of extreme heat and pressure, like on the sun, or when the hydrogen bomb exploded. Basically, all that Fleischman and Pons did was to take a jar of heavy water, stick a cathode of palladium in it, and run an electric current through it. It was that simple. The current started a low-level nuclear reaction they claimed was 'cold fusion.'"

'I don't remember anything like that. The '80s? I was only just born in the '80s," Susan said with a sheepish grin.

"Well, me too. But I read about it. Turned out, almost nobody could reproduce the experiment, and what at first seemed like a new, clean, cheap energy source that was going to solve the world's energy crisis wound up being labeled a complete fake. At least that's what most scientists, the media, and even the scientific journal editors believed.

"The National Science Foundation and government agencies like the Department of Energy wanted no part of it, but researchers kept experimenting, and they kept getting results showing a weak nuclear reaction was taking place. The beauty of LENR is that it doesn't put out dangerous radiation or hazardous wastes. It uses up only tiny amounts of the components. And compared to nuclear reactors, LENR devices should be cheap and easy to produce."

"What Mac says is true," Bunker announced. "I checked into it after I got Mac's call. "The phenomenon itself was noticed as far back as the 1920s, but what was happening remained a mystery. Pons and Fleischman produced the nuclear activity, but their explanation was flat wrong. Scientists for another twenty years got it wrong too. Their explanations always broke with known laws of physics. Then in '06, physicists Lewis Larson and Allan Widom published what is now an accepted theory of the phenomenon, calling it a Low Energy Nuclear Reaction, LENR. And their theory is consistent with the laws of physics."

"So, if everybody knows about it now, what makes Professor Wentworth's LENR device so valuable?" Clay asked.

"Well, now we've got an explanation for what's going on," Mac said thoughtfully, "and all those successful experiments have proved that LENR is potentially a major power source. But the trick now is finding the right combination of materials to produce a practical device. Research on that is in what they call 'the Edisonian stage.'"

"What?" Susan said with obvious frustration.

"Edison tried hundreds of different materials for the filament of his light bulb before he finally found the right one," Mac answered. "Research lately has shifted from explaining LENR to engineering a practical device. Until Wentworth came along, LENR just promised to be the 'Holy Grail' in the search for a solution to the world energy crisis. Seems like his device will actually do what LENR theory predicted. If it does, LENR technology will end our dependence on oil, and that will be a world changer. Must be why the Chinese are willing to pay $1 trillion for it."

"And why the Muslim terrorists called it a sin against Allah," Bunker speculated. "They must realize that at the very least LENR technology will end our dependence on Mideast oil and eliminate the leverage Arab countries have had with our government."

"And cut off the flow of petro dollars they've been getting fat on," Clay added. "Some of those countries have been helping fund the radical Muslim groups, so the terrorists must know they'd get hit in the pocket book too."

"Only five virgins to a martyr then," Mac joked.

"I'm impressed Mac," Clay said after everyone stopped laughing. "You really know your stuff about LENR. What bothers me now though, is that we really do have to get my cell phone back. We're talking a world-changing discovery here. The photos of that file on my phone must be the only other copy besides the one Conrad has. And I don't think we should let him steal the discovery. Or let the Chinese get it either."

"Sneaking into those tunnels was one thing, Clay," Mac said. "But I don't see how we'll get back into the main house without an invitation. Especially now that Conrad is on to us."

"You're right about that, Mac. Bunker, I don't suppose you could get Homeland Security or the FBI involved?"

"Officially? Not without some sort of a smoking gun. Conrad has a lot of friends on the Hill, a couple in the White House even. I believe you and all. But anything you claim to have seen would have to be backed up by evidence, and so far, all we've got is speculation. If you had that cell phone, that would work. Otherwise it's a case of you said, he said, and we'll never get a warrant based on that."

"Damn!" Clay balled his fist in frustration, then opened his hand and laid it down flat on the kitchen table. "Okay. I think we can get as far as the mansion all right. But if things get hot, we're going to need a back door, a way to get out fast, especially if Conrad's people get on our tail." Clay looked at Susan. She looked decidedly unhappy at the thought, having been through just that. Bunker rubbed his chin, thinking it over.

"I suppose," he said with hesitation, "I could help out unofficially. You know, hang around up there in the wings so to speak, in case you need an emergency evac."

"Well, that's a start."

"Start? What do you mean, a start?" Susan blurted out. "You're not really going to try this, are you? Remember, Clay, Krieger tried to kill us."

"I know, Susan, I really do. It's a big risk, but I don't see any other way. We can't let Conrad get away with this. And what if something happens to his copy? Then where will the world be?"

Susan wanted to answer him, but something made her keep silent, an instinct maybe, that told her that in the end, this had to be his decision. He was right about how important getting that cell phone was, she knew that. And his courage was, after all, one thing she admired and loved about him.

"What kind of alarm system does he have?" Bunker asked, after he was sure Susan wasn't going to say anything more.

"Don't know," Clay responded. "My bet is that it's nothing too exotic. He probably relies more on armed guards than hi-tech stuff. He's probably got alarms on doors and windows, but most likely doesn't activate the system until he's ready to hit the sack."

"Okay, so our window is after dark, between say 7 and 10 p.m.," Mac said. "Let's hope he doesn't go to bed really early."

"Yeah. Jeez, I wish *you* could call Maria," he said with a wink at Susan. "She'd know about all this stuff."

"If she has a cell phone of her own, it won't do us any good out there. It's too far out. No bars out there."

"There's a land line to the mansion," Clay said. "I saw that phone in his study, in back of his desk. But I'll bet there are a ton of extensions, so Conrad or a servant could always listen in if we called her. I didn't see a computer, so my guess is he doesn't want to deal with the Internet and email. Maybe Krieger does, but that won't help."

"Bunker, do the Germans have an alternate way to contact her?" Mac asked.

"That's a thought, Mac. I don't know, but I can check."

"Next question," Clay interjected. "If we need you, how do you find us? Have you got something we can use to help you home in on us? Can we use GPS equipment? If we have to resort to flares, those Muslims will come a runnin'."

"Sure. Longitude and latitude coordinates from a handheld GPS navigator will work fine. Just radio me the 8-digit coordinates. My chopper's got GPS equipment. I can even punch the coordinates into my autopilot and come in right on top of you."

"I've got a handheld two-way emergency radio we can use," Clay said. "Range is about twenty miles."

"Okay." Bunker paused, giving the plan more thought. Since it's Foxhaven, I'll know within a few miles of where you'll be. But maybe you should take an IR beacon too. It's not likely Conrad's friends will have the capability to see infrared. Night vision optical goggles, maybe, but not infrared. The beacon emits a coded flash, so I can tell it from small arms fire, if I have to."

"Oh, great!" Susan complained.

"It's okay, honey," Clay said putting his hand on her shoulder. "It probably won't get to that. But if it does, we've been there before, right Mac?"

"You bet."

"Clay, you do what you have to," Susan said in an exasperated tone. "But I can't listen to any more of this. Please, please, be careful."

"You know I will, honey," Clay said as he watched her leave the room. "She worries, but she'll be all right. Now, the other problem is the pickup point. The property is heavily forested, and if we stir up any trouble, our best bet will be to retreat into the woods."

"Okay. If you can find a clearing, that's best. But I'll bring a fast line. I can hover over the trees and drop it down to you."

"What do you think, Mac. Tomorrow night? If we go at about 8 o'clock, everybody at Foxhaven should already be settled in for the night."

"The sooner the better. One question though, Bunker, how long can you stay on station?"

"Not all night, that's for sure. How about if we do this: I'll stick around for the first half hour as close by as practicable. You call me by your two-way radio, if you need me. If I don't hear from you in that first half hour, I'll have a spot where I can land safely and wait. Depending on where, I might not be reachable by radio. So I'll get airborne once every hour after that. You'll have to hole up between those times, but that way fuel won't be a problem."

"I'd say we're a go."

"You two are taking a big risk. I'm not saying it isn't worthwhile, considering what's at stake. But those guys are playing for keeps, Clay. And you don't even know that he hasn't already found your cell phone."

"The only way would be if he cleaned out the whole drawer."

"Maybe so, but I'd hate to see you risk your necks and come up empty."

The following night at 7:30, Susan dropped off Clay and Mac well past the drive leading into Foxhaven. They were dressed in all black and had blackened their faces and hands. Except for the M-16s and backpacks they carried, they looked like full-fledged cat burglars.

"Okay, Susan. Take off for home. And don't worry, we'll be fine."

"Clay," Susan answered as sweetly as she could muster, "it's my job to worry. Yours is to be careful and get back safe, okay?"

"Yes dear," he deadpanned.

Susan watched them melt into the darkened forest, then turned around her Volvo and headed back to Staunton. It was going to be a long night. She could feel it.

So far as Clay and Mac were concerned, they had every reason to be confident about their ability to move in on a target undetected. They had had plenty of training in that as Rangers and they weren't going up against a hardened target. Because of thick cloud cover, moonlight was not a factor tonight, so the forest terrain became their biggest problem. Brush and branches of small understory trees tore at them, tangles of fallen trees blocked their way, and even though Clay's eyes adjusted to the darkness, the forest floor was a minefield of chuck holes and rock outcroppings. Worse was the thick carpet of fallen leaves on the ground. It made moving quietly almost impossible without coming to a near standstill. Clay's hope was that any guards Conrad may have outside would be walking the perimeter close to the house.

Clay and Mac had covered about a mile when they encountered the rushing mountain stream. They carefully worked their way down a steep rocky slope before stopping atop a large boulder. The stream was only about ten feet across, but thanks to a recent rain, the water was moving fast around and over the rocks dotting the streambed.

"Do you see any way across, Mac?"

"Just an exposed rock here and there. Not close enough together to rock hop across. I don't know how deep that water is, but it's moving pretty fast."

"Yeah, I don't suppose we'll do any better farther up stream. If we're on course, we should be pretty close to the driveway now. I don't remember seeing a bridge, but there must be one. Suppose we head over there."

Not long after scrambling out of the ravine, they reached the driveway. Farther on, they came to a small stone bridge, with the stream rushing madly under it. They were about to cross when Clay stopped suddenly and put a hand out to restrain Mac.

"Look there, Mac," Clay said pointing to a small box mounted to the rustic stone bridge, about halfway across. Another box stood about the same height on the other side. Clay dropped his pack and rifled through it before finally extracting a small infrared night vision scope, which looked like a small camera with a lens mounted on the front and binocular-like dual eyepieces on the back.

"Yup, just what I thought. Infrared, Mac," he whispered. "Here take a look."

"Just the one beam," Mac said after scanning the bridge. "He probably uses it to warn of incoming vehicles."

"Easy enough to walk along the bridge's stone walls to get past it. And we'll make better time, I think, if we stay on the roadway until we get close to the house. Then we can take to the woods again."

"Better keep an eye for more of those beams, Clay."

"I've got to remember to thank Bunker for insisting we pack this," Clay said as he scanned the road ahead. "You keep an eye out for laser beams, and I'll keep checking for infrared. Then all we have to worry about is a car coming." Mac gave him a thumbs up and they headed up the drive, keeping to the shoulder.

Another mile passed with nothing more than the rustling of their clothing and the sound of their breathing. Then the noise of small engines roaring flat out shattered the night air. And they were coming this way fast. Clay and Mac sprinted into the forest shadows, not a minute too soon.

Roaring around a bend in the driveway up ahead, Clay saw two headlights coming straight at them. He and Mac took cover behind big tree trunks, watching while shafts of light sliced deep into the forest behind them. Clay flicked off the safety of his M-16 and aimed at the left headlight without thinking.

Just when it seemed they were coming straight at them, the headlights turned to follow the driveway. They flashed by going flat out, attached to two ATV's running side-by-side. One driver yelled a redneck, "Yeee-hah!"

"Racing, Mac. Bet they're drunk. If we're lucky, the rest of the guards will have had a snoot full too."

"That sure woke me up," he said with a grin.

"This stuff does keep the blood flowing, doesn't it Mac?" Mac smiled as they set out again.

When the two were about a quarter mile from the estate proper, they ducked into the woods. Trekking in several hundred yards, they stayed roughly parallel to the lower boundary of the grounds. Along the way, Clay looked for distinctive features to help navigate the darkened landscape. Then in a grove of pine trees, they found two twenty-foot high boulders resting against each other. At the base, the uneven sides of the two giant rocks formed a small cave, a perfect place to stash their gear. Better yet, the big boulders created an opening in the tree canopy.

Clay and Mac hid their packs and their M-16s in the cave. Their plan was to get in and out without firing a shot by using the infrared binoculars to avoid the guards. But they carried their .45 cal. side arms just in case. Clay checked their position with his GPS navigator. Then he turned on an IR beacon as a backup to help Bunker get a fix on the position. The preparations completed, Clay and Mac worked around the boulders, heading on a direct line for the estate grounds. They hadn't hiked far before leaving the pine grove and returning to the hardwood forest.

They moved slowly, quietly, navigating along as straight a line as possible. Gentle breezes helped them by rustling the trees and providing a covering background noise. Before long they spotted the lights coming from the mansion. The imposing edifice, sited on a hill, loomed above them, ominously, like a fortress. They crossed a well-worn fire road, probably used for patrolling the perimeter, and stopped before a tall, cut-stone wall marking the edge of the grounds.

"This is it, Mac," Clay whispered. So far it had been easy, but Clay had expected that. From here on out, the risk of getting caught jumped off the chart. They had surprise going for them. Conrad would not expect them to try breaking and entering. And they had the infrared binoculars. Still, it was a long way from where they stood to that darkened mansion and Conrad's study, and anything could happen. "Mac," Clay whispered, "you did leave a GPS navigator back with our gear, right?"

"Yes. Hate to say it, though. I lost my rabbit's foot somewhere back there. Must have fallen out of my pocket by the cave." Mac, the superstitious one, didn't look at all happy about that.

"Not to worry. We'll make our own luck then, Mac."

"If you say so."

Clay scanned the wall with his IR binoculars. No beams. Conrad apparently did put more stock in his guards than hi-tech devices. That was a good sign.

Mac gave Clay a leg up the wall, and once Clay had scrambled up top, he gave Mac a hand. The two dropped down into the bushes in one of Conrad's formal gardens, next to a small pond. A statue standing in the middle spouted a small stream of water. Beyond the garden, a long upward sloping lawn lay between them and the mansion. Very open, but not directly lighted. Clay tapped Mac's shoulder, then pointed progressively to the pond, the house, and then the side of his head. The pond would be an important landmark for their trip back out.

Clay scanned the sloped lawn and didn't pick up any sign of infrared beams anywhere. Better yet, they had come onto the grounds right about where he thought they'd have the best shot at seeing the South Porch, their key point of reference. Looking up the slope, Clay thought he recognized the lighted garden and the curved railing, but from this angle he also noticed, for the first time, the long row of garage doors below the garden.

That momentarily confused him, because he saw another curved railing above the opposite end of the garage. But, he decided, it was probably a second porch modeled on the same pattern, and in any event they had to circle around to the right of the mansion to get into Conrad's study. Clay scanned that whole area looking for infrared signatures of patrolling guards. Suddenly, on his far right, he picked up one coming their way. He signaled Mac, and they hunkered down in the bushes.

Clay held his breath. The guard, carrying a rifle on his shoulder, swung a flashlight beam this way and that as he approached, then let the beam linger for what seemed forever on the bushes in front of them. Clay and Mac stayed perfectly still until finally, the light swung forward as the guard continued on.

The two waited several minutes before moving out. They traced a long curving button hook, staying in the shadowed lower lawn before closing in on the gardens at the mansion's right-hand corner. Clay guessed that Conrad would want his privacy and wouldn't have any guards patrolling close to the mansion. So now their biggest risk was being spotted by someone on the inside.

Clay and Mac sidled up to the mansion's foundation, keeping a thick wall of rhododendron and boxwoods between them and circular drive out front. They had passed by a porch entryway, but Clay wanted to locate Conrad's study from the outside first. Lights blazed from the library's ganged windows and one double window that Clay took to be Conrad's study, but the window sills stood eight feet off the ground here. Times like these it paid to have a tall, strong partner--Mac knitted his fingers together and nodded to Clay. Clay stepped into the foothold, and rising up on one leg, saw Conrad and Krieger in the study.

Back down again, Clay silently mouthed "Conrad" and "Krieger" and pointed to the study. Mac grimaced. They had no choice but to wait until those two left, and then hope to hell they didn't bump into them somewhere inside. That became the subject of considerable hand signals between Clay and Mac, with Mac suggesting they go in through the double windows. Clay countered that the windows were shut, and because they were casement windows, they probably couldn't be opened from the outside.

By the time he and Mac had settled on the porch entry door, the light in the study flicked off. Clay rechecked the darkened study with his IR binoculars, confirming the room was empty. Back at the porch, Clay scanned it too.

Sneaking up the porch steps, they found the entry door unlocked, and as easy as that, they were in and standing in a wide hallway. Clay felt suddenly naked in the hallway's bright light. With no choice but to gut it out, he and Mac strode down the hallway like they owned it, finally stopping at what Clay thought was the library. He cracked the door to the now darkened room to be sure, and then backtracked to the study's door. He couldn't believe their luck as he opened the unlocked door. They were home free.

Or so he thought. Conrad picked that instant to spring his trap. The lights suddenly blazed on. Caught in the blinding light, Clay and Mac froze for split second at the sight of Conrad, Krieger, and two oversized Chinese gorillas pointing guns at them. Turning to bolt out of the room, they found two gun-wielding Chinese in the hallway behind them. Stymied, Clay wondered about the Chinese, then put it down to them wanting to protect their interests in the LENR. Did that mean the deal had gone through?

"Come in, gentlemen. Please, we've been expecting you," Conrad said, mocking them. With gun barrels jammed in their backs, they had absolutely no choice. On Conrad's orders, the Chinamen removed Clay and Mac's gun belts and patted them down, finding Clay's GPS navigator in the process.

"So nice to see you again, Conrad," Clay replied to Conrad in kind. He thought about saying they were there to see Maria, but decided she was best left out of it. "Expecting us?"

"But of course. I was fairly certain you'd try again for the file. You don't really think I'd be so foolish as to believe that phony story you handed me the other night, do you?"

"What file?"

"Oh come on, Clay. You know what I'm talking about. Who are you working for?"

"Well, myself, Conrad. If you'll remember, you wanted to buy Fairview from us. By the way, Krieger, how are you feeling? Looks like you've had a bit of an accident. Run off the road did you?"

Krieger, wearing a large bandage on his forehead, sneered back at Clay.

"Did you enjoy my little house buying ruse?" Conrad replied, choosing to ratchet up the sparring contest with Clay. "That was just to keep you around, in case Krieger needed to do what he tried and failed at. A rarity for him, by the way, gentlemen. He will have the opportunity to right things soon enough. You might say you'll have a couple of days reprieve while we take care of business. Something rather larger than Fairview, Clay. So you will have time to reflect on your lives, and Krieger can think about how he will end them." Krieger broke into a sardonic grin.

"Lying is a pretty big pastime for you, isn't it Conrad?" Clay said, trying to keep Conrad engaged.

"When it becomes necessary," Conrad said matter-of-factly. Then he smiled. "Or advantageous. Did you enjoy your day in court, Clay?" Conrad said with great satisfaction.

"You arranged that?" Clay replied angrily. Conrad saw that he had hit the mark.

"I most certainly did. Wanted to keep you busy while my friends got their operation into gear," he said with an evil smile. He couldn't resist adding, "And I'm sure Mac enjoyed my little Susan look-alike. Amazing what money will buy."

For a second, Mac looked as though he'd been shot with a bolt of electricity, but he caught himself. Conrad smiled at that victory too. He truly enjoyed holding all the cards.

"So, gentlemen, who are you working for? And how did you know to look here?" Conrad said with a steely look.

"Okay, you win, Conrad." Clay wracked his brains for an answer, any answer that would keep Maria out of this. He could pin it on somebody in Conrad's staff, but he didn't have any names that he could remember. He needed to stall while he thought of some way he could have found out about where the file had been hidden, if he had to admit that at all. "Weiss told me what you were up to before he died."

"Weiss? That wormy bastard! He knew about this?" Conrad seemed momentarily confused. Then he recovered. "Not possible."

"Not all of it, maybe, but a lot." Clay was working out the story as fast as possible. He needed to come up with enough detail to make it work. "He knew about the front end from his neighbor, the man your Muslim buddies killed. So Weiss knew what Prof. Wentworth's LENR generator was worth, and he said he knew you wouldn't ever pass up that much money. He was sure you'd sell the Muslims out."

"He was, was he?" Conrad said flatly, obviously getting angry at having discovered a hole in his operation.

"Weiss's friend also told him the Chinese had been sniffing around the lab." Clay lied about that, but decided to push it. He wanted to give Conrad something to worry about. "That's when the FBI started listening in on every Chinaman in shouting distance of you. That's how they found out about your deal, Conrad." Clay gave him a big, very fake smile, hoping he'd sold his story. Conrad shot a worried look to Krieger, who returned a tight-lipped, angry grimace.

"He's lying," Krieger sneered finally. "They can't have found out about Hwang Ho."

Conrad shouted at him, "Shut up, Krieger. If he didn't know before, he does now."

"It doesn't matter. He's in no position to be telling anything to our Muslim friends. Those two are not long for this land of the living."

"Yes, but not here. Not anywhere near here. And not until we've completed our business. Take them to The Cliffs and lock them up until we come up with a plan for disposing of them. An accident of some kind perhaps, but far from here. Understand?"

Krieger and the four Chinese thugs led Clay and Mac down some stairs and out through a narrow passageway to Conrad's massive garage. They marched past limousines, Mercedes sedans, and three or four sports cars before stopping in front of a Land Rover. Krieger motioned them into the back seat. Krieger drove, while one Chinaman in the front seat and three others in the rear cargo bed all kept guns trained on Clay and Mac.

Taken into the ruins of The Cliffs, Clay and Mac were led down a stairway into the badly burned out part. The guards' flashlight beams revealed that here fire had raged even in the basement level, leaving behind nothing but charred wood and remnants of the masonry walls. Another stairway took them down into a subbasement. Krieger stopped before a heavy wooden door, turned a large iron key, and then swung the door open.

Clay and Mac exchanged worried looks before being shoved into a long, completely dark corridor. Krieger's flashlight revealed four iron doors, each locked by a sliding iron bolt. At the fourth, Krieger opened the door and motioned his prisoners in. The door slammed shut, echoing on the solid rock walls. What little light the flashlight had provided suddenly disappeared. Clay felt a sudden pang of fear in the pit of his stomach. They were in a hell of a fix now.

16

THE DUNGEON

"Man, it's dark in here," Mac said after hearing the outer door slammed shut and locked. "If we don't figure something out quick, we're screwed."

"Yeah, we'd better. But I'll tell you, for a minute I thought Conrad was going to do us right there."

"You were kind of pushing him, Clay."

"Well, I was hoping to get more out of him. And I definitely didn't want them suspecting Maria."

"That girl's going to be the death of you yet. And maybe me too. I can't believe Conrad set up that whole thing with me seeing a fake Susan. Man, having to tell you what I saw about tore me up. And all along it was nothing but a con. I feel guilty as hell about causing all that grief between you and Susan."

"It's okay, Mac. He almost nailed me too, with that fake witness. You had no way of knowing--*we* had no way of knowing. And just between you, me, and these stone walls, Maria did get to me. I really love Susan, no question about it, but Maria got under my skin. I told

Susan the truth about what she saw the other night. We really were holding each other to make it look like we were lovers. But truth is, Maria was getting me worked up being that close. And when she kissed me, without even thinking, I kissed her back."

"She kissed you...?"

"Yes, it was after I told her I was going to copy that damn file. She told me to be careful and then she kissed me. It seemed so natural. Man, did I get my wires crossed. Susan saw us holding each other out there on the porch--she was really hurt. I explained that, but I didn't tell her about the kiss. And I don't want to hurt her any more, so keep that to yourself, partner."

"Don't worry, I won't say anything, not even to Rita. That one stays with us."

"In that case, maybe we should get to work finding a way out of here."

"I'm with you on that. And I'll bet Bunker can probably do something with that name you got out of Krieger. Hwang Ho, wasn't it?"

"That's right. Now, how about we start by finding out if there's anything in here to work with."

To orient themselves, they felt their way along the walls until they found the iron door. From all they could tell, it was rusty but solid. Then they methodically searched their cell. They found nothing, just bare stone walls and a stone floor. Returning to the cell door, they sat side-by-side on the stone floor.

"There must be a way out of here," Clay said idly, half to himself.

"Too bad Blakes's buddies didn't use more dynamite. Might've taken out this cell block if they had."

"Yeah, that was one hell of a fire up there. All that charred wood. Kind of reminded me of what Fairview looked like after that bastard George burned it down. Not a pleasant sight."

"No, it wasn't...*Hey! Wait a minute!*" Mac exclaimed. He stood up and started feeling the wall to locate the masonry joints between the rocks in the wall next to the door. He started out about chest high, and then started working his way higher.

"Mac, what *are* you doing?"

"Clay, don't you remember what happened to the foundation out at Fairview? The heat of the fire turned the cement to dust."

"Mac, by God, you're a damn genius!" He stood up next to Mac.

"It's still solid at chest height, Clay. But up here, shoulder height, it's almost loose enough for me to scrape it out with my finger."

"Our belts, Mac. The buckles are metal. We can use them for scrapers!"

They quickly traced the outline of a big stone whose mortar joint was powdery all the way around. Working furiously, they scraped out enough of the mortar to work the stone loose and pull it out. That put a dent in the wall. But because it had been built with rough stones of varying sizes, there had to be at least another layer between them and the corridor. They would also have to make the opening big enough to get through. So, they next traced out two more stones, and each man set to work on one.

Finally doing something to escape buoyed their spirits and helped brush aside thoughts of the second door they would somehow have to get through--before Krieger came back for them. If they got to the corridor, they could always surprise him and get his gun.

Two more stones fell to the floor. The dent was now almost large enough that they'd be able to crawl through. They traced the joints of the last two rocks needed to make the hole big enough. With them out, they would work on the outer layer of rocks to complete the hole. At least they hoped that was the outer layer.

It was tedious work though. Scrape, scrape, scrape until the furrow got deep enough to wiggle the rock free. As they dug deeper still, the sharp edges of the rock scratched and cut their fingers. But this was no time to sweat the small stuff. They kept working as quickly as they could. Clay pulled his rock loose first and took a breather, listening to Mac scraping away at his in the darkness. Clay heard the hollow thud of another rock dropping to the floor.

"What do you say, Mac, the hole seems big enough now. Shall we start on the next layer?"

"Don't say next. Say outer layer."

"Okay, think positive." It was harder to find the actual joints--the mortar seemed to have been slopped in place between the layers, but it was still soft. They were making real progress now, enough that the tension of being trapped had all but disappeared.

"You know, Mac. We've gotten into a hell of a lot of trouble over this LENR thing. And I still don't know how LENR works. Did you ever find out?"

"Well, sort of. From what I've read, there's still some stuff they don't completely understand, but the theory explains a lot. It's kind of complicated, but I can give you the basics."

"At the moment, Mac, I've got all the time in the world. So don't keep me in suspense."

"In a way, it's like this wall here, except we're talking molecules not rocks. The surface of certain kinds of metals amounts to a flat face of interlocking molecules. Except that under certain conditions, little cracks form here and there between the molecules."

"Like the mortar joints we're scraping away."

"Yes, like that. Except they're really, really tiny. Nano-sized cracks. Anyway, if you put that metal, like palladium or nickel, into an electrolyte of water--I think heavy hydrogen works better--and run a current through it, you begin to get hydrogen atoms migrating into those cracks. That's when things start to get strange. For some reason, the hydrogen atoms link up, forming a line inside the crack. But the linkage is not stable. When the atoms break apart, they release energy in a tiny flash. Get enough of them going at once, and suddenly you have quite a lot of heat being released."

Clay went silent, suddenly engrossed in scraping the joint he'd been working on. Mac kept on digging around his rock.

"So, if it's a nuclear reaction, why isn't there radiation released?"

"There is, but it's a very weak form in most cases. A few experiments have produced some stronger radiation, but something seems to happen in the way LENR usually works that prevents the creation of radioactive byproducts. Maybe because the stuff breaks down to something stable right away. What you end up with is usually helium, but that varies, depending on what metal you use for a cathode and what the electrolyte is."

"Oh," Clay said thoughtfully. "You know, Mac, my rock feels kind of loose and wiggly. I've tried pushing on it, but it won't go. How about you give it a try?"

Mac groped around in the hole until he found the rock. It was definitely loose, but it refused to break free when Mac tried pulling it inward. So he pushed it hard, and gained a little more. Frustrated, he jerked it back and forth and then, with a low growl, shoved it with all his might. That's when it gave way and fell into the corridor with a thud.

"I hope nobody heard that, " Mac said, trying to hold his breath and listen for someone coming.

"I'm betting they have so much confidence in this cell block that Krieger isn't too worried about us escaping." Clay went silent while he felt inside the hole. "You did it guy. We're definitely through. Now all we have to do is make the hole bigger."

Both men reached in and started working vigorously to loosen more rocks. No longer a solid mass of interlocking parts, the rocks began coming out faster and faster. When the hole was finally big enough, Clay squirmed through first, with Mac close on his heels. They dusted themselves off and went to the wood door at the head of the corridor.

"What do you see?" Mac whispered as Clay peered through a small metal grate. Outside, a lantern flickered against the darkness, and a heavyset guard lay fast asleep, sitting propped up against a wall. An empty liquor bottle lay on the ground next to him.

"Looks like one of Conrad's regulars. Dead drunk and fast asleep. No wonder he didn't hear us."

"I guess he won't mind then, if we get the hell out of here."

"Probably not. But how, Mac? This door is really solid."

"More scraping?"

"Might have to. But first, let's see if there's anything we can use in these other cells."

As Clay felt his way along the wall, he wondered out loud, "You know Mac, I thought those Muslims would be long gone after the raid. But from what Maria said, they're still here. Do you suppose they're sticking around for another raid?"

"Yeah, it's kind of strange. Conrad's got the Chinamen guarding the house. Maybe the Chinese are insurance, in case the Muslims get wise to his deal."

"Might be," Clay said. "Here's one," Clay said as he felt a metal door. Sliding the bar back, he pulled hard and the old iron door opened, its rusty hinges protesting loudly. Clay stepped cautiously into the pitch dark cell. Two steps in, his toe bumped into something.

"Mac, it feels like wooden boxes, crates of something."

"Another weapons stash?"

"Probably. These crates are long and thin. Rifles maybe."

"Well grab one, will yah?"

"I don't have anything to open the crate with, Mac. Plus they're probably packed in Cosmoline. Let's try the other doors."

"More crates," Clay announced a minute later. "These are smaller and heavy as hell. Must be ammo. This place is their damn armory." And again, after opening the third door. "More crates."

"That's great, Clay, but how do we get out of here? Sooner or later somebody's going to come back and find that guard."

"Let's try the other side of this corridor. I didn't notice any doors when they brought us in, but I wasn't really looking." Returning to wood door, Clay began feeling his way along the opposite wall. About halfway, he found a flimsy wood door that opened easily. He probed the darkness beyond it with his foot.

"Hey, it's steps, Mac. Steps going down."

"Let's take 'em. Anything is better than here."

Feeling their way down, they came to a landing and more stairs leading down. From there they saw light pouring in through an open doorway at the bottom. It was like air to drowning men, and they hurried toward it. Clay waited a moment for his eyes to adjust to the light before peering cautiously out into a tunnel.

"Mac, this looks very familiar. I think this is the tunnel we were in before."

"Good. Then let's head uphill and get the hell out of here."

"Not so fast, Mac. If those terrorists are gone, I'm thinking we might find some weapons down there. We're probably going to need something to fight with before we get out of here."

Mac agreed, even though he thought their chances would be a lot better above ground. Down here they might run into a Muslim terrorist or armed Chinese guard at any moment. Even though the tunnel lights were on, it seemed singularly deserted, so Clay thought the Muslims were long gone. He was dead wrong. When they reached the gallery, they saw not the six from before, but a full dozen lounging about in the room below. And there in the middle of them was "Vanilla." Clay had no choice but to signal Mac and retreat back up the tunnel.

Passing by the two arms caches they had investigated previously, Clay thought "My kingdom for a crowbar." But they kept on and passed through the secret door into the mansion's basement kitchen. Then, finally, they broke out above ground on the first floor of the ruins, relieved to be breathing fresh night air and savoring their freedom.

But they weren't out of the woods yet. Until they got back to that cave and their gear, they had no weapons, no radio, and worst of all, Clay's cell phone remained out of reach in Conrad's desk. Clay toyed with the idea of taking another shot at retrieving it. Until word got out that they'd escaped, nobody would be expecting another attempt. But that guard could wake up at any moment.

The night air seemed noticeably cooler and ground fog was settling in. That could help with their escape, Clay thought. Taking no chances, he and Mac crept cautiously through the ruins and out to the fire road leading back to Foxhaven. Clay suddenly put out a hand to stop Mac. A Gator sat unattended on the fire road. Where was the driver?

Clay scanned the shadows and finally spotted a guard seated nearby on the ground, smoking a cigarette. Clay tapped Mac's shoulder, pointed to the cigarette's faint glow, and signaled him to work around behind the man. Clay waited until Mac was in position and then stood up, his hands in the air.

"I give up," Clay shouted as he walked with arms raised toward the man, hoping the guy wouldn't take a shot at him. The surprised guard scrambled to his feet and was reaching for his rifle when Mac came up from behind. Mac's single powerful blow hit the base of the guard's neck, knocking him out cold.

"This is our ticket out of here," Clay said as he checked the Gator for the key and started it up. "Grab his rifle, Mac, and hop on. We're going for a ride!"

"Hold on Clay! Let me get his walkie-talkie too."

Clay revved up the machine and, with Mac hanging on for dear life, he swung the Gator into a sliding U-turn, then sped off down the fire road toward Foxhaven. What was going to happen when they got there was very much an open question, but at least now they had something to fight with. And if they were lucky enough to get to that little cave, then they'd be home in time for breakfast. Mac would appreciate that, Clay thought, smiling to himself.

"Mac," Clay shouted over the Gator's roaring engine, "I was just thinking...."

"Uh-oh."

"How are we going to find that pond again? We need that marker to figure out where to turn into the woods below the mansion. We'll have to ditch the Gator and sneak past the mansion somehow."

"Yeah sure," Mac replied, not thrilled with that plan. "Conrad's sure to have guards out patrolling the grounds. They're liable to spot us."

"They won't," Clay said confidently. Then he saw the headlights on the trail ahead. "Yes they will. Shit, Mac, company's coming."

Clay didn't slow, instead impulsively rammed the Gator up to full throttle. It was a flat out gamble. The darkened tree trunks whipped by now at over forty mph, and he could only hope the two lights careening toward him came from two ATVs running side-by-side, not the Land Rover. On this narrow woodland road, if it was the Rover, he'd have nowhere to go but smack into the those trees. He'd know in a few seconds. Clay held his breath. He was closing fast, a hundred yards, now seventy five, now fifty.

"Hang on, Mac." The headlights started to wobble. Clay leaned forward, as if pushing the Gator to go still faster.

"Yes!" Clay yelled to Mac. The two ATVs behind their headlights chickened out, suddenly peeling off to either side of the fire road. Clay blasted right between them, catching a glimpse of two gaping rednecks.

"Yee-hah!" Clay yelled as he whipped by them.

"They're calling it in, Clay!" Mac yelled a few seconds later, their confused messages coming over the captured walkie-talkie he now held up to his ear.

"So we shouldn't stop in and say hello to Conrad, then," Clay joked, still caught up in the exhilaration of the moment.

"Nope, definitely not. I think that was Krieger bitching them out for letting us get away. Those two guys on ATVs are coming after us now. You can bet they'll have another welcoming committee waiting for us, if we make it as far as Foxhaven."

"Good point, Mac. They definitely will be looking for the Gator. Time to take aggressive action here," Clay said, skidding the Gator to a halt. "Do you see them yet, Mac?"

"No, but I hear them. They're getting close."

"You take one side, and I'll take the other. Let's nail them before they call in again," Clay said as the two melted into the trees lining the fire road.

The two rednecks on ATVs pulled to a stop a few yards away, removed their helmets, and with guns drawn, approached the still idling Gator on either side. After giving it a once over, they holstered their revolvers. Bushes behind them rustled and they turned just as two darkened figures sprang at them in a surprise attach. Clay grabbed hold of his man by the neck, pulled him over backward, and knocked him out by pounding his head against the Gator. Mac throttled his man with lightning quick punches that sent him to the ground unconscious.

"Find their radios, Mac. I'll grab their guns. This keeps up, we might actually be able to defend ourselves.

"Okay, Mac, time to adapt and improvise or we'll never get the hell out of here. The way I see it, Krieger will be looking for us in the Gator. What I'm thinking is that we take the ATVs and approach the grounds at normal speed. But instead of going in, we turn off at the fire road that runs outside the stone wall. We'll follow that around to about where that pond would be. Then head for our stash in the woods. Krieger won't be expecting us outside the wall. That should buy us extra time. When these two monkeys wake up, they won't be able to call in. If they go back to the mansion in the Gator, Krieger's liable to think they're us. That might add to the confusion and get us even more time."

"Once they catch on, they'll be after us for sure. It's 1:30 now," Mac said looking at his watch. "Bunker won't be up looking for us for another half hour."

"Short of hoofing it out of here, I don't know what else we can do. Just keep 'em chasing their tails as long as we can."

"Okay, Clay. It's worth a shot. I'd say let's get going before these guys wake up."

"Be wonderful if they'd drive that Gator right onto the grounds."

Mac grinned as he and Clay donned the helmets and hopped on the ATVs. They took off at half speed and minutes later stopped at the trail around the stone wall. Clay couldn't believe their luck. He heard the Gator's engine revving high and heading for the mansion. He and Mac turned onto the perimeter road and disappeared around a bend before the Gator roared past and flew into a waiting gauntlet. A fusillade of small arms fire erupted just seconds later, the shots crackling in the cool night air. Clay and Mac gunned their ATVs, racing now for the spot where they would turn into the forest.

Finding that spot would be little better than guesswork, but Clay kept checking their position relative to the mansion. After coming around its back side, Clay slowed and stood up on the ATV. He could just see the South Porch. Judging by the angle, Clay estimated they had only a few hundred feet more to go. Then the guard's two-way radio crackled.

"You bastard," Krieger shouted over the airwaves. "You're dead. Slowly. I promise."

Clay pressed the talk button. "Gotta catch me first, Krieger!"

"You think he isn't pissed enough already, Clay?" Mac asked plaintively. "I'll bet he calls in the Muslims now."

"Come on, let's go. Up there, where this road bends, we take to the woods. All we've gotta do is find that pine grove and we're home free."

"Yeah, at two. Still twenty minutes to go." Clay had already started off and didn't hear. Mac popped his ATV in gear and both veered off into the woods, bouncing over rocks and skidding down the short slopes, branches of small trees whipping at them the whole way. Clay noticed the ground fog getting thicker as they worked their way farther down the slope, especially in the hollows.

Weaving in and out around the trees, rocks and logs, he was having a hard enough time trying to keep to a straight line. If the fog got any thicker, they might have to give up trying to find that pine grove and their packs. Except they needed Mac's radio to contact Bunker. Otherwise, it would be a long walk home, with Krieger and his gang combing the woods all the way.

Clay signaled Mac to hold up, then called over to him, "We should have seen that pine grove by now, Mac. I'm guessing, but I think we've gone about as far down this mountainside as we went up. Maybe we should start zigzagging to see if we can find it that way."

"Whatever you say, Clay. But do you hear what I hear? Sounds like ATVs. A lot of them. Coming this way."

"We probably left a dead easy trail to follow with these things. Let's try a left turn here and see if we can find those pines. Maybe this fog will throw them off our trail," Clay said, looking around. Visibility in the low spots was down to ten feet or so.

Mac gave him a thumbs up, and the two turned and started running across the mountain slope. A few more minutes of bobbing, bouncing, and weaving between trees and they ran smack into the fog shrouded pine grove. Wheeling right, they skidded down alongside the boulders, and stopped at the cave.

"How's that for dead reckoning, Mac?" Clay bragged in a loud whisper as he ducked into the small cave to retrieve their equipment. Meanwhile Mac circled around the front of the cave, kicking the leaves and looking at the ground. "What are you doing, Mac?" Clay asked as he hauled out their M-16s and backpacks.

"Looking for my rabbit's foot. I must have dropped it around here somewhere," Mac said, keeping his voice down.

"Mac, how can you believe in that stupid rabbit's foot? I mean, you're Mr. Science right? What good can it do you when we're surrounded by a bunch of bad guys. Like right now!"

"I don't know. But that's exactly it, Clay. When my butt is on the line like this, I figure I need all the luck I can get. *I believe.*"

"That's what it's all about I guess. But we need to get out of here, and quick."

Mac stopped and bent over. "Here it is!" he announced happily and slipped the rabbit's foot into his shirt pocket. Then he cocked his head, listening to the ATVs. "See it works, Clay. Sounds like those guys missed our turn. They're running downhill past of us now and well over to the right."

"I'll never doubt your rabbit's foot again," Clay joked.

"Should we put some more distance between us and them?"

"Not unless they wind up right on top of us. These big boulders give us a break in the canopy. That'll make it easier for Bunker to drop the fast line. And the fog's pretty thick right here in this hollow. Maybe we can hide out until Bunker gets here."

Mac handed Clay the two-way radio and GPS navigator from his backpack. Then they strapped on the waist harnesses for hooking onto the fast line Bunker would be lowering for their escape.

"How much time?" Clay asked.

"Ten minutes." Mac looked uphill. "Sounds like more ATVs coming downhill. Like they're really spread out."

"Must have figured out they lost our trail. Be really great if Bunker was early."

The forest echoed with the sound of ATV engines, too many to count. The thick fog hiding Clay and Mac also made it impossible to see where the ATVs were. But they were definitely close now.

"How much more time, Mac?" Clay asked, turning his head trying to locate the closest ATVs.

Mac didn't have a chance to answer. Suddenly an ATV flew overhead, it's engine screaming at full throttle with no load as it sailed over the lip of the boulder above them. The heavier ATV followed a steeper curving arc, separating from the terrified driver. The ATV crashed into the ground, bounced and then slid, tumbling downhill, lost in the fog. The driver hurtled over Clay and Mac, his arms and legs flailing. He flew headfirst into a tree trunk with a terrible thud and dropped like a sack of potatoes to the ground a few feet away. Clay rushed over to him.

"He's one of those Muslims, Mac. Dead. Krieger's called out the cavalry," Clay whispered. "But look, they're using NODs. If they get too close, we can surprise 'em with the flash bangs."

"They're not using thermal imaging?"

"Nope, optical. No wonder they haven't found us. They can't see us in this fog."

"How much more time, Mac?"

"Five minutes by my watch. But do you hear that?"

"Man, am I glad he's early." Clay clicked the talk button on the two-way. "That you, Bunker?"

"Yeah man. You hot or cold?"

"Very hot, but in a bunch of fog. I hear 'em pretty close by. IR beacon is on. Mac says glad you're early. So am I."

"Worried about you. Are you in a clearing?"

"Sort of. Not big enough to land. Better come in, hover, and drop that fast line. Company's close by." Clay then read him the GPS coordinates for the middle of the clearing.

"Roger that, I've punched it in. Wait one, while I check my IR screen. I see six of 'em moving slowly toward you. Two very close, just west of you. Have you got those flash bangs?"

"Roger. Got 'em out now." Then, with hand signals, he and Mac took up positions behind trees on opposite edges of the clearing. Clay stepped behind the tree where the dead Muslim lay and flicked off the safety of his M-16. Problem was, if he fired it, the sound would bring the rest of Krieger's army down on them. So would the flash bangs.

The sound of Bunker's chopper overhead was music to Clay's ears. He couldn't see it, but he heard it and that was all he needed now. He imagined it must be confusing the hell out of Conrad's men, wondering what it was doing there. Bunker was close now, hovering overhead just above the fog. The chopper's rotor wash swirled the ground fog in a frenzy. Looking up from behind the big tree trunk, Clay saw the fast line drop and then dangle about waist level, like a miracle from heaven. So near, yet so far. He couldn't go to it, because two ATVs had just pulled into the clearing.

Clay pulled back behind the tree as two Muslims spied the dangling rope and then looked curiously around the clearing. One headed toward the cave, flipping down his NODs as he did so. The other walked straight for the tree where Clay hid and leaned over for a closer look at his dead comrade. He was so close, Clay could hear him breathing. It was now or never.

Clay stepped around the tree with gun butt raised and brought it down with all his strength on the back of the Muslim's neck. The man went face first to the ground as Clay hit him again. Then Clay took a flash bang off his belt, pulled the pin and tossed it into the cave. "Mac," he yelled. "Eyes!" Clay turned away and covered his ears just before the flash of light and incredible explosion. "Second man down, Mac. Let's get the hell out of here!" Clay said running to the fast line. Mac appeared a second later and the two quickly latched their harnesses onto the fast line's D-rings.

"We're on," Clay yelled into the two-way. "Take her up fast!"

"Roger. Thought you guys got lost."

It was as though they'd been snatched up on a giant rubber band. Twenty feet, forty feet, then suddenly they were clear of the ground fog. A second later, still hurtling upward, Clay looked down and to his horror, saw muzzle flashes erupt from the woods below, outside the perimeter of the heavy ground fog. He and Mac were sitting ducks. Clay grabbed Mac's shoulder, showed him a flash bang, and pointed down at the muzzle flashes.

They were about a hundred feet off the ground when he and Mac tossed flash-bang grenades, mentally counting out the seconds before they would go off. Then they covered their eyes as the bright flashes blinded the shooters down below.

Clay hugged the fast line as Bunker turned the chopper toward the clearing he'd been using to land and wait. Sailing along at forty or fifty miles an hour, Clay marveled at his intense feeling of relief, despite hanging from a thin tether several hundred feet above the blackened forest. He'd never felt safer, but then maybe it was only relative to the last few hours. Soon though, he and Mac found themselves hovering over a clearing, gradually descending earthward. Home free and damn glad of it.

For the trip home, Clay sat in the cockpit next to Bunker, and put on the headset Bunker handed him. Long-legged Mac sat sideways in the rear passenger seat and promptly fell asleep. The view through the bulb-shaped windscreen was like looking out of a fishbowl, interrupted in the middle by the lighted instrument console. Clay watched as Bunker lifted the collective and the chopper began a steady vertical climb. Once they were above the treetops, the chopper tipped forward slightly and began the homeward journey.

"Did you get it?" Clay heard Bunker ask through the headset.

"No, dammit. Somehow, Conrad figured out we were there. We made it to Conrad's study, but he had some Chinese gunmen waiting for us. I got him talking though. I told him Weiss had pretty much figured out what he was up to. That pissed him off."

"Chinese gunmen? Do you think Conrad's deal has already gone down?"

"No. Well, probably not. He said he'd kill us *in a couple of days,* after he had taken care of some business. I assume that's the China deal. Then he threw us in a dungeon underneath that ruined mansion by the lake. More arms caches in there, by the way, and we saw a dozen Muslim terrorists in the living quarters in the tunnel under The Cliffs. Vanilla was there too."

"Vanilla?"

"Didn't I tell you about him? White guy, I think he's American."

"Jeez. One of our own."

"Yeah. And I thought they'd all have skipped by now, but maybe they have something else planned. Before I forget it, Krieger slipped up and gave me the name of their China contact, Hwang Ho. Can you check him out?"

"Sure. If he's foreign, it'll be easier to set up surveillance on him too."

Clay was silent for a long time, thinking over the night's events. They'd had a narrow escape, and Conrad's estate would surely be well guarded from now on, albeit by a mongrel force of Conrad's regular thugs, Chinese, and Muslim terrorists too. Clay knew they'd been lucky to get out whole this time. Prospects for another trip into that hornet's nest did not look good, but his cell phone was still in there. He told himself, he would have to be crazy to try again.

They were passing over Staunton now, the sun just peeking over the horizon. Clay finally spoke up. "You know that deal is going to go down soon, Bunker."

"Yes, looks like it."

"Can your guys do anything to stop it?"

"Sorry to say it, Clay, but probably not. I'll try, but I got shot down pretty hard when I tried the first time. He's on our radar now, but Conrad's got a lot of juice up there in DC. It'll take a while to build a case and push back against his friends."

"Yeah, I understand," Clay said, but it left a sour taste in his mouth. He couldn't let go of the fact Conrad might get away with it. Somebody had to stop him. "You know, I was thinking maybe Maria could get in there and get the phone without getting into trouble. She's pretty much got the run of the place. Did you ever find out if the Germans have a secure way of communicating with her?"

"They do. Her mother."

"What?"

"Her mother calls her and they talk for a while about family stuff, how she's doing, that kind of thing. When her mother talks about her migraines that's the signal for Maria to go shopping in Trustlow. That's where her handler is. Severe migraines means ASAP."

"Can you get them to do that this morning? Get a message to call me on Susan's cell phone. I've got to talk to her."

"I can try. What are you thinking? You're not going back are you? I've got a couple of bullet holes to explain from this sortie, Clay."

"Right now, I'm not sure. It'll depend a lot on what Maria says. For sure the file's been moved, but if we can get my cell phone out, we won't need it."

Bunker landed at the mill house, and after dropping off Clay and Mac, he headed back to DC. Clay made him promise to contact the Germans first thing when he landed in DC.

The mill never looked so good to Clay. After Mac drove off for home, Clay was torn between his gnawing hunger and his drooping eyelids. Sleep won out and Clay bypassed the kitchen for the bedroom. Susan was awake when he fell into bed with his clothes on. She kissed the top of his head to avoid the blacking still on his face and asked what had happened. "Didn't get it," he mumbled before falling sound asleep. It had been a long, discouraging night.

17

THE HISTORY LESSON

Maria went down to breakfast early the next morning, hoping to catch her uncle and ask him about all the gunfire the previous night. She had been frightened to death and suspected the worst--that Clay had been mortally wounded. After all the commotion had died down, Conrad sent a maid to her room to reassure her that all was well and tell her to have a pleasant night's sleep. As if she could.

Conrad was surprised to see her so early and was in an unusually noncommunicative mood. It was a rare time when he didn't submit to her charms and open up. All he would say was that an intruder had gotten onto the estate and shot at the mansion. They'd wounded him, Conrad said, and Krieger took the man to the hospital. That's when Krieger came into the dining room and whispered something to Conrad. Maria saw an angry look cross Conrad's face before he excused himself, saying he had business to attend in the library.

Maria waited until he left, then hurried to her room and took the secret passage to the library. From the peephole she saw four Middle Eastern types and one Caucasian, none of whom she recognized. They were obviously angry, as were Conrad and Krieger.

"What were they doing here?" the Caucasian man insisted in perfect English.

"I told you," Conrad snapped, feeding them yet another lie. "We think they were looking for you. They know about your attack on the LENR laboratory. Somehow they came to the conclusion that you might be here. We caught them, and left them securely locked up at The Cliffs. We posted a guard, but he let them escape."

"Allah will tell you how to punish your guard. *I* will tell you your prison cell is no better than a piece of Swiss cheese. You should have killed those two while you had them."

"Perhaps. But you know my policy is to never allow anything to happen on this estate. And now it has. If I cannot control this situation and word leaks out, the police will come with warrants to search the house and grounds. Call your people. Tell them you must leave here before tomorrow evening. By the seaplane to a ship in international waters would be best, but that decision is yours. Tell them I absolutely insist on it. Sooner would be better. And use your radio, not my telephone, to make contact, understand?"

The Caucasian was obviously still angry, but nodded his agreement and the five left, eyeing the four armed Chinese guards in the library as they did so. The presence of the Arabs and the Chinese puzzled Maria, especially since there seemed to be bad blood between them. Was this somehow connected to the sale of the LENR plans? Was Conrad talking about Clay and Mac? At least she knew now that whomever it was had escaped Conrad's clutches alive.

Maria returned to her bedroom unsure of what she should do. Something was coming to a head, but what? The sale to the Chinese? A revolt in the ranks by those Arabs? Who are they and what are they doing here? she wondered. An hour later, Maria received a phone call from her mother, and now she knew something really important was happening. She waited until lunch, when she casually mentioned to Conrad that she was going shopping in Trustlow. She asked if he wanted her to get anything, but her question barely broke through whatever thoughts were occupying his mind. He barely smiled and wished her a good time in town.

What weighed on Conrad's mind was his father's demand that he explain last night's events. Conrad had been putting his father off all night--and this morning--sending messages by servants that all was well. Thankful that the old man had remained in his room, Conrad had kept him there by promising he would explain everything after lunch. That time was upon him now.

Conrad entered his father's room with far more hesitation than on his recent triumphal visits. He knew that he would have to tell everything, but presenting it in the best possible light was what worried him. There really wasn't any. The deal would go through tomorrow as planned, but that damnable Clay was still alive. He could throw a monkey wrench into the deal. Had already tried to. And might have succeeded if it hadn't been for an alert guard manning the security cameras. Most of the guards were useless drunks, but at least one had earned his pay.

"Afternoon, Sir. Was lunch satisfactory?" Conrad asked cheerfully as he strode into the room, exuding false confidence.

"No, and you damn well know why. People out there shooting up the estate last night, and you wait to see if I'm all right until now?"

"Really, Sir. There was never any danger to you."

"Well, I couldn't see it from here, but Ludwig tells me that two men were shot to death out there."

"That was a mistake."

"Mistake!"

"Yes. We caught those two I told you about trying to steal the LENR plans from my study. Caught them red-handed. I had them locked up, but they escaped. Krieger had word they were driving a Gator, but they'd switched to ATVs. When two of our guards drove the Gator back, they were shot and killed. Unfortunate."

"I told you that LENR business was going to be trouble," Klaus declared without so much as a thought about those two lost guards. "Haven't I taught you anything? How can you forget what happened to your grandfather? To me?...To be forced to flee your own house?" Klaus's voice became shriller still as his scowl morphed into red-faced rage at the painful memory.

"*My God, Conrad, my mother and I barely got out alive! I was only fifteen and she had to drag me into the escape tunnel. I was determined to stay and help him, but she dragged me. Those bastards blew up The Cliffs while we were still in the tunnel. My whole world shook, and I knew...I knew they had killed him. Those bastard Americans, they did it. I know they sent those murderers.*"

"Sir, you have told me this hundreds of times. I could not possibly have forgotten how horrible it was. Don't you see, what I am doing will repay them for what they did, just as you have--"

"I never put you or Foxhaven in jeopardy, Conrad," Klaus shot back. "You know that."

"Yes, and you never managed more than a pinprick here and a pinprick there. I cannot be so timid. *I* want to hurt them in a way they will remember for a long time," Conrad said with bravado. "*And become rich doing it,*" he added with relish.

"You fool, you overreach yourself."

"*I will succeed, Sir.* Make no mistake about it. Tomorrow," he said with satisfaction, "the Chinese will bring the down payment for the plans."

"If those two don't stop you," Klaus said with an angry satisfaction.

Conrad stared at his father, momentarily lost for words. How could the man wish him ill luck? His own son!

"They were lucky to escape with their lives," he said finally. "They won't be in such a hurry to try again." He gave his father an indignant look, but it was theater for the heat of the moment. Clay and Mac probably *had* learned their lesson. But Conrad knew full well that if those two breached the stone wall his political allies had erected in Washington, the authorities would come down on him like a plague of locusts. Once the Chinese came through with their first payment, though, there would be plenty of money to shore up any chinks in that wall. Conrad broke into a sneering smile and took his leave of Sir. He had more important matters to attend.

* * * *

One o'clock that afternoon, Susan gently shook Clay's shoulder. "Clay. Clay! Wake up. Maria's on my phone. She said it's really important."

"What?" Clay said groggily. "Maria?" Coming out of a deep sleep, he was momentarily confused, unsure where he was until he realized he was in his own bed.

"Yes. She said she was supposed to talk with you." Susan handed him her cell phone.

"Oh. Right," he said coming back to reality, then took hold of the phone. "Hello, Maria?"

Susan started to get up from the bed to give them some privacy, though she really didn't want to. Clay caught her by the sleeve. "No, you stay," he insisted and pulled her back onto the bed.

"Maria, yes I needed to talk to you. It's urgent. Migraine urgent." He listened for a moment and smiled. "Yes, I thought it was clever too. But listen, I'm sure you heard a lot of commotion last night. That was Mac and me. Conrad caught us trying to get into his study. We were trying to get my cell phone. I took pictures of everything in that LENR file with it, but he came in right when I finished. I barely had time to put the file back, and my phone slipped out of my hand. It fell into the bottom of the file drawer.

"From what Conrad said that night, I think the deal with China is going down tomorrow, so we don't have much time. I need your help to get my cell phone, Maria. Without that, Conrad could walk away scot free. Can you sneak into Conrad's study without getting into trouble?"

Clay still held Susan's arm loosely, squeezing lightly at points during the conversation without realizing it. Susan watched him, realizing how intently focused he was on Maria's reply.

"A secret passageway? You're kidding, aren't you? That sounds like something out of a '40s movie." He listened again as Maria described the argument this morning between Conrad and the Muslims. "That doesn't sound good Maria. I don't think you should go back to Foxhaven at all. This thing is a powder keg that's liable to blow up any minute."

Listening again, he exhaled an exasperated breath. "Well, you're right. I do need that cell phone, and I can see that your necklace is important too.

"Mac and I will come get you tonight...I don't know, Maria, let me think. A car. We need a car. Can you get keys for one of those in Conrad's garage?...Well, what are you driving?... A sedan? That will work. Can you have the keys with you tonight?"

Clay's hand slid down to cover Susan's. He gave hers a squeeze and then smiled at her. A plan was coming together, and he might yet get the better of Conrad Nebel, impossible as that might seem. Memories of last night's near disaster and narrow escape receded, pushed aside by thoughts of a second chance now in the offing.

"The only way, Maria, would be with some kind of diversion. I don't know. I'll have to think about that. But it's not your worry. Mac and I will have to come up with something. You be on the South Porch at nine tonight with the cell phone and the car keys. Be close to the stairway to the garden. Mac and I will sneak in after dark and meet you there. We're going to drive out."

Clay listened to Maria's final protest. "We'll think of something, Maria. I don't want him to get away with this anymore than you do." Clay closed Susan's cell phone and handed it back to her. "We're back in business, honey. Would you be available to drive Mac and me over to Foxhaven tonight?"

"I suppose you'll be wanting breakfast now too," she said with mock irritation.

"Absolutely. I'm famished."

Shortly after three, Mac arrived at the mill house and joined Clay and Susan in the living room.

"You really want to go back there again, Clay?" Mac chided.

"Truth be told, I've had my fill of high society, Mac. But we need those plans and it's getting pretty dicey for Maria too. If those Muslims figure out Conrad's sold them out, there could be a small war between them and Conrad's Chinese buddies. I really don't know who would win."

"Maybe they'd kill each other off." Mac smiled as he said it.

"Yeah, but odds are Conrad would get away. Anyway, we need some kind of diversion to cover our exit from Foxhaven. Maria's going to be out on the South Porch at nine. We should be able to sneak her through that garden and down to Conrad's garage below it. Maria's going to have the keys for one of his cars. We'll drive right out."

"Assuming nobody's following us."

"Yes. That's where the diversion would help. Keep Conrad's attention--better yet Krieger's--focused somewhere else while we hightail it."

"What have you got in mind, Clay?"

"Besides explosives, loud rock n' roll music, or flying pigs? I haven't a clue."

"Jeez."

While Clay and Mac grinned at each other, Susan spoke up. "You already know the answer, Clay. Do what Mr. Hill did. Remember? He got the communists to put a stop to Conrad's grandfather, just by feeding them some information. That's all you'd have to do."

"What, like tell the Muslims what Conrad's up to?"

"Yes, exactly."

"Why should they believe anything we tell them," Mac asked.

"Good point. But from what Maria told me, the Muslims met with Conrad this morning wanting to know what we were doing there last night. Conrad said we were after *them* because of the LENR attack."

"Guy's a damn agile liar, that's for sure. Suppose they would believe you. You can't exactly pick up the phone and give 'em a buzz at nine, can you?"

"No, and timing isn't the only problem. We obviously can't call them at their hideout in those tunnels. But Bunker said that Moktar is probably connected to them somehow--you remember that mosque above the Halal Meat Market we staked out? He's the imam there and from what Bunker says, they've got him making calls to a sheik in Qatar. Very circumspect conversations that appear to be about nothing, so Bunker thinks it's code talk. He's also made calls to what Bunker says was their safe house in Fairfax. Unfortunately nobody's home there now, which may be why they're still at Foxhaven. Moktar probably figured out the Feds were onto the safe house."

"What you're saying is that we don't really have a way to rat out Conrad?"

"No, only that we *may* have a way. Maria told me she heard Conrad tell the Muslims to use the radio in The Cliffs hideout. They were supposed to contact somebody to transport them out by tomorrow. That means Moktar might be able to get a message *to* them. It's a gamble, I know. But Susan's right, if they get word Conrad's sold them out, they'll blast him right out of Foxhaven. That would be one hell of a diversion, Mac. And I don't mind the thought that it would also blow his deal with the Chinese sky high."

"So are you going to try Moktar?"

"Yes, but we need a backup, in case it doesn't work. Suppose we toss some sticks of dynamite around while we make our getaway. That ought to create lots of confusion."

"Flash-bangs would work too. They'll blind anybody following us."

"That's better yet, Mac. Flash-bangs it is. Timing is still a problem though. I can't call Moktar from anywhere around Foxhaven. There's no cell service. Once Moktar gets the message, my bet is they'll move pretty quickly. Especially if he thinks he can screw up Conrad's deal. But how do we make sure he's around to get the call?"

"Call him with a teaser first," Susan suggested. "Later today, say at four. Tell him you know about his soldiers holing up at Foxhaven.

Say you can't talk now, but a friend will call him at--when do you want, 8:00?--with some very important, very urgent information."

"Takes a woman's touch," Clay exclaimed. "That's just what we'll do. Jimmy's been itching to do something to help out. He can make the second call. I'll fill him in on what he needs to say."

Everything was going like clockwork that night. Jimmy made the second call at eight o'clock, and Moktar picked up on the second ring. He was hooked, and Jimmy could tell from the conversation that he already had his suspicions about Conrad. Susan again served as the duty driver, dropping off Clay and Mac, dressed in all black and armed with their M-16s, by the side of the road, not far from the beginning of Foxhaven's long driveway. The only hitch was the thickening fog. It would give Clay and Mac plenty of cover for their approach, but Clay worried out loud about Susan getting back safely. She replied she'd be taking it slowly, and added that would mean she was probably safer than if he were driving. Mac stifled a laugh as the two headed into woods. It was just eight o'clock.

Fairly sure they hadn't tripped any alarms before getting to the mansion previously, Clay and Mac stayed close to the driveway all the way to the outer wall surrounding the grounds. With eight minutes to spare, they again scaled the wall at the little pond, then began working their way toward Conrad's garage and the South Porch above it. The approach was going so smoothly Clay couldn't shake the feeling it was almost too easy.

Maria, anxious to get Clay his cell phone and to escape Conrad's clutches, had seemed distracted during dinner. Conrad noticed, but couldn't fathom why. Certainly a call from her mother had never upset her before. Then, out of an abundance of caution, she went down to the South Porch at fifteen minutes early. With nothing to do but wait, she sat idly at a table, purse in hand, staring out into the fog. She'd never done anything like that before, and the guard viewing the monitors thought it prudent to alert Conrad. She only takes her purse when she's going somewhere, Conrad thought, and realized what was about to happen. He called Krieger. They would have to work fast.

Clay and Mac checked the entry door to the garage, found it open, and then scaled the slope up to the garden over the garage. A winding path took them through the garden toward the stairway to the South Porch. As they approached, the mansion loomed as a vague shadow in the fog. Yellow blurs filtered out from the windows of lighted rooms. Finally, Clay saw the shadowy figure of the princess standing by the stairs, backlighted by light streaming through the French doors.

Clay hurried to Maria's side. Surprised by his sudden appearance, she threw her arms and around him and looked up expectantly at him. He'd learned his lesson, though, and returned her look with only a smile.

"We're here, Maria," he whispered. "Nothing to worry about. But we'd better get moving before the fireworks get started."

"Hold it right there, Clay!" burst out of the foggy shadows surrounding them, followed by the clicking sound of guns being cocked. Krieger, armed with a Glock pistol, and a half dozen henchmen, four Chinese and two Americans, toting AK-47s stepped out of the shadows. Then the lord of the manor, Conrad himself, casually stepped through the French doors.

"Going somewhere, my dear?" Conrad asked icily. Maria, recoiling from the frightfully evil look in his eyes, clung to Clay tighter still. "And you, Clay? Well, I should say Krieger will get his second chance at dispatching you and Mac after all. I wonder what imaginative demise he'll conjure up for you. Perhaps he'll throw you to the Muslims and let them decide what to cut off first." He laughed fiendishly at that, then officiously commanded, "Get their weapons and bring them to my study."

As Conrad disappeared through the French doors, Maria stepped back from Clay while he and Mac were frisked and relieved of their weapons. Krieger and the men, busy with those two prisoners, did not notice Maria put her hands behind her back and secretly open her purse. Probing with one hand, she latched onto Clay's flip phone, extracted it and closed the purse. She stood there innocently, palming the flip phone, until Krieger herded them to the French doors. Clustered together with Clay and Mac, she pretended to stumble into Clay from behind. In that instant, Clay felt something slip into his back pocket. A moment later he knew what it must be.

Conrad, holding an old German Luger, sat casually astride the corner of his desk as his captors were shoved roughly into the study. Clay and Mac represented the last stumbling block to his deal of the century and the almost unimaginable fortune it would bring. The only pain for him in all this was the loss of Maria. He had hoped she would come to love him and become his wife. Now that was impossible. Nor could he let her live.

Such a loss. But perhaps not entirely. He had waited patiently far too long to taste her pleasures. Once Clay and Mac had been dealt with, he decided with a flush of arrogance, he would take her, and after a day or two give her to Krieger to dispose of. He didn't care, at this moment, how.

"Now, where were we?" Conrad asked, faking pleasantries. "Last time, Clay, you left without telling how you knew that file was in my desk. Did a little bird whisper in your ear? Like my little darling Maria?"

"I told you what we were doing in here. I had no idea what was in your desk," Clay answered adamantly.

"Do you see this here?" Conrad said, patting the leather briefcase standing on top of his desk. "This is what you were looking for. The plans are in here. Doesn't it hurt you to be so close, yet powerless to have it?" He sneered triumphantly.

"I'm the one you should be worried about, *uncle*," Maria cried out. She saw no point holding out. It had been a long, agonizing year of spying on Conrad, play acting her affection for him. She was sick of it, sick of him and what he was. This was an end she had not foreseen. No one had foreseen. But it was here. "I've been spying on you for the past year."

"You what?" Conrad exclaimed through a disbelieving laugh.

"The BND recruited me because they know you smuggled arms and explosives to those terrorists in Hamburg. And I've overheard everything about your big deal with the Chinese," she said forcefully. "The secret passage."

"You know about that?" Then he answered his own question. "Of course you do."

"Yes, and now the BND knows all about your China deal and what you did to arrange it. I passed it all to them today in Trustlow."

"Why you nasty little bitch," Conrad screamed. He stood up and with a roundhouse swing hit her face with the Luger so hard she fell to the ground, bleeding from a cut cheek. Both Clay and Mac made a move to jump him, but the guards raised their weapons in a warning to stay put. Conrad stood over her, screaming, "I fed you, I practically raised you, you ungrateful little whore."

"Whore! I'm a saint compared to you, *uncle* Conrad. Always so sweet and caring. Always fawning over me. Don't think I didn't know what *you* wanted. *Uncle.*"

Conrad was momentarily embarrassed to have that thrown out in front of everyone, then sneered, "I'll have that tonight, Maria," and laughed at her. Things were spinning out of control now, tidal waves of contrary emotions raging inside him. It was not so easy to truly deny a decade of hoping for her love.

"How could you help those Muslims, Conrad?" Clay threw it out, hoping to draw him off Maria. "They're nothing but barbarians!"

"That is their chief asset," Conrad snarled back at Clay. "They can be counted on to do their worst. *They believe in brutality.* It is their passion, *their* religion. Don't you Americans believe in the freedom to practice your religion?" he asked, feeling exceptionally clever, despite the fire inside his head.

"*You* should be worried about their passion for revenge, Conrad," Clay sneered. "They know you have used them. They know you have the plans."

"So you say, Clay," Conrad smirked, still confident they had been completely duped. "Nice try though."

"I'm not lying, Conrad. That's your department." Distant sounds of automatic weapons gunfire rattled in bursts like Morse code, long, short, long. Conrad and Krieger exchanged puzzled looks. The six guards looked suddenly alert. "Hear that Conrad? That's the truth coming to get you."

"Shut up, Clay! Krieger, take our Chinese friends and get everybody you can round up on the windows. Then find out what's going on outside and report back to me." The fever inside Conrad's head raged. He felt like he might explode, but he had to think.

Krieger and the four guards weren't gone but a few seconds, when Conrad's wheelchair-bound father appeared in the study like a bad dream, a scowling nightmarish avenging angel.

"Who told you to bring him here?" Conrad shouted at Ludwig, who stood behind the wheelchair.

"Why he did," Ludwig answered servilely. "He insisted." Ludwig disappeared the moment Conrad's attention shifted from him to Klaus.

"Conrad! You fool. How many times have I told you this would happen!" the old man shouted shrilly in a quaking voice. "That's it! They've turned against you, haven't they?"

"No! Yes!" Conrad hardly knew what he was saying any longer. "Krieger will stop them."

He believed that. Had to. It couldn't all end here. He had to hold on. Tomorrow he would have it all. Just hang on for another twelve hours.

A bullet crashed through the study window. Everyone ducked at the sudden intrusion of breaking glass. The gunfire was very close to the mansion now and Klaus came unhinged.

"It is happening again!" he yelled angrily at Conrad, shaking his fist. "They will destroy our house. Mein Gott! They will kill us all, just like they did Father!"

"Sir! Shut up!" Then to the guards, he ordered, "You two, go to the window and shoot. Shoot them! I'll guard these three."

Krieger lurched back into the study, followed by a loud explosion outside.

"What was that, Krieger?" Conrad barked.

"RPG. They probably stole them from the armory. They've killed three of ours so far and they're directly outside now. We've got men in the windows firing back, but *they've* got those damn rocket propelled grenades. I don't know how we're going to hold them off."

Conrad wiped his brow. Suddenly he didn't know what to do. Another explosion shook the mansion and the sound of gunfire and breaking glass seemed to be coming from every direction. A guard ran to the study door and reported breathlessly, "Sir, the west wing is in flames."

Conrad wheeled and shouted, "Put it out then! Fool, don't stand here telling me!" The guard disappeared, abandoning ship by a back door as the fire spread to the roof. Conrad was sweating now, pacing back and forth like a trapped animal. "They can't know," he repeated over and over.

"It does not matter!" Klaus cried out. "You idiot, you've ruined us just like my father." That revelation stunned Conrad. In all the stories, Klaus had never blamed his father, never said that the disaster at The Cliffs was anything but the fault of the Americans. Klaus had been lying all these years and for Conrad it was a punch in the gut that knocked the wind out of him. He revered his grandfather. *How could he?*

More gunfire crashed through the windows, and a guard at the window slumped to the floor. Then Klaus jerked suddenly and his head fell forward. A spot of blood appeared on the left side of his chest. It was that quick. Conrad gawked at his father, feeling nothing but confusion. Everything that wasn't being torn apart was falling apart in front of him.

"How the hell could they have found out?" Conrad demanded of Krieger. Krieger just stood there.

"I told them," Clay said flatly. He wanted Conrad to know where it had come from, a last shot at revenge. "I called them and told them what you'd done."

Conrad's eyes filled with rage and he raised his Luger at Clay. Maria, standing next to Clay now, cried out "Nein" in her native German and stepped in front of Clay as Conrad fired. The sight of Maria falling to the floor shocked Conrad to the core. He rushed to her and knelt down. Clay glanced over at Krieger, who was still pointing his Glock at Mac and him, but watching Conrad cowering over the crumpled princess.

Conrad took her chin in his hand and lifted her head up. It was as though someone had flipped a switch in him. "My darling. What have I done?" he cried in the sincerest tones. She spit in his face.

A grenade crashed through a library window and the thunderous explosion blew the communicating door into the study off its hinges. In that split second Clay lunged at Krieger, grabbing his wrist and pushing his arm down and away as Krieger squeezed the trigger. Five shots spit out of Krieger's Glock, two of them ripping into Conrad's shoulder. While Conrad rolled on the floor in agony, Mac dove for the remaining guard, a giant of a man--even for Mac--who was returning fire out the window.

Clay bull rushed Krieger up against Conrad's precious desk and tried banging Krieger's gun hand against it, but Krieger was strong and refused to let go. Gaining some leverage, Krieger shoved Clay backwards. Losing his balance, Clay grabbed hold of Krieger's shirt with his free hand and pulled him to the floor as he fell backwards. Clay was already rolling sideways as he hit the floor, still holding onto Krieger's gun hand. Up on his knees, Clay landed several hard blows with his free left hand to Krieger's face.

Both men struggled to their feet, this time a sneering Krieger rammed Clay backward into a wall and landed punches to his chest and face. Desperate to get free of the pummeling, Clay stomped his heel down hard on Krieger's foot, then pushed off the wall, driving Krieger backwards across the room until they ran into the now dead

Klaus, overturning the wheelchair and tumbling the three of them into a heap. Krieger got the advantage this time and rolled over on top of Clay. Using all his strength, Krieger slowly wrenched his gun hand around, grunting for breath as he fought against Clay's strong arm. Clay threw an upward punch at Krieger's contorted face, but the German kept his evil grin as he inched the Glock toward Clay's chest.

For Clay, it was now or never. The growl came from deep in his gut as he poured every bit of strength into turning Krieger's gun hand back and up into his chest. Suddenly the Glock fired three times in quick succession and a look of complete surprise froze on Krieger's face.

Clay was rolling out from under Krieger's now limp body when he saw Conrad disappear through the doorway to the garage passageway, his left arm hanging limp and the briefcase in his right. Maria cried out weakly, "Clay. He's getting away."

Rushing over to her, he started to sit her up, but she cried out in pain. She'd lost a lot of blood from the wound in her chest, and was already very weak.

"Hang in there, Maria. We'll get you some help."

"Clay, no. Get him. Get Conrad. He's got the plans. Get out of here before the Muslims break in. They'll kill us all."

The crash and thud over by the windows drew Clay's attention. Mac and the giant guard were locked together, rolling around on the floor. Mac saw Clay staring dumbly at him as the giant attempted to gouge his face. Pulling at the guard's sausage-like fingers, Mac managed to grunt, "If you're not doing anything useful, Clay, how about a little help here!"

Clay scrambled to his feet, grabbed the chunky marble pen holder from Conrad's desk and swung it down in a smashing blow to the back of the giant's head. Then he helped Mac untangle himself and get to his feet.

"Clay go after him," Maria cried.

Clay and Mac looked at each other. To be sure, she was dying. Moving her now would likely kill her that much faster, but they couldn't leave her. Not to the Muslims. Or to a new sound that had raised its voice above the gunfire and shattering grenade explosions, a throaty, fierce roar he had heard before. Fire. Big fire. A massive, hungry monster was consuming the mansion around them.

Clay reached into Maria's purse, pushed aside the diamond necklace, and retrieved the keys.

"Maria," he said forcefully. "Where is the car?" She was dazed, going into shock. "Maria! Where is the car?"

"Bay 5. The Mercedes," she said weakly.

"Mac, we can't leave her. Help me carry her down to the garage." They were as gentle as they could be, but she cried out in pain as they went down the stairs and into the garage. They found the Mercedes sedan and eased her into the back seat.

"I'll start the car, Mac. Get the garage door, will you?" Clay looked down the line of luxury cars. One garage door was already open and Conrad's black limo was gone. Clay wondered if Conrad had escaped unseen, or if the Muslims had gotten him. Mac jumped into the passenger seat.

"Go, Clay. The coast is clear."

"Okay, get ready to duck, Mac." Clay eased out of the garage, but instead of following the paved drive back around to the front of the mansion, he turned onto the grass and made a beeline for the gateway in the stone wall surrounding the grounds. With no lights on, the sound of gunfire, and a shroud of fog, they made it through the gate and out of danger without drawing a shot. Finally in the clear, Clay turned on the lights, but he could only go so fast because of the thick fog.

"How is she doing, Mac?"

"She's hanging in," he lied. Her eyes were still open, but glazed, and her breathing was labored.

"My bet is that Conrad is heading down the mountain, not up. There's nothing going up but more mountains and West Virginia. And Maria needs a hospital. That's down the mountain too."

"Okay by me. But Conrad's got a good head start on us. I doubt we're going to catch him, especially in this fog."

"The fog might just help us, Mac. He's been shot, so he's going to be getting weaker. He'll be more concerned about staying on the road than making good time. Besides, he probably thinks nobody will be getting out of Foxhaven alive."

"Except those Muslims."

Clay smiled and stepped on the gas. He had to pay close attention, but he found he could make a pretty steady thirty to thirty-five miles an hour in the fog. They were about midway down the mountain when Clay caught up with Conrad's limo, crawling along at fifteen miles an hour and wavering unsteadily through the corners.

"We got him, Mac. Look there."

"You sure it's him?"

"Must be. The limo was gone from the garage. I'll get up close and check the plate." Clay closed to a few feet from the limo's bumper. "Yup. FXHVN-1. It's Conrad all right. Think I'll let him know we are here." With that he gunned it and smashed into the limo's rear bumper. Clay laughed as a startled Conrad looked up into the rear-view mirror and accelerated.

"Woke you up, eh Conrad?"

Now Conrad was doing twenty-five and clearly having trouble going through the turns on the winding mountain road.

"Not fast enough, you bastard." Clay floored it and again rammed into the limo. Conrad was now doing thirty or so and weaving badly through the turns, and even on straightaways. The fog was thick enough that Clay couldn't safely go much faster, but he had one advantage. He remembered this section all too well. Clay floored it again and rammed the limo at about forty.

"I hope you know what you're doing, Clay," Mac said nervously.

"Turn about's fair play, Mac. This is where Krieger tried to run me off the road. It's pretty straight for a while, no bad curves, then ends up in some wicked hairpins. Just got to watch for a big yellow Runaway Truck Ramp sign on the right. The hairpins are a little past that. If I can keep him going fast, he might run off the road like Krieger did."

Conrad tried slowing down after nearly running off the road on a gentle curve. Clay rammed him again, forcing him back up to 40.

"There's the sign," Mac called out.

"I see it." Clay hit the brakes and Conrad's taillights shot ahead, nearly disappearing in the white mist. Then Clay heard squealing tires, hollow banging and crashing up ahead. As he pulled to a stop, he shouted. "Maria. Maria, wake up. We got Conrad."

Mac turned around and saw the vacant look in her eyes."Awh damn," Mac moaned. "Clay, I don't think she made it." He reached over his seat, and pushing forward, put his hand to her neck. Turning back around, he looked at Clay. "I'm sorry, Clay."

Clay banged the steering wheel with his fist, then stared ahead blankly, overcome by the terrible feeling Conrad had somehow won. It wasn't true. He knew that, but it felt that way now.

"Come on, Clay," Mac said finally. "Let's go find out what happened to Conrad."

He practically pulled Clay out of the car. A short way down the road they found the skid marks and a break in the trees where Conrad had gone over the cliff and into a deep ravine. Fifty feet below, the crumpled remains of Conrad's limo lay in a burning heap, a flickering light blurred by the fog.

"We'd better get some fire trucks up here. Mac, this is going to take a lot of explaining."

"Maybe we should talk with Bunker first. Those guys are pretty good at sweeping stuff under the rug."

Clay grunted a laugh. "I suppose his copy of the plans burned up with him."

"That makes yours the only copy then. Where the hell *is* your cell phone, anyway?"

"Maria. She slipped it in my back pocket. I'd forgotten all about it," he said pulling it out, still intact, to show Mac.

"Well, it's a damn good thing you didn't get shot in the ass, partner. Where would the world have been then?"

Mac's joke jarred Clay free of the frustration coiled within him for a moment and he laughed out loud. It hurt, but it felt good to finally laugh again.

Down off the mountain the fog was so thick it took them a good hour to reach Trustlow. With Maria's lifeless body still in the back seat, her death weighed heavily on Clay. She did not deserve to die, he told himself, and those few seconds kept replaying in his mind. The image of Conrad's gun pointing right at him, that look of rage in his eyes. That awful feeling at being completely powerless, sure he was about to be shot. Then shock--surprise--as Maria stepped forward to take a bullet intended for him. It was all still too brutally clear in his mind. He wanted to believe she was just doing her job, but knew there was more to it. Either way, she had given him his only chance to get out with the LENR plans. And kept him alive. He owed her for that, but he could never repay her. Not even the mixed feelings of guilt about wanting to hold her again would do that.

"That was a goddam mess, you know Mac?" he said after a long silence.

"What, you mean at Foxhaven? You got Conrad."

"Yeah, with us getting caught, again, with Maria getting shot. Conrad, he didn't get near enough of what he deserved."

"Beats me how Conrad knew we were coming. He sure was ready for us."

"Maybe he's got perimeter sensors we didn't spot. You know, in ground sensors--EUGs like we used over in Afghanistan," Clay said. "Or surveillance cameras. Probably really well hidden cameras."

"Could be. Didn't figure him for a hi-tech security type. But maybe Krieger."

"Doesn't matter now. He sure got the drop on us. And that got Maria killed. I don't suppose moving her helped her any."

"No changing that now, Clay. And I'll tell you, there's no way we could have left her there. Not with those hadjis closing in. Not with that fire burning the place up. And she didn't want us to let Conrad get away. Don't forget that," he said emphatically. He knew what Clay was going through. "Conrad's days of playing games are over. There was a whole lot of hate in that family. We sure put an end to that."

"Yeah, we did, didn't we?"

Mac called Bunker as soon as they got cell phone coverage, so Bunker was already airborne by the time they reached Trustlow. Per Bunker's instructions, Clay drove directly to the house of Maria's German intelligence contact, a man named Meyer Hochstein, and there made an anonymous call to the local authorities about an accident on the road to Foxhaven. Nothing was said about the fire at the mansion, for fear the fire department would wind up in the middle of a running gun battle. A Homeland Security Strike force would have to go into Foxhaven first, aboard three big Black Hawk helicopters, and that mission was about to get underway. Bunker's last words to Clay were, "Make damn sure nothing happens to your cell phone, Clay."

About four a.m., Bunker landed his helicopter in the middle of the Trustlow High School football field, which was located on high ground and so was clear of fog. Clay and Mac were waiting for him, along with Hochstein, in Hochstein's car. Bunker joined Mac in the back seat and introduced himself to the fellow agent.

"You guys don't do anything half way, do you?" Bunker said to Clay with a sly grin. "Can I have the cell phone now? My people are really hot to download those photos," Bunker said holding out his hand to Clay.

"Sometimes you do have to take the bull by the horns," Clay quipped, feeling better now that they had left the Mercedes and Maria's body behind in Hochstein's garage. He handed the precious phone over to Bunker. "Those Muslims got there quicker than we thought. Kinda glad they did, though. I might not be here jawing with you, if they hadn't. Don't forget to put in your report that we just handed over the only copy of that file in existence."

"The Muslims really messed up that mansion," Mac added. The whole second floor must have been in flames when Conrad lit out with his copy of the plans. Thanks to Clay he didn't get very far. Like I told you, he crashed and burned."

"Our people will check the wreck," Bunker replied. Conrad's body will have to be identified, of course, and they'll look for the file, but it sounds as though it probably did burn up with his limo.

"All things considered," Bunker continued, "you two definitely did your government a service. Not exactly in keeping with the laws of the land, but a service nevertheless. A whole lot of government people, who might not see what you did in the proper light, are on their way. It'll definitely be easier for me to run interference, if you're not here. So, I'm thinking right now the best thing would be if I flew you back to Staunton. Meyer, we've got people on the way to take care of Maria's body and Conrad's car."

"Meyer," Clay said, "will you see that Maria's personal effects get back to her mother? I mean her real mother, okay, not Mrs. Migraine. You'll find a very beautiful and very valuable diamond necklace in Maria's purse. It's a family heirloom, and she was really proud of it."

"Yes, of course, Clay. I'll get her purse out of the car as soon as I get back. Thank you for telling me about it."

Minutes later, Clay waved at him as the helicopter rose up into the still dark sky with navigation lights flashing and the steady roar of its turbine engine drowning out all conversation. Before he knew it, Trustlow was gone and the still flaming ruins of Foxhaven, now just a distant point of light, were receding into the darkness.

18

JUST REWARDS

The lights were still on at the mill house when Bunker touched down just long enough to deposit Clay and Mac on his way back to Washington. He had before him a long bureaucratic nightmare of dealing with the fallout from what he was certain would be remembered as the Foxhaven Conspiracy. A lot of bigwig politicians up there in DC were going to be mightily embarrassed by their one-time friend and source of campaign cash. But Bunker did promise, in exchange for a home cooked meal, to return in a few days with whatever new information he had uncovered.

Susan draped herself on Clay the minute he walked in the door, every bit as thankful he'd come back home as he was to be there. Lost for a time in a long kiss, Clay came up for air, brushed aside her hair to put his hand on the nape of her neck, and kissed her again. He barely noticed Mac slip by him to lock Rita in a bear hug and lift her off the floor as they kissed. Glad to be back? You bet. But you don't just hop off the plane from combat. It takes time to put the brakes on and find your way back to normal, even for two guys as exper-ienced as Clay and Mac.

"You know, I think I could use a drink right about now," Clay said, pulling back a bit from Susan. "Mac, what do you think, bourbon and soda? How about you Susan?"

"Make mine a double," Mac answered. Susan and Rita both shook their heads.

The drink was cold in Clay's hand as he drained off a large slug with a strong feeling of relief. Not long after, the warm, boozy glow spread through him, and he noticed the coiled tension inside him begin to loosen a little. He and Mac clinked glasses and drank some more while Susan sat watching Clay, wondering about what was going through his mind. Rita already knew. She'd seen them both there often enough before. She waited until they both started on a second drink.

"What happened," Rita asked, putting her hand on Mac's broad shoulder. She and Mac sat together on the sofa in Clay's living room. Clay and Susan sat on the floor across from Mac and Rita.

"Conrad must have seen us coming," Mac answered. Clay let him tell it. Was more than happy to let him do the talking. Mac continued, "He had us surrounded when we got to Maria on the porch. Things got messy after that. The Muslims hit the mansion with RPGs and submachine guns, and as far as I know, the place burned to the ground. Conrad and Krieger are dead. Maria's dead too, but she got the cell phone to Clay. Bunker's got it now."

"No walk in the park," was all Rita said. She knew better than to push for more details from Mac tonight. "I suppose you two could use some breakfast to go along with your bourbon."

Mac brightened instantly. "That'd be perfect, Rita honey."

Susan looked at Clay. He smiled and said, "I'm starved too."

The first, faint light of the new day had just peeked over the horizon when Mac and Rita finally drove off. Relaxed by the bourbon and revived by the full breakfast under his belt, Clay almost felt normal again. It had always been like that after a mission in Afghanistan. Returning to base, you shed your gear, shook off the dust, and unwound the stress any way you could. He was almost there. And though the beginnings of fatigue from last night's action tugged at the edges of his consciousness, he wasn't ready for sleep just yet.

"Come on Susan. Let's go for a walk around the millpond."

"What? It's still dark out there."

"Get your coat. As long as we're still up, we might as well watch the sunrise."

Bundled up now, they went down the two flights of stairs, walked past the wheels, cogs, and axles of the mill's idled machinery on the lower level, and stepped out onto the deck. Looking out over the millpond, Clay drank in the nighttime stillness and the sight of stars innocently flickering high above in a cloudless sky. Gloriously peaceful, it was tonic for his soul.

Clay's and Susan's breath fogged in the chill night air, and a white frosting of frozen dew clung to the grass and low shrubs. Apart from the steady rush of water spilling over the mill's dams and sluices, all else was quiet, expectantly awaiting the approaching dawn. The sky above began to glow grayer with new light and somewhere a bird chirped. As they set out on the path around the millpond, Clay put his arm around Susan and she leaned against him. More tonic for his soul.

"Was it bad?" Susan asked softly.

"Bad enough. After Conrad got the drop on us, they took us to his study. That's when the Muslims started shooting up the mansion. Heh, they were really tearing it up."

"You were still in there when they attacked?" she asked with an alarmed expression.

"Yes. They moved quicker than I thought they would."

"Maybe my idea of telling them wasn't such a good one."

"No, it was good. The way it worked out was, well, like calling in an artillery attack on your own position. Risky, but sometimes necessary. Turned out we really needed that diversion." He wasn't about to get into graphic details. Didn't want to think about them, at least not now. "When the Muslims attacked, Conrad started coming unglued. I finished it for him when I said I'd tipped them to his double-dealing. That's when he took a shot at me, and Maria jumped in front. She took the bullet for me," he said sadly.

"I guess now I shouldn't have said it," he continued, "because of what happened after. But Conrad was such a smug, lying bastard, I couldn't resist. Then a grenade went off, all hell broke loose, and Mac and I got free. The diversion worked, just not the way I wanted."

"Well, *I'm* glad it wasn't you he shot," Susan gushed. "What happened, happened. If it's anybody's fault, it's Conrad's. He shot her."

Clay gave her a hug and a tenuous smile. They were standing on the old wooden bridge, which crossed the stream below the overflowing millpond dam. Clay stopped to watch the water tumbling over the rocks in the streambed below.

"Well, I know, Susan. I know. And I sure as hell wasn't going to let Conrad get away with it." He paused, still looking down at the stream. "That may turn out to be a problem when all this hits the fan. I took one of Conrad's cars and caught up with him right about where Krieger tried to run us off the road. The fog was really heavy and I kept ramming the back of Conrad's limo, forcing him to go faster. I thought he'd lose control and run off the road like Krieger. I never actually pushed him off the road, but I kept him going faster than he wanted. I knew enough to slow down before those hairpin turns. He didn't, and that's where he went over the cliff. Conrad got what he deserved, but I may get some heat for helping it along."

"Do you really think you'll get into trouble for that? I mean the man's a murderer, a thief, and he helped carry out a terrorist plot. How could the government possibly come after you?"

"That's just it, Susan. It's a helluvah mess." Then Clay brightened. "I do have an ace in the hole. I came out of this with the only surviving copy of the LENR plans. That will count for something. Maybe a lot. Bunker took my cell phone with him to DC. He's probably going to spread copies of it all over the East Coast, so this can never happen again."

They turned to follow the path on the other side of the pond, heading back toward the mill.

"You really cared for her, didn't you?"

"Maria?" He looked into Susan's eyes. "You knew?"

"A girl knows these things."

"How the heck do I put this?" he said after a moment, "It was like slipping on ice you don't realize is there. I love you, Susan. I want to marry you. No question about it." He put his arm around Susan and started walking again. "Maria was an attractive, flirty kind of girl, and I got my feelings sort of tangled up with her before I knew what was happening. Nothing was going to come of it, not like us. It's just that the attraction was there and I figured out I had to walk carefully after that. Does that make any sense?"

"Yes it does, Clay."

"Funny thing is, once I found out she was spying on Conrad, I figured she was just flirting with me as part of her work. You know, stringing Conrad along by making him jealous or something. I guess maybe her taking the bullet changes that."

Clay stopped and they turned toward the rising sun, now a promising sliver of an arc peeking above the ridgeline a quarter mile off. Though deep shadows still blanketed the rolling pasture spread before Clay and Susan, the rising sun nevertheless lit the sky with a brightening blue and excited their eyes with the spectacle of dawn and a new day. The bright orb seemed in a rush as it rose and swelled and, climbing past midway above the ridge, became too bright to look at any longer.

Clay and Susan turned to look back across the pond at the mill, its big water wheel hanging motionless in the shadows. The first rays of morning light struck the roof and upper stories now, turning the windows into blazing reflections of the sun. Susan turned and put her arms around Clay.

"Clay, when we're married, can we live here?"

"You want to?" he said, surprised. "I thought you'd want to live somewhere else. You know, start off with something different."

"I suppose a lot of couples feel that way, but I don't, Clay. I love this place. I feel so safe and comfortable here, and we'd never find a home with as much charm as this. I want this to be our home."

"Then that's what we'll do."

"Some window boxes, I think, Clay. Do you think you can make me some this winter, so I can grow flowers in them this spring?"

"Oh boy, here we go," Clay said with a laugh. "The 'honey do' list begins!" Susan swatted his arm playfully.

Clay and Mac only managed to get a few hours sleep before Bunker's calls rousted them with the news they were to be debriefed that afternoon at the courthouse in Staunton. The still sleepy pair dutifully appeared in an upstairs conference room commandeered by Bunker and four bigwigs from Homeland Security. For three hours Clay and Mac stifled yawns and answered a barrage of questions, including pointed ones regarding Conrad's demise. As was usual with formal debriefings, the questions all came at Clay and Mac. Their interrogators, even their pal Bunker, remained adamantly tight lipped when it came to giving out any information whatsoever. So Clay and Mac weren't able to find out what had happened with the strike force, or even if any of the Muslims had been arrested. They left the courthouse feeling totally drained, but determined to have a beer or two before going back to their beds.

Bunker, meantime, decided that he had enough information now to pay a visit to his father at Sunnyvale. When he walked into his father's room, Blakes was sitting upright on the bed, feet dangling over the floor and staring out the window. He seemed surprised when he realized Bunker was there.

"Feeling better, Dad?"

"Better, yes, still not tiptop though."

"I think you will be, when you hear the news."

"Really? What's that?"

"Conrad is dead. So's his father Klaus. FBI's rolling up that network of Muslim fanatics, the ones who killed Weiss."

"Thank God. Who took care of Conrad? You?"

"No, that would be Clay and Mac. You know, those two who were in here."

"Yes, I know who you mean."

"Worked out about the way you figured, I'm guessing." He gave Blakes a pointed look. Blakes's eyes betrayed a momentary surprise. Then he smiled, as though he'd just remembered a private joke.

"You always were a smart one, Bunker."

"Want to tell me about it?"

"I guess it's safe to come clean now that Conrad's dead and his buddies are on the run." He patted the bed. "Sit down, son. This is going to take a few minutes to explain.

"You have to understand," he continued, "that neither Klaus Nebel nor his son Conrad ever knew who sicced those communists on them, the ones who killed Gerhard and destroyed The Cliffs. They suspected the bureau, of course, but even the bureau had no idea who had done it. The only guy I ever told, before a little while ago, was Weiss, and I knew he'd never spill it to anybody unless I told him to. He was that kind of guy.

"Weiss had a neighbor, a Muslim named Khalid--they were good friends--who worked as a lab assistant at a small Babcock Chemical Co. laboratory over in Loudon County. It was pretty hush-hush stuff, but Khalid told Weiss all about it, well, because Weiss was his friend and had worked for Babcock for years as a research chemist. Weiss realized right away how important the work was, and how it could really solve the world energy crisis, global warming, all that.

"One day Khalid tells Weiss some other Muslims are putting the squeeze on him for information about who is working there, that kind of thing. Said that when he refused to talk, they threatened to denounce him as an infidel. Under the Muslim's Shariah Law, he could be executed for being an infidel. He was so scared he told Weiss everything. Weiss told him to keep his mouth shut and he'd check into it, but a couple days later his neighbor turned up dead.

"When the cops called it a random killing or drug deal gone bad, Weiss raised hell, told them he was sure those guys trying to squeeze

Khalid had killed him. But he had no way of knowing what they were really up to. And he couldn't say anything about the lab to the police without spilling secrets about the research. So there wasn't much he could do when those Muslims gave the cops solid alibis. Solid, but bogus, I'll bet.

"That's when he came to me. He had the names of three likely suspects his neighbor had given him, so I called an old friend who's still got contacts at the bureau, and bingo! One of the possibles works for a local imam, a guy named Moktar, who's on the FBI radar. Nothing too serious, but there are suspicions. They've had a watch on him in the past, because a Qatari oil sheik is a big bene-factor for Moktar's mosque. So now this darn case is getting mighty interesting.

"Next thing you know, Weiss tells me people are following him, and that I'd better be careful. Well, he's a lot spryer than I am, so I'm getting worried. Thinking I'd better be sure about what Weiss got us into, I asked my friend to see if he could twist some arms at the bureau. See if they turned up any other bad actors connected to the oil sheik. He came back with a pretty good list. That sheik has been busy all right, but I can tell you my eyes about popped when I saw both Klaus Nebel and Conrad Nebel on that list. They own a fleet of oil tankers and do a lot of business in the Mideast. I checked to be sure, of course, but it was as if the Nebels had just jumped out of the past to haunt me.

"That's when I decided I'd better go under cover." He lifted the edge of the hospital blanket and grinned at Bunker.

"Oh jeez, Dad. Just tell the story."

"Testy today, are we? Well, my doc agreed to help me fake the Alzheimer's diagnosis, so if anybody got onto me, the Nebels or any-body else, they'd figure I'm no possible threat."

"Dad, why didn't you come to me!" Bunker blurted out. "I could have protected you."

"No offense, Bunker. Homeland Security has a lot bigger fish to fry than a decrepit old FBI agent with nothing but some suspicions about very rich and very powerful people. Who also happen to be very resourceful. No, I couldn't take that chance. And besides, I know you, son. You'd beat yourself up for the rest of your life, if anything happened to me."

"You could have at least let me know. That really hurt when you pretended to not recognize me."

"I'm sorry, son. But the act had to be convincing. Especially after those bastards killed Weiss. I couldn't even feel completely safe here. They could have had people here, nurses, janitors, whatever keeping an eye on me. I did see a white Camero hanging around out there in the parking lot for a while, when your friends started coming here."

"So did you plan to use them from the start?"

"No, not really. At first, I was trying to feel them out. See if they really were your friends. Could have been somebody Conrad sent to find out if I was faking. Then they seemed pretty serious about getting to the bottom of Weiss's murder, and I started thinking, 'Why not?' Those two, Clay and Mac, looked like they could take care of themselves. You know, ex-military. So I just told them the story, figuring that the apple never falls far from the tree--that Conrad and his father were probably no better than Gerhard was, maybe worse, if that's possible."

"You mean you didn't know Conrad was double-dealing? That he used the Muslims to destroy the lab so he could sell the LENR device to the Chinese for a trillion bucks?"

"Is that what he did?"

"He tried to! If you didn't know that, why did you set up Clay and Mac to go after Nebel?"

"Mostly a hunch. I couldn't really tell what Conrad was up to, but like I said, it was probably no good. So I told them about The Cliffs knowing that would probably get them interested in checking up on Foxhaven. Figured they might find something out, give you enough to go after Conrad. Turned out, they already knew Conrad and had seen the ruins of The Cliffs."

"That's all? You were just playing a hunch?"

"Well, I had one more clue from Weiss. By itself, it probably meant nothing. You see, Weiss told me that Khalid had overheard one of Prof. Wentworth's assistants talking about money she was going to get. A whole lot of money. Like she'd never have to work again. It could have been nothing. But I figured the research was important enough that she could have been selling information to someone, very valuable information."

"Could have been those Muslims."

"No, they weren't offering money, Bunker, just threats. I agree it could have been anybody, but I had a hunch it was probably Conrad. And if it was him, what would he likely do with information worth that much?

"At first, I wasn't going to tell Clay and Mac about using the communists to get back at Gerhard. But to be truthful, I got carried away, remembering how mad I was about being pulled off the case."

"Turned out," Bunker said, "Clay and Susan picked up on that, Dad. He found out about Conrad's double-dealing and told the Muslims Conrad was using them. Stirred up a hornets nest. About a dozen terrorists attacked Foxhaven. Killed Conrad's father and several of Conrad's people and set the building on fire. There's nothing left of the mansion, from what I'm told."

"No kidding? Who'd of thought history would repeat itself. But you know what they say, son. Conrad and that whole goddamned family finally got what was coming to them. Took way too long, but we're finally rid of them. "

"All of it because you had a hunch, eh?"

"Sometimes you have to listen to your gut, Bunker. I taught you that. When you only have little bits and pieces to go on, you have to. That's how you see through the fog."

"Yes, Dad," Bunker said a bit sourly.

"Those two did all right, didn't they?"

"Yeah, they created a hell of a mess, but they got Conrad."

"And I'll bet Conrad had you pretty well stymied, didn't he?"

"Yes," Bunker admitted and shrugged.

"Looks like I did you a favor, recruiting those two. Not so many guys willing to go out on a limb anymore. Keep 'em around, Bunker. My gut tells me they'll prove useful again."

"Okay, Dad." He smiled weakly at his father. The man looked so frail, and yet here he'd been running a case from a hospital bed. "I'm glad you're okay," Bunker said finally.

"I'm sorry I hurt you, son. I didn't like doing that."

"I think the worst was not knowing if the next time you would remember me at all."

"Well, that's not going to happen. If I haven't gotten Alzheimer's by now, it won't get me." He put his hand on Bunker's shoulder and smiled warmly. "I haven't forgotten your mother either, Bunker. It's almost fifteen years now, and I still miss her. You know, that woman, Susan, she reminded me so much of Martha when we were young. It was like she'd come back to me so I could talk to her again. I think that's another reason why I spilled the beans about the communists. All that happened before our marriage, and I never told your mother about it. Only Weiss."

* * * *

"This your first ride in a helicopter?" a grinning Bunker asked Susan, who was strapped in one of the sling seats lining both sides of the chopper's cargo bay. The big Black Hawk helicopter was at that moment swooping upward, leaving stomachs struggling to catch up. Clay, an old hand at this, smiled at Mac, as Susan nodded yes. Neither Susan nor Rita, another first timer, looked entirely comfortable, but they were holding up fine. And underneath their winter coats, they were dressed to the nines. Clay and Mac, for their part, had on coats and ties under their long formal dress coats.

Bunker hadn't told them much, just that the Homeland Security director wanted to express his thanks personally for having broken the Foxhaven case wide open and returning the LENR plans to their rightful owners. Clay and Mac were to be given VIP treatment for the afternoon, but Bunker had made it clear that no one outside the Department of Homeland Security would be there. Too many bigwigs were still licking wounds caused by the exposure of Conrad's treacheries. Clay smiled at that thought. And the knowledge that the government had chosen to ignore his transgressions, understandable though they were.

So, he and Mac were to be given the hero treatment. Clay certainly didn't feel like a hero, given what had happened to Maria, but Conrad had been stopped and that was worth celebrating. Clay had read in the newspapers a sanitized version of the big fire at Foxhaven and Conrad's death in a crash that same night. The real story might come out later, but Clay didn't really care one way or the other. From what Bunker had told them, Moktar and his cronies had been arrested, but Vanilla and six others of the Muslim fanatics had escaped, apparently melting into the forests surrounding Foxhaven, along with the surviving members of Conrad's gang. Bunker seemed confident they'd catch the rest of the Muslims, but Clay wasn't so sure and that was a concern. If the truth about the Foxhaven Conspiracy had proved anything, it was that a cancer has to be killed completely. Halfway doesn't do it.

Homeland Security Director Bud Algrin--a bronze-tanned, smooth-skinned bureaucrat--stood at the podium in the fifty-seat auditorium, the department's press conference room. Today, though every seat was taken, there were no reporters on hand. With Clay and company sitting up front, the director was preaching to the choir--Homeland Security's department heads, assistants, section chiefs, and the like. Over the past few days, juicy details of the Foxhaven Conspiracy had spread through the agency like wildfire, it's secure computer networks buzzing with speculation, gossip, and photos of the burned remains of the mansion. Algrin was doing a bang up job of belting out--in his deep, throaty voice--a thumping speech about the need for vigilance against the forces of terrorism in our midst.

"The majority of Muslims are peace-loving people," he reminded the audience, "but Islam is at a crossroads, and faces a deep schism between moderate, modern-minded Muslims and the fundamentalists and their jihadist sidekicks. Terrorist attacks, once reserved for those of us in the West, have now become a problem for moderate Muslims too. That is not to say we can relax and sit on the sidelines while Muslims battle Muslims. Given the opportunity, Islamist groups would still strike at us. But more importantly, they have been actively recruiting volunteers from Europe and the United States to fight in their wars in Syria, Iraq, Yemen, and elsewhere. Once trained, these volunteers--who can legally use their passports to return to their home countries--can foment homegrown terrorism.

"Defeating homebred Muslim terrorists on our own turf means watchfulness by every citizen, a readiness to report suspicious people and actions, no matter how trivial they might seem. We are at war with a smart and determined enemy," he said with a flourish, and then called Clay and Mac to the stage.

"Let me introduce two heroes in our fight against terrorism, Clay Cantrell and Mac Harper. These men refused to knuckle under to Muslim fanatics who tried to intimidate them into silence. Then, at great personal risk, they took it upon themselves to investigate suspicious activity. Not everyone is capable of such heroism, but these men were, and we are extraordinarily grateful for their determination and their bravery.

"By their efforts they not only uncovered the perpetrators of the recent terrorist attack on the Babcock Chemical laboratory, they also exposed what can only be described as a wanton act of industrial espionage and profiteering by a highly regarded American citizen collaborating with the terrorists. We are so very fortunate to have men like this in our midst.

"Your brand of heroism, gentlemen, deserves something rather more special than medals. I am pleased to announce that the Babcock Chemical Company, in appreciation for your successful return of their very valuable plans for the LENR device, has issued each of you a very generous check for the sum of $1 million dollars." As the room erupted in spontaneous applause, he turned and one after the other, handed the two very surprised awardees their checks.

Clay and Mac returned to their seats, and Director Algrin raised his hands to quiet the applause. "It's been a heck of a ride these past few days, and I want to thank you all for your efforts in containing the fallout. I know it's been stressful, but it's behind us now. So, if I may be allowed a bit of levity here, ladies and gentlemen, I'll pass along a message to our two heroes from their friend, Agent Bunker Hill. He asked me to say, 'Next time you two plan a weenie roast, do us a favor and pick a smaller house.'" The roar of laughter literally shook the building.

Their moment in the limelight over, Clay and Mac relaxed on the flight back to the mill house.

"Man this was a surprise," Clay said, tapping his breast pocket, where a folded fortune resided for safekeeping. "But you know, Mac, I don't feel quite right about it."

"I think I know what you're going to say, but go ahead."

"I figured you would. First place, we never would have known about those plans if it hadn't been for Maria. Granted, she was doing her job, but she paid for it with her life. I can't help feeling at least partly responsible. I'm thinking I should split my check with her. Send it to her family. Then there's Jimmy. He helped out too. It's always been the three of us, since we started that treasure hunt."

"Clay. What can I say? I already have more money than I know what to do with. I don't mean to sneeze at a million bucks, but you know what meant more to me? After that ceremony, every one of those people in that room stopped to shake my hand and thank me personally. I'll remember that until they plant me in the ground."

"Me too, partner."

"A four way split is okay by me."

"Thanks, Mac."

Rita smiled warmly. "I hate to tell you two guys, but Trisch is going to want to kill you. I know giving him a share is the right thing and all. But she's already having enough trouble keeping Jimmy's spending urges in line. Now you want to give him another half million?"

*　　*　　*　　*

Everybody made it to the celebration at Clay's parents' estate that evening, including Jimmy and Trisch. Bunker brought a swanky red-headed beauty from an office down the hall at Homeland Security. The party started at six and wound through cocktails, dinner, dessert and coffee, and came to rest finally with more coffee in the sitting room, in front of a roaring fire in the fireplace. Inevitably, the conversation circled around to the events of the past few weeks.

"To me, it's easier to understand Conrad's motives, than the Muslims'," Jimmy said. "Seems like he was all about pure greed to me, but you probably have a better sense of that, Clay."

"Maybe. Greed figured in it for sure. And there had to be an inherited hatred for this country after what happened to Conrad's grandfather. I'd bet that the sheer thrill of pulling off such a gutsy play was part of it too. But there was something else, I think. Control.

"That night when we were in his study and the Muslim's attacked, Conrad's father--Klaus--appeared out of nowhere. I didn't even know he was at Foxhaven. He was old, obviously weak, and in a wheelchair, but really pissed--sorry--really angry. He came in yelling at Conrad for being a fool, for getting them attacked the same way Gerhard did. Conrad just stood there and took it for a minute, like he didn't know what to do.

"But you know the really weird part? Conrad called him 'Sir.' He screamed 'Sir! Shut up.' To his own father. Here's Conrad, a grown man, a very wealthy and successful businessman, and he calls his father 'sir.' Like he'd been packed off to boarding school as a kid and raised to bow down to his father, the king. The way I read it, Conrad must have been brought up in a really controlling family. So control became everything to him. And the lies and treachery gave *him* the control he wanted, needed, over people."

Clay's father, Carl, stopped puffing on his pipe and cast an amazed look at his son. "You know, Clay, that's a damned astute assessment."

"Thanks, Dad," Clay replied. "Thanks especially for *not* raising me like that."

"That's one side of it," Susan said. "But what about the Muslim terrorists? I mean, how did they get so cold-blooded?"

"I think part of it is their religion," Carl answered. "Peaceful Muslims will tell you Islam is a religion of peace, but the jihad--war against the nonbelievers--is part of that religion too. So are some pretty brutal punishments under the Muslim Shariah law. The rigidity and brutality embedded in those old Islamic teachings is, I think, what really resonates with the fundamentalist fanatics and in their eyes legitimizes them.

"Islam is an ancient system of beliefs, parts of it, like Shariah Law, being better suited to ancient times than the modern world," Carl continued, puffing thoughtfully on his pipe. "On the one hand, that cultural heritage is a source of pride for Muslims, but on the other it threatens to strangle them unless they can adapt to the modern world. Much as the Muslim fundamentalists hate it, Western culture, is a very powerful force within the Muslim world.

"You mean like the Arab spring revolts?" Susan asked.

"Yes. But what started as a revolt against dictators in the name of democracy is failing. Look at what happened in Egypt. And now, out of the revolt in Syria comes ISIS with it's brutal conquests and barbaric caliphate. It's a counterrevolution by the fundamentalist fanatics preaching the harsh cultural dictates of old Islam and jihad, not only against nonbelievers like us, but against the moderate Muslims too."

"We'll keep fighting the terrorists," Bunker said, "but I think the change will have to come from within Islam itself. Somehow the moderates will have to reform, modernize the Muslim teachings. I don't know how that will happen. But change is the only way to eliminate the legitimacy in the Islamic teachings that the radicals have laid claim to, to justify what they do."

"That's true, Bunker," Clay said. "But how do you change what a person believes? For the fanatics, Shariah Law, the Koran, Allah's will--that is their reality."

"How does anybody know what is real?" Jimmy interjected. "Conrad is a case in point, isn't he? The guy was just a bunch of lies, a house of cards."

"In a way," Carl replied, "I suppose that's what it is for all of us. It's layer upon layer of experiences, sensations, perceptions of the world around us, emotions, memories, which we *believe* are real. Philosophers have wondered about the question for centuries. How do we know what is real...?"

"Carl, dear," Catherine scolded. "I can see where this is going. I don't know about the rest of you, but it's my bedtime."

"Just when I was getting started," Carl said with a sheepish grin. "Well, maybe it's time to leave questions like that to the young folks. It's been a long day for me too. The rest of you are welcome to stay, but the missus and I are going to have to say good night."

The party broke up shortly after Carl and Catherine retired. Since Clay and Susan were staying the night in the mansion's west wing, they saw everyone out and locked up. With the lights off downstairs, Clay and Susan climbed the grand staircase arm-in-arm, trying--but not really succeeding--to talk in hushed tones. When they reached the hallway at the top of the stairs, Susan hesitated.

"Are you sure this is all right with your parents?"

"Of course. Why wouldn't it be?" Clay replied with some surprise as they walked down the corridor to their bedroom.

"I mean us sleeping together. Here. In their house."

"They're fine with it, honey. Don't worry."

"Are you sure?" Susan stopped outside the door to their bedroom.

"Yes, I'm sure. You're wobbling, Susan."

"No I'm not. I'm perfectly sober."

"You're wobbling. I can tell when you're nervous. Look, it's really okay. Mom asked whether she should have one or two rooms made up for us. I told her you've been staying over at the mill most of the time now."

"Oh, great, Clay!" she cried out, then whispered, "Now your mother is going to be mad at me for wrecking your morals."

Clay laughed out loud, then took her in his arms and said in a low voice, "They think the world of you, honey. The only way my parents will be mad at you is if you don't show up for the wedding. I'd be mad at you too, you know."

Susan looked up into his eyes and gave him a hint of a smile. "How do I know you really mean that? What is real, Clay Cantrell? Like your father said, philosopher's have wondered..."

Clay pushed open the door to their bedroom. "*I'll show you what's real,*" he said.

She laughed like a schoolgirl and slipped from his arms. Ducking into the bedroom in a flash, she jumped onto the old fourposter bed.

Caught up in the game, Clay called out "You can run, *but you cannot hide!*" He closed the bedroom door behind him and eyed the bed's end posts--looking for all the world like goal posts. With arms spread wide, he took a flying leap onto the bed. Susan laughed as he landed in an ungainly belly flop beside her, then screamed in surprise as the old bed's slats gave way and their mattress suddenly dropped to the floor with a resounding thud.

Clay was every bit as surprised as Susan by the sudden flight floorward. He sat bolt upright, and in a high-pitched, very bad imitation of Susan, exclaimed, "Clay, what will your parents think!" Clay and Susan looked at each other and as one, roared with laughter.

EPILOGUE

Killer Fog is a work of fiction, but I have kept faith, wherever possible, with the actual historical events surrounding the fictional characters and their imaginary doings. So I believe I can say there is some truth to this fiction.

The events leading up to World War II were politically and ideologically every bit as tumultuous as portrayed, and I wrote the story to be consistent with the dates of the major events mentioned, especially Hitler's ill-fated attack on the Soviet Union, which played such an important part in the book. I am particularly indebted to one excellent nonfiction work, which provided a basis for my portrayal of America at this time, *Those Angry Days: Roosevelt, Lindbergh, and America's Fight Over World War II, 1939-1941,* by Lynne Olson.

While Nazi Germany's interest in producing gasoline synthetically served my purposes as a temporary foil for the LENR discovery and to keep you, my reader, aware of the importance of energy in this world of ours, synthetic gasoline has in fact been produced from coal since the early 1900s, and the Nazis did indeed produce huge amounts of gasoline synthetically before and during World War II. But synthetic gasoline also holds a certain sentimental importance for me personally. My father, you see, was in fact a research chemist, and during World War II, he worked on a government project that successfully discovered a way to make synthetic gasoline from silica gel, which as I understand it, is derived from sand! Alas, because of my father's premature death (he was just thirty-six), I know little about this discovery, except that the process is too expensive to be practical even when oil prices are high.

Nevertheless, the discovery was important back in the day, though I cannot say whether Nazi spies ever tried to steal it. That much was a work of my imagination and, of course, necessary to the novel. Someday I'd like to spend a day or two combing through the National Archives to see if I can learn more about my father's work during the war.

The revolutionary new energy source at the heart of *Killer Fog*, LENR, is real as well, though research has not yet progressed as far toward a practical device as portrayed in this novel. I regret that I could not include a more detailed description of how LENR works down at the atomic level, but that is something that scientists are still working to explain fully. But the fact is, the phenomenon is real, appears to be as promising as portrayed in this novel, and is only now beginning to get the attention it deserves from energy researchers. To my mind, it holds greater promise for our future than anything else out there. Whether a practical LENR device will be developed before we spend billions on hi-tech windmills, bird-frying solar arrays, and dubious genetic modifications of plants is anybody's guess.

Alas, the schism between moderate and fundamentalist Muslims that figures in *Killer Fog*, is all too real. Until recently, I doubt many people outside the Muslim community were aware of the fundamentalists' grand plans for establishing Islam as the world's only religion, much less their idea of reverting to a harsh Seventh Century Islamic society, or the fact of these fanatical Muslims attacking their own, more moderate-minded brethren. The recent act of establishing the Islamic State, along with its brutal adherence to Islamic Shariah

Law, has made that plain enough for all to see, as did the now notorious attempt by Muslims to impose Islamic Law in Egypt.

There are obvious precedents for overt, violent terrorist attacks here in the US, of the kind portrayed in *Killer Fog*. Thankfully, though, they are far fewer in number than in places like Afghanistan and Iraq. The scenario of a fundamentalist cell operating underground here for less violent subversive purposes, which also plays a role in the novel, is rather less on the minds of most people today, but that fiction is grounded in reality as well.

Bunker Hill's threat assessment in *Killer Fog* was primarily informed by a think tank threat analysis, *Shariah, The Threat to America,* produced by the Center For Security Policy in 2010. This very good, and I might add prescient, study provides an understanding of Shariah Law, of the jihadi mentality, and of Islamic supremacism, by examining the roots of these phenomena within the Koran and other key Muslim texts. In addition to shedding light on the split between moderate Muslims and the fundamentalists, the analysis delves into the very real threat from the fundamentalists' concept of "stealth jihad," including background on activities here in the US. It is available online and for downloading by simply Googling the search term: *Shariah, The Threat to America.*

In addition, I have also relied on news reports and analysis, and a somewhat older book, *Infiltration, How Muslim Spies Have Penetrated Washington,* by Paul Sperry 2005. As to Bunker Hill's conclusion that ultimately reform by moderate Muslims will have to come from within the Muslim Community, I can cite one encouraging news report now only a few weeks old at this writing: Shiite and Sunni clerics from about eighty countries met in Iran's Holy City of Qom, vowing to "counter extremists through mosques and Islamic teaching centers...." The irony of their meeting in Iran will have to be left for another day.

--Bruce Wetterau, December, 2014

Reviewers praise the first book in the Clay Cantrell series, *Lost Treasure:*

"An engrossing work of knife-edge suspense. Lost Treasure is enthusiastically recommended." *--Michael Dunford, Midwest Book Review*

"Wetterau does a superb job in weaving fact with fiction...I look forward to reading future entries in this series, which is why I give this book 4/5 stars. *--Jud Hanson, reviewer, Bestsellersworld.com*

www.ingramcontent.com/pod-product-compliance
Lightning Source LLC
Chambersburg PA
CBHW060601310726
48982CB00008B/1202/J

* 9 7 8 0 6 9 2 5 6 5 1 1 7 *